HUMANITY UNLIMITED
VOLUME 1

TERRY MIXON

YOWLING
CAT PRESS

This book was previously published as Humanity Unlimited Publisher's Pack 1.

Published by Yowling Cat Press ®

Digital edition date: 7/6/2023

Print ISBN: 978-1947376540

Individual Works

Liberty Station Copyright © 2015 by Terry Mixon

Print ISBN: 978-0692531907

Freedom Express Copyright © 2016 by Terry Mixon

Print ISBN: 978-1947376052

Cover art - image copyrights as follows:

DepositPhotos/innovari (Luca Oleastri)

DepositPhotos/zittto (Rui Miguel Morais Vale Sousa Pereira)

BigStockPhoto/Creativemarc

Donna Mixon

Cover design and composition by Donna Mixon

Print design and layout by Terry Mixon

Audio edition performed and produced by Veronica Giguere

Reach her at: v@voicesbyveronica.com

ALSO BY TERRY MIXON

You can always find the most up to date listing of Terry's titles on his Amazon Author Page.

Note: the links below (ebook only, obviously) redirect you to my website where you can click a button to go to Amazon. This allows me to participate in Amazon's associates program and earn a little more. Sorry for any inconvenience.

The Last Hunter

The Last Hunter

Bonds of Blood

Alpha Strike

The Enemy Revealed

Command Authority

The Grand Conspiracy

Shield of Humanity

Fog of War

Ships of the Line

Operation Liberty

The Empire of Bones Saga

Empire of Bones

Veil of Shadows

Command Decisions

Ghosts of Empire

Paying the Price

Recon in Force

Behind Enemy Lines

The Terra Gambit

Hidden Enemies

Race to Terra

Ruined Terra

Victory on Terra

When Luck Runs Out

Gunboat Diplomacy

The Imperial Marines Saga

Spoils of War

Imperial Recruit

Enemy Action

The Humanity Unlimited Saga

Liberty Station

Freedom Express

Tree of Liberty

Blood of Patriots

Single Novels

Scorched Earth

Storm Divers

The Vigilante Series with Glynn Stewart

Heart of Vengeance

Oath of Vengeance

Bound By Law

Bound By Honor

Bound By Blood

Box Sets

The Empire of Bones Saga Volume 1

The Empire of Bones Saga Volume 2

The Empire of Bones Saga Volume 3

The Empire of Bones Saga Volume 4

Humanity Unlimited Volume 1

Humanity Unlimited Volume 2

Want to get updates from Terry about new books and other general nonsense going on in his life? He promises there will be cats. Go to TerryMixon.com/Mailing-List and sign up.

DEDICATION

This book would not be possible without the love and support of my beautiful wife. Donna, I love you more than life itself.

ACKNOWLEDGMENTS

Once again, the people who read my books before you see them have saved me. Thanks to Tracy Bodine, Michael Falkner, Cain Hopwood, Kristopher Neidecker, Bob Noble, Jon Paul Olivier, and Jason Young for making me look good.

I also want to thank my readers for putting up with me. You guys are great.

LIBERTY STATION

BOOK ONE

Harry Rogers uses his military training to rescue the innocent. His domineering and powerful father uses that to lure him to the jungles of Guatemala.

Harry thought the mission only meant rescuing a beautiful scientist at a Mayan pyramid. Wrong.

What they find puts them in a deadly race against his diabolical family. The first to solve the thousand-year-old mystery gets a ticket to the stars.

1

Harry Rogers watched the target's house through his night-vision scope. A guard patrolled the roof of the Italian villa slowly, with no idea that someone had him dead in his sights. Satisfied the guard wasn't going anywhere, Harry clicked his transmitter once to let his team know he was ready. A pair of clicks on the encrypted frequency acknowledged his signal.

The other members of his team were already in place. All they needed to move this mission from recon to assault was for him to give the word.

He scanned the rooftop once more and spotted a second guard near the rear of the house. That one was smoking. Didn't he know that was bad for his health?

Harry clicked his transmitter three times. Then he took a deep breath, lined up on the farthest man, and fired. The target stood just over two hundred feet away from the tree Harry had chosen for his nest. That range was a snap with a sniper rifle but chancy with a tranquilizer dart. Good thing he'd practiced.

The man made a small cry, scrabbled at the dart embedded in his back, and collapsed. The closer man turned toward the commotion, giving Harry a clear shot at his unprotected rear. He went down just as easily as his friend had.

His people checked in once they'd neutralized the two guards at the back of the property, the two in front, and the man in the gatehouse. Time to move the operation to phase two.

Harry climbed down the Italian stone pine as noiselessly as he'd ascended. Tree climbing spikes made the ascent easy.

The tall trees at the edge of the yard made for dark shadows this early in the morning. He enjoyed their scent as he made his way toward the clearing. A hint of the sea mingled with the trees. He really needed to take some time off to unwind.

He crossed the clearing below the imposing mansion and up to the back of the villa just as his people were securing the unconscious prisoners. The next set of guards would find them just before dawn, and the manhunt would be on. The clock was ticking.

Less than a minute later, the rest of his people ghosted in out of the dark. They were almost invisible in their gray-on-black camouflage. Their night-vision goggles made them look like monsters to the uninitiated.

If this had been a hard entry, they'd have blown the doors and come in firing. He and his people had more experience at that than any seven people should have. War did that to people.

Thankfully, this was a snatch and run. They'd only kill if they had to. These guards were only doing their job. They didn't deserve to die for their master's poor decisions.

That wasn't always the case. Some opponents deserved lethal force.

The interior guards on this mission expected their exterior compatriots to warn them of any intrusion. Hopefully, his people would take them out before they realized their error.

Jeremy Gonzales, his security expert, had the doors open in just a few seconds. The target hadn't activated the electronic alarm. Of course not. He had armed guards. Harry and his team raised their night-vision gear as they came into the lighted interior.

The staff lived on-site but in a different building. At three in the morning, they wouldn't be up for a few more hours. All Harry needed to worry about were the two guards in the building. Infrared had one of them in the kitchen —probably snacking, another bad habit—while the other was up on the second floor.

The team split without a word. Two of them moved toward the kitchen, two of them went toward the front of the house, and he led the remaining pair up the stairs.

The interior of the villa was every bit as lavish as he'd expected. Fine antique furniture filled the side rooms, and expensive-looking art occupied the niches. The thick carpeting deadened even their careful steps as they went up to the next level.

A tiny fiber-optic wire around the corner showed the upstairs guard examining one of the paintings near the far end of the hall. The man had a magnifying glass. He must be an art lover.

Harry leaned out into the hall and shot him in the ass with a dart. That was going to be tough for him when his friends teased him later.

That's where the plan went off script. This guard managed to bring his weapon around and squeeze the trigger before he collapsed.

Harry ducked back as the automatic weapon ripped through the silence and disintegrated the corner beside him. The man only got off one burst, but that was enough to ruin the element of surprise. Hopefully, it wouldn't be loud enough to wake the staff.

"Blow the power and communications," he said over the team channel as he surged around the corner. He flipped his night-vision gear down just as the lights went out. They'd cut the landline, and a cell jammer would keep anyone from calling for help.

He raced to the end of the hall and kicked the door open. There were two people in the room, a very fat man digging in the nightstand and a shrieking woman in the bed with the sheet pulled up to her chin.

Harry darted the man and watched him crumple with a sense of satisfaction. A second shot took out the unknown woman. She'd wake up in the morning with a headache and damaged pride.

There hadn't been any shots from below, so his people had neutralized the man in the kitchen. Clean sweep.

He made a pass through the bedroom and attached office, just to be certain that no one was hiding there. The master bedroom could've come from a palace. The NVG didn't allow him to see color, but the furnishings here looked even more refined than the ones downstairs. They had to be hundreds of years old.

The office wasn't just for show. It looked as though the man used it extensively. The large desk had a messy spread of papers and data chips. Expensive paintings covered the walls, and a few cases held knickknacks. Mostly Egyptian stuff, Harry thought.

A spread of old-looking parchment pages under glass took up one wall. The illustrations of plants and people looked medieval. The flora had to be a monk's flight of fancy. He was sure some of them weren't real.

Satisfied that they hadn't missed anyone, Harry headed back to the hall. It was time to collect the client and withdraw. He stopped outside the door closest to the master bedroom and knocked.

"Emily Schultz, your mother sent us. It's safe to come out. She said to tell you that she'd take you out with your friends Hannah and Cheryl as soon as you get back to the States. I believe cinnamon swirl ice cream is on the menu."

The door opened a moment later, revealing a young girl with dark hair dressed in a nightgown. Ten-year-old Emily Schultz, the kidnapped girl. Her scumbag father had thought his money and influence could keep her American mother from enforcing the custodial agreement that the US courts had ordered. Not this time.

"Am I really going home?" she asked. Her voice was timid and soft.

"Yes," Harry said in a serious voice. "Dress fast. We only have a few minutes. Only take the important stuff. One bag."

One of the two women on his team ducked inside with the client. Two minutes later, they exited the way they'd snuck in. They piled into a plumbing van and left the scene at a sedate pace.

No need to draw attention. If you acted as though you belonged, the man on the street seldom questioned your right to be there. In the case of service people, they rarely even remembered what you looked like.

The trip to the coast went off without a hitch. No word of their invasion had made it out of the house, so no one had raised the alarm. Harry looked at his watch as they hustled the girl from the van to their borrowed boat. They still had maybe an hour before someone found all the unconscious people.

Unless they had completely crappy luck, they'd be back on the ship and into international waters before the search even moved beyond the general area around the villa. The man driving the boat would take them to their ship, return to shore, and get the plumbing van back to his shop before anyone got excited. He'd get a very large bonus for his part in the operation.

Harry didn't relax until they were several hundred miles in the clear. The news was all over the airwaves by then. Girl from rich family kidnapped, police looking everywhere for the villains. Good luck with that.

Only then did he turn on his satellite phone and call the girl's mother. She hadn't known when the snatch would take place, so she had to have been anxious for the last week. It was almost three in the morning on the East Coast.

"Hello?" Harry could hear mixed notes of fear and hope in the woman's voice.

"Miss Schultz? Harry Rogers. We have Emily, and we're safely away."

"Oh, thank God!" He could hear the anguished relief in the woman's voice. "Can I talk to her? Is she okay?"

"She's perfectly fine. Here you go." He handed the phone to the little girl and stepped back to let them have their reunion.

Once they finished their long and tearful conversation, he took his phone back. The woman was still crying. "Thank you. Thank you so much."

"It's my pleasure. We'll have her back to you tomorrow evening. Try to get some rest."

He hung up with a sense of satisfaction, knowing that the woman wouldn't be able to sleep a wink. Another family reunited. Those were the best jobs.

That's when he noticed he had a voicemail from an all-too-familiar number. His father. Great. That man could ruin a wet dream.

Harry stepped onto the deck and looked out over the waves. The smell of the sea calmed him. It reminded him of a less complicated time when his family had taken long trips on the ocean. He must've been two or three. They'd hardly been a model family, but at least they'd been together.

He could ignore the message, but his father was resourceful and determined. One didn't build one of the most powerful companies on the planet by rolling over at the first setback. He'd get more and more irritating if Harry didn't call him back.

He sighed and listened to the message. His father's deep voice came out of the speaker.

"I'm sorry for disturbing you while you're at work, Harry. I hope you're enjoying the Med. It's wonderful this time of year."

How had the man known where he was?

"Anyway, something has come up. I know that we don't have the greatest relationship, but an innocent woman is in grave danger. I'm willing to pay triple your usual rate, and you can attach a substantial surcharge for working for me. Please call me back as soon as you get this message."

The fees Liberty SOG—Special Operations Group—charged for the simplest operations were substantial. Private military groups took a lot of money to keep in specialized gear and weapons. And Harry paid his people very well indeed. They deserved every penny.

The amount of money his father was talking about was... substantial. Enough to tempt Harry, even against his better judgment.

He sighed. Might as well get this over with. He dialed the number, smiling a little at the time. At least he got to wake the bastard up at an inconsiderate hour.

* * *

THE PHONE beside the bed jarred Clayton Rogers from a sound sleep. Only a select few had his private number, or the code to make it ring through, so he knew it was his son before he checked the caller ID.

He noted the hour with resigned amusement and answered the call. "Harry, it's good of you to get back to me so promptly. I hope your work bore fruit. Kidnapping children is a nasty business."

"And you know more than your share about nasty businesses, don't you?" his son said coolly. "Let's cut the pleasantries short. I'm not inclined to take your money. I know how you earned it."

His son's antipathy was no surprise. He really couldn't blame the boy. Clayton was honest enough to see his own failures. The things he'd done to climb to the top of his business were sickening, despicable, and occasionally horrific. And quite necessary. Something his son had never been able to understand.

Business in 2035 had very little in common with what it had been even two decades earlier. The largest international corporations were almost governments in their own right. Cutthroat didn't begin to describe some of the things they did to one another.

Rainforest—his company—was no exception. He'd like to believe that his behavior was less ugly than most of his compatriots, but that was only rationalizing. He did what he had to. The project was too important to fail.

"I strongly urge you to reconsider. If you walk away, it's likely that dozens of innocent people will disappear into hidden graves. Most of them are in no way associated with my business interests. These are the kind of people you help every day. On that, I give you my word."

The long silence made him wonder if his word was no longer good enough. That day would eventually come.

"When the bill arrives, you'll pay it without a peep," Harry said. "Who are these people, where are they, and what pickle have they gotten themselves into?"

Clayton let out his breath slowly. He'd made it past the most difficult hurdle. Whatever Harry charged would be worth every cent and more. "They are a team of archaeologists excavating a Mayan ruin deep in the jungles of

Guatemala. Communications there are quite spotty. For their own safety, they need to be brought out."

He could hear the surprise in his son's voice. "Archaeologists? Why in the world would people like that be on your payroll? You own the world's largest online store. Is Rainforest selling priceless relics now?"

"Only one of the people is associated with me. The rest are innocent bystanders."

"Who is this person, and what do they do for you?"

"Her name is Jessica Cook. She's an engineer with specialties in space construction."

That silenced his son for a moment. "What is she doing at an archaeological dig in Guatemala?"

"I'm not precisely certain," Clayton admitted. "The man in charge of the site—a friend of hers—asked her to come look at something. Her office is at the Yucatán Spaceport, so it wasn't too much of an inconvenience, I suppose.

"I found out after she departed that your mother has taken an unhealthy interest in her. One of my spies in Kathleen's organization tells me that your mother has dispatched Nathan to collect her. And to make certain there are no unfortunate questions asked later."

His ex-wife was always on the lookout for chances to harm him or those around him. With cause, he admitted. Their marriage of convenience had become most inconvenient when he terminated it.

Scratch the CEO of any global corporation, and you'll most likely find a high-functioning sociopath. The ability to look past the harm people suffered during the course of making a company succeed was a prerequisite to doing business on that scale.

Kathleen Bennett had led her own company when he married her. One that had been in her family for generations. It had made up half of Rainforest when they merged. And he'd stripped it from her via a hostile takeover when they divorced.

The generous payout had done nothing to quench her burning rage at his outright theft of her family's company. Instead, it had given her the tools to wage war against him.

She'd started a new company, but something had broken inside her. She'd become a psychopath determined to hurt him in any way possible, no matter the cost, laws broken, or who she hurt doing so. She'd become the poster girl for the apocryphal corporate monster.

And an almost-cartoonish enemy. It wouldn't be unreasonable for most people to imagine Kathleen sat around rubbing her hands together while cackling madly and muttering "revenge!" to herself.

One day her insensible rage would bring her down. She'd do something so heinous that even her wealth couldn't save her. And he had to admit that she'd recovered her fortune quite well. She was worth almost as much as he was these days. Perhaps more.

The cruelest irony had been finding out she'd been pregnant with their second child after the split. He'd managed to gain sole custody of Harry, but she'd hung on to Nathan. He was almost as bad as she was now.

Harry and Nathan had clashed before, so Nathan's involvement was actually a plus for Clayton. Nathan was one of Harry's buttons.

"Why didn't you say that up front?" Harry demanded. "That would've made this conversation go much more smoothly. As much as I despise you, those two are a completely different level of bad news.

"I'll need all the information you can give me about Jessica Cook, her friends, and the site. A secure upload to the Liberty SOG servers would be the simplest solution. I'll email you a link and a public encryption key. I have a child that I need to deliver. That will complicate the timing."

Clayton had planned around that contingency. "I have a ship in your general area. I can take the child off your hands and assure a safe and speedy delivery. It's something Rainforest prides itself on. Time is of the essence in this matter. Your brother is already on his way."

"Fine, but I hold you personally responsible. If the girl doesn't make it home safely, I'll come for that visit you've been pestering me about, but you won't enjoy it. Look for the email."

The call ended abruptly. Clayton returned the phone to its cradle and rubbed his face tiredly. Days like this made him wonder if his schemes were worth the pain they caused.

The only positive aspect to this situation was that he now had a way to bring his son into the plan. Only stage one, but possibly enough to whet Harry's appetite to learn more.

His son didn't know it, but Clayton had always intended to bring him in on his grand undertaking. In fact, his boy was a critical component of its eventual success. Even if he had to keep lying to his son until he'd ensnared him too deeply to extract himself.

Clayton glanced at the clock on his nightstand and rose. He had a lot of work to do if he wanted to salvage his undertaking and stymie his ex-wife.

2

J essica Cook removed her Astros cap long enough to wipe her face and reapply her insect repellent. The jungles of Guatemala were even hotter and more humid than she'd feared. What had she been thinking?

The trees towered over her, filled with life that called out to attract or warn off others that she would never see. The cover didn't stop the undergrowth, though. Someone had cut a path through the worst of it, but that wasn't saying much. And God, the humidity! She was soaked in sweat.

Besides being far more uncomfortable than she'd counted on, this jaunt was taking her away from her job as the chief construction engineer for Liberty Station. They were coming up on some very important deadlines, and she really should be preparing for them.

The rest of the world—those that even paid attention to such things—thought Liberty Station was going to be a space hotel for the uberwealthy. The truth behind that story was a lot more impressive. Clayton Rogers was building the first spaceship to take humans to Mars and beyond.

If the truth got out, plenty of people would try to stop them. The only players in space these days were the Indians and the Chinese. Both had Mars locked in their sights and were determined to be the first to put a human on the Red Planet. They'd lose that race when Liberty Station stole a march on them. Just one more reason to keep things quiet, since those governments might be able to stop them if they had enough warning.

The United States had given up on space, turning their attention to purely terrestrial problems. Oh, they'd tried to keep up appearances, but the ISS2 space station project had imploded financially. Mister Rogers had bought the unfinished skeleton, and they'd corrected its flaws and expanded on it.

They'd be the first global corporation to focus on the rest of the solar system, and the riches—both financial and scientific—awaiting them. With their technological lead, they'd have years to set up infrastructure that the rest of the world would be hard-pressed to match.

She stumbled a little and forced herself to focus on the here and now. A broken leg would slow her down even more than this side trip.

The boat had dropped her and her guides off that morning, but it had taken them all day to traverse just a few miles of thick jungle. The workers had it much harder than she did, though. They had boxes and bags of equipment and supplies to carry. The sight of them all moving in a long line reminded her of an old Tarzan movie. She could've used a pith helmet.

A stone column was the first indication they'd entered the Mayan ruins. With all the people behind her, she couldn't stop to examine it. Not that she could see much anyway. The thick vegetation hid it almost completely.

She began looking at the hills around them. The ones behind the caravan looked normal. The ones in front of them were more angular. They weren't hills at all. They were pyramids covered in jungle growth.

They'd arrived at the city.

The ghost of a road led them deeper into the long-abandoned capital of some forgotten Mayan kingdom. Her imagination filled in the missing details, and she could see it as a bustling metropolis. Considering the Mayan's technological level, the city was a marvel.

She spotted a few young men and women with survey equipment on a small rise ahead. They waved as she and her party walked past them. Jess cheerfully waved back.

The caravan leader took them to the central camp in what must have once been a great courtyard. Tents stood in neat rows just past a large, dark hole in the ground. A small tumble of stone marked what she imagined had been a short wall surrounding it.

Doctor Abel Valdez stepped out from one of the tents and waved at her. "Jess! You made excellent time! Come! I must show you what we found."

Even though she ached to sit and rest, she wanted to see what had gotten her old friend so excited. And to find out what possible assistance an orbital engineer with degrees in mechanical and nuclear engineering, and several minors in space sciences, would be at an ancient ruin.

His enthusiasm was as infectious as she remembered from college. He'd almost convinced her to become an archaeologist before she'd dedicated her life to engineering. The past had called to him even as the stars seduced her toward space.

Jessica pulled him into a hug. "Abel! Take a breath! How are you? This place is amazing!"

His expression turned sheepish. "Better than good. I apologize. I should let you rest and recover from your trip."

"And miss this mysterious find of yours?" she asked with a smile. "No way. Maybe now you'll explain what the hell is so important that you couldn't tell me over the phone."

She'd been at the Yucatán Spaceport, so it had only been a matter of hours to fly to Guatemala. And then three days of rough travel involving overland driving, a boat she'd been certain would capsize, and a full day hiking through almost impenetrable jungle.

Abel grinned. "This is the most important find of this century and possibly any other. This city is probably from the late classical Mayan period, so around AD 700 to 900. I need your help in deciphering something critical."

She gave him a skeptical look. "I'm an engineer. What I remember about archaeology wouldn't fill a small notebook."

"It would be much easier to show you. I've kept details on this particular aspect of the dig quiet. If word gets out, it will draw the wrong kind of attention. You've studied astronomy and other esoteric space skills for your work in orbit. That is the kind of assistance I need."

Jess blinked in surprise. "Seriously? How can that possibly be useful?"

"Come inside, and I will show you."

Abel led her to a formidable pyramid. Someone had cleared part of it, and she could see the ancient stones as they climbed the steps to the top. He grabbed a pair of flashlights sitting with some equipment and took her inside. They'd strung lights, but there were still pools of darkness between the widely spaced bulbs.

He led her down through a confusing series of shafts and rooms. They moved too quickly for her to do more than glance at the stonework. Carvings worn with age covered some sections of the walls. She couldn't tell much about them. The stone beneath their feet was rubbed smooth by the passage of unnumbered feet. The almost oppressive weight of the ancient building above them made her crouch lower as they walked.

He finally reached a large chamber with a well in the center of the floor. Now every bit of stone contained images that tugged at her memory. She'd seen similar carvings in textbooks back in college. The room looked very important.

Oddly, they had passed no other people while getting here.

"Where is everyone?" she asked.

"Outside. I couldn't allow them to see the last chamber I found."

Jess saw that someone had put a wooden ladder inside the well when she stepped close. Rather than leading to water, it took them down to a chamber with four evenly spaced tunnels leading away into the earth.

Unlike the chamber above, this area was purely functional. None of the tunnels looked very stable, but one seemed particularly shaky. Someone had braced it with makeshift wooden beams. That was, of course, the direction Abel led her.

She eyed the ceiling warily. "That doesn't seem very safe."

"It's good enough for the moment," he said. "We'll bring in stouter timbers once we have the find fully documented. Word cannot be allowed to spread, or looters will descend on this place like a biblical plague."

She ducked down and followed him through a twisting passage that led to another chamber. It was at least twice the size of the one above them. Rather than the rectangular shape she'd expected, it was circular. Except for the far wall, which was flat. The center of the room held another well. This one might even be real, as she could hear what sounded like water below.

The wall froze her in place. It held something impossible.

Though stylized, the inlay was obviously a map of the solar system. She remembered enough to know the Mayans didn't display their representations of the planets like this. They made sky bands showing the planets and representing the paths they followed overhead.

Yet the scene before her wouldn't be out of place in modern America. It clearly showed the sun as the center of the solar system. Something she wasn't certain the Mayans had known. Even the spacing between the planets looked approximately correct. Each world had a line of inlayed gold for its orbital path.

Abel gestured toward the wall unnecessarily. "You see why I contacted you? This cannot exist, yet it does. I need you to tell me if this is some kind of elaborate forgery. It seems to be as old as the ruin, but I can no longer trust my judgment."

Jess stepped closer and examined the jade insets representing the planets. They were about the right sizes, even for the worlds the Mayans shouldn't have known existed. "Correct me if I'm wrong, but they only knew about the visible planets, right?"

"That's correct," he confirmed. "They knew of Mercury, Venus, Mars, Jupiter, Saturn, and the moon. They might also have been aware of one or two of the largest asteroids. Ceres and possibly Vesta. That's it."

She pointed at the worlds outside Jupiter's orbit. "Yet here we have the outer planets. This shows the moons around them as little chips of jade. Even Pluto, Charon, and Eris.

"And one even farther out. A big one. I've read that scientists suspected that there were a few undiscovered bodies out there of significant size, but this one is almost as big as Earth. Quite the discovery, if true. How could the Mayans know any of this?"

The archaeologist shrugged. "I have no idea. And that's not all. See this?" He pointed to another orbit, this one going around the sun inside Mercury and out beyond Eris. Its orbital path was inlayed with what looked like oxidized silver. "This looks like a comet. And here along its path? These markings are faint, but I think they're dates from the Mayan calendar."

The marks meant nothing to her, but she could look them up at some later point. "May I take pictures?"

"Of course, so long as you promise to keep them confidential."

"I don't imagine I'll need to talk to anyone about it. There's a very large database of heavenly bodies and their orbits. I can check it myself and use some computer time to see if these marks indicate a real time that matches any known orbits."

He nodded slowly. "Take your pictures, and we can go back to camp. Dinner will be ready soon. We have much to discuss."

* * *

NATHAN BENNETT SCANNED the endless jungle outside the helicopter door. How could anyone find anything in this green hell? They could've flown over the target a half-dozen times and been none the wiser.

His money had gotten them information that led to the river drop off, but none of the people he'd bribed had known where the ruins were located. They might be an easy day's walk or a week down some hidden trail. He had to keep looking, though, because Mommy Dearest wanted this woman.

Not that he cared, but the target was an important cog in his father's space hotel scheme. That idiocy seemed to matter to the old man, so his mother knew any disruption she could manage there would hurt him. And that's what she wanted most in the world: to hurt her ex-husband, no matter the cost.

He'd rolled his eyes and loaded a team on his private jet when she'd ordered him to do so. He couldn't imagine what use his mother would get from a space engineer. That made no sense at all.

Perhaps it was because she'd lost a lot of money and prestige when the US space program had collapsed. A decade ago, the liberal politicians in charge of the federal government had wanted the money being "wasted" on the new ISS2 space station to go to public projects for the people who'd elected them.

The conservative minority had gone along so that some money could go to military spending. Unsurprisingly with the reduced budget, the project had come apart. Massive computer-design failures crippled the control center when none of the software worked as promised. And his mother had already fired the people who could've walked the systems back to something workable to increase her profit margin.

In space, the station construction fell far behind schedule, even with the corners she'd cut, and the estimated costs rose precipitously. The government didn't do what his mother had expected, which was to pay through the nose to complete the work.

Instead, they terminated the contract. Lagrange Multinational—his mother's space company—had gone bankrupt, saddling her with massive debt and splashing egg all over her face.

The Russian government bought out all the international partners for pennies on the dollar, though he knew they didn't have the spare cash to complete the proposed station. They were far too busy subverting and invading the nations of the old Soviet Union while the US stood around uselessly waving its hands.

Not that Nathan cared. Whatever his mother wanted, she got. So long as she paid.

"Smoke at two o'clock," the pilot said over the intercom.

Nathan looked ahead of them and spotted it. Thin and gray, but undoubtedly smoke. "Find a place to set us down."

"I might be able to drop you in the river, but that's six or seven miles away. I haven't seen a single break in the canopy."

"Keep looking," Nathan snarled. "I'm not dropping into the water and hacking my way through the jungle. I need a place where you can pick us back up." Carrying an unwilling guest through this would be a nightmare.

His second in command, a bruiser named Jake Farley, jerked his chin toward the open door. "Why not drop in on top of them? We can rappel into their camp and get this over with."

Nathan gave him a steady look. "Because this isn't going down like the job in Syria. There's far less paperwork for me if we don't kill everyone that might recognize the helicopter or us."

"It's easier for me," Jake said indifferently.

"Right up until one of the local guards shoots you while you try to get untangled from a tree. We do this my way."

The man shrugged. "Whatever."

Nathan really needed to get some new blood on the team.

The pilot circled around the ruins at a distance. The jungle would dampen the sound of the helicopter rotors to a soft murmur. Technology couldn't completely eliminate the noise, but it was a lot better than it had been around the turn of the century. In his line of work, getting in and out quietly made the high cost of the equipment a no-brainer.

He finally caught a break about ten minutes later. A tree-covered hill rose above the canopy. The area it shaded from the sun had a relatively bare spot they could rappel into. He tapped the pilot on the shoulder and pointed. "We'll go in there. How long for you to get here when I call?"

"About ninety minutes. Add half an hour to get the bird ready."

"Bullshit. Keep the bird ready to roll. When I call, I want you in the air in ten minutes."

The pilot's acknowledgement was more than a bit surly, but Nathan knew the man would do what he'd told him. He'd seen firsthand the kind of pain Nathan could inflict on those who failed him.

It was already late in the day, so Nathan would get them settled in and wait out the darkness. Under other circumstances, he'd prefer to attack at night, but it would be far too easy to break legs and fall into holes stumbling through the wilds of Guatemala. Or to be eaten by something. They'd strike out at dawn, locate the camp, and take the woman.

The pilot brought the helicopter to a hover over the bare patch, and Nathan tossed his rope out the open door. He watched it fall to make sure it didn't kink. That could cause someone to lose their grip and fall right to the ground. That would be their problem, of course, but he didn't want to have less than a full team when he got to the camp.

Nathan checked his harness, took off his headphones, and stepped out onto the helicopter's skid tube. One last check below and he kicked off, using his braking hand to control the speed of his descent. He slowed to a crawl just above the ground and landed lightly on his feet.

It took only a moment to disconnect his D-ring and raise his weapon to cover the landing zone. He stepped away from the rope and watched as his people come in with mild satisfaction. All six of them made it to the ground safely.

They spread out to watch every approach to the LZ as the crew chief pulled the ropes back up. The helicopter turned and headed back for the airfield.

Nathan led the way into the jungle. It stank, and there must've been a million different creatures making suspicious noises in the gloom. He couldn't imagine why anyone would choose to live in a shithole like this.

The already-faint light dropped off to almost nothing under the canopy. The way became congested with undergrowth so thick he had to put his rifle away and draw his machete.

This job was going to be a real pleasure. Thank God he'd fought hard for a bonus.

3

The rented boat dropped Harry and his team off at what he might charitably call a dock just after dawn. It only extended into the river far enough to allow a shallow-drafted craft to use it. That was just barely enough, but it beat swimming.

He showed the owner of the boat a small wad of American dollars. His Spanish was good enough to get his message across. "You come back when I call you, and this is yours."

The skinny man shook his head. "Yes."

Harry gave him a steady look. "If you don't come when I call, I'll take back what I paid you up front, even if you've already spent it. Understand?"

The man swallowed hard. "I understand. I will do as you say."

"That will make me very happy. And when I'm happy, everyone else is happy too."

The team hefted their packs and stepped onto the dock one at a time.

His sniper, Sandra Dean, watched the boat head back the way they'd come. "Did you really need to go all hard-ass on him, Harry? We look like mercenaries in an action movie. He's not crazy enough to double-cross us."

He grinned. "I'm living up to the image. If we need to get out of here in a hurry, we don't want him stopping for a beer." He eyed the trail and shouldered his pack. "Time to hit the road. I'd prefer to be long gone by the time my unlamented brother arrives."

* * *

JESSICA STEPPED out of her tent and stared groggily at the cheerful people preparing breakfast. Actually, a glance at her watch showed they were getting ready for lunch. It was almost ten in the morning. She'd slept far longer than she'd intended.

Of course, she'd been up late studying all the pictures she'd taken yesterday. Not just of the amazing art deep in the pyramid, but of everything else inside the ancient building that they'd seen on the more sedate trip back out.

As far she could tell, only the one work was unusual. None of the other carvings, inlays, or paintings Abel had showed her after the big reveal held even a hint at the great secret buried deep inside the base of the ancient structure.

Abel said that the false well leading down to the secret level was unusual. The only reason he'd discovered it was that he'd tried to get a water sample and found stone instead. He'd taken some water from the real well in the secret room, but he was already certain it would be identical to the water in the well in the courtyard. He believed an underground river fed them both.

One of the graduate students waved. "Good morning! Would you like some lunch? The stew is almost ready."

Jess stretched her back and walked over to the young man. The day was already getting hot. "That sounds good. I hadn't intended to sleep so long. Where's Doctor Valdez?"

The young man gestured toward the pyramid. "Where else? Deep inside the secret chamber."

He laughed at the surprised expression on her face. "What? You thought no one knew about it? We snuck in the same night he told us not to go inside the pyramid. Well, it took us several nights to find the fake well. That was pretty clever. What do you think the wall means?"

"I think it means Doctor Valdez needs less inquisitive graduate students," she said sternly. "You need to keep this quiet."

The young man waved away her concern. "We've been with the doctor for years. His secret is safe with us."

"That's not really the point. If you talk about it, someone will overhear you." She gestured at the local workers all around the camp. "Do you think none of them understand English? You're almost certainly wrong. Some of them understand it well enough, even if they don't speak it.

"Others might be in the employ of Doctor Valdez's competitors. Under normal circumstances, that wouldn't be a major problem, but the wall changes everything. It might bring a horde of people determined to strip this find of everything of value to sell on the black market."

The graduate student stared at her with an expression that indicated he was waiting for her to deliver the punch line.

Jess shook her head. "You really don't get it, do you? People will kill for something like this. Forget you saw that thing, and tell your friends to zip their mouths if they care about Doctor Valdez. And, yes, lunch sounds wonderful."

The bemused young man led her to the tent they'd set up for dining. She accepted a bowl and some water. The scent of the stew had her mouth watering before she took her first bite.

Whoever the cook was, they knew their business. It had enough spice to make it interesting without burning her mouth. She wolfed down her meal and went looking for seconds. She'd need to watch her diet, or she'd get back to the spaceport with a few pounds to shed.

She washed her bowl and eating utensils then went back to her tent to retrieve her camera and carry bag. After reading the graduate student the riot act, she probably shouldn't leave her sensitive notes lying around.

With her bag in hand, she headed into the pyramid.

* * *

NATHAN CHOSE an observation post near the summit of what looked like a hill, but was probably a Mayan ruin, and watched the camp. There were more workers than he'd accounted for in his planning, but that wouldn't be a problem. Seven men armed with automatic weapons could intimidate an amazing number of people. Particularly if they made examples of a few loudmouths.

A flash of pale hair drew his eyes toward a woman walking across the central square. He focused his binoculars on her and quickly confirmed that she was the target. He'd chosen his hide with care so that the sun wouldn't reflect off the glass.

She was a real looker. Short, stacked, and curvy. Getting to know her was going to be a pleasure he'd savor for as long as he could.

He watched her head into one of the pyramids before he spoke softly into his headset. "Target confirmed. She just entered the pyramid on the north side of the square. It looks like they're getting ready for lunch, so we can catch them all at the table. Solidify a count of the people and stand fast for now. Note any other stragglers."

The team acknowledged one by one.

Nathan considered the tactical situation as he waited for them to serve the midday meal. The trip through the jungle had gone faster than he'd thought possible. In the daylight, they'd found game trails leading them in the general direction they needed to go. Now all he had to do was get the woman into custody.

He smiled at the thought of how she'd probably fight. Some women only resisted in the beginning, but he hoped this one might put up a prolonged struggle. Women with spirit were always more fun to break.

The workers finally came streaming to the dining tent. He watched the pyramid the woman had entered, waiting for her to join them. After half an hour, he decided that she wasn't coming. He'd have to go in after her. Which could be fun too.

"She's not coming out," he said over the radio. "Move in on the workers and get them under control. No shooting unless they have guns. I don't want to warn the target that we're coming. Zip-tie and gag everyone."

He backed away from the hide and climbed down the building where the workers couldn't see him. By the time he'd circled the rise, his people had everyone under the gun. His men wore balaclavas, and their camouflage was of an old pattern still heavily used by every stripe of mercenary and guerrilla fighter in the area.

One of the men he'd chosen for this mission spoke the language like a native. He was doing all the talking. With only moderate luck, the Guatemalan National Civilian Police would lose his trail hunting for the wrong people.

Nathan tugged his mask over his face and strode out of the jungle. Four of his men split off to search the area, looking for stragglers. There was always someone.

The roving teams found half a dozen workers at two sites and brought them back. There was still no sign of the woman emerging from the pyramid.

He motioned for two of his men to come with him and headed after her. The explorers had thoughtfully strung lights. That would make the job of finding them that much easier.

* * *

HARRY SLOWED his team as they started seeing signs of ruins. He didn't want to appear threatening, but he was cautious by nature. "Rex, scout the area."

"Roger." Rex Jamison, his main scout, slipped into the thick jungle and was invisible within seconds. They held their position, waiting for word that they could proceed.

Rex ghosted out of the foliage three minutes later. "Hostiles have the camp locked down. I counted four with automatic weapons. They look like locals, but that might be to throw off the police."

Harry cursed under his breath. "Nathan beat us here. Dammit. Rex, go around to the right. Sandra, take the left. Get as close as you can. If they make the wrong move, take them down."

Sandra nodded. "Can do. Going tactical."

Everyone opened their packs and pulled out their weapons. Encrypted radios only from this point forward.

His people melted into the jungle while Harry made his way cautiously into the ruins. He'd opted to carry a heavy pack with an extra weapon. In this case, the tranquilizer rifle. With the right timing, he might be able to take out the hostiles. Or at least some of them.

He didn't feel any qualms about using lethal force on his brother's men. They were literally the scum of the earth. However, if his brother wasn't out in the open, he'd prefer to keep him in the dark about their arrival.

Once he found a good place to observe, he slowly scanned the prisoners, looking for Jessica Cook. He didn't see any women with blonde hair. The client was still in play. And that's how he thought of her. Screw his father. She was the one that mattered.

He focused his attention on the four men. Two of them watched the jungle while two intimidated the prisoners. The high-tech tranquilizer he used could drop a man in seconds, but with everyone so close together, someone would react. And when a man with an automatic weapon felt threatened, people died.

Well, he'd just have to distract them. He keyed his encrypted radio. "I need to get them looking in the wrong direction for a few seconds. Rex, make a noise. Something subtle, so they don't start shooting."

"Yeah, I'd like to avoid that," his friend said dryly. "If I can startle some birds, that'll probably be good enough. I'll give you a heads up before I do it."

"If I can take them quietly, we go that way," Harry said. "Sandra, if one looks like he's going to shoot a hostage, take him out."

"Copy. Call the targets as you engage."

"The one closest to me is home base. I'll start at first and make my way in for a home run."

"Copy."

A minute later, Rex called in. "I'm set."

Harry settled his sights on first base. "Go."

He didn't hear the noise, but he saw the birds take flight. First base, one of the mercenaries watching the jungle perked up. He turned his head and said something to his companions. Second base headed for Rex's location at a jog. Home base turned his attention in that direction too. Third was looking Harry's way.

"Change of plan. Third, home, first, and then second."

He lowered his aim to the man facing him and put a dart in his chest. The man staggered back a step and collapsed.

Harry was already moving his aim to home plate. The target must've heard something because he pivoted toward the fallen man. He continued the turn all the way to the ground when Harry shot him.

First base called out a warning and ducked for cover. Unfortunately, for him, he didn't know where Harry was, and his ass was exposed. Harry put a dart in it.

Second base sprinted for the jungle. Harry fired at him but missed.

"Runner down," Rex said after a moment. "He was grabbing for a radio, but I don't think he got off a call."

"Tie him up and bring him back to the camp," Harry said. "Everyone, move in and keep a lookout for more hostiles."

Harry rose from the bushes and jogged into the large open area, scanning the buildings. He pulled out zip ties and secured the prisoners. He left searching them for weapons and other goodies to his team.

He chose a young woman who looked as if she might be an archaeological student and cut her loose with his combat knife. He held a finger to his lips when she started to say something.

"Keep your voice down," he said softly. "How many others are there, and where did they go?"

She pointed to one of the pyramids. "Three men went in there after Doctor Valdez and his guest. They're in the secret room at the bottom of a fake well, but those men will spot the ladder if they look hard enough."

Harry gestured toward the workers. "I want you to head down the path toward the dock. I'll send some of my people with you. Grab food and water, nothing else. Keep quiet, or those men will come out and start shooting. You give the orders to the locals as I cut them loose."

He made his way from person to person, slicing their bonds as the woman whispered instructions to them.

That didn't keep him from sending orders to his people. "Rex, you and Leann secure the prisoners. Have some of the workmen carry them off with you. I don't want Nathan grabbing them on the way out. Move the civilians a mile off. We'll call when it's safe to come back."

"Copy."

"Allen and Paul, you're with me. Sandra and Mark, you keep watch from out here. If they come out with the client, use lethal force to stop them from taking her. Discourage them from going down the trail too."

"Copy," his sniper said.

She'd do it without qualm too. When she got in the zone, it became nothing more than a numbers game to her. Distance, wind speed, and elevation. If Nathan tried to escape with Jessica Cook, she'd stop him. Permanently.

He caught up with the woman coordinating the workers. "Do you have a map? How can I get down to the well fast?"

"Go to the center of the pyramid and down as far as you can. The well is at the bottom. It comes out into a chamber with four tunnels leading off. The one that looks almost collapsed is the one that leads to the secret room. The others meander around a while and go nowhere. Can you save them?"

She was putting on a brave face, but the woman was terrified. And for good reason.

"We'll do our best. Now get out of here."

He and his people kept watch on the pyramid until Rex and Leann Branson, their com expert, herded the crowd of workers down the trail. Harry waited until he couldn't hear them anymore before heading into the pyramid.

It was time to save the woman of the hour.

4

Nathan was ready to pull his hair out. The damned place was a maze. The lights were no help at all. They went everywhere.

They'd stopped several times to listen and heard nothing. Or worse, they'd heard something and went looking only to come out somewhere else no closer to finding the woman.

Where the hell had she gone?

"Maybe you should've asked someone for a map," Jake said.

It took every ounce of Nathan's willpower to stop himself from shooting the smug bastard in the face.

"We must've missed something," he snarled. "There's some hidden passage somewhere."

He led them back down to the ornate well room deep in the center of the pyramid. The room had a string of lights going around the ceiling but nowhere else. He glanced inside the well and saw a ladder a few feet down.

"Goddammit," he muttered. "They're down there. What could they possibly be looking for at the bottom of a well?"

He aimed his light down the hole and saw a stone floor. No water.

"Shit. These Mayans suck." He pointed to the second man. "Keep watch here. I don't want them stealing the ladder if they aren't down there. Jake, you're with me."

He slung his rifle and climbed cautiously down the ladder. Once he reached the floor, he looked around. Four tunnels. He noted scuffs in the dirt that indicated people had used all of them.

Once Jake was beside him with his weapon ready, Nathan turned off his light. None of the tunnels gave even a glimmer. He turned his light back on and listened closely, but there weren't any unusual sounds. They'd have to do this the hard way.

None of the tunnels looked exceptionally safe, but one looked markedly worse. He leaned close to Jake and spoke softly. He didn't whisper, because that carried farther. "We go a little way down each of these. Come back after five minutes. Mark the path."

Jake took the tunnel directly across from the shaky one. Nathan wasn't surprised. It wouldn't be his first choice, either. He selected the one to Jake's right and went in. This hunt was almost over.

* * *

HARRY FOLLOWED the woman's instructions slowly. He didn't want to give Nathan any warning. He slung his rifle and went with his pistol. It would be a lot more useful in these tight spaces.

He reached what looked like the final bit of corridor leading to the central well chamber and motioned for his men to slow down even more. One was backing him up while the other kept watch behind them. If they ran into any of Nathan's people, Harry wanted to take them out quietly, if he could.

That plan almost went out the window when he entered the chamber and someone knocked his pistol out of his hand. It clattered loudly across the floor, but Harry didn't go after it. He swung in close to his opponent instead, even though his hand hurt like hell. The bastard had used his rifle butt.

Harry grabbed the rifle with one hand and clamped down on the man's free wrist with the other. He yanked the two apart, which left him open for another attack but prevented the mercenary from firing his weapon.

The bastard staggered to his left, directly toward the well. Harry tried to alter their course, but the man seemed determined to fall in.

Harry released him at the last moment, but the man grasped desperately at his equipment webbing as he tumbled over the low rim.

The fight had taken place in relative silence up to that point, with only grunts and growls between the two of them. That changed when they smashed the wooden ladder in the well to splinters.

Harry landed on top of the man when they slammed into the stone floor below. Momentum sent him rolling into the far wall. He saw stars, but staggered to his feet. The light from above only cast a dim glow down here, but he didn't see any movement.

That wouldn't matter. Someone would come looking for the source of all that racket.

The man he'd fought with lay twisted in a way that could only mean he was dead. The ladder was in splintered chunks. He wouldn't be going up without assistance from above.

"You okay, boss?"

He glanced up long enough to see Allen looking down at him. "Better than the other guy. You have a rope?"

"Of course."

"Rig something to get me back out of here. And toss my pistol down."

A sound from the tunnel behind him made Harry turn. There was light coming toward him.

His pistol bounced off the dead man and clattered on the stone beside him. Harry grabbed it and moved to the side of the chamber, aiming toward the potential hostiles.

Two figures came out from the tunnel. Though their bright flashlights obscured them, Harry could tell they didn't have camouflage on. And one of them was a woman. He could tell when she let out a scream at the sight of the body.

Definitely not Nathan's people.

He opened his mouth to make some awkward introductions, but footsteps from the other direction warned him of an oncoming threat.

"Back into the tunnel," he snapped. "Unless you want to end up as dead as he is."

"Who the hell are you, and what's going on?" a male voice demanded.

He didn't have time for this. "Move!" He advanced on them, causing them to retreat in the direction he wanted them to go. Harry made it to the tunnel entrance just as a man with an automatic weapon came into the chamber behind him.

The hostile opened fire as Harry shoved the woman back around the bend in the tunnel. She sprawled on her face, hopefully safe from the incoming rounds.

Harry returned fire to force the other man back. He doubted he hit the bastard, but the action bought him time to hunker down.

The other man emptied a full magazine into the tunnel. The shooter yelled into the ringing silence afterward. "Give us the woman, and we might let you live."

"Pass," Harry said. "Give up now, and you won't end up like your friend."

The other man laughed nastily. "Him? He was an asshole. No loss. I bet you think you got me where you want me. You probably have friends upstairs. So what? I got something for them."

Harry saw him dodge across the room and fired. Too late, as it turned out. The man threw something up the well and made it to the far side of the room safely.

A loud blast upstairs told Harry it had been a grenade.

Dirt and falling pebbles pelted him from the roof of the tunnel. He spun on his heel and tripped over something. A man lay on the floor, his eyes open and staring. The woman was giving him CPR, but from the amount of blood, Harry knew it wouldn't do him any good.

He scrambled to his feet, grabbed the woman's arm, and yanked her along in his wake. "He's gone! Run!"

She still had her flashlight in her hand, which allowed him to see ahead. There was a room around the next bend. They barely made it before the tunnel collapsed. A huge cloud of dirt and debris whooshed into the air, making him cough and shield his eyes.

A flash of light from the side gave him just enough warning to dodge and throw up his arm. The woman's flashlight hurt like hell, but better than if she'd caught him on the head like she'd intended.

"Whoa! I'm on your side!"

She took another swing at him, catching him in the shoulder. The light from her makeshift weapon made the room twist wildly. Her hair fell crazily across her face as she snarled at him. "You killed Abel!"

He caught her third swing and twisted the light out of her hands. He managed to turn his torso and catch her knee on his thigh.

"No! The people trying to kidnap you did. Your boss sent me to rescue you."

"I'll bet."

"He said to tell you that you're too important to Project Liberty to let them take you. The security passcode is kiwi."

She didn't look completely convinced, but she stopped trying to maim him. She wiped tears from her eyes and coughed. The dirt in the air was like being in a sandstorm. "Who the hell are you?" she demanded. "And why would anyone want me so badly that they'd kill a kind, gentle man like Abel?"

"That's a long story."

She gestured toward the collapsed tunnel. "We're not going anywhere soon."

"Hang on." He activated his radio. "Paul? Allen? Are you all right?"

"Harry?" Allen asked. The reception was poor but comprehensible. "We're good. Are you okay? Part of the well room collapsed."

"Yeah, I'm seeing that up close and personal. I'm fine, and I have Miss Cook with me. There's no way you're getting to us, and the pyramid might be unstable. Get out now and organize a rescue."

The other man's tone sounded dubious. "Copy. We'll be back as soon as we can."

Harry turned to the woman now that he knew his people were safe. This was the first real look he'd gotten of her. The picture his father had given him didn't do her justice. She was beautiful. Even covered in dust, with her large eyes streaming tears. His greater height and weight didn't intimidate her at all.

"Miss Cook, my name is Harry Rogers. Your CEO hired me and my team to come after you when he found out his ex-wife had taken an interest in you."

She stared at him. "I've heard of you. The estranged son. Your feud with your father is legendary. Why would you ever work for him?"

He used her flashlight to examine the walls and ceiling for cracks. "That's an even longer story. The short version is because he's paying well and you're not one of his usual corporate douchebags."

"Thanks, I suppose. I'm just an engineer. Why in the world would his ex-wife be after me?"

"Because she's a vindictive bitch and a psychopath. If she can hurt my father, she will, even if it makes more sense to do something else. Were these cracks here before?"

He had his light focused on the wall. Large cracks ran down from the ceiling, and the facing had fallen off. Glimmering bits of gemstones and gold twinkled in the debris.

"Oh, no!" Jess ran over to the wall, horrified. "It's gone! The artwork is gone."

"I'm sorry to hear that, but on the scale of our troubles, I think that ranks pretty low."

"That painting was the most important archaeological find in the last century," she almost snarled. "It was the crowning achievement of my friend's work. His life's work."

Harry held his hand out, palm forward. "Then I'm truly sorry." He reached past her and poked the cracked stone. It shifted easily, and he could see darkness behind it. "This looks hollow. Maybe there's a passage behind it. We need to look without bringing the ceiling down on our heads."

Together, the two of them began gingerly pulling the stones out, revealing an open area beyond the wall. Perhaps their fate wasn't quite as sealed as he'd feared.

* * *

NATHAN CAME BACK into the central chamber ready to shoot, but things were quiet. They weren't promising, though. The guard from above lay sprawled dead on the floor and the tunnel that had looked ready to collapse had done so.

Jake was working with his rope and a shard of the ladder. He was making a jury-rigged grappling hook.

He grinned at Nathan. "Well, things could've gone worse. We're done here."

Nathan gave him a cold stare. "Tell me exactly what happened."

"Your asshole brother showed up. He killed that poor bastard, whatever his name was. We exchanged shots, and he retreated down the tunnel. His people upstairs were a threat, so I tossed a grenade. Took them out."

He finished tying off the rope. "Looks like I took care of your brother too. No need for thanks. I'll take cash."

Nathan's gut burned cold. "You absolute imbecile. What in the world made you think I wanted you to kill my brother?"

He shot Jake in the head.

"That's my job," he informed the newly created corpse.

The tunnel was well and truly gone. He hoped his brother could find another way out. It would gall Nathan for the rest of his life if he hadn't been the one to eliminate that self-righteous prick. The woman's death was a shame. A lost opportunity.

Fortunately, Mother had paid him up front. The loss of the success bonus would sting, but he could live without it. And he didn't have to pay Jake or that other dumb bastard.

At least he had another way out. The tunnel he'd explored had led him out beyond the massive building and toward the surface. It ended at a mostly concealed stone door that the Mayans had cleverly balanced. He'd opened it enough to see the jungle. He'd get out of here, gather the rest of his team, if they were still alive, and get to the extraction point. This mission was over.

He salvaged the weapons and radios from the dead men. They might prove useful.

Now it was time to get rid of any evidence. He opened his pack and pulled out several sticks of plastic explosive. He planted them around the chamber and into the three remaining tunnels. He rigged the wireless timer to blow them in twenty minutes.

Now he might be able to convince himself that he'd killed his stupid brother after all.

"See you on the other side, brother mine. After I send our father to join you in hell." He ran down the tunnel with a laugh.

5

_____

J ess tried to keep her mind off the heavily armed man beside her, but it wasn't easy. How did she know he was really who he said he was? This could all be a trick. He might have been partners with the man that had killed Abel.

Yet, what choice did she have? The tunnel was gone. Hell. That by itself argued in his favor. What kind of idiot collapsed a ruin on himself to build a cover?

She was inclined to believe his story, simply because she could see the familial relationship between him and her boss. Admittedly, Harry was a taller and more ruggedly handsome version of his father. On any other day, his wide shoulders and hard body would warrant a closer look. Today, she just hoped they survived.

Reality dashed her optimism as soon as she grabbed the flashlight and took a good look at the area on the other side of the wall. It looked like some kind of tomb. One without another exit.

Jess's knowledge of Mayan burial chambers was sketchy at best, but this one looked important. Effigy figurines, polychrome pottery, masks, and mushroom figures packed the chamber. Other works of art, carved of jade and marble, sat around the chamber. She could also see a sarcophagus in the back.

"Do you see a way out?" the man asked. Harry Rogers. The man who'd renounced his own father.

"No. It looks like a burial chamber."

"Then we need to find another way clear."

She turned and gave him a look. "The way I see it, we have three options. We dig out the tunnel and hope it doesn't bury us, we go down the well, or we die. We can look in here and maybe we get lucky. If not, our best chance is the well."

He stared at it. "I don't have any breathing gear. We'll end up wet and dead."

"Maybe not. Abel seemed to think it's connected with the courtyard."

"Which way is that? If we go the wrong way, it will be just as deadly."

She pointed into the burial chamber. "That's a clue. I did some reading on the trip down here. The Mayans buried their dead facing either north or west. The pyramid is north of the courtyard. If you don't have a compass, we can make an educated guess and head toward the bottom of the sarcophagus."

He pulled an object off his belt. A compass. "The chamber is facing north-south. So we can try south. Come on."

"I'm not leaving without taking a few pictures. This site might be lost forever. Surely you can spare ten minutes."

By his expression, he didn't think so. She short-circuited his options and ducked through the opening. It was just wide enough for her, so he couldn't get in.

"We don't have time for this." His tone told her he wasn't used to other people arguing with him. Too bad.

She had to get what pictures she could. The art meant they'd buried someone special or unusual here. Perhaps a great astronomer. If she didn't document the site, Abel would never get the credit he deserved, and she couldn't tolerate that.

"I suggest you look for a good spot to tie off the rope while I take pictures. Please tell me you have a rope."

"Christ. How sturdy does that stone box look?"

She aimed her light at the sarcophagus. "It's stout. We can run a line around it. It should support our weight."

"Then take your pictures fast. The chances of the pyramid coming down on top of us increases every minute."

Jess stuck the flashlight into her pocket so that it illuminated the ceiling. She took pictures from the entrance, catching every angle to the room. Every time her flash strobed, she saw the glitter of gems and gold.

She wanted to get the layout before she tried to walk through the funerary offerings. She bent to get the statues and carvings in as much detail as she could. There were too many pieces and too little time to do them justice, but she tried to get a sampling.

Jess took some of the smaller pieces and slipped them into her pack. It was supposed to be waterproof, so she hoped everything made it through undamaged. Including her camera, which the manufacturer also claimed was waterproof.

Mayan carvings covered the stone slab lying across the top of the sarcophagus. The edges had markings that probably said something about the deceased. The top had more around the sides, but the central area was a scene. Well, a scene mixed with all kinds of ritual details.

A man seemed poised to leap off the top of a pyramid. Other men stood nearby, mostly kneeling. They all had the same kind of appearance with long hair and fairly primitive clothing.

The man in the center had some kind of harness over his bare chest, short hair, and an expression of beatific happiness. His arms were spread as though he were about to take flight.

She snapped pictures from every angle. It was magnificent.

"You about done in there? We really need to hit the road."

"Why? Hot date?"

"This place could come crashing down any second. The rocks and dirt are shifting."

She set her camera down on top of the sarcophagus. "I'm almost ready. Just one more thing to look at."

The heavy stone slid a few centimeters when she shoved it. Jess put her back into it, and it opened almost a foot at the head. Time to grab a picture of the man of the hour.

What she saw inside froze her in place. The dried human husk was expected. His clothing was not. It wasn't primitive at all. It looked similar to the woven shirts men wore today. It had buttons. And what certainly looked like a name tag, though the lettering was unfamiliar to her.

"Harry," she said softly. "You need to come in here and help me right now."

He peered through the opening. "You look fine. Come on out."

Jess shook her head. "No, there's something really strange in the sarcophagus. A man with strange clothes. Modern clothes."

He looked suitably doubtful. "In a secret room at the bottom of a previously undiscovered Mayan pyramid? I read that book a few years ago. Pure fiction."

She stepped back to the opening and handed him her camera. "Then what is that?"

Harry stared at the image on the screen. "Is this some kind of joke?"

"Do I look like I'm laughing? Get in here and help me."

He hesitated a moment, cursed, and handed the camera back to her. "I sure as hell hope we don't live to regret this. Or not live at all."

The two of them widened the opening in just a few minutes. He took off his pack and forced himself through, leaving it beside the entrance.

He stepped carefully through the priceless art on the floor and played his flashlight into the sarcophagus. "Holy shit. It really is someone in modern clothes. Sort of."

She grabbed his hand when he started to reach into the sarcophagus. "Wait. It might look intact, but it'll probably turn to powder if you touch it. Help me move the lid aside so we can see the entire interior. If we can keep from breaking the lid, we might be able to cover him back up. They might be able to recover him later."

They managed to get the lid off and leaned it against the side of the sarcophagus, revealing the corpse completely. He looked as dried out as an

Egyptian mummy. His clothes seemed mostly intact and looked far too modern to be possible.

Jess started snapping pictures. His shirt was light in color. Perhaps it had once been white or tan. The name tag was over his right breast pocket. A real pocket. The letters didn't look at all familiar. The shirt had buttons that looked like some kind of plastic.

"How long has he been down here?" Harry asked. "The Mayans have been gone a long time, right?"

"Abel was sure this place was late classical, so AD 700 to 900. This site has been abandoned for over a thousand years."

"Then where the hell did this yahoo come from?"

"I'm an orbital engineer, not an archaeologist. Or a science fiction author. Actually, this kind of seems more like a Dane Maddock adventure. If we survive, you can write a letter to David Wood and ask him how he'd set up this kind of story. I'd love to hear what Bones has to say about it."

The dead man's pants were more like shorts. Jess checked the fly, which caused the fabric to powder. It used buttons too. She pocketed the one that came off in her hand. He wore low-slung shoes that didn't use laces. They looked like leather. A satchel sat just below his feet.

Harry looked at the man's shirt closely. "He has a patch of some kind on his shoulder."

It was too tight for her to see any details. His shoulder was only a few centimeters from the side of the sarcophagus. She put her camera into the space and took half a dozen pictures, changing the point of aim slightly each time.

"Are we about done?" Harry asked. "The hair on the back of my neck is standing up. Something's about to go down."

She prayed, opened her backpack wide, and slid the satchel into it. The thing came apart, but the contents were inside. She tossed her camera in, cinched the pack tight, and strapped it onto her back. "Ready. Let's get the lid back in place, get the rope tied off, and get out of here."

It took all her strength to lift her end, but they got the lid back in place. She sighed. They'd done it.

That's when a sharp shock sent dirt flying off the walls and made the ceiling groan.

"Time to go," Harry said. "Run."

She slid through the opening and watched the ceiling with growing horror. There were cracks, and they were growing. "Do you have the rope ready?"

"Nope. Hold your breath."

He snatched up his pack and rifle, grabbed her in his arms, and hopped over the lip of the well.

She screamed as they fell into the darkness. The fall seemed to last an eternity, but it couldn't have been more than a few seconds. They slammed into the water, and the force of the impact tore her from his arms.

Jess lost her flashlight, plunging her into pitch darkness as she floated in the cool water. She held her breath and let her head figure out which way was up.

She exhaled and felt the air going up the side of her face. She righted herself and kicked for the surface.

The air tasted wonderful when she finally reached it. She took rapid, deep breaths.

Harry broke the surface to her left. "Jessica!" His voice echoed weirdly.

"Over here."

Something splashed into the water beside her. Something big. She swam to the side as rocks from above fell into the water. The chamber had collapsed. The man and his secrets now rested under tons of rock and dirt.

The two of them came up against a wall of stone, and she waited to see if the whole cavern caved in. The rocks finally stopped falling, and they were still alive.

"Well," she said. "That was a little more exciting than I prefer. I don't suppose you managed to hang onto your light. Mine is at the bottom of the pool. It wasn't waterproof, either."

"Mine is." A bright light came on, pointed at the ceiling. She could see where the well pierced it. Or where it used to be. A massive boulder plugged it now. If that had fallen on them, they'd be dead.

Harry played his light around, revealing that they were in a natural cavern. "If there's a connection between the courtyard pool and this one, it's underwater. Let me go look."

He pulled out his compass, and they moved around until they were at the southernmost wall. "I'll be back in a minute."

She watched his light vanish into the depths with more than a hint of trepidation. What if there wasn't a way out?

That question had a simple answer. They'd die.

Jess sighed. It wasn't as though she had any control over what happened now. She had no choice but to wait in the dark and hope for good news.

* * *

HARRY DOVE, his light showing the wall as it plunged toward the bottom of the pool. He could see something glittering dully in the sand below him and to his right.

He made it all the way to the bottom quickly and easily. With all his gear, that was a forgone conclusion. He shed his rifle and pack next to a low opening in the wall. He could feel a sluggish current coming from it.

Then he looked into the passage. It wasn't too tight, but he didn't see it widening, either. It made a turn just at the limit of his light. He set his flashlight on the sand and undid his boots. He'd be able to swim more easily without them. He tied the laces together so that he could carry them around his neck when the time came to go.

That took him to the limit of his air. He grabbed his light and headed back to the surface.

"Did you find anything?" She asked as soon as he broke the surface.

"A tunnel," he said as he caught his breath. "It looks natural. I left my gear down below and came back for more air. I'll get farther that way."

"Do you think it leads to the courtyard pool?" She sounded half hopeful and half afraid.

"It goes in the right direction, so maybe. There's something that reflects light in the sand down there."

"Offerings, probably. Jade, I'll bet. They probably threw other things into the well as gifts to the gods, but they might not have lasted this long."

He was as oxygenated as he could get. "Be back, hopefully with good news."

Harry dove back down and veered toward the glinting object. It looked like polished stone, so it was probably jade. He tucked it into his pocket. That's when he spotted something near the wall. It gleamed like silver, but more dully.

The object wasn't big, so Harry stuck it in his pocket too. Then he kicked his way into the passage. It led him around the turn and into a tighter area. He took a chance and swam into it. The tunnel was only three or four feet across at the narrowest point, but he thought it opened back up.

He turned off his flashlight and let the darkness enfold him. Yep, there was dim light from ahead. The two pools did connect. They might survive after all.

Harry turned his light back on, but it didn't work. Crap, the water must've gotten into it. This would be fun. He turned around and felt his way back. He kept a hand on the stone above him so that he'd know when to head up.

Once the roof turned into a wall, he went up. He was almost out of air when he broke the surface.

"Are you okay?" she asked. "What happened to your light?"

"The water got to it, I think. Rest assured, I'll be leaving a negative review about my experience on the Rainforest website. I went far enough to see light on the other end. I think we're good to go."

"But you're not totally sure? Great. We get to swim into a dark tunnel and hope it stays wide enough for us to make our way through. If not, we drown."

Grim, but true enough. "We can't tread water forever. I'll make the trip all the way and come back for you."

He could hear her breathing heavily in the dark. She sounded on the edge of panic. Her voice was steady, though.

"No. I'll go with you. We'll make it together or not at all. I'm a decent swimmer. How do we do this?"

"I'll take you down, grab my stuff, and lead you through. Hold onto my belt and follow my lead."

Once he was certain that she had a tight grip, he dove down, following the angle he'd used before. His hand felt the wall, and he kicked his way to the sand.

He found his boots, slung them around his neck, grabbed his pack and rifle, and headed in. She kicked along behind him, but her grip on his harness was slowing him down.

It felt like an eternity before he felt the turn in the tunnel. He followed it around and into the narrowest area he'd explored. The gray glow of light ahead lured him on.

The brightness grew as he kicked his way forward, but the tunnel narrowed again. At least he could see it. This would be tight.

Harry tugged Jess forward and gestured for her to go first. If he couldn't get through, he'd only kill himself.

Once she was through, he shoved his gear to the other side and pulled himself into the narrow opening. He got stuck almost immediately. He struggled to push his way through, but didn't budge.

Jessica had stopped even though he'd motioned for her to go on. She grabbed his hand in hers, planted her feet on the rocks, and pulled. That gave him just enough leverage to tear free. She spun and launched herself into the growing light.

He grabbed his stuff and followed. His lungs screamed for air, so lunged for the surface. He made it. Barely.

The two of them gulped air and looked up. It was fifty feet to the roof of the cavern, then maybe twenty more to the opening. There was no way they were climbing those walls, either.

"You should've left me," he told her, "but thanks. You saved my life."

"So, we're even. And you're welcome. Now what? That's a long way up."

"We call for help."

His pistol was soaked, but the damned thing was almost indestructible. "Hold your hand out."

Harry locked the slide back, letting the chambered round fall into her hand. He held the pistol up to the light to make sure there was no dirt or mud in the barrel. That had the potential to blow the weapon up in his hand. The water wasn't doing it any good, but it would fire. Of that, he had no doubt.

Once he was sure it was clear, he took the round back from her, put it in his pocket, and let the slide chamber the next round.

"This will be loud. Plug your ears."

He aimed the pistol out of the well and fired three shots. The sound echoed off the walls, even more loudly than he'd expected.

"Are you calling for help or just catching dinner down there?" Rex shouted.

"I am kind of hungry," he said. "It's damned good to hear your voice."

"I thought you were gone, man. They blew up the whole pyramid. You got the civilians?"

"I have Miss Cook with me. Doctor Valdez didn't make it. Did the boys get out?"

"Just before the thing collapsed. I left Leann with the civilians and came hauling ass back."

A wave of relief rolled through him. "Thank God."

"Are either of you hurt?" Rex asked. "We've just about got a rope secure. I'll come down for you if I need to."

"We're fine. Rig one of the rappelling harnesses, and we'll handle our end."

He looked at Jessica. "I assume you're fine with being hauled out of here."

"Hell, yes. The ride can't be any scarier than having a pyramid dropped on you."

"Probably not."

Harry holstered his pistol and waited for the harness. When it came swishing down, he strapped Jessica into it. "Just hold onto the rope, and they'll get you out. Safe as houses."

"Thanks for coming for me."

"My pleasure. Haul away!"

They lifted her out of the well and quickly dropped the harness back down for him. Getting it on while treading water with his gear was a bit of a challenge, but he managed. "Pull!"

They lifted him into the bright sunlight. Ready hands yanked him over the rim of the well, and he rolled over onto his back.

"Today has totally sucked. I'm charging my father extra."

Rex pulled him to his feet. "Let's get you into a tent to change into something dry. Sandra will help Miss Cook."

"I want eyes all around us. If some of them made it out of the pyramid, I want them found. Nathan is too damned selfish to blow himself up just to get me. He probably had another way out. Find him."

His people spread out as he lugged his waterlogged pack into the nearest tent. He'd be lucky if anything was dry. If not, he'd borrow something from Rex.

* * *

NATHAN WATCHED them fish his brother out of the well with mixed emotions. It would've been nice to have Harry off the playing field, but he wanted to see his eyes when he killed him.

He had his crosshairs on his brother but wasn't tempted to fire. He'd have too much trouble making it back to the LZ with Harry's team hunting him every foot of the way. If the copter crew was even ready when he called.

No, not the time to take chances. "I'll be seeing you soon, big brother," he said softly.

When the others began fanning out to search the general area, Nathan knew it was time to put some distance between him and them. He'd have to report a complete failure. They'd missed the target, and his team was captured or dead.

Well, that was occasionally the price of doing business. They'd failed, so they could take the fall with the local authorities. They wouldn't talk. The money waiting for them when they got out ensured that.

Oh, well. He backed away from his hide and slung his rifle over his shoulder. He'd watch his brother for a while and then call for a pickup when things calmed down. This was not over.

6

Thanks to her waterproof pack, Jess had dry clothes to change into. The female mercenary left her alone to change, saying she'd be outside if Jess needed anything.

What she needed was a stiff drink and some time to grieve for her lost friend. Time she suspected she wouldn't have. Not until they were safely out of this jungle.

She stripped off her wet clothes, twisted as much water out of them as she could, and packed them in a trash bag. They'd be nasty by the time she washed them, but that was a manageable problem. She then dried off and changed into the dry clothes she'd laid out.

The next thing she did was check her camera. It was dry and working, so she synced the pictures to her tablet, which was also intact. Thank God.

While that was happening, she eyed the contents of the dead man's satchel. It was mostly still together, but she needed to secure it better. They'd be traveling in a hurry, and the fall into the water might have irretrievably damaged something already.

She saw several wrenches and a flat-bladed screwdriver similar to the one on her belt back at the spaceport. The tip was removable. There were other tips that looked as though they could fit on the screwdriver handle, but their purpose was murkier. They looked electronic, but there was no indication of a power source. Or what they might do.

She examined the screwdriver handle. The grip had a removable base that revealed a hollow. It held what certainly looked like a battery. It had strange writing on it, similar to the name tag on the mummy. No signs of corrosion, so there must not be an acidic component.

After all this time, the battery was certainly dead, but examining it in the lab might tell them the power level it was supposed to deliver.

At the bottom of her pack was a notebook. It was about the size of a diary and seemed intact. The cover looked like leather, but it wasn't cracked. The pages hadn't come apart either, so she risked touching her finger to their edges. No, it wasn't paper. It felt slick, like some kind of plastic.

Jess took a deep breath and opened the cover.

The first page had tight rows of handwriting in a language that she didn't recognize. Maybe it was a diary. The beginnings of some of the paragraphs were different, so that could mean dates. The inside cover had a few lines of text, maybe the man's name and how to return it to him if it was lost.

She took a chance and lifted the book out to lay it on the cot. She wanted pictures.

That's when she saw the tablet under it and stopped breathing. She set the book carefully down and picked up the device. The surface felt like glass, but that didn't mean much. It could be any number of materials.

The back was made of light metal and had a strange emblem centered on it. A tree of some kind with text in a circle around it. It shared some similarities with the Rainforest logo but wasn't enough like it to feel creepy.

There were several recessed buttons, but she restrained herself from pressing them. The power supply had to be dead, but she didn't want to take any chances. She'd examine it more closely once she had it back in the lab.

Returning to the book, she starting taking multiple images of each page. The first third of the book only had text. The middle of the journal had a number of drawings as well. Some of plants that she wasn't familiar with but also what looked like contour maps of terrain. One whole page had what was certainly a rough map of the Mayan city.

There were sketches of men and women she assumed to be Mayan. Not just the well-to-do but workmen building a wall. Women tending to plants in a terraced garden. Even children playing some kind of game. The man had a good hand.

A second map seemed to show a path away from the city. There were notations in the strange language that probably meant distances or landmarks. The end of the trail had a heavy circle around it. More text beside that might indicate what was there, but she couldn't make heads or tails of the words.

Jess finished taking pictures, synced them, and put everything except her tablet back into the pack. She shouldered her bag and walked out of the tent. The woman was waiting. Another man was slowly turning, watching the jungle. The rest were gone.

"Is it safe out here in the open like this?" Jess asked. "If you think there are still some bad guys out there, maybe we should get under cover."

The woman shook her head. "We've already cleared the general area. We'll withdraw down the trail as soon as Harry is ready."

He stepped out of another tent as she said that. He was dressed in dry fatigues but still had his wet pack on his back. And his weapons, of course.

She walked over to him. "What's your plan?"

"A couple of my people are looking to see if they can find any other bad guys, but I wouldn't hold my breath. Once they get back, we'll move toward the river and meet up with the workers. We'll call for the police when we get to the river."

Jess stepped closer to him and lowered her voice. "I took a few minutes to look over the artifacts. I found something you might want to see." She handed him her tablet with the map of the area on the screen.

He looked at it closely. "What's this?"

"A page from a book inside the satchel. I'm thinking it's a journal. This is the Mayan city here. This path leads somewhere the dead man thought was important. The police will be all over this area. We should see what's there before they accidentally destroy it. Or lead looters to it."

He gave her a stern look. "In case you forgot, there are people in the jungle that want to kidnap you. I don't think wandering around where they might get a second shot is the smartest thing to do."

"I know it's a risk, but this is important. Really important. Come on, surely even a man like you can see that the first extraterrestrial visitor and the things he brought with him need to be protected at all costs."

The corner of his mouth quirked up. "A man like me, huh? Perhaps it would surprise you to know I don't grunt when I walk or drag the backs of my hands on the ground. And we don't know this guy came from outer space."

Jess felt her face heat. "That wasn't what I meant." Actually, it had been exactly what she'd meant. It just wasn't polite to rub his face in it.

"There was a tablet computer in the satchel. Where else would someone with something like that come from? Atlantis? No. Humanity would've found some trace of a terrestrial civilization that advanced. This person came from space. With the condition of the body, he might not have been human."

Harry looked skeptical. "I've seen enough pictures of mummies to know that was a human being. An alien, even one that was bipedal, would almost certainly have some aspect of the face that was noticeably different. Unless, of course, you'd like to propose that humans were seeded all over the galaxy."

"I'm keeping my options open. Think of this from another angle. The artifacts we're recovering could lead to any number of breakthroughs. The technology would have to be very advanced." She thought of another angle. "It might even have military applications."

He shook his head slowly. "You really need to check your prejudices at the door, Miss Cook. I'm a warrior, not a warmonger. Perhaps you're right, though. If there were weapons or technology that could lead to a weapon, I'd rather not see it make its way into the world. There's already too much violence and killing for my taste."

Harry spent a minute examining the map. "I think the best course of action is to accompany the workers to the river. We can call for help from there. Then we'll set out for this place. If the scale is anything close to accurate, we might make it there by midday tomorrow. Maybe. What language are these comments in?"

"I'm not sure. I've never seen anything like it, but I'm not a language expert."

"Someone will figure it out. Come on. Let's get moving."

She watched him get his people into motion. They took down several of the tents and packed them. Probably so they'd have shelter overnight. That had her full approval.

While he organized things, she went back into the tent she'd come from and let the emotions she'd been holding back roll over her. Better to cry now than when she had an audience. Her friend was dead and that hurt. If she ever had an opportunity, the people behind Abel's death would pay.

* * *

HARRY HAD the team ready to roll in ten minutes but stopped when Sandra held up her hand. "Is something wrong?"

"The client is pulling herself together. Give her a few more minutes."

Not the time for it, but he could hardly blame her. He was sure the events of the day would give her nightmares for months.

He'd already cleaned and oiled his weapons, so he made one more pass around the camp. If they were going to be stuck in the jungle for a few days, he wanted to be sure that they had everything they needed.

They had enough water, but taking more would help if they had problems. The tents he'd commandeered would see them through until he arranged a pickup. The extra food and cooking utensils would make them a bit more comfortable.

When he had nothing else to do, he decided he owed his father a call. He reluctantly stepped away from the tents to get it over with.

"Harry," his father said when he answered. "Did everything go as planned?"

"Nothing ever goes as planned, but this went a little further off script than usual. Nathan and his team beat us here. We managed to get Miss Cook away from him, but his people killed the archaeologist leading the dig. At least one of Nathan's people died as well. Both of them are buried under a collapsed pyramid."

"That is unfortunate news, but it could have been much worse. Well done. What's your extraction plan?"

Harry considered what he could say over an open line. Any unencrypted communication might have extra ears. "We're getting the workers to the river, but we're not evacuating with them. There are aspects of the situation that require our attention before we can get clear. We'll be here at least one more night."

The tone in his father's voice expressed his disapproval. "Miss Cook's safety is paramount. I'm certain that whatever issue you're concerned with can wait until she's safely away."

"I disagree, as does she. I'm not able to go over the specifics on an unsecured line, so you'll need to trust my professional judgment." He smiled at defying his father. The small pleasures in life were the sweetest.

"In any case," he continued, "I'll call when we're ready to evac. If you had a plane nearby and perhaps a helicopter capable of picking us up via cable from the jungle, that would make this go more quickly."

"I'm not happy with this turn of events, and I expect a full briefing once you're clear. And, Harry? This better be more than just tweaking my nose, or you'll enjoy our next meeting even less than you usually do."

The line went dead.

At least they understood one another. He cleared his throat outside the tent. "Miss Cook, it's time to go."

She came out, her eyes red, but her expression resolute. She shouldered her pack. "Ready."

He gave her a sharp nod. Her steadiness was admirable. Most civilians, male or female, would've come to pieces under the strain of the last few hours. Jessica Cook was made of sterner stuff.

They hefted their borrowed gear and moved down the path at a steady pace. The workers were only about a mile away with Leann. He took the time to brief them on the general events and to break the news that their boss was dead.

The students took it hard, but he got them moving again in short order when he told them that some of the bad guys had probably gotten away. They made it to the river faster than he expected. No doubt, everyone was eager to be away from this place.

Harry called the Guatemalan National Civilian Police. He kept the details to a minimum and feigned a bad connection before terminating the call. All they needed to know was that there'd been an incident with a fatality. They'd come in enough force to get the workers to safety.

Next, he spoke with the young woman now in charge of the workers. "You need to keep word of the secret room under wraps," he told her firmly. "The men that attacked you can't know about it, or you'll all be in danger. You can't tell the police about it, either. Does anyone else know?"

"About the art? Just the other graduate students. I can't lie to the police."

He hadn't seen her standing there, but Miss Cook intervened. "Don't lie. Just don't mention it."

Harry gave her a quelling glance. "Word will get out if you speak of it. Your boss found something unprecedented down there. Unless you want to see this whole area stripped bare, stick to the basics. These men attacked you, they killed your boss in the pyramid, and they blew it up. You don't know why."

"I don't know why!" the woman almost shouted. "Those people almost killed us. Then you came in and saved us? Why? Who are you?"

Harry put on his least threatening expression. "We're Miss Cook's security team. Her boss should've sent us along with her, but there was a breakdown in communication. I'm certain that he'll give the police a full statement about us and provide access for the police to question us."

In a pig's eye. The old man would shut them down quick.

Miss Cook took the woman by the shoulders. "Do you really want the police to think you might have had some part, no matter how small, in Doctor

Valdez's death? You'd be better off keeping quiet unless you like the idea of a few months in jail being questioned."

The woman's expression went from outrage to fearful.

Harry didn't like the idea of lying to the woman, but they couldn't tell her the truth. Miss Cook was surprisingly adept at managing the situation. She had hidden depths.

"Just keep things simple," Harry said soothingly. "Tell them the truth, just not all of it."

The woman nodded and walked over to her fellow graduate students. Time would tell if the scare kept them quiet.

"I'm a little surprised you told a whopper like that," he said softly.

"I'd tell a bigger lie if it meant safeguarding this secret," Miss Cook said. "I'm more concerned about what the prisoners will tell the police."

He looked over at the bound men shuffling along under Rex's guard. "They won't say a word. I'm sure the penalty of ratting out Nathan and my mother would be fatal. There's probably a financial sweetener to keep them quiet too. And that reminds me, I need to send some money to the guy who was on the hook to pick us up. He still deserves to be paid."

They made the rest of the trip to the river in relative peace. Once they arrived at the dock, Harry trussed the prisoners up like prized turkeys and hitched them to handy trees. No way they'd get loose without assistance.

Surprisingly, it only took an hour before Harry heard a boat on the water. It came around the bend, and he recognized the uniform the men wore. The Guatemalan National Civilian Police had arrived.

He tugged on Jessica's arm, and the two of them backed into the lush vegetation. The rest of the team had spread out to keep watch for hostiles. They'd meet up at a predetermined rally point. Time to see what other secrets this jungle held.

7

J ess discovered that going through the jungle without a cleared path was significantly more difficult than walking down an open trail. Progress was slow, and the insects were all over them. Time to give up that fantasy about exploring the wilds of Africa in a pith helmet.

The mosquitos were even more vicious in the deep jungle. The repellant seemed to be attracting them. She swatted them, but more came to take their place.

The mercenaries took turns hacking at the growth and politely declined her offers to assist. Instead, she followed Harry Rogers. She still knew virtually nothing about him, other than the rumors that she'd heard.

Those stories revolved around him and his father having a huge falling out when he was younger. Of him joining the US Army and becoming some kind of special-operations officer. Him leaving the service to become a mercenary. Obviously, that last was true.

She still had no idea why someone that hated his father so deeply would get involved in rescuing her. It made no sense. Maybe she should ask.

"Hey," she said.

He glanced over his shoulder at her. "You need a break?"

"No. Why did you come for me?"

He smiled. "Because you needed rescuing, and my father is paying heavily for the operation."

"You and he don't get along so well."

"That's something of an understatement. As far as I'm concerned, you're the client."

"It seems like I'm missing something important. You're a mercenary, right? Isn't this kind of job a little off the beaten path for you?"

He looked around at the trackless jungle surrounding them. "We're all a bit off the beaten path, but I get your meaning. No, I do this sort of thing for a living now. Rescuing people stuck in situations they have no way out of. We mainly recover kidnapped children held overseas by noncustodial parents."

Jess blinked. That wasn't what she'd expected at all. "So you're not mercenaries?"

"That's a matter of debate. Liberty SOG has people from the best US military units: SEALs, Delta Force, Marine Raiders, and others less well known. When the government decided to neuter the military, there were plenty of excellent candidates to choose from.

"We've done purely military operations, and honestly, we occasionally still do. But only if the moral reasons for doing so outweigh the trouble. Frankly, with all the problems in Europe, there's plenty of business that we don't need to hold our noses over."

She understood that well enough. It used to be that only the Middle East had issues with violent groups espousing virulent forms of Islam. Now Western Europe was fighting a cancer in its body. It wasn't politically correct to call them Islamic extremists, but honesty compelled her to say that was the right name.

The news organizations, with a few exceptions, and the government preferred to leave the religious part out. They said those people had nothing to do with Islam. That might even technically be true, but those people had no problem using Islam to justify terrible acts.

The European Union had opened their arms to an enormous number of refugees when the violence in the Middle East and Northern Africa spun out of control. War between Saudi Arabia and Iran quickly spread over the entire area around them.

Iran used nuclear weapons they weren't supposed to have on their enemies. Armed with US-made defenses, the Saudis and Israel fended them off. Israel, of course, nuked Tehran and several other military strongholds inside Iran.

Others were less able to defend themselves, and millions died.

That fractured Iran but didn't stop the violence. It only shoved it underground. Groups like Al Qaeda and ISIS now openly recruited from, and infiltrated into, any country they could. With the general collapse of most governments in the Middle East, they saw their chance to create a Caliphate. Saudi Arabia and Israel were islands in a violent sea.

It wasn't looking so good for Europe, either. France was the worst off. Paris was more like Beirut these days. Roving gangs of militants kept the police penned into certain neighborhoods. Sharia law was the rule not the exception. The French government was helpless, and she suspected the militants would finalize their takeover before too much longer. How much longer until the rest of Europe caught the cancer too?

The situation made her sad.

Frankly, she believed in the US government's viewpoint. Profiling was wrong. People should be judged by what they did, who they were, not what they looked like. You couldn't just label everyone of a specific ethnicity as something and rob them of their rights.

Only that open-mindedness hadn't worked out so well. Thankfully, she didn't have to fix the world. She'd be leaving it soon enough for Liberty Station.

Huh. His company had the same name as the project she headed. That couldn't be a coincidence. His father must've been making some point.

"Why call your company Liberty SOG? What does that mean?"

"Liberty is part of what we do. It plays into every aspect of our work. SOG stands for special-operations group. Technically, we're a private military company. We have a number of teams spread out around the globe."

They arrived at a clearing. It looked like the team was setting up the tents for the evening. Good. Her legs felt like rubber.

She dropped her pack and sat on a fallen log after making sure nothing was waiting to bite her.

They had the tents up before the light faded. The guy named Rex built a very small fire and cooked some of the food from the dig. It tasted good after a long terrible day. She turned in early and fell asleep before her head touched the sleeping bag.

* * *

HARRY TOOK the last watch of the night while Sandra cooked breakfast. Frankly, he wished he could just declare Rex as the sole cook because he had the touch. Sandra made a much better sniper than homemaker.

He let Jess sleep in. She'd insisted on him using her first name. Apparently, she thought saving her life entitled him to stop being so formal. That was fine with him.

Once the food was ready, he tapped her foot through the flap of the tent. She sat up abruptly and blinked at him. Her hair was poking out in every direction, and she looked disoriented.

"What?" she asked. "Are we under attack?"

"Only if you consider Sandra's cooking a war crime. Breakfast is ready. We have a latrine set up to the south. Leann will provide overwatch while you take care of business."

He returned to the fire and did what he could to salvage breakfast. He handed Jess a plate when she came back. She'd brushed her hair and actually looked awake.

"Sorry I overslept. That's two days in a row." She took a bite of the food and made a face.

He almost smiled. Everyone did that. "Sorry about breakfast. It was Sandra's turn. She says it builds character."

"That's okay. I'm happy to have it. How long do you figure it will take us to get to the site?"

Harry shrugged. "No telling. We'll be in the general area by lunchtime.

Finding whatever is there might take days. Or never happen. Look around. There could be a city a hundred feet away, and we'd never know."

She glanced around at the almost impenetrable jungle. "True. That would be very disappointing."

"If we don't find anything, I imagine my father will send someone else to look. So, all things being equal, I'd rather find it first."

"Competitive much?"

He took a few bites of something that might once have been eggs. "I make it a habit to never let my family get one over on me. Nathan almost captured you, so I have to make up for it by screwing things up for my father. It's complicated. Even if it takes a few days, I want to know what that site is before he does."

They broke camp half an hour later and resumed their trek. In the end, they didn't have to do a lot of searching. There was a big hill overlooking the general area. Sandra climbed a tree at the top to get a look.

"I have something to the northeast. A gap in the trees. It might indicate ruins."

All Harry could see was undergrowth. He waited for Sandra to climb back down and sent Rex off in the indicated direction. Odds were that he wouldn't find anything.

And, in fact, Rex didn't find any ruins. He did find something strange about the clearing. The gap was a perfectly circular clearing about a hundred feet across.

Even the undergrowth was missing. The limbs from the surrounding trees hid the spooky symmetry from the air, breaking up the curve. Bare ground was all that greeted them. Only a few dead limbs lay in the open.

Harry stopped at the edge, his finely honed subconscious screaming at him to back up. It thought he was about to be ambushed. He wasn't entirely certain it was wrong.

He glanced over at Jess. Her expression told him this wasn't what she'd expected, either.

"Can you tell me why there aren't any plants in there?" he asked.

She shook her head. "No. I've never heard of anything like this." She stepped out into the open before he could grab her and ran her hand over the ground. "It feels like regular dirt."

"Maybe you shouldn't be out there. What if it's some kind of poison?"

"One that works in a perfect circle? Doubtful. And even in poisoned areas, some plants are hardier than others. There's no natural reason for a clearing like this."

Harry couldn't think of one, either. "Spread out, everyone. If there's a group of people cleaning this spot, I don't want to be surprised if they come calling."

He stepped out beside Jess. "Why would someone clear a random spot in the jungle?"

"Because it isn't random. It means something to them. Let's give the ground in the middle a better look."

She marched to the center of the clearing resolutely while he followed behind her, his weapon up and scanning for threats. It felt like the trees were staring at him.

Jess squatted and ran her hand across the ground. "This feels different. More compacted." She opened her pack and dug inside, producing a small hand pick. "I grabbed this from the camp in case we needed to dig."

Within a few minutes, she had a section of the dirt dug up. It didn't go down far. Maybe fifteen centimeters under the surface, she found stone.

"This isn't natural," she said. "See the tool marks? Someone put this here."

That made him shake his head. "Why cover something with stone and then bury it?"

"Because you want to protect whatever is under it. We might not be able to find out why the man marked this area by his book. We're not set up to dig anything like this."

"How far out does it go?"

"Let's find out."

She moved a few feet over and dug into the ground. "More stone here. And this looks like a seam. Maybe there's a buried trapdoor."

Rex came out of the jungle as she started digging again. "I found a trail off to the east. There were some bare footprints. That might mean locals. It doesn't appear to have been used in the last week or so."

Harry stared off in that direction. "Post a watch. Tripwire protocol."

"Copy that. I'll put people out in the other directions too. If we see anything, I'll warn you trouble is coming."

"Hey," Jess said. "I found a handle."

Harry examined it as Rex headed back out to set the perimeter watch. Sure enough, the stone slab had an area carved out so that someone could lift it. That wasn't to say that the two of them would be able to do so by themselves.

"Let's see how big the door is," he said.

It took them working in turns for half an hour to uncover the slab. It was a dozen feet across. That meant it was far too heavy for the two of them to budge. It must weigh tons. Still, it only had the one handhold.

He grasped the stone and pulled upward. The rock groaned and rose on his end. "It must have a counterbalance. That's pretty advanced. Did the Mayans know how to do something like that? And should it still be working?"

"Damned if I know." A flight of stairs descended into the darkness. They also looked like worked stone but were carved and fitted together. It was obvious from the undisturbed dirt that no one had been down there in a long, long time.

He pondered their options and decided he wanted to know more. "Let's go take a look. Watch out for hidden death traps, Doctor Jones."

"Call me Indiana," Jess said with a grin. She pulled an appropriated flashlight from her pack and started carefully down the steps.

8

J ess proceeded down the steps with caution. Just because Harry had been joking when he mentioned Indiana Jones didn't mean there weren't traps for the unwary. She slid over to the right as far as possible. That way she wouldn't trigger something under the center of a step. Unless she was supposed to be on the left.

The stairs went a lot farther down than she'd expected, spiraling gently to the right. Was that a Mayan feature? She wasn't sure. By the time she reached the bottom, she guessed they were at least fifty feet below ground level.

She expected a corridor but found herself standing on the edge of a vaulted chamber. The walls looked like closely fitted stone. Heavier blocks made up the floor just in front of her, but that wasn't the most interesting thing in view.

"Holy crap!" Harry said as he stepped up beside her. "Is that a spaceship?"

Jess had to admit that it certainly looked like one. Its high-tech lines were completely out of place in the ancient hiding place. As if the tablet she'd recovered weren't enough, this proved that the man in the burial chamber had come from space.

It stretched out about the length of a commuter bus, with wings that looked extendable. Much of its bulk was lost in the darkness. Her flashlight was totally inadequate to see the ship as a whole.

Something had mangled the front of the vehicle. The very lines of the frame seemed skewed. This ship had crash-landed.

Jess took a deep breath and turned off her wonder. It was time to be a space construction engineer. "Okay. We need to take some pictures of this thing and, if possible, get inside."

Harry seemed unconvinced. "We might have unhappy visitors before very long. My team is good, but we don't have enough people to stop a howling mob. We need to get a real security team to cover this area before we go all gaga over the spaceship." His expression soured. "Even if they are my father's people."

Jess shook her head. "Harry, this thing has been buried for a long, long time. I'm safe here. Go up and use your sat phone to call for help. Your people, his people, I don't care. This site must be protected."

He tugged a small box off his belt. It had an earpiece with a long cord, so it must've been a radio. "Put this on. I'll try to stay in range so you can yell if you run into trouble. And so that you can get word if we have guests."

After a moment's hesitation, he continued. "Have you ever shot a pistol?"

Deadly weapons weren't really her thing. "I've been to the range with friends a few times."

He shucked his pack and dug a holstered pistol out of it. "This belonged to one of the bad guys. Hang it on your belt. You probably won't need it, but if the crap hits the fan, I want you to be able to defend yourself."

She wasn't comfortable with the idea but didn't turn him down. Yes, she'd been to the range, but it hadn't been the most comfortable experience. Guns were loud and scared her more than a little. She believed they caused more problems than they solved. He obviously had a different worldview.

Still, she was in the middle of the Guatemalan jungle with people trying to kill or kidnap her. It seemed like an appropriate precaution.

Jess listened to his short safety lecture carefully. If circumstances forced her to use the damned thing, she wanted to do it correctly. And, his warning to be certain what she was shooting at was only common sense. With her luck, she'd shoot at a bad guy, and it would be him. No doubt, that was exactly what he was afraid of.

She slid the holstered weapon onto her belt and pocketed the spare magazine.

Once Harry was gone, she turned her full attention to the ship. She doubted it had made such a neat hole in the ground. That meant the Mayans had dug this area out, lowered the ship into it, and built the roof and stairs to conceal it.

That was a lot of work.

A rough estimate of the ship's weight convinced her they hadn't lowered it in. No primitive ropes would've been able to support it. Perhaps they'd dug out the hole, created a gentle slope, and used logs to ease it into place.

Jess dismissed that line of thought. Someone would figure it out. She needed to examine the vessel.

She circled the ship, taking pictures to document it. Once she had the ground-level exterior covered, she made a closer pass. She didn't want to spend too much time on any one thing, but she couldn't stop examining the external fixtures.

Time had damaged so much. Metal left out in the air for long periods often decayed in ways many people didn't consider. Rust was only the most common kind of damage. It was a testament to its builders that this thing still existed at all.

The ship, of course, would never move under its own power again. The stresses would tear it apart. Yet the technology it contained could hurl them into the future with a number of leaps and bounds. Some of the exterior equipment was recognizable, most was not.

"You okay down there?"

Jess jumped at Harry's voice in her ear. She ordered her racing heart to slow down and searched for the button to transmit.

"I'm fine. Just taking pictures and looking at the equipment on the hull. Any sign of visitors?"

"Not yet, but I have Rex putting out some tripwires. We have some that will warn us silently if anyone is coming. I need to call my father too. I really can't justify keeping you in a dangerous situation like this any longer. Dammit."

She could hear the frustration in his voice. She didn't understand the circumstances behind their relationship, but she sympathized. Her brothers occasionally sounded like that when complaining about her.

"Someone else was always going to take over this site," she said reasonably. "He'll guard it, but the Guatemalan government will find out soon enough. We're only temporary caretakers."

"Maybe I should've called them directly. Probably not. The corruption is so endemic down here that we wouldn't have any idea who'd take possession. How long will you be down there?"

"How long until the new protective force arrives and kicks us out?"

He laughed. "I should've guessed. Call me if you find anything dangerous or if you need any help."

"Will do."

Jess returned her attention to the ship. How could she get in?

* * *

Nathan watched Harry from the safety of the hill. He couldn't see him directly, but the microdrone he'd sent in transmitted the visual in maximum HD.

His brother's strange actions convinced him that he'd been right to take a risk and follow them.

What was he up to? Why come all the way out here to this hidden site? And how had they known it was even here?

Harry had left the workers to the police and came out to the middle of nowhere. They'd dug up some kind of stone slab, and now the woman was underground. It was a mystery, and he hated mysteries. Someone always died, and it was rarely the self-righteous prick that deserved it.

With the forces opposing him, Nathan couldn't do anything but watch, but that was interesting enough. Something in the pyramid must've led them here. Or something the archaeologist had discovered. There was no telling.

Actually, he might be able to get an idea, but only if his idiot brother moved away from the hole in the ground. That meant Nathan needed to exercise patience. How boring.

He settled in to wait and watch. If the opportunity presented itself, he'd send the drone down the hole.

* * *

HARRY MULLED over what Jess had said and called his father with a sigh. Best to get this over with.

"Harry. Are you ready to tell me what this is all about?" his father asked when he answered.

"Not over an unsecured line, no. We're ready for a pickup, though. We'll also need a security force. There's something here that needs guarding."

"So call the police. That's not my problem."

Harry smiled humorlessly. "Oh, I think you'll want to send some people. You know how you're always raving about how good your word is? Well, this is the time to trust what I'm saying. You want a strong security force as soon as possible at the coordinates I'm sending you. You have an interest. You just don't know it yet."

His father was silent for a moment. "Very well. I can have a small team to your general area in about an hour. It will take at least two more to get a larger group of guards in place. Which is better?"

"Both. We're not in immediate danger, but that could change on very short notice. I'll send you the coordinates. There's a clearing large enough for landing a small helicopter, but rappelling in would be faster and safer. I'll talk with you again once I get Miss Cook in your hands."

He hung up before his father could respond.

Things could still go to hell in an hour, but they were making strides toward getting Jess to safety. He'd best go check up on her. Make sure she wasn't doing something dangerous. Of course, with strange technology, how would he know?

* * *

CLAYTON CONSIDERED the phone in his hand for a moment. This kind of behavior wasn't typical for his oldest son. If Harry had something to say, he'd say it and damn the consequences. Whatever he was hiding, it must be important.

He'd already relocated to the Yucatán Spaceport, so he'd pick them up personally. He wouldn't go to this kind of trouble for just anyone, but this hinted at fast-moving and important events. Events that he needed to know about as soon as possible.

His personal assistant looked up from his computer as Clayton came out of his makeshift office. "Yes, sir?"

"Hold all my calls, and notify my pilot that I'm on the way. I want to be in the air as soon as I buckle in."

He didn't wait for a response. His man was more than capable of handling simple instructions.

* * *

IT ONLY TOOK Jess a minute to find the way into the ship. Of course, that didn't mean she had a clue about how to open it. Or even the assurance that it was possible after all this time. It might be corroded shut. Or need power to function.

The hatch itself was about the size of a double doorway. More than big enough for a person but small for cargo. The hatch failed to budge when she tugged on the handle, so she was pessimistic about her chances of getting inside.

"Coming down," Harry said over the radio. "Don't shoot me."

She glanced over at the stairway and saw his light. "You're good. This time."

"Thanks," he said dryly. "How's it going?"

"I'm trying to open a hatch with no success. Maybe you have a crowbar?"

"I have a wrecking tool, but let's hope you're not seriously thinking about destroying things."

Jess waited for him to arrive and gestured at the hatch. "This doesn't seem to have an exterior unlocking mechanism. The handle doesn't turn. It looks as though I should just have to slide it open, but it won't budge."

He played his bright light over the hatch. "Is it an airlock?"

"Probably. Even so, there has to be a way to open it from the outside."

Harry examined the area around the hatch. He pointed to a dimple on the hull to the left of the handle. "What's that?"

She examined it closely. "I'm not sure." It looked like a fold of metal in the hull. She pushed on it with her finger. It opened a little. "Good eye. Maybe it's some kind of keyhole. Too bad we don't have the key."

He frowned. "It's reminding me of something I found in the well." He set his pack on the floor and dug around inside it. After a few minutes searching, he produced a flat strip of metal about the size of a data chip. It gleamed with a sheen that told her it was made of something from the platinum group.

Jess took it from him. "You found this little thing in the water? I'm impressed. Definitely not something produced by the Mayans. Unfortunately, I'm certain that any power supply for the hatch is long dead. We can see if it fits, though."

The tip of the strip fit into the dimple, and she slipped it in with a click. The hatch moved slowly to the right. She jumped back in shock.

Harry raised his rifle and covered the newly exposed area. "I think it still has power."

"Thanks, Captain Obvious. I'm pretty sure that we don't have to worry about live threats inside this thing, though."

"I wouldn't be so certain. If the hatch works, any internal defenses might work too. That does kind of look like an airlock."

The ones on Liberty Station weren't very different. Some of the equipment inside looked like oxygen containers and spacesuits.

The suits looked more like coveralls than true vacuum gear. The fabric had rotted, of course, but she was already salivating over the construction techniques she might be able to learn from them.

At the far side of the compartment, the other hatch was open. Not surprising, as they were in a breathable atmosphere. She hopped into the airlock and aimed her light inside. A fine layer of dust covered everything.

The rear area looked more suited to cargo, but the forward section had bulky acceleration couches. The most forward of those had a wide, wrap around control console, similar in appearance to the tablet she'd recovered. The rear of the cargo area had an interior hatch. Two long bags lay on the floor of the cargo area.

Harry jumped in beside her and lowered his weapon so that it hung on his chest by a strap. "I suppose it does look fairly safe in here. Considering the condition of the exterior, things are in amazing condition. Our ride gets here in an hour, so you might want to pick up the pace."

"I'm not going anywhere until I give this a thorough look," she said firmly.

"Don't touch those."

Jess looked up from the long bag she'd been about to open. "Why not?"

"Because, unless I miss my guess, those are body bags. They don't look empty. Unless your plan is to dump some poor bastard's remains on the deck, you'd best steer clear of them."

She pulled her hand back. "Thanks. No, that wasn't on my list of things to do. These must be the man's crewmates."

He peered into the front of the craft. "The interior of this thing looks remarkably intact."

Jess tried the hatch at the rear of the cargo area, and it opened without a problem. The inside, as she'd expected, was stuffed full of equipment. Most of it was engines, she thought. They didn't look like anything she'd ever seen before. She wasted no time getting her camera into action.

"Do you think this is the power supply?"

She looked over at where Harry was pointing. A cube about ten centimeters across sat behind a clear panel. It glowed a soft blue. Jess took some pictures.

"Maybe. I can't imagine how any of this still works. Any kind of battery should be long dead. Also, there's no indication of reaction mass."

"Excuse me?"

"A spaceship gets thrust by igniting flammable fuels or heating something to high temperatures and letting it escape in the opposite direction from where they want to go. There's nothing like that on this ship. How did it fly?"

The mercenary shrugged. "Magic? Little blue elves? Black holes? Does it matter?"

"Yeah, kind of." She examined the cover over the cube. It didn't seem heavily shielded or all that secure. A simple latch kept it closed. It looked as though a tug was all it took to remove it.

Once she finished taking pictures of the engineering space, she led the way to the front of the cabin. She couldn't pilot a spaceship, but she knew acceleration couches. These could handle three or more gravities, she guessed.

The restraints looked heavy duty. It would've taken a very bad crash to kill someone strapped into one. She was willing to wager that the people in those bags hadn't died in these couches.

Gingerly, she sat in front of what she guessed was the pilot's console. The curved panel in front of her was dark and covered with dust. She swiped her hand across it. That cleared a swath of the surface and caused it to light up. Another curved panel at window level lit up too, showing the room outside. Since it was pitch dark in reality, there must've been some kind of enhancement taking place.

"Holy crap," Harry muttered. "That looks like something out of a movie."

It sure did. The controls were incomprehensible to her, but she recognized the writing as similar to the script from the book. She kept her hands far away from the glowing icons and graphs, afraid she'd activate the engines if she touched anything.

Jess looked up at Harry. "Call your father again. Tell him to speed things up."

* * *

NATHAN RAN the drone down the stairs as far as he dared. Communications were getting spotty, and he didn't want to lose control of it. That's when he saw what looked like the bottom of the stairs.

He gnawed his lip. To chance it or not? If he lost the drone, they'd probably find it. That wouldn't be good. Still, he needed to know what they were doing.

Deciding to risk it, he nudged the drone deeper into the underground area. It still had communication with the controller unit when he reached the bottom, but only just. He didn't dare go any farther than the bottom of the stairs.

The room was darker than the pit of Hades. Where were they? In some other part of an underground maze? He flipped the visual to mixed mode. Two bodies appeared in the infrared spectrum. One of them was sitting, and the other was looking over the first one's shoulder. They were somewhat indistinct. There was a significant barrier between the drone and them.

He activated the small UV spotlight. For a moment, he didn't understand what he was seeing. Then he almost dropped the controller.

That couldn't be right. Was that some kind of aircraft? In the bottom of a Mayan tomb?

Nathan stared at the image for several moments, not really comprehending what he was seeing. Where had that thing come from? Who'd put it there? Why were his idiot brother and that bimbo looking around inside it when they should've been getting the hell out of there?

With a shake of his head, he decided that he'd better pull the drone out before someone came down the stairs behind it. He goosed it straight up when he reached open air.

His timing was good. One of Harry's men ran from the trees and down the underground stairs moments later. He looked a little panicked. Curious, he scanned around the area.

His brother's mercenaries were still out there, but they weren't alone anymore. Dozens of people were creeping in from the east. Nathan smiled. His brother was about to be ambushed. Oh, this was going to be good. He wished he'd brought popcorn.

9

"Possible hostiles inbound," Rex said over the radio. "Estimate thirty-plus."

Harry cursed and keyed his microphone. "Copy. I want visual confirmation. Pull back to the prepared positions."

He turned to Jess. "Get ready to leave at a moment's notice, but stay down here. If these are locals, we should be able to drive them off."

"And if they're more of your brother's men?" she asked.

"Then we're in serious trouble. Hang tight, and don't do anything until I call for you to come out. If someone else comes down, shoot them."

"That's a bit hasty."

"You can comfort yourself with the thought that you'll probably miss."

Jess gave him a steady look. "That's not comforting."

He headed toward the hatch. "Keep your head down."

It only took a minute to run up the steps and meet up with Rex. "Status?"

"I'd say they're locals. They're using the terrain very well, but they don't move like trained fighters. If so, that means no body armor and probably no heavy weapons. We should be able to turn them around without killing the lot of them."

"Unless this is a religious site. We both know that changes things."

Rex's expression soured. "Yeah. Let's hope they aren't as fanatical as those buggers in the sandbox. I figure we have about ten minutes before they think they're close enough to attack."

Harry went to the position they'd dug for him. He didn't like having his people scattered on all sides of the clearing, but he'd had no way of knowing which direction an enemy would come from. They'd consolidate quickly if things went into the crapper.

"Liberty Six, Long Gun." It was Sandra.

"Go, Long Gun."

"I have eyes on the intruders. They look like locals. No armor. Some guns. Some machetes. They're sending scouts toward the clearing. Orders?"

"Do not engage unless they make the first move. I'd prefer we scare them off."

"Copy. Shoot to defecate."

He smiled. "Orders confirmed."

Harry settled in to wait.

* * *

NATHAN WATCHED the primitives come closer and considered his options. He grinned and brought the drone's explosive package online. If he used it just right, he might be able to screw his brother over. It wouldn't stop him in the end, but he owed the bastard.

He sent the drone slowly down.

* * *

JESS FINISHED TAKING pictures of everything she thought was interesting. The pilot's console had gone dark again, so she brought it to life once more and took detailed close-ups. Maybe one of the mission pilots could help her make sense of the icons and graphs.

She'd just finished when a sharp explosion went off somewhere above her. The ship didn't move, so it couldn't have been too bad. She stood there listening, dreading. If the ceiling collapsed, it would probably crush the ship and her.

Something small bounced off the hull. She waited in dread, but that was it.

Once she was relatively certain that she wasn't going to die, she ventured to the hatch and looked out. Her light showed she was in trouble again. Rocks covered the stairs leading up. Perfect. She scanned the ceiling with her light, and it looked intact. Jess hoped it stayed that way.

"Harry," she said over the radio. "Can you hear me?"

No response.

She ran her hand over her face. Now what?

* * *

THE UNEXPECTED EXPLOSION made Harry throw himself down. There wasn't any follow-up gunfire, so he peeked over the log behind him. It had come from somewhere back toward the clearing.

Shit.

He ran back as fast as he could. The trapdoor had fallen into the stairwell. He skidded to a halt and stared at the damage with dismay. Only a small opening remained. The entrance had collapsed.

Harry keyed his radio. "Jess, are you okay? Jess?"

No response. The ceiling was obviously intact, so she was probably safe. As long as he could get her out before her air went bad. Or the roof really did collapse.

Where had the explosion come from? Did the locals have a mortar? He doubted it. He'd have heard the round on the way in, and the damage would've been significantly worse. This was a surgical strike.

If it wasn't the locals, odds were it was Nathan. His father's men hadn't arrived. He'd have heard the helicopter. That little bastard was still around here somewhere.

"Liberty Team, this is Liberty Six," he said over the radio. "Be advised we have advanced hostiles in the area. If you see someone, light them up. Long Gun, what is the status of the locals?"

"Holding position and conferring," Sandra said. "I don't think they liked the sound of that explosion. Some of them seem to be circling around, maybe to get a look from the other side of the clearing."

"Keep the main group in sight. I'm going after the client."

"Scout to Liberty Six, you need to charge extra."

As if he wouldn't make his father pay through the nose for everything. "I will. Go find that bastard, Rex. Bring me his head."

"Copy that."

The opening looked wide enough for Harry to wriggle into. Hopefully, the slab wouldn't shift and crush him.

* * *

JESS LOOKED at the rock pile with dismay. It completely cut off the stairs, and there was no telling how much rubble was there. If she started digging, it would continue to fall out. All she had were her hands anyway.

A few minutes later, the sound of stone scraping stone startled her. That wasn't falling rock. It came from the other side of the chamber, from the collapsed stairway.

The sound was too steady to be natural. It was as though someone was dragging a rock across the floor every few seconds. She jogged to the side of the spacecraft and aimed her light over at the wall.

Part of it was open a little. It slid a few centimeters more as she watched. Its jerky movement gave her the idea that it was almost jammed. She couldn't see inside it, but it had to be some kind of hidden entrance. That meant there was a way out.

And that someone was sneaking in, probably to do bad things to her.

What should she do? Hide in the ship? If she closed the hatch, she'd probably be safe for the time being. And trapped. If she stayed outside the ship, they'd see her.

She could try to bluff them with the gun, but that seemed stupid. What would she do if they called her on it? Give up, most likely. She didn't see herself getting into a gunfight.

Jess decided stealth was her best course of action. She ran back into the ship, ducked into the engineering space, and chewed her lip. Taking a deep breath, she opened the cover shielding the glowing cube and yanked it out.

Nothing terrible happened. Hopefully, she wasn't getting soaked in lethal radiation. She couldn't leave this for them to find. She stuffed it into her pack.

She raced back out of the ship and yanked the key from the lock. The hatch slowly slid shut. The cube must not be its only power source. It didn't budge when she tugged on it.

Most people were right-handed, and they tended to go around things on their dominant side. She slid to the other side of the ship and turned off her light.

The door scraped along for another minute and stopped. She knew her eyes would reflect any light they carried, so she looked at the ceiling. There was one source of light moving toward the other side of the ship.

So far, so good.

Once she judged that they were rounding the ship, she started around her side. With the bulk of the vessel between them, they'd be none the wiser as long as she didn't give herself away.

The reflections of their light were just strong enough for her to see the door. Refusing to run, she walked toward it as quietly as she could.

The door opened onto a dirty chamber scarcely three feet across. A passage led straight up from there with holes cut into the rock for climbing. Dim light filtered in from somewhere above.

She considered closing the door, but even if she could move it, she might be trapping those people down here to die. She'd just have to take the chance that they wouldn't come up and catch her in the act of escaping.

Jess made it about two-thirds of the way up when someone shouted below her. A glance down showed someone climbing rapidly toward her while a second person shined a bright light upward.

Time to pick up the pace.

She threw caution to the wind and raced toward the surface. If she fell now, they'd kill or capture her, so she jammed her boots into the holes as deeply as she could.

Which, in hindsight, might have been a mistake. Her foot got stuck just shy of the surface.

Jess cursed and wiggled her foot. When she felt it give, she yanked hard. Her boot came loose, and so did the stone. It fell straight down and smashed into the man behind her. Much screaming ensued.

"Sorry," she said as she pulled herself up to the surface. Hopefully, it didn't kill either of them.

She came out into the dim light filtering through the trees and jumped to her feet. It looked as though they'd rolled a rock out of the way to gain access to the passage.

"Well, well. It looks like I get a second chance after all. There must be a god."

Jess whirled and stared at the man in camouflage leaning against a tree. He had a pistol held loosely in his hand. "Come along quietly, and I won't have to use this. Resist, and my idiot brother can carry your corpse home in a body bag."

* * *

HARRY WAS STILL TRYING to widen the hole enough to wedge himself inside when shots rang out to the west. A lot of shots. He sprang to his feet and headed for the tree line at a jog.

"Shots fired," Rex said. "Somewhere back toward the clearing."

"Who's engaged?" Harry asked.

A chorus of negatives came back.

He looked around the tree he'd chosen for cover. "Enough of this crap. Pop smoke and drive our visitors back. Rex, you and I will find the source of those shots."

It had sounded like a pistol. Someone had let off at least a dozen shots in short order. He wondered what the hell they'd been shooting at.

A sound off to his right caught his attention as he eased into the undergrowth. Someone was hauling ass. He headed in that direction, stopping occasionally to listen.

He knew he'd focused on the movement a little too closely when the tree beside him took a bullet that sent splinters into his face. He dropped and rolled, looking for his attacker.

"You think you can sneak up on me, shithead? Wrong answer!" The voice was obviously a very stressed out Jess.

"Do you kiss your mother with that mouth?"

* * *

"HARRY?" She stared at the source of the voice, trying to ignore the ringing in her ears.

"I'm going to stand up," he said. "Don't shoot me."

He rose cautiously out of the undergrowth. "You want to put that thing away?"

She stared at the pistol for a second and then lowered it to her side. "Sorry. It was your brother. He ambushed me."

"It looks like that didn't work out so well for him. Where the hell did you come from? I was about to dig my way in."

She gestured behind her. "There's a secret tunnel back there. There were two guys in the chamber, and I dropped a rock on them."

Harry shook his head in amused disbelief. "Aren't you the resourceful one?" He took her pistol from her, checked it, and held out his hand. "You're almost dry. Give me the other magazine."

She handed it to him as Rex came through the trees at a run. He hefted his rifle and scanned the area, making her feel a whole lot better.

Harry swapped out the magazines and slid the pistol into her holster. "Are you hit? Turn around."

"No. He missed me. He said he was your brother. He shot at me, and I drove him off."

"So you said. Where's this hole down?"

Jess felt like she was in shock. Her vision was all weird and tight, and she couldn't seem to think straight. She took a deep breath, focused, and led him into the trees.

He grabbed her arm when they spotted two men hobbling away. One was supporting the other. "No need to shoot at people who're retreating. Just let them go."

"I wouldn't have shot them," she said indignantly. At least she hoped not. She'd been reaching for her pistol when he grabbed her.

The man supporting what looked like a teen saw them and hobbled faster. In moments, they were gone in the trees.

Rex came into the small clearing. "I found a few blood drops, so I think he took a round. You want me to chase him down?" He inclined his head toward Jess. "Good shooting."

Harry grunted. "No. We can't afford to let him ambush one of us alone. Help me close this off. We'll post a guard and make sure the new people know about it. I don't want that asshole slipping in there to blow anything up. Pardon the language."

She smiled. "I said something like that a few minutes ago. How long before the ringing stops? That gun is loud."

Jess cocked her head. She heard something in the distance. It was the distinctive sound of a helicopter. "We have more company."

The two men rolled the rock back over the opening. "Rex, stay here."

He led her back to the clearing. A helicopter was hovering overhead, and men in Rainforest security uniforms were rappelling down.

"Thank God," Harry said. "We'll let them get deployed, and then I'll fill their team leader in. Once they're good, we'll hoist you up and get the hell out of this damned jungle."

She felt relieved. "That's the best thing I've heard since this sorry trip started."

10

Once the security team was in place, Harry quickly briefed the Rainforest team leader as the helicopter searched the area, looking for signs of Nathan. There wasn't much chance of spotting him, but it was worth a try.

He dialed his father's private number as soon as he finished the briefing.

"Are you on your way out?" his father asked.

"Almost. Nathan showed back up. We drove him off, and we're about to take to the air. You'll want a total lockdown of the two sites, particularly this one."

The line was quiet for a moment. "I'll call my friends in the Guatemalan government. With the generous application of some bribes, I should be able to gain control of the Mayan site. At least in the short term. It will take significantly more money to extend that into the long term, and I'll need a compelling reason for doing so."

"You'll want to talk to Miss Cook about that as soon as she gets back to the spaceport. I believe you'll find her reasoning and evidence compelling."

"Speaking to her is my highest priority. There's a chartered plane waiting for all of you at a private airport nearby. It will fly you directly to the Yucatán Spaceport as soon as the helicopter delivers you."

Jess walked over to Harry. "Are you talking to Mister Rogers? Give me the phone."

He handed it over. "Don't go into any detail over an unsecured line."

She put the phone to her ear. "Good evening, sir. Jessica Cook here. I need to meet with you as soon as possible. This information has some bearing on the project, and it's literally earthshattering."

After a moment of listening, she continued. "Yes, sir. It's that important. Thank you."

Harry took the phone from her. "We'll be there sometime tonight." He disconnected without waiting for a response.

"You're not looking forward to seeing him," she said.

He allowed the corner of his mouth to quirk up. "You're very perceptive. No. He and I haven't seen eye to eye for a very long time. But that's me. He's your boss. God save you."

"What happened? Your split with him, his split with his ex-wife and his other son, and your not-so-subtle war with your brother. That's a bit dysfunctional."

"It's also a bit personal."

"We've saved one another's lives. We're like blood brothers now. Blood siblings? Something like that. We're supposed to bond."

Harry laughed in spite of himself. She was a bold one.

"Let's just say that the two of us didn't see the world the same way. My mother is like him, only worse. As for my brother, he's a homicidal maniac that I'll take out of play one day very soon."

She nodded seriously. "I can't argue with that."

"And what about you?" he asked. "I didn't think there were many orbital engineers left after the collapse of the American space program. Nobody is building anything anymore. Well, except for the Indians and the Chinese. Who'd have expected those two to get into a race to Mars? It's kind of sad, really."

"Once the government liquidated NASA and sold off all their assets, those kinds of jobs pretty much went away," Jess said. "The Russians bought the skeleton of the ISS2 station from the other partners and sold it to a private firm. It's not common knowledge, but if you dig through all the shell companies, Rainforest is where they all lead. And that's how I come into the story."

He frowned. "What the hell does a global seller of everything need with a space station? Aren't drones fast enough?"

"We're always looking for new ways to deliver things more quickly. You'd be surprised how fast a package dropped from orbit can get to your house."

"Nice."

A grin lit up her face. "I use that at parties. Would you believe we're turning it into a space hotel?"

"Actually, I might. I heard my father talking about something like that a few times when I was growing up. How could you make a profit? The construction costs must be ruinous. Even with the skeleton already in place when you bought it."

"That wasn't any help, cost-wise. I did an inspection after we purchased it, and there were flaws in a number of critical struts and supports. Your mother's company cut some very serious corners. The thing would've probably come apart when they spun her up. It certainly wouldn't have lasted the entire planned lifecycle."

He felt his eyebrows rise. "You've been in space? Impressive."

"I know, right? I've been up there six times."

"And this thing can turn a profit?"

"I'm just the construction boss. You'd need to talk to someone on the business side for that."

The helicopter circled back around and dropped lines for them. The crew chief handed out earplugs and hauled them up one at a time.

On the flight to the airport, he thought about his father's plans. The idea of building a hotel in space was ludicrous. He must've spent billions on the project. No way he'd make that money back with paying guests. There must be a different angle.

Harry hadn't figured out any answers by the time the helicopter landed. It was after dark. They walked over to a private hangar.

The interior was lit up brighter than day. A sleek private jet with the Rainforest logo on the tail waited for them. A woman in an immaculate light-green uniform stood at the foot of the fold-down stairs.

"Good evening," she said. "I'm Alicia, and I'll be your attendant tonight. If you and your party will board, we'll take off immediately, Mister Rogers."

The faint smirk on her lips told him she was one of the shrinking minority of people that had seen the old television program. At least she hadn't felt the need to sing the damned song.

He let his people board while some men opened the hangar door. A small tug backed in and attached a tow bar to the front wheel of the aircraft.

The interior of the plane smelled like money. Leather and dark wood everywhere. Wide seats that looked more inviting than his bed. His father knew how to live.

That's when he saw him come out from a door at the rear of the cabin. The Devil had come to Guatemala in person.

* * *

CLAYTON LOOKED his son over with a critical eye. "You look like hell, boy."

His son's expression hardened. "Let's see how you look when someone drops a pyramid on you. I didn't expect to see you so quickly."

"Obviously not. Everyone, get your gear put away, and Alicia will serve dinner and drinks while we fly out of this hellhole."

He stepped up to the cockpit as everyone found places for their gear. The pilot looked back at him questioningly.

"What did the tower say when you didn't file a flight plan?" Clayton asked.

"The same thing they said when I didn't give them a tail number. Thanks for the money. I'll fly us out on a course that doesn't lead to Mexico. I'll turn when we're safely away."

Clayton nodded. "Excellent. Carry on."

He returned to his seat and openly studied his son. Which no doubt led to the steam he could almost see rising from the boy's ears. Harry had never been the best at concealing his emotions. Especially the hostile ones. Perhaps that was a plus in his line of work.

Alicia made the rounds and had everyone secured by the time the pilot started the engines. They'd only landed a short while ago, so the warm-up time was minimal. They took off and rose into the night sky without incident. Once they leveled off, Alicia took orders for food and drink.

Clayton gestured for Miss Cook and his son to join him at the rear of the craft. He had an office there that would give them privacy to probe what had sent the levelheaded engineer into a tailspin. He couldn't imagine how she intended to link an ancient Mayan ruin to Project Liberty, so it was undoubtedly going to be a surprise.

Because he knew that sitting behind the desk would only make matters worse with Harry, he arranged all the seats in the open area in front of it. He'd already eaten, so he sipped a fine single malt whisky as the others put some food in their bellies.

Once the intensity of their hunger diminished, he spoke. "Miss Cook, I'm delighted to see you alive and well. I heard your friend didn't make it. Please accept my deepest condolences. I regret that my ex-wife and son perpetrated this vicious attack. If I may be so bold, what did you find that warrants my immediate attention?"

She opened her bag, which she hadn't stored, and pulled out a moderately expensive-looking digital camera. "Do you have a screen controller?"

He gestured to his desk. "Please have a seat and load them up on the wall screen."

She removed the memory chip from the camera and inserted it into a slot on his desk. The wall screen came to life a few moments later. There were a number of images. Some of jungle, some of ruins, a few of people, and many of chambers indoors. The interior of the pyramid, he assumed.

He pointed at a picture of a man standing beside a pyramid. Presumably the one that had collapsed. He was young, Hispanic, and grinning widely. "That must be your friend."

Her face sagged a little. "I took that the day before everything went to hell. He was on top of the world. I suppose that's a lesson in how wrong we can be."

"I'm not certain that's the lesson I'd take away from this terrible situation. Perhaps that the world is more dangerous than we expect. To always remain vigilant."

"I doubt that would've helped him. He found a chamber hidden deep inside the pyramid. It had some art that is literally game changing. Though it's not the reason I asked you to come, it's a good place to start."

She selected an image and zoomed in. The art and inlay of polished stone was impressive. It took him a moment to realize what was wrong with it. It showed the outer planets.

"That can't be right," he said after a moment. "This has to be faked."

She shook her head. "We found something later that indicates otherwise in the strongest terms possible. One more thing to note. There's something marked here that comes from the outer system to the inner. An extinct comet, most likely.

"There are dates in Mayan script beside it at several points. We should be able to figure out its orbit based on that. Also, it shows a large body in the outer system that we don't know about."

"That is extraordinary," he admitted. "Now I understand why your friend sought you out. This is indeed the find of the century. How could the ancient Mayans possibly be aware of the outer planets? They had no telescopes, if memory serves."

"Allow me to show you what else we found in the pyramid."

The next picture showed the devastation that used to be the Mayan artwork.

"What a loss," he murmured. "This happened when the pyramid collapsed?"

"No, it came apart when a grenade caused the tunnel leading up to this point to cave in. We thought the cracks in the wall might lead to a hidden tunnel, so we opened it up."

"Is that how you escaped?"

"No," Harry said. "We had to jump down the well in that room and search for a passage to the one in the courtyard. We were lucky."

He considered the two of them. "Exceedingly so. I'm not certain that I would play the lottery going forward, if I were you. You may have used your allotted share of good luck."

"Actually, I think the lottery is a good analogy," Miss Cook said.

She skipped ahead and showed him what was behind the wall. The burial chamber astounded him.

"Amazing," he said.

She showed picture after picture until they opened the sarcophagus. He stared at the impossible image on the screen. "This cannot be correct."

"It was there," Harry said bluntly. "I saw everything from the moment we opened the tomb. The wall was old. Really old. This wasn't planted."

The lie his eyes told him warred with his bedrock certainty that his son's word was good. If he said it was true, it was true. He watched as she scrolled through the pictures. The clothing was definitely anachronistic. Similar to modern clothes, but not in every way.

The pockets, buttons, and name tag stood out. And the patch on the man's shoulder. The angle wasn't very good, but it looked like a tree surrounded by text. Well, by gibberish in text form. Not something that anyone found in an ancient tomb should be wearing.

Clayton stared at them. "What the hell does this mean?"

"It means a lot more than you think," Miss Cook said. "Let me show you what we found at the second site."

The image changed, and he slowly stood as he realized what he was seeing. "Is that…"

"It's a spaceship," she confirmed. "One that's been buried in the jungle for about a thousand years."

* * *

JESS WATCHED her boss's expression with satisfaction. He got it. He knew what this find meant.

"The man in the pyramid undoubtedly came from this ship," she said. "Harry found the key to opening it in the well once we escaped the collapsing pyramid. I saved what I could from the burial chamber, but we need to recover the body and go over everything that survived the collapse with a fine-tooth comb. We also need to recover Abel's body. His family deserves to have him back."

The elder Mister Rogers nodded. "Of course. I've already called a few people, but I'll start working every contact I have to get complete control of both sites. We'll need to have everything you recovered gone over very carefully and protect it from deterioration. I'll arrange for some restoration specialists to preserve everything. Those artifacts are literally priceless."

Clayton looked at her with a very serious expression. "Do you realize the scope of what you've found here? The immensity of it? The value of this find is incalculable."

"Even before we found the ship, I knew," she said. "Even the Mayans knew. Look at the lid of the sarcophagus. See how they have him as though he were about to take flight? He came from above, and they knew it."

The older man stared at the image. "It certainly seems that way. I realize you have many duties awaiting your time on Project Liberty, but we need to debrief you in detail."

Harry cleared his throat. "Perhaps you've forgotten, but this isn't your find. It's hers. As in she owns everything in that pack."

Mister Rogers paused. "A valid point. Thank you for the reminder. Miss Cook, if you'll allow me to bring some experts in to conserve and examine the artifacts you've recovered, I believe that it might be worth a great deal to me. And you."

"And to Harry," she said. "He was there every moment of this exploration."

The younger Rogers shook his head. "I was under contract to rescue you. I have no claim to anything in that chamber or the data you found."

"You risked your life to get this. I say you do."

"And I say I don't."

Clayton Rogers made calming gestures with his hands. "I'm sure the two of you can work that out at your leisure."

His son's jaw shot out. "She'll want to contact an attorney she trusts to review whatever you offer. You're a shark, and I won't let you gobble her up."

"I bet your military group has an attorney," Jess said. "If you were my partner in this, you could loan him to me."

Harry gave her a look. "Maybe. I'm going back out front. Don't let him bully you into signing anything. I'll give my lawyer a call tomorrow and arrange for her to review your contract." He shifted his gaze to his father. "I might have to take a small share just to keep you honest. Don't cross me."

She stared at the door after he'd departed. "Is he always this muleheaded?"

"My son is many things, including stubborn. He's also honorable to a damned fault. My advice is to listen to him. This find is valuable. Very valuable. Well worth killing for or cheating someone out of their share."

"Would you do that?" she asked as she retrieved her memory chip.

He steepled his fingers. "I've done things in business that would horrify you, I'm certain. I could swear my intentions are honorable, but that should fool neither of us. I'll strike as good a bargain as I can while still being fair."

He leaned back in his chair. "We'll talk tomorrow. Please, take your bag and stow it near your seat. I want you to have sole custody of it until we settle the details of what this means."

She made her way back up to the front of the plane and sat down beside Harry. "I'm not sure what to do next."

"Get some sleep," he advised. "Tomorrow is going to be a long one. Also, make sure to count your fingers once you shake on this deal."

He stuck a pillow behind his head and quickly went to sleep.

She ordered a stiff drink, and it wasn't long before she joined him.

11

Harry slept like crap. He'd run through collapsing tunnels chasing Jess for what seemed like hours. He woke when the plane touched down, more exhausted than when he'd dozed off.

His people gathered their gear and deplaned once the pilot shut the engines down. To his annoyance, Jess seemed rested and ready to take on the world.

The view of the Yucatán Spaceport was rather limited in the middle of the night. He couldn't see any of the launch towers. Hills blocked the no-doubt inspirational view.

His father directed them to cars that would take them to the hotel. They'd sleep again and join him for a late breakfast. Jess sat beside Harry in the one he piled into.

"So, how careful do I need to be?" she asked. "He might be your father, but he's my boss. I don't want to overly antagonize him."

It took a moment for Harry to squelch his instinctive response that Clayton Rogers couldn't be trusted. That was his bias speaking. "Have a lawyer look everything over before you sign it. Mine, yours, or someone else you trust. Bargain hard. My father will slip something past you if he can. Once you both sign on the dotted lines, though, he'll honor the agreement.

"And by that, I mean what's spelled out in black and white. Oral agreements don't count. Read the fine print, and look for things he can twist. This is worth a lot of money, and he plays hardball when it comes to stuff like that."

She nodded slowly. "I'm not really interested in the money. I want to follow the mystery."

Harry snorted. "Don't tell him that. He'll value what you found more highly if he has to pay for it. Show him that while you might've been born on a Tuesday, it wasn't last week."

"You're funny. Give me the name of your lawyer so I can have someone check her out."

He gave her the woman's name and number. "Tell her I sent you and that the work is highly classified. She'll keep it under her hat."

"You seem to trust very few people. How can you be sure about her?"

"I rescued her son from Eastern Europe about five years ago. She's as loyal as any human can be."

Jess's expression softened. "You're like a knight in camo. I'm not kidding."

Harry shook his head. "Don't make me into something I'm not. I've done as many bad things as anyone else. War sucks."

They pulled up to a brightly lit hotel. It was almost four in the morning, so things were quiet. Someone expedited the check-in and had them in their rooms a few minutes later.

Harry put his pack in the closet, locked the door, and put a chair under the knob. He didn't like sleeping in places he didn't control.

His pistol sat on the toilet seat while he took a quick shower. It went on his nightstand when he face-planted.

It only seemed as though a few minutes had passed when someone started pounding on the door. One glance at the clock showed it was only seven. "Go away."

"You'll miss breakfast," Jess yelled through the door. "They might have blueberries."

"Is that your criteria for a high-end breakfast?" He rolled out of bed. "Give me a few minutes to get dressed."

"You want the clothes in the hall?"

"Hand them through."

It only took a moment to pull the chair back and crack the door. She stood in the hall looking well rested. She wore a pale-blue blouse, a dark skirt, and shoes without heels. If he didn't know better, he'd never have suspected she'd been on an adventure in the Guatemalan jungle yesterday. She had her pack over her shoulder.

"I had no idea you were shy," she said with a grin.

"I could be naked over here."

She raised an eyebrow. "Are you? What if ninjas attacked?"

"Then I'd kill them naked."

"I'd pay good money to see that."

Harry grabbed the clothes and headed for the bathroom. He closed the door most of the way, took care of business, and washed his hands and face. "How can you be so chipper? You were awake as long as I was."

"I thought you military types got up early every day so you could run ten miles and do an obstacle course."

"That doesn't mean we have to like it. You learn to sleep when you can."

"That's rough. I'm a morning person."

"Figures. Nobody's perfect."

He dressed, combed his hair, and started shaving. "I dreamed about that damned spaceship last night. I can't believe it, even after seeing it with my own eyes."

"I'm in the same boat," she said. "The scope of this find is mind-boggling. Advanced humans long before the Europeans discovered the American continents. Where did they come from? Space? That seems almost inconceivable."

"Why not time travel?"

"Let's stick to reasonable possibilities."

He grabbed his boots and headed back into the bedroom. She was sitting on the edge of his bed. "Why? Because advanced humans from outer space is a more likely alternative than time travel? You said that ship didn't use reaction mass. Maybe it's a time-travel ship."

She opened her mouth to say something and stopped. "I guess I shouldn't dismiss the idea out of hand. I should let the evidence tell me what's possible. How much do you think a find like this is worth?"

"A lot of money. It's proof that others visited our world and educated some of us to work for them."

He smiled at her surprised expression. "I read science fiction. I get this has implications with aliens. That's big stuff. And, if word of it gets out, everyone and their third cousins will be after the technology. It means weapons, star drives, and possibly any number of other things. I'd be real careful who you mention this to."

"Aliens might be a jump. We've only found evidence that humans were involved."

"Since there's no indication of a high-technology center on Earth a thousand years ago, the tech had to come from elsewhere. That means aliens. Unless you believe in Atlantis."

She rolled her eyes. "At this point, I'm not ruling it out, but I don't think so. Plato almost certainly used the fictitious island allegorically. Even he said the events he supposedly chronicled took place something like 9,000 years before his time. But, with this find, it makes me wonder if he was being literal. This just boggles my mind. I want to see where this leads."

"Me too," Harry admitted. "If anywhere. I figure other signs of this are long gone."

"Except in space. The only place we've been to in person is the moon. NASA wanted to go to an asteroid a couple of decades ago, but that never happened. They killed the idea of returning to the moon and gave lip service to manned missions to the asteroids and Mars, but they never did anything more than blow hot air. That was the end of American leadership in space. Hell, recent events were the end of America going into space at all."

Harry snorted. "I had a ringside seat when my mother did her part to put NASA out of business. Corporate greed and governmental incompetence at its worst. Now China and India are locked in a race to Mars"

"Yeah, both of them are a few months away from leaving orbit, but the ships are complete. The planets just need to line up."

He nodded toward her bag. "That might just change things. Maybe make my father pony up some cash to get a mission out to that comet."

She gave him an odd look. "Could be. We need to get moving if we want to eat."

They stopped talking about the find once they got onto the elevator with other people. Jess changed the subject adroitly. "What will your people be doing while we talk? Shouldn't they be out saving the world?"

"If they're smart, they're sleeping in. Depending on what I hear this morning, I'll either send them back to the US or keep them here."

The doors slid open, and everyone hustled out. A rotund man in a suit came from behind the desk when he saw them. "Mister Rogers, Miss Cook. I'm Thomas Quincy, the hotel manager. I hope you had a pleasant night. The elder Mister Rogers has arranged breakfast in a private conference room. If you'll come with me, I'll see you there."

Jess took the man's offered hand with a smile. "It was perfect, thank you. Tell me, do you have blueberries?"

"Of course."

She grinned. "Excellent."

He turned to Harry. "Do you have any specific breakfast requests, Mister Rogers?"

"No, I'm pretty pedestrian in my tastes. I'll want some good coffee, though, and lots of it."

"I'll make that happen. This way, please."

Harry followed the two of them and watched Jess almost skipping along. Blueberries. He might never understand her at all.

* * *

Jess walked to the conference room with the manager. Two large men in dark suits eyed them with disfavor but opened the door. The elder Rogers was already there, sipping on coffee and talking with two women in lab coats. All three looked over as she and Harry made their way in. The manager did not accompany them, and the guards closed the door.

Clayton Rogers rose from his seat. "Miss Cook, Harry. Meet Doctors Paulette Young and Rachel Powell. They are two of the most experienced professionals on the planet at restoring and protecting delicate artifacts. If you have no objections, they will remove everything you found from the pack and begin the preservation process. They are independent contractors and will answer to you unless we come to an agreement."

Jess slid the backpack over to the women. "Us. Harry is part of this."

She watched Harry look to the ceiling, probably praying for strength.

"That again? I told you, I was under contract to rescue you. I'm a hired gun. One who has finished his work, by the way. I expect to be on my way shortly."

Harry's father pursed his lips. "It's true that you were there at my behest. However, I've consulted with my attorneys, and they tell me that the find is unrelated to the work I hired you to do. Which I have paid you for, by the way, with a significant bonus."

The mercenary's eyes widened for a moment and then narrowed. "You don't give anything away for free. What are you up to, old man?"

"Why don't you eat your breakfast while we discuss that? We've shielded this room from monitoring of any kind. No transmissions in or out. The good doctors have signed strict nondisclosure agreements, and my people will search them closely when they leave their laboratory. If we can come to an understanding, the items will be under heavy guard and 24/7 observation by the most paranoid security people I employ."

Jess watched the interplay between the two men with interest. Harry's antipathy couldn't be plainer, yet his father accepted it as though it was normal. Dysfunctional didn't begin to describe their relationship.

At her nod, the women took possession of the pack, and one of the guards from outside escorted them down the hall.

"And how do we order breakfast if we can't call out?" Jess asked once they were gone.

"The old-fashioned way." He slid a pen and pad of paper over to her. "Write whatever you want on that. When we have everyone's order, we hand it to the paranoid men outside. They send it to the kitchen and examine what they bring back. The coffee is in the carafe. It's quite good."

She raised an eyebrow. "And how do I know what I can order without a menu?"

The older man smiled. "You tell them what you want, and they figure it out. The sky is the limit. Do you want caviar and champagne for breakfast? Something even more esoteric? Make it so."

That set her back for a moment. "I'm a woman with fairly simple tastes, so I don't expect to break your bank account."

"As long as you have blueberries, she'll be happy," Harry said with an amused glance at her.

"Then you're in luck," Clayton said. "I had some with breakfast yesterday. Now, to address your earlier comments, I'm not giving anything away. From my point of view, it doesn't matter how the two of you split my offer. Or even if you do. Your objection needs to go to her. Frankly, I hope you stand your ground. That would simplify matters a great deal."

Harry stiffened, and his demeanor shifted. "I'll bet it would. Well, maybe it's better that I keep an eye on what you're up to. Not only for her sake, but to keep you from misusing this find."

"Let's eat before you become even grumpier."

Jess suppressed a smile as she wrote out her breakfast order. Her boss had just played his son. She could see the satisfied gleam in his eye. As sharp as Harry was, he had baggage.

And, to be honest, so did she. Mister Rogers was her employer. A wealthy man in a position of great power over her life. She'd best keep that front and center as they talked. She had a fine line to walk while guarding her interests.

Jess gave Harry a pleading look. "I hope you reconsider. No offense to your father, but I've worked for him for years. I'm not sure I'd push a hard-enough bargain."

The younger man nodded. "Maybe. For you." He started writing an order for himself.

While he focused on that task, she looked at his father. He inclined his head slightly with a hint of a smile. He'd seen through her plea.

Once Harry slipped their orders under the door, the elder Rogers leaned back in his chair. "The doctors are aware that these items are of an indeterminate age and unknown origin. They'll be working exclusively on this project for at least the next year, with options to extend that by two one-year periods. They know nothing of the ship, and it's probably best we keep it that way for now.

"As there was no choice, they are aware that some or all of the items in that pack may be of extraterrestrial origin. They're being exceptionally well compensated for their isolation and discretion."

She took a deep breath and picked her purse up from where she'd set it on the floor. "There's something else that I think I'm more qualified to look over." She took the cube out and set it on the table along with the key to the spaceship.

Harry gave her a disapproving look.

"You took that and didn't tell me? What if the ship had blown up?"

"I couldn't leave it down there. What if the ceiling had collapsed? Again."

The older man gave her a searching look. "What is that, and why is it glowing?"

"I think it's a power supply," she said. "I'll need to get it into an engineering lab to work on it, but based on the fact it still had enough charge to power the crashed ship after a thousand years, I think it's pretty damned important."

"So, it's a battery?"

"I think it's a power generator of some kind. Given that there was no indication the ship used reaction mass, it had to require a significant amount of power to move. I'll need to do a lot of testing to figure out how it works."

Her boss took a sip of his coffee. "That will be a priority, I'm sure. The potential applications are enormous. I'd say they might be useful in our current endeavor, but I think the project is too far along."

"You can never have too much energy," she said.

"True enough. I see several paths going forward. First is the pyramid. I've volunteered Rainforest's services to the Guatemalan government in recovering Doctor Valdez's body from the ruins. That will take some time, of course, and may not generate any recoverable artifacts.

"The second site with the spaceship is self-evident. The third possible recovery site is the astronomical body you found reference to. If it was important enough to note, it may have some interesting ruins of its own."

Harry frowned. "How will you search there? A probe? That's going to be difficult and take a while, especially if it's not near Earth."

His father steepled his fingers. "You might not be aware of it, but I purchased the ISS2 space station from the Russians and have begun converting it into a hotel. That's actually a deep-cover story. We've added a concealed propulsion section, beefed up the superstructure, and built it substantially larger than the original planners envisioned. Liberty Station will be the first ship to Mars. It's also capable of making a trip to other portions of the solar system. Even the outer system."

Harry's eyes widened, and he looked at Jess. "You knew this?"

She smiled. "It would be hard to design and direct the construction of a spaceship without knowing that part. I couldn't tell you because the project is classified.

"We're getting the last of the supplies loaded now. We also need to get the engines ready. We saved that part for the end, because if word gets out, there might be enough outcry to cause Mister Rogers some trouble."

The older man grunted. "It's nuclear, so every environmentalist crackpot on the planet will burst into flames. As if the universe doesn't already have enormous amounts of radioactive material. Idiots."

Jess poured herself some coffee. "I'm sure that any number of governments would disapprove too. It doesn't use weapons-grade material, of course, but they might worry that it's a weapon held over their heads. Once the reactor is loaded and the fuel secured, the project can't be stopped short of using force."

Harry could see how that might get people all excited. "Where's the material coming from? The US? That might be difficult."

"The source of the material is a closely guarded secret," the elder Rodgers said, "but I'm willing to share it with you. The reactor core is an experimental prototype your mother has been developing in France. I plan to steal it. And, if we can come to an agreement, I'd like you to help my security forces make that happen. Your people are even better at that sort of thing than they are."

"We might be able to work out a deal," Harry said. "I owe Mother some payback. Isn't that leaving things up to chance? What if you don't get your hands on it?"

"They have a demonstration for her major investors scheduled for this week. The invitations are already out. We'll hit them before they have a chance to realize anyone else even knows it exists. Obtaining the fuel is rather more straightforward."

* * *

CLAYTON WATCHED his son out of the corner of his eye as they ate and chatted. The woman was a moderating influence on him. Normally by this point, Harry would be snarling.

She was clever too. She'd seen his reverse psychology for what it was and used herself as a lever to get Harry on board. He'd reward that behavior with a good final deal. If she were the tie he needed to bind his son to the plan, he'd use her and make certain she had no cause to complain.

Harry took a bite of his pancakes. "So, now I know what you want to do. Go to Mars. Why?"

Clayton sipped his coffee. "Actually, while the ship can go to Mars quite speedily, that isn't its primary purpose. It'll find a suitable asteroid, set up a mining outpost, and then beat everyone else to Mars.

"With the resources harvested in space, we should be able to fund additional construction and use the raw materials as a means to do so. Liberty Station is intended to be a self-sustaining home to explore the solar system."

"The ship has a lot of room in the torus," Jess said. "That's what we call a habitat ring that generates artificial gravity via centrifugal force.

"We've designed and built multiple sets of mining and refining equipment, so we can leave teams on at least three asteroids. With the right kinds of raw material, it could be quite lucrative in a short period of time."

His son mulled that for a moment. "What about that wandering asteroid? Any idea where in the solar system it is now?"

Clayton inclined his head. "A fairly good one, actually. The dates on the painting gave us a timeline to trace it. If they're accurate, it's just about to pass Earth on the outbound leg of its eternal journey. The experts concur that it's most likely an extinct comet, by the way."

He considered them as they took in his words. It wasn't quite time to push for closing the deal, but he already knew he'd offer more than Jessica Cook expected. And he'd come through too. The potential of this find could put his plans ahead by decades. He might even live to see them come to fruition. When it came to the potential of this deal, the sky was quite literally the limit.

12

Kathleen Bennett stared at the trembling man on the other side of her desk. She eyed the distances and gestured for the guards to drag him back a few steps. Burmese teak was naturally resistant to moisture, but she didn't want to chance getting any blood on the golden wood. The desk was worth far more than the wretch in front of it.

The slight man quivered in barely restrained terror. Only the two guards gripping his arms kept him from falling to the floor and pleading for his life. Again.

She shook her head. "You disappoint me, Vincent. Exactly how did you expect this to play out? Did you think your other employer would whisk you away once you'd done his dirty work? That was foolish. Once he had what he wanted, you became a liability he could safely dispose of.

"I realize you information technology people are insulated from the real world, but this goes a few steps into blindly stupid. You stole from me. I certainly hope you enjoyed the extra money while you could, because it won't do you any good now."

Vincent Cruz, the former assistant director of her IT department, swallowed noisily. "There's been some kind of horrible mistake, Mrs. Bennett. I would never betray you."

She smiled like a shark. She knew so because she'd perfected that expression in a mirror. "Don't insult my intelligence. You copied files from the classified database. You didn't quite manage to erase the entire trail of evidence, though. Sloppy. You'd best be forthcoming, because your punishment will reflect your cooperation. Or lack thereof."

He started in on another round of denials, but she stopped him with a raised hand. "If you don't tell me, Donald will break something you value. Who were you working for, and what programs did you access?"

"No one, Mrs. Bennett. I was just—"

"Donald, if you please."

Her chief of security grabbed the man's hand and bent one of his fingers back with an audible snap. Vincent screamed and thrashed in the guards' arms.

The door opened, and Nathan sauntered in. Her son raised an eyebrow at the scene and dropped into one of the comfortable chairs with more panache than grace. He winced a little at the landing. "What did this one do, Mother? Steal your parking space?"

She sighed. Her son's timing was execrable, as usual. "Donald, please take Vincent back to your office and determine the particulars of the security breach. Vincent, I advise you to cooperate. If you satisfy Mister Reynolds before I arrive, I'll let you live. You won't enjoy it, but that beats an unmarked grave. And remember, the longer you take, the more broken bones you'll have to suffer through."

The security team dragged the blubbering fool out of her office. Kathleen focused her attention on her son. "It took you long enough to get back. This was supposed to be a simple kidnapping. Do you have any idea how much of a scene you've caused? You destroyed an entire Mayan pyramid, and you allowed your idiot brother to capture your entire team. On reflection, Harry isn't the stupidest of my children."

His face reddened. "I had no idea he would be there, and I didn't blow up the pyramid. That was the moron I hired. He paid for it."

She shook her head. "You still don't get it. Take poor unfortunate Vincent as an example. He stole classified data from me, but I hired him. The ultimate responsibility for this situation falls on me. I don't make the mistake of trusting the wrong people often, but when I do, I don't blame them for their failures. I blame myself."

"So that's why you're sparing his life? I thought that was uncommonly generous of you."

"Don't be stupid. He condemned himself the moment he conspired against me. Donald will let him babble on until he's certain that he's gotten every bit of useful information and then take the poor bastard off to his private torture chamber. I'll never see Vincent again and good riddance."

"You hire some real winners, Mother. You're living up to your nickname. Has anyone accidentally called you Cruella to your face recently?"

She ignored his jab and walked over to her bar. She'd earned a drink. "Donald delivers everything I could ask for in a security chief. He keeps the riffraff out and the employees in line. His personal quirks are none of my business.

"You, on the other hand, disappoint me. You can't even carry out the simplest of tasks without creating an international incident. The police have your team in custody."

Nathan smirked. "They won't talk. I have a very generous bonus for situations like these. They'll keep their mouths shut and retire when they get out of prison."

"They won't be getting out," she said flatly. "I've already made arrangements. There will be a riot. Your people will not survive it."

Her son sat up abruptly. "You can't do that! If word gets out that my word isn't any good, then I won't be able to—"

"To sweep your failures under the rug? No, I imagine not. Too bad. My security is worth more to me than your reputation is to you. Frankly, your performance has been so questionable recently that I'd liquidate you if you weren't my son."

His smirk returned. "I'd watch that kind of talk if you want those grandchildren you occasionally pine after. And there's more to this situation than you're aware of."

She turned toward the wide windows and stared out over the company grounds. Modern buildings surrounded by exquisitely manicured lawns and parks lay before her. Hundreds of people in her employ walked around like little ants.

This was her kingdom. All she surveyed was hers. She controlled every aspect of anything that happened here. Her word was law. That always shot a thrill up her spine.

She sipped her gin and glanced over at her son. "What am I unaware of? The fact the woman I sent you after escaped with your brother? One of my spies saw them arrive at the Yucatán Spaceport early this morning in the company of your father. They're all closeted in a secure hotel discussing God only knows what."

"I know what." Nathan pulled a data chip from his pocket and tossed it onto her desk. "You'll never believe what they found."

She loaded up the video and stared at it as it played, her drink stopped halfway to her mouth.

When it finished, she stared coldly at her son. "What kind of garbage is this? As excuses for your failures go, this is a whole new level of ridiculous."

"That's just it. It's real. I tried to capture the woman again when she came out of the second area, but she proved to be more resourceful than I expected." He shifted in his seat and winced again.

Kathleen considered her son for a long minute. "If I find out you're lying to me, you'll envy poor Vincent."

"I'm not worried."

"Then I need to call Donald. I think the files Vincent stole went to Clayton. If so, I want to be certain that we get the true and complete story as quickly as possible."

She took another sip of her drink. "Don't unpack your bags. Gather a competent group of associates and go down to Mexico. I want you to capture the woman when she reveals herself. She will eventually."

Kathleen leaned forward. "Listen closely. You may detain your brother if circumstances allow, but you may not kill him or the woman. If one of your people makes another 'mistake,' you'll suffer for it."

She gave him a cold look. "And as for grandchildren, you'd best remember how well some of my genetics projects are proceeding. I can take care of your progeny without you, if need be."

* * *

CLAYTON CONSIDERED JESSICA COOK. He finally had her alone. His son had excused himself to check on his people.

"Harry has no doubt cautioned you to scrutinize every word I say and every angle of the deal we're about to discuss. I urge you to do the same. What I'm about to propose is complicated by our already existing employment relationship. One I do not want to disrupt. Still, we need to discuss matters at a high level so that we can come to an understanding before we proceed. Agreed?"

She took a deep breath and nodded. "No offense, but I will have his attorney look over the papers, and I'll discuss the framework with someone I went to college with that does corporate work."

"An excellent idea," Clayton said. "One thing, though. Are you certain you can trust the second individual? I've had Harry's attorney vetted quite thoroughly. We cannot allow this information to go public."

"I've never shared a secret with my friend that would be a challenge to his morals, but I trust him implicitly."

Clayton smiled. Her trust in her friends was adorable. "I can discreetly arrange a test through an intermediary, if you like. I'll make him a very generous offer if he reveals something he shouldn't. If he accepts, then no one will ever hear about it from me, but we will know. If he rebuffs my advances, then he's reliable enough to go over the framework."

"Forgive me, but what's to keep you from making up a story that he's unreliable to keep me from seeking his advice?"

His smile widened. "That's a wise question to ask. My associates will record the conversations. While that still leaves me some methods that could taint the results, I think any failure on your friend's part should be clear enough. We need to trust one another to some degree for this to work."

She gave him a name that he jotted down. He slipped the piece of paper into his jacket. By dinner, he should have a comprehensive dossier on the man.

"What do you have in mind going forward?" she asked. "It may be months or years before we have even the most basic grasp of what this technology means."

"Spoken like an engineer. There are no certainties in business, only opportunities. You risk money on the chance to make even more money. Sometimes you win. Sometimes you lose. Every venture is a roll of the dice. It's my job to evaluate the possibilities and make an offer consummate with what I think the reward might be when counterbalanced with the risk of failure."

She shook her head. "No. It's your job to make the most profitable offer. That's why people negotiate, to get the best deal they can. I'm not a negotiator like you. I have no idea how much something like this is worth."

"In this case, circumstances dictate that the best deal isn't the one that earns me the most money."

Miss Cook turned a little in her chair and frowned. "You lost me."

Clayton allowed himself a small laugh. "Contrary to what my son believes, money isn't the altar at which I worship. It's a means to an end. Some things are worth doing, even at a loss. Project Liberty, for example. Though, to be fair, I eventually expect to see a return on that too."

She inclined her head, conceding the point. "Project Liberty is worthwhile even if it never makes back the investment."

"And there lies the basis of an agreement between us," he said. "I could make you a very generous financial offer, but I have a better idea. You're an integral part of the project. One I don't want to risk losing. What I propose is giving you a stake in Project Liberty."

That made her sit bolt upright. "Are you joking?"

"Absolutely not. Think of everything you found as the tip of an iceberg. Where did this man come from? What kind of civilization would it take to make those devices? What examples of this technology still exist, where might they be, and what could they teach us?"

She shook her head. "We have no way of knowing. There might not be anything left of them."

"Or there might be something incredible on that comet. Whoever they were, they didn't show themselves lightly. There has been no contact, other than this one instance over the course of recorded history. We might never know why, but it seems to me that this man was somehow cut off from his fellows."

"You make it sound like he didn't come from Earth at all. He certainly seemed human."

Clayton rose from his chair and stretched. "I suspect he was. That doesn't mean that he came from Earth in the way you're imagining. Someone, or something, trained him. Educated him. Whoever they were, they didn't want humans in general to know about them."

"Harry said something similar." She scowled at him. "We have no proof to back that up. Those are just theories."

"Ones I have every confidence that we can find more evidence to support, if we look in the right places. We have a trail of breadcrumbs that could lead us to the biggest discovery in human history."

"Aliens?"

"Aliens. Someone took humans and raised them to a technological pinnacle in advance of our own achievements more than a thousand years ago. Something like that would leave signs. So, where are they? I say they came from the stars. Perhaps only to visit. Perhaps they stayed a longer time and some calamity took them down. I hope to find out.

"In any case, that's the value I see behind this find. With luck, we might find examples of technology that would allow us to create ships capable of visiting other stars. That's Project Liberty writ large. Are you ready to hear my offer?"

"Shouldn't we wait for Harry to get back?"

"I'm not asking that you accept anything this very second. I just want you to understand how seriously I'm taking this. I'm offering you a 30 percent stake in Project Liberty."

She blinked at him for a moment. "That's ridiculous."

He felt the corners of his mouth rise. "Very well. Make it 40 percent, and Harry can have the extra ten. That's my limit, though. I insist on maintaining operational control of this project."

Her lips firmed into a thin line. "That's not what I meant. With the amount of money you've poured into this project, that's a tremendous sum. Tens of billions of dollars."

"If you take the research and side projects into account," he said, "Project Liberty has cost me most of my personal fortune. Almost $100 billion. You didn't know that I was broke? Well, one must keep up appearances. If the project fails, I go down with it. When my enemies finally grasp how deeply invested I am, they'll swarm like carrion birds. Only success will save me."

She visibly gathered her wits. "But the return on your investment will be in the trillions. Personal wealth unimaginable to anyone alive. Even you, I suspect."

"Beyond a certain point, it's really only keeping score. That said, there's something magical about skunking your opponents so badly that they realize they were never in your league to begin with."

He stood and straightened his jacket. "Consider my offer. Forty percent ownership of Project Liberty, or whatever I decide to rename it to because of this find, for you and 10 percent for my son. Don't worry about what he brings to the table. He's quite resourceful. And very soon, unless I miss my guess, we'll be fending off military incursions. He's quite capable of taking the lead in that area."

She smiled. "And you get to pull him back into your life again. Is my cooperation in that area part of our bargain?"

"I'd make it so, if I thought I needed to. You see him for who he is. In fact, you maneuvered him into accepting part of the deal. Well done, by the way. And much appreciated."

Miss Cook stood. "Now what? You need to check my guy, and I need a contract to submit to Harry's lawyer. And, since we're going to be partners, you should call me Jess."

He extended his hand. "Clayton, then. I can't tell you how eagerly I'm looking forward to working even more closely with you." He gestured toward the door. "You should go give my son the good news. You'll want to get the yelling out of the way before dinner. It's bad for the digestion."

13

It took a few hours, but Harry had spoken to all his teams. If he knew his shithead brother, there'd be an attempt at payback. He'd expedited the missions he could and delayed those that hadn't kicked off.

Liberty SOG employed half a dozen full-time strike teams. He knew enough reliable semiretired pros to put another half-dozen teams in action with a few days' notice. He summoned those he could to join him here.

Once he had things in motion, he called Rex in for a private chat. The scout had changed into a pair of jeans and a mind-numbingly bright Hawaiian shirt. He lounged back with one leg over the arm of his chair, chewing on something that looked like grass.

Harry shook his head. "Seriously?"

Rex grinned. "You know the deal. Blend in. Have you seen the tourists on the commercial side of the spaceport? Who knew seeing cargo launches to the space hotel would bring in so many retired Floridians."

"Apparently you did. I hope you enjoyed the break, because it looks like we have a new job."

The scout's grin dropped away, and he sat up. "That was quick. Where next? Libya? The Black Sea? Disney World?"

"As if we'd ever be lucky enough to get Disney World. I'd love to see Jeremy try to crack their security."

"Give him a chance, and he'll make you proud. What's up?"

Harry considered how much he could tell his friend. He trusted Rex with his life and had done so for years. Still, he didn't know how much of this fantastical story he'd believe if he hadn't seen it with his own eyes.

"I can't tell you everything," Harry said. "For now, treat this as a classified mission brief. We found something in the pyramid and something even bigger at the second site. Things I can't fully explain to you, either, but they're seriously important."

"Like a supervillain's lair? I've always wondered where they hid those things."

"Just about that unexpected. The bottom line is that it's something worth killing over. I've made preliminary arrangements with my father to work in tandem with his people on certain aspects of something he calls Project Liberty."

"Hey! That's our name! Did he steal it?"

"Probably. In any case, our interests are aligned in this matter."

Rex's eyes widened. "With your father? That's some serious shit. Does it have something to do with that asshole brother of yours?"

"Not really, but he might make another appearance looking for Jess."

The scout smiled. "Jess, is it? You know, I hear shared danger makes for hot sex."

He gave his friend a stern glare. "And lousy long-term relationships. Focus. I've summoned all available teams, including those on standby. We'll work with my father's security forces, but we don't take orders from them without my say-so."

"I'm totally focused. She's hot. Besides, blokes like us don't live long enough to have long-term relationships. As for the teams, that's a lot of people. Why do we need so many shooters?"

"That's classified too. The basic outline is a heist. Something large and valuable. While I'm not normally prone to grand theft, my mother was the one pulling Nathan's strings, so I'll make an exception. My father's security people have been working on a plan for some time. We'll integrate with them to make it happen, hopefully with me in overall command. This is going down in less than a week, and once it does, I expect all hell to break loose."

A knock at the door interrupted them. Allen stuck his head in. "Sorry for the interruption, Harry. You have a call from that lady we rescued."

Harry stood. "I'll be right there. Rex, get the team together and briefed. I don't trust my father, and I want to be ready to move at a moment's notice. As far as I'm concerned, Jessica Cook is still our client. Get a two-person guard detail ready for her."

"On it."

He followed Allen back to the sitting room and picked up the phone. "Rogers."

"Harry, it's Jess. We need to talk about something that came up in the meeting after you left. Do you have a few minutes?"

"Sure." He gave her the team's suite number and hung up when she ended the call.

* * *

HARRY OPENED the door when Jess knocked. He'd changed into khakis and a dark shirt.

She took a moment to admire the view. "You clean up nice. Now you look like a secret agent."

He smiled. "I'm sure that isn't quite the case, but thanks. We searched the rooms for listening devices. All clear, and one of my people is here 24/7. Let's go and have that talk."

Harry led her back to the room they were using for conferences and closed the door. "I haven't told them anything about what we found. I'll eventually need to, but I'd rather do it once I know what's really going on."

Jess sat and crossed one leg over the other. "I'm seriously considering taking your father up on his offer. Not that it's any of my business, but what happened between the two of you?"

"We don't have enough time to explore that. Suffice it to say, he's not the humanitarian of the year. He's done things that hurt people. Saying he's good in comparison to the other corporate oligarchs isn't saying much. He's a mile better than my mother, but he's still a son of a bitch. Be very careful of any offer he makes you."

"We discussed the framework of a deal already. No agreement or anything, just an idea of what he's looking at paying. An offer that includes you."

His expression soured. "That fails to fill me with joy. I'm not quite sure how this happened."

"Maybe you just wanted to keep him from taking advantage of me. In any case, he's offering an interest in Project Liberty."

"The mission to Mars? Honestly, I'm still not really seeing the return in something like that. How much money could mining in space bring in?"

She decided it was time to pull the curtain back a little. Harry's father was offering a stake in the project, so he deserved to know what that meant.

"Let me lay it out for you. The most common asteroid is a C-Type. That stands for carbonaceous, by the way. Those make up something like 75 percent of all asteroids. The outer part of the asteroid belt and beyond may have an even higher percentage of them. That's the critical takeaway from this. They're extremely common.

"While the specific breakdown of each asteroid is different, even within a narrow classification like this, we can make some basic assumptions about them. First, the average density is between 2.9 and 3.5 grams per cubic centimeter. About 40 percent of the density of iron, give or take. You with me so far?"

Harry tried not to smile. "Barely. I'm not an engineer, Miss Scott."

"A gratuitous *Star Trek* reference. Nice, but my Scottish accent stinks. Anyway, let's assume a median of that density and a decent-size asteroid. Say 1,000 meters, or maybe a bit larger for the math. At that density would be about 2 billion metric tons of material. There are roughly a thousand asteroids of that size in near Earth orbit by current estimates. Again, once someone is out there looking for them, they will almost certainly end up finding more."

He nodded. "Okay, I'll grant that's a lot of material. It would cost a mint to mine it, wouldn't it? Also, you'd need to get the ore back to Earth. That seems like a limiting factor to me."

"It is. Iron makes up a bit more than 20 percent of the total material, almost 440 million metric tons. The cost of extracting the raw ore here on Earth varies, but it usually sells for around fifty dollars a metric ton. That makes the iron on one asteroid worth $22 billion. That, of course, doesn't count how much it would cost to ship it into orbit for use in space, which is a lot more expensive."

"That's a lot of money," Harry admitted. "You're not talking about bringing it back to Earth? Isn't that where the market is?"

"I'll get to that. That one element is literally only the tip of the iceberg. Let's talk platinum. They'll be able to pull about 2,000 metric tons of that out of the asteroid. That'll be worth about $80 billion. And there are many other valuable minerals. It only makes economic sense to ship the most profitable back to Earth. We can use the rest much more efficiently in space."

He considered that for a moment. "It looks like you're thinking big."

"We are. On average, each metric ton of raw material will bring in about $1,500. A few decades ago, that number would've been somewhat lower, but scarce minerals are getting even harder to find.

"So, let's roll this up. One asteroid. Two billion metric tons. Three trillion dollars. It would be more if we selected an asteroid even heavier in platinum-group metals. It might approach twice the value.

"As I said, we'd only ship the most valuable elements to Earth for sale. We'd use most in space to create infrastructure and habitats. This would fuel the spread of humanity to every part of the solar system. It would free humanity from the bonds of Earth. Hence, Project Liberty."

Harry was quiet for a while. "Ambitious. How long would it take to mine something like that?"

"When the prospective mine is fully operational, which might take a few years, we figure it can process between 50 and 100 million metric tons per year. So, that one asteroid would take twenty to forty years to fully mine. And the best part is everything is useful. No waste.

"The majority of the output could go right into setting up other mining sites and habitats. There's a significant amount of water tied up in these kinds of asteroids too. That means air, water, and fuel. Life for people in space."

He took even longer to digest that. Jess sat back and let him think about it at his own speed.

"Okay, I know why a normal person might think this is a good idea, but what does my father get out of this? Control of humanity? Something else? He doesn't do charity."

"You'd have to ask him. I assume he's doing this because it's in his own long-term interest. It'll make him the wealthiest man who ever lived. Anyway, that's enough detail for you to understand the scope of the project. Your father is offering me a 40 percent stake in Project Liberty. You'd get 10 percent."

"Wow. That's a lot of money. He has to have something else up his sleeve. Make sure you get the contract examined closely."

"I will. As long as the details check out, I'm going to accept the offer. Even a minority stake in something like this would give me so much more input going forward."

Harry gave her a skeptical look. "I hope it works out the way you expect. I need to go confer with my father's security people. If he can't get the engine for this thing, the project is deader than the guy in the pyramid."

14

Getting onto the spaceport wasn't as difficult as Nathan had feared. It wasn't on total lockdown. His new team had an ally that helped get them into the area around the hotel, though he'd said he couldn't get them inside.

Nathan wasn't convinced that was true. With the right motivation, the man could probably come up with a way.

First, though, he'd listen to what the man had learned. He sat behind his borrowed desk and adjusted his backside to ease the discomfort. The woman's shot had only grazed him, but it hurt, and it was his ass. The bitch would pay for that when he caught her.

His mother's spy wasn't much to look at, scrawny and short. The bones of his dark face stood out as though someone had starved him for a month. Not even the pricy suit he wore could make up for the air of starvation that seemed to hang over him.

Nathan's temporary headquarters were inside an unused office with a view of the hotel. One of his men had found a spot on the roof to use as a sniper hide, though that really wasn't anyone's idea of a good plan. The odds of successfully extracting were slim if every security guard was on alert.

Two of his people flanked the man as he sat gingerly in front of Nathan. Their silent presence kept the man a little on edge, just as Nathan intended. The sweat on the man's forehead was a pleasant addition to the proceedings.

With a studied, cold expression, Nathan gestured for the man to speak. "Tell me everything you've learned about the mercenary and the woman he came in with. Leave nothing out."

The man's smile was fleeting and perfunctory. "Of course, sir. They came in early yesterday morning with Mister Rogers. The hotel is in lockdown. We moved all the guests to other accommodations. The elder Mister Rogers and

Miss Cook were in a secured conference room all morning and part of the afternoon.

"The owner's son spent a short while there but retired to a suite occupied by his companions before lunch. I was unable to gain access to the conference room, but I did manage to spy on some of the other occupants as they left."

He slid a data chip across to Nathan, who handed it off to one of his people. The man booted a tablet and loaded the video. It showed a guard escorting two women. The women wore lab coats and carried a pack as though it contained something very fragile. The clip lasted less than ten seconds.

Nathan wasn't impressed. "That's all you have? Who are they? What's in the pack?" He, of course, already knew more than he'd said, but the little bugger needed some extra motivation.

The sweat on the man's face grew heavier. "I'm sorry, sir. I don't know. Security around Mister Rogers is exceptionally tight, and the two women are isolated. I did manage to get a list of the equipment they brought with them, though. It's also on the chip."

The mercenary found the file and opened it. Nathan scanned the list. It looked as though they might be setting up a clean room, though some of the equipment just didn't make sense for something like that. He'd need to have a technogeek look at the list.

"And when did my brother leave?"

"He's still here, sir. Mister Rogers indicated that they would remain for at least several days and possibly much longer. It appears that the two of them have some type of arrangement. One of my associates is procuring some equipment and clothing for them. It's being charged to Rainforest."

That made no sense at all. Nathan knew his brother hated their father as much as he did, though for all the wrong reasons. He wasn't sure what had convinced Harry to rescue the woman, but he certainly wouldn't be doing long-term work for their father.

Nathan leaned forward and smiled coldly. "I want you to get something into their rooms. I'll give you a device to plant."

The little bastard had the gall to shake his head. "They aren't allowing anyone into the rooms. Not even maids to clean up. As far as I can determine, someone is always present there. It just isn't possible."

"I'm not interested in excuses. I want results. You will make that happen. I'll leave it to you to fill in the 'or else' part."

The frightened man nodded. "I'll try."

"You better do more than try, little man. Get him out of here."

Once his men had roughly escorted the weasel out, Nathan pulled out his phone and dialed his mother's private number.

"This better not be bad news," she said after a single ring.

"I'm sending you a video of two unknown women. They seem to be part of whatever scheme father has cooked up."

"How so?"

"I expect their identities might provide a clue. I also have a list of equipment and a mystery."

"Don't drag this out, Nathan. What mystery?"

"The one where dear Harry and your ex-husband are working closely together."

The connection was quiet for a minute. He could imagine his mother racking her brain for the cause of such an unlikely alliance.

"Get me some answers." She hung up without another word.

* * *

JESS EYED the two guards that Harry had sprung on her with disfavor. They seemed unmoved. Sandra Dean didn't look all that intimidating, but Jess knew she was a very capable sniper and all around badass. Allen Ellison towered over both women, muscled and tough.

Yet he deferred to Sandra, which told Jess all she needed to know about which was the more dangerous of the two.

Both wore the same kind of camouflage uniform that they'd worn in the jungle, a liberty bell patch with the numeral one on their left shoulders. Instead of allowing them to blend in, it made them stand out. As did the pistols on their hips and the automatic weapons that hung in front of their chests.

"Don't you think this is a little over the top?" Jess asked Sandra. "We're in the middle of a hotel under heavy guard. There's no one here but us."

The wiry woman shrugged. "That's assuming we can trust the security, which I don't. If I think one of them is making a move on you, I'll cap him." She smiled sweetly at the uncomfortable-looking man in a suit that trailed them. He'd easily overheard every word.

"That's harsh." Jess thought Harry was being overprotective, but she couldn't blame him. His brother had almost gotten her twice. The memory of drawing her borrowed pistol and shooting the hell out of the jungle trying to hit that bastard would haunt her for a while.

Which reminded her. "I need your advice," she said to Sandra. "I appreciated Harry loaning me the pistol, but I'm not going to cart something like that around on my hip. Can you recommend something smaller that I can carry in my purse?"

"Mexico is pretty restrictive on weapons unless you have a permit. Especially concealed. If they'd have caught us in the jungle, I'm sure Guatemala would've locked us up too. You'll need your boss to make some calls."

The Rainforest security guy took the hint and called someone on his radio. After a brief conversation, he looked back at Jess. "My boss knows someone who can expedite a permit. He's making some calls."

"Thanks."

Sandra darted her eyes toward the ladies' room they were just passing. Jess didn't need to go, but she took the hint and angled over toward it. "I'll just be a couple of minutes."

The mercenary woman followed her in without a word to her companion.

Jess frowned a little. "Are you going to follow me into the ladies' room every time I have to go?"

"Duh. It's a great ambush spot. The bad guys can literally catch you with your pants down."

Sandra cleared the bathroom stalls. One had an occupant. The mercenary banged on the door. "Security. Wrap it up, and move along."

"I'm busy," a woman said acerbically. "You'll just have to wait."

"If you're not done in sixty seconds, I'm coming in to help you with that." She keyed her radio. "One extra in the bathroom. Stand by."

The woman in the stall sighed and finished quickly. She washed her hands and glared at Sandra as she exited.

The mercenary was apparently immune to embarrassment. She finished searching the stall and called the all clear to Allen.

"Now, let's go over a few ground rules," she told Jess. "First, you don't pull this gun unless you really need to. Allen and I are here to provide security. If there's trouble, you do exactly what we tell you to do, which will not be to shoot at anyone. Clear?"

Jess nodded. "I only used the pistol last time because I didn't have a choice."

"I heard. You got a piece of him, right?"

"Rex found a little blood, so I think so. It must not have been anything important."

"That's good. It'd have been better if you shot the bastard in the head, but take what you can get. I've heard stories about cops and thugs emptying their pistols at one other while standing a few feet apart where they missed every shot. Adrenalin screws up your perception, so you have to train hard to overcome it.

"Rule two, if you draw your weapon, shoot to kill. Do not shoot to wound. That never ends well. If you need a salve for your conscience, surprisingly few people die from gunshot wounds unless the shooter is really good or lucky. Odds are that anyone you cap will make it to the hospital and survive the experience. Don't give the enemy any advantage. Clear?"

"Yes. Don't draw unless I have to, only draw if I intend to kill someone, and then shoot to kill." Her stomach roiled a little at the cold-bloodedness. A few days ago, she'd never have considered anything like this. Her worldview was changing in ways she didn't really like.

Sandra looked her in the eyes for a moment and then nodded. "Good enough." She unclipped her rifle and set it on the counter. She then tugged her shirt up, revealing a black bra with a pistol butt poking out from beneath it.

"Seriously?" Jess asked. "You have a gun attached to your bra?"

The mercenary grinned. "Last place you'd expect to see one, right? The holster snaps around the center between my tits. Guys never see past them to what they're hiding. Boobs of death."

Sandra unsnapped the holstered weapon and gestured for Jess to lift her blouse.

"You're more stacked than I am, which is a good thing for keeping something like this hidden," Sandra said as she attached it to Jess's bra. "This keeps the pistol under your breasts horizontally so that you can lift your shirt and draw. The gun comes free with a good tug. You'll want to practice with the weapon unloaded. I want you to be able to draw from a dead sleep."

"You want me to go to bed armed?"

"No, but you need to get the muscle memory in there. In a crisis, you'll do what you've trained to do. You want your first response to be the right one, especially when someone is trying to kill you."

Once the holster was in place, Sandra pulled the pistol free and unloaded it. It looked very much like the one Harry had loaned her, though a little smaller.

"This is a Glock subcompact 9mm," Sandra said. "The one you had in the jungle is its big brother. You have ten rounds in the magazine and one in the pipe. I have a spare magazine that can go in your purse. Twenty-one rounds total. Most confrontations take place inside of ten feet and are over in seconds. That should be enough ammo.

"We'll be training you more on how to use this later, but it should make you feel safe enough for the moment. You'll be self-conscious for a while, but no one will see it under your blouse. Hell, they might not even find it during a pat down if they cop a feel. Pretend it isn't there. If this isn't to your taste, we can go shopping for a different kind of holster or gun later."

"I don't want to take your stuff. I need to buy my own."

Sandra shrugged. "You can buy me some new toys later. A girl can't have too many hand cannons. Remind me to show you my .50 BMG single-shot pistol."

"BMG?"

"Big Mutherfracking Gun."

Jess shook her head. She'd never understand some people.

They walked through loading and unloading the pistol safely. Then Sandra put it in the holster unloaded, Jess slid her blouse down, and she practiced drawing it a few times. The pistol came free surprisingly cleanly, though it did feel odd exposing herself a little to get at it. She supposed the distraction was a plus.

She examined herself closely in the mirror. She didn't see the gun at all.

"It's not exactly the most comfortable thing, but I suppose I'll get used to it."

Sandra clapped Jess on the shoulder and handed her a spare magazine from her belt. "A gun is supposed to be comforting, not comfortable. You need to hit the can?"

Jess shook her head and put the magazine into the side pocket of her purse. She could get to it quickly, and it wouldn't be popping out if she needed her brush. "I'm good. They've got to be wondering what we're doing in here."

"Guys have no clue what women do in the bathroom. They might be impatient, but they'll never guess the truth. Come on."

They walked out of the restroom, and Jess headed down the hall with the group at her heels. "Sorry I took so long. I'd like to go see the restoration specialists."

The Rainforest guard stepped ahead of them. "The doctors are in a suite on the sixth floor. This way, please."

15

Harry walked into the head of his father's security forces' office with a chip on his shoulder and two armed guards at his back. His father's, not his.

The man across the desk from him eyed Harry for a few seconds. "Wally, close the door on your way out."

The guard in question, who looked like a boxer that had taken a few too many shots to the nose, looked at Harry uncertainly. "You sure?"

"I'll yell if I need you," the man's boss said.

Harry waited for the two men to leave and stood next to the bookcase, ignoring the chair set out in front of the desk. He wasn't going to play these head games. He'd play his own.

The selection of books looked professional, most relating to the security industry. The ones that didn't fit that meme were thrillers of one kind or another.

He allowed the silence to go on. That, too, was a power game. People abhorred silence. They wanted to fill it. Patience and keeping your mouth shut often gave one an advantage. He'd wait for hours, if need be.

As he'd expected, the other man spoke first.

"I'm John Cradock, Mister Roger's head of security. I want to start this meeting off by making it clear that I'm in command of the operations around here. I don't give a shit if my boss is your dad or not. You got that?"

Harry took one of the thrillers off the shelf and read the back cover. A military thriller. Snipers and terrorists. Sandra might like to read it for laughs. He slid it into his pocket, turned toward the desk, and basked in the glow of the man's dismay at his petty theft.

"And, for my part," Harry said, "I don't give a shit that you don't give a shit. My father can go to hell, and you can escort him there. That said, someone I do care about needs this heist to go off without a hitch. Unless you have a lot more experience than I expect at this kind of thing, I'm going to be calling the shots."

The way the man was glaring, it was a wonder that the books behind Harry didn't burst into flames. "That isn't going to happen."

"Then we're done here. You can explain to your boss why I'm pulling out, and he can flap in the wind. Or we can work out a mutually agreeable plan. I have years of experience getting into places where I'm not meant to be and taking things that other people don't want to give up. People, mostly, but we guard the ones we love the best."

Cradock ran his hand through his hair. "Shit. I don't know you, and I'm the one responsible for this mission. If it fails, I'm going down for it."

"Then let's make sure that doesn't happen. We'll go over your plans, and I'll make suggestions. I'll have almost a dozen spec ops teams here in two days, every one of them with experience being on the sharp end. Surely you and I can come up with a plan to use them effectively once we've gotten past this pissing contest."

"Shit. Fine." He pounded on the keyboard with his thick fingers, and a street map came up on the screen across from the desk.

"This is the satellite view of the target. It's an industrial park on the outskirts of Paris. BenCorp owns the entire park. Why they built in that cesspool, I'll never know. The outer buildings are empty. The central building is where they designed and built the reactor.

"I imagine they'll bring in other tenants after the secret project is complete. Or maybe things will go so bad that they'll abandon it. Some parts of Paris seem to be on fire 24/7 these days."

The map showed how isolated the target was. Fences topped with razor wire surrounded the facility. Based on the markings, guard teams heavily patrolled the grounds. The public wouldn't get within a thousand feet of the research facility. Not even the terrorists virtually running Paris these days.

"Where are the guard posts?"

"There are a dozen along the perimeter and roving patrols all over the place. Random times and patterns. Dogs, bomb-sniffing robots, and automatic weapons. They're ready to repel the strongest attack force."

Harry nodded. "But you've found a weak spot."

"Right." Cradock added a layer to the image. "Sewers. BenCorp has them wired, but we've spent the last six months hacking the security protocols. We'll be able to bypass the alarms and slip inside their perimeter when the time comes. The tunnels have a spur that services the target building. We'll be inside it with no one the wiser."

"If you believe that, you're an idiot."

Cradock bared his teeth. "You don't know me, and you don't know how carefully we probed this thing. It's a real weak spot."

"It's a trap. My mother is like a spider. She likes people to think they've gotten one over on her, right up until the bear trap snaps shut on their hand. There's no way she'd leave something basic like that unprotected."

"I just said it was protected. We've spoofed all the security monitors. I had a team probe the sewers all the way to the basement of the target building."

"I'm sure you did. And when your teams come in force, something you never saw coming would blow the shit out of you. I have a genius at security on my team. Let him go over what you have. If he agrees that my mother is slipping into dementia, fine and good. If not, you don't lose dozens of men."

"Fine," Cradock said unwillingly. "Call him down. Use the desk phone. Cell traffic is blocked."

It only took a moment to call Jeremy Gonzales. Harry returned his attention to the security man when he finished explaining the situation. "Is that where the fuel is too?"

Cradock shook his head. "No. Mister Rogers has a factory in Northern Africa. They made deuterium-tritium pellets there for years. They have a large stockpile in storage. Unfortunately, the government collapsed, and a warlord has taken over the area. He's probably not aware of what he has under his nose, but there are militants all over the facility. They think it's something they can use to make nuclear bombs."

Harry chuckled. "As if anyone sane would allow that to happen after Tel Aviv. Israel turned most of Iran into glowing craters. Good riddance. You're right. That's a solvable problem. We can focus on the tough nut first."

* * *

NATHAN PAUSED the porn on his tablet and answered the call on his encrypted cell. "Mother."

"The women in your video are experts at restoring and safeguarding ancient artifacts. The kind of thing one finds in a Mayan pyramid. Or, I suppose, in an ancient spacecraft."

"Not exactly helpful. Your man on the inside isn't able to get a bug into Harry's room, and I've seen no sign that he or the engineer are coming out any time soon. We're just sitting here spinning our wheels."

"Perhaps not. I've heard that Harry is calling in his special-operations strike teams. Some are on the way down to the spaceport right now. Your window to make any gains is short."

Nathan sat up abruptly. "He's calling in his shooters? How many of them?"

"How the hell should I know? All of them, as far as I can tell."

"Shit. Once they lock the hotel down with that kind of force, we won't be able to do a damned thing. We need to go after them right now."

"Exactly my thought," his mother said. "Except they're not the most important thing in that building. If you can catch them, great. What I really want are the artifacts. I'm working with my people in Guatemala to take the sites away from Clayton, but he's spent a prodigious amount of money. It won't be easy, if it's possible at all. We need to know what they're looking at and get samples of it."

Nathan nodded thoughtfully. "We'll go in just as the sun goes down. The other teams will be close to landing, and their guard will be more relaxed. He only has one team here, and they're probably not guarding the artifacts. In and out. We'll need to evade the security response long enough to escape the area, though."

His mother smiled. The small picture didn't do her justice. "I know just the right kind of distraction to give you the time you need. Call my man and get this rolling."

* * *

THE DOCTORS HAD SET up their lab in a large conference room. Jess didn't recognize most of the equipment but imagined they used it to stop the deterioration of delicate artifacts. The two women had their heads together over the book.

They looked up as Jess and her entourage entered. Security was tight. There were two Rainforest guards outside and two inside, all in body armor and armed with automatic weapons. Clayton Rogers was taking security very seriously.

Jess's guard detail peeled off and took up spots against the wall opposite the Rainforest security team.

"How are things going?" Jess asked.

Paulette Young gestured toward the book. "This is amazing. The pages are made from a material somewhat like plastic but almost as flexible as paper. It's obviously much more durable. The pen used an ink that bonded with the pages. It's quite ingenious. I hope the pen turns up."

"What about the writing itself? Has anyone looked into what language it might be?"

"We haven't had any luck identifying it yet. It's written from left to right and isn't similar to any lettering that I'm familiar with. Rachel scanned it in, and we have a search of our offline database running now."

Rachel Powel gestured toward a computer. "We have samples of every known language on file. If it's been used on Earth, we'll find it."

"What about the tools?"

"They seem to be made of the same material. We took a sample and sent it off to the lab. The tools don't seem to have lost their tensile strength over the centuries. The only object that seems to have broken down is the satchel, and even it has held together surprisingly well. I'm not sure there's much for us to preserve, other than that."

"There are other... objects being brought in. You'll probably need more space."

The scientist nodded. "Mister Rogers said that he has a lab building that will be ready for us tomorrow morning. It will be more isolated and not disrupt the hotel."

A flash of light outside caught Jess's attention. It was getting dark, so the flare was quite visible. Was a cargo shuttle launching off schedule?

She'd taken one step toward the window when Sandra tackled her like a linebacker and covered her with her body. The larger Allen was right behind the sniper and planted himself between the two scientists with his back to the flash.

The large windows blew out in a maelstrom of broken glass. A massive explosion roared in the distance. A few shards nicked Jess's exposed arm, and the sting of pain was surreal.

Her head rang with the aftereffects of the explosion. It was worse than when she'd fired the gun in the jungle.

Dazed, she almost fell over when Sandra yanked her to her feet. "Time to go," the mercenary said. "Allen, clear the hall. We're going back to the suite." She keyed her radio. "Liberty Base, Long Gun. Condition Gamma. We're returning via the stairs on the south side of the building."

Jess didn't have much of a choice. The woman almost dragged her back to the hall. Allen had his weapon up and covered the Rainforest guards as the three of them withdrew.

She didn't think they were much of a threat. They'd been looking right at the windows when they exploded. The two interior guards were down, clutching their bloody faces. The guards from outside were staring at the destruction in shock.

The Rainforest guard assigned to them must've ducked. He had a long gash on the back of his hand but was otherwise okay.

"Wait," Jess said. "This had to have been an accident. Something exploded at one of the launch pads."

Sandra didn't seem to care. "That's someone else's problem. I'm getting you back where I can protect you."

"What about the scientists and the priceless artifacts? We need to keep them safe."

"They aren't my responsibility."

"Bring them with us. At least grab the book."

"The other guards can see them to safety. Let's go." She dragged Jess down the hall. Allen sprinted ahead to clear the stairs.

The big mercenary had just disappeared when Sandra jerked to a halt and collapsed. Jess had just enough time to turn and see the grinning Rainforest security man pull his stun gun back from Sandra's neck.

"Don't make me hurt you," he said as an automatic weapon started firing in the stairwell. "Mister Bennett wants you in one piece."

16

Harry sprinted out of the Rainforest security center and appropriated one of their vehicles. He cut off a car full of tourists and floored the gas. He figured he'd be back at the hotel in less than three minutes.

"Liberty Base, Liberty Six. Client status?" He had a lot of experience multitasking in combat, but swerving to miss idiots in traffic was new.

"Shots fired upstairs. The protective detail is not responding."

"Retrieve the client."

"Copy."

He cut across a field and made directly for the hotel. Jess didn't have seconds to spare.

* * *

NATHAN STEPPED over the body in the stairwell. Another mercenary, a woman, lay sprawled on the hall carpet. The Rainforest guard on his mother's payroll stood behind the woman who'd shot him in the jungle. He held a stun gun to her neck.

"Well, well. What an unexpected surprise!" Nathan said with a chuckle. He gestured for his team to continue past him. "Hit the lab. Take anything of use, and kill everyone. Leave my father's gift on the table."

The woman trembled, deliciously terrified. It warmed his heart.

"Have you searched her for weapons?" he asked. "She has hidden depths."

The man pinned the woman face first into the wall and started patting her down. His reach was limited with the stun gun planted on her neck.

"Idiot," Nathan said. "Keep her still while I check her."

He started at her ankles and felt his way up. She squirmed when he roughly checked her privates. "Get used to that. I'll be examining you much more closely."

"Bastard. I'm going to kill you."

Nathan laughed. "If only you knew how many women have said that to me over the years. It's almost an endearment at this point."

He made a point of fondling her breasts as he finished patting her down. They were his favorite part of a woman, and hers were magnificent. Gunfire erupted down the hall. It ended quickly, and his team called back in that the room was secure.

"She mentioned a book," the guard said. "She made it sound like that was the most important thing in the room."

"Why didn't you say that earlier, moron?" Nathan updated his team. They quickly reported that they had it.

The woman glared at him. "Harry won't let you get out of this building alive."

Nathan grinned nastily. "My brother will be very late to the party. And if you think his people will rescue you, well, you're in for a very disappointing day."

The floor jumped, and the stairwell door swung open a little. The booby trap he'd left below had found some customers.

He glanced at his watch. "Time to make our way to the roof. Move it along, people."

* * *

JESS KNEW that time was running out. If the bastard got her out of the building, she'd never escape. Right now, she only had him and the turncoat guard to deal with. She needed to do something while she could.

The guard had relaxed a little now that the heavily armed team had arrived. The damned stun gun wasn't on her neck anymore. That gave her a small window of opportunity.

Nathan had his attention focused down the hall waiting for his people to leave the preservation room. Jess had to make her move now.

She jammed her hand under her blouse and pulled the pistol free. The guard gaped, probably having no idea what she was doing.

He recognized the pistol, though. She stepped away from him even farther, wanting to keep him from grabbing her gun. He was still drawing his weapon when she had hers lined up on his head and pulled the trigger.

The results of that shot would feature prominently in her nightmares for years to come, if she survived.

She turned her attention to Harry's brother. He had body armor and an automatic weapon. One that was swiveling in her direction.

Jess threw herself into the stairwell just as he opened fire. The doorframe disintegrated, spraying her with splinters of wood.

Allen Ellison lay sprawled on his back in a pool of blood. He didn't look like he was breathing, and his eyes stared sightlessly at the ceiling. His weapon still hung around his neck.

She set her pistol on the floor, grabbed the rifle, and waited. If Nathan just came around the corner...

At the first sign of movement, Jess yanked the trigger. She quickly lost control of the automatic weapon. The barrel rose unexpectedly, but she forced it back down on target. The man's burst went harmlessly to the side as he slid down the wall, leaving a trail of blood. Her gun locked open surprisingly quickly.

It wasn't Nathan. Dammit.

Jess listened to the shouts down the hall as she grabbed her pistol and retreated up the stairs to the next landing. If they came this way, she'd give them something to regret.

* * *

HARRY WAS ALMOST to the hotel when his windshield shattered. He'd just hit a big bump in the ground, so the bullet aimed at him blew out the dashboard instead.

He couldn't stay in the sniper's kill zone, so he floored the SUV and started swerving. The main entrance to the hotel was right there.

More bullets hit his vehicle but missed him. He entered the area where passengers unloaded at what some might kindly call an unsafe speed and went right through the big glass doors.

He stood on the brakes and stopped just short of the front desk. He jumped out and ran past the shell-shocked staff to the stairs. Automatic-weapons fire came from above.

He passed what looked like an exploded booby trap on the third-floor landing. The lifeless bodies of a number of Rainforest security guards lay around it. He reached the hotspot and found his team already in place. Two of them were working on Allen, but it looked bad. Two more had just dragged Sandra in. A dead hostile lay sprawled just inside the hallway.

Jess stood on the stairs above them, a pistol in her hand, looking as though she were going into shock. "They went after the preservation room," she said. "They used a stun gun on Sandra."

The man working on Allen shook his head. Dammit.

"Rex, grab Sandra and get Jess clear. Everyone else is with me."

"Your brother said he was leaving a gift in the room," Jess said over her shoulder as Rex hustled her down the stairs. "Be careful!"

A Rainforest security man lay dead a few feet down the hall, his head shattered. The team moved as a unit past him to the open door. Three—no, four—dead men lay scatted around the room. There was no sign of the two scientists.

There was also no sign of the alien gear recovered from the tomb, at least not in plain sight. And he didn't have time to go looking for it.

A small stack of plastic explosives sat in the middle of the central table. A helpful timer indicated there was less than two minutes remaining before the device exploded. Not enough time to exit the building.

That was enough explosives to bring the hotel down. The device almost certainly had some kind of antitamper protection too.

Harry pondered his range of options. The bomb's sensors would know if he moved it, but there was some play. Otherwise, even minor shaking would set the thing off.

"Hold it steady. Lift it just a little."

Two of his people held the bomb while he cut the straps securing the explosives. He held his breath and slid the lower packages to the side. The ones on the edges of the top layer also fell away. Leann tossed them out the broken window.

That reduced the scope of the explosion enough to spare the building. Maybe. At his gesture, they set the bomb down carefully and ran like hell.

* * *

REX HUSTLED Jess out the side door of the hotel just as a helicopter took off from the roof. It had medical markings. She saw Nathan through the open door. He waved at her.

She was tempted to take a shot at him, but she knew she wouldn't hit anything.

Dammit.

Less than a minute later, the side of the hotel blew out. Debris showered around them even as Rex dragged her behind a parked minivan. Something heavy landed on the vehicle, crushing the roof.

She screamed. Who wouldn't?

When the rain of debris finally stopped, she stared at the devastation. The hotel was mostly intact. It had a huge divot in the side, and it was on fire, though. Steel and concrete littered the parking area. Every car alarm within a mile seemed to be going off. The stench of the explosives made her nose itch. And her ears were ringing even more loudly.

She turned to Rex. "Is Harry okay? Did he get out?"

The big man nodded grimly. "He made it down a few floors. It sounds like they're okay."

"I saw the mercenaries. They flew off the roof in a medical helicopter."

"They won't get far, but it'll probably be enough to slip away. Dammit. That's twice that assclown tried to kill some of us, and this time he did it."

His eyes shifted toward the hotel. "At least we took one of them out."

"Two," she said as she watched fire engines pull up to the hotel. "One of the Rainforest people was a traitor. He zapped Sandra. I shot him. Then I used Allen's weapon to kill the mercenary in the hall."

He blinked in surprise but said nothing.

She knelt beside the sniper and was happy to see signs that Sandra was waking up. Since slapping her cheek seemed like a very bad idea, Jess just waited.

The other woman sat up abruptly, reaching for her weapons. Jess held the rifle down. "Whoa! The fight is over."

Sandra blinked and felt the back of her neck. "What happened?"

"You know where you warned me that trouble could sneak up when I least expected it? It did. Allen didn't make it. I'm sorry."

The sniper said something particularly foul. "Help me up. Rex, what's the situation?"

He filled her in while they watched the building. Jess was happy to see other people streaming out of the damaged structure, including the two scientists from the preservation lab. They must've gotten the hell out of there right after the explosion at the launch pad.

Jess didn't relax until she saw Harry and his remaining teammates come out. Then she allowed herself to cry in a mixture of relief, terror, and horror.

* * *

HARRY HELD Jess when the reaction set in. He wanted to ask her exactly what had happened, but this wasn't the time. He stayed with her until he saw his father climb out of an SUV. Harry passed the wrung-out engineer to Sandra and headed over.

His father looked at the building. "This was Nathan, wasn't it?"

"Yes. He made off with some of the artifacts but not the scientists. Or Jess. He killed a bunch of your guards too. One of my people died in the stairwell, but it looks like he dropped one of the enemy and allowed Jess to escape. Rex said he flew off the roof in a medivac helicopter. What did he blow up?"

"The fueling station for pad three. He killed some of the staff. Security said the helicopter landed outside the fence, and they climbed into some vans. They're gone. The police are scouring the city, but it wouldn't surprise me if Nathan had some cops in his pocket. I'll put out a massive reward for their arrest, but don't hold your breath."

Harry considered the hotel while he thought. The fire was spreading quickly. It might be a loss.

"Nathan knew," he said after a moment. "He must've gotten a look inside that second chamber and saw the ship. The race is on now. What next?"

His father turned toward him, his expression as cold and hostile as Harry had ever seen. "We make them pay. If we want to stop Kathleen from derailing our plans completely, we need to act quickly.

"I know corporate contracts are supposed to be almost incomprehensible with legalese, but we don't have time for that luxury. If I write out a short deal swapping an ownership stake for access to the items already provided and anything recovered in the future, will you accept my word that it will be good? You can send it to your attorney for confirmation."

"On one condition. Mother has obviously compromised your organization. I want to be in charge of all security operations for Project Liberty. That includes the upcoming missions because your guy is fighting me on it."

"Done," his father said immediately. "Once your mother gets a chance to think this through, she'll realize what we're doing. You need to move the Paris timetable up."

Harry shook his head. "Your guy's plan feels like a trap. There's something going on there. We need more information about the facility and what they really have planned."

His father considered that. "I have a man in your mother's IT department. He was supposed to get me the final plans on this and a number of other secret projects, but he's gone quiet. She must've picked him up. If he got the data, it would be very helpful to retrieve it. And it would hurt her badly."

Harry smiled coldly. "Get me what you have, and I'll see about returning Nathan's visit."

17

———————

Jess turned down the doctor's offer of something to calm her nerves. She needed her wits about her. Mister Rogers had presented her with a ridiculously short contract that matched what they'd discussed in astonishingly plain language.

Harry had already run it past his lawyer, and she'd found no issues. The company would own the finds—past, present, and future—and profit from them. The ownership was unambiguous, and Jess would have her say in the new company, Humanity Unlimited.

Clayton was the chief executive officer, she would be the chief operating officer, and Harry would be the chief of security for the organization. Each would share the profits according to their stake.

Harry had said he'd sign it if she did. Time to do her own check. She looked up the number for her college friend and dialed.

"Dawson and Treadwell, Aaron speaking. How can I help you today?"

"Aaron, this is Jess Cook. How's it going?"

"Jess! I was just thinking about you the other day! Things are great. I made partner last year. Are you still building bridges while dreaming of space stations?"

She smiled at the joy in his voice. Aaron had always been a happy one.

"Actually, I'm working in space. In fact, I wanted to see if I could beg a favor about that."

"You need me to come up and turn a wrench? Bad call. My wife won't let me do home repairs due to liability concerns."

Jess queued up the contract on her tablet. "I found something that the owner thinks is worth a lot of money. He made me an offer, and I need someone I can trust to look it over."

"Sure. Do you have my email address? Send it, and I'll take a look. I can probably have an answer for you in a couple of days."

Jess sent the contract. "Things are moving pretty quickly on this end. If you could just take a peek, I'd appreciate it."

"Contracts are nothing to skim," he said seriously. "The devil is in the details. One little word in the boilerplate can change the whole... Wait a second. This isn't complete. It's only one page."

"That's it."

The silence on the other end of the line dragged on as her friend read. "This is pretty plainly stated. You cede control of the listed artifacts to the company, as well as those discovered in the future, and you get an ownership stake in the sole entity that will profit from them: Humanity Unlimited. This list of items you found seems pretty pedestrian. Wrenches, a book, and... wait. A crashed spaceship? Is this a joke?"

Sometimes, it seemed like it. One on her. "Nope, completely serious, though I need you to keep the details confidential. I'll send the general assets list for the company too."

Once he had it, he continued. "This says the company owns a spaceship constructed from the ISS2 skeleton. It lists tens of billions in assets. And you're getting an outright stake of 40 percent? Jess, I've never seen a contract so straightforward. I don't see any gotchas."

"That's what I needed to know. Remember, keep it under your hat and watch the news over the next few weeks. I owe you one."

Jess hung up and signed the contract. She sent a copy to Clayton, Harry, and herself.

They'd relocated to the spaceport proper. To say that security was heavy was an understatement. Several of Harry's special-operations teams had arrived, and all of them seemed to be keeping an eye on her. And the building they were in, to be fair.

Sandra was back on her feet and mad as a wet cat. For her, that meant brooding silence. The rest of the original team was off doing other tasks. The room Jess and Sandra were in had four men standing guard, armed for war. Four more stood in the hall outside.

"Sandra, I'm sorry about Allen."

The other woman looked up with cold, hard eyes. "Me too. He was a good man. It's not your fault. It's mine. I let that traitor get behind me and almost lost you too."

The sniper visibly shook herself. "Sorry. My mind is already on payback. That'll come in time. Allen took them out and got you free. That's what matters."

"Actually, no. I wish he had." She gave Sandra a rundown of what had happened.

The other woman's eyes widened as she listened. "Oh, God. I'm sorry you had to do that. To see that."

Jess shrugged. "I didn't have a choice. They had it coming, but I'm going to have some bad nights. I just know it."

"You need to talk to someone," the sniper said firmly. "If not today, then soon. PTSD isn't a joke, and you don't want to let something like that take over your life. I don't know if you're religious or not, but you might see someone there too."

"I will. When I have time. Harry's figuring out what we're doing next. I need to be part of that."

"Then what the hell are we doing sitting here? Let's go."

Sandra stood and keyed her radio. "Scotty is on the move."

"Scotty? Seriously?"

"Harry suggested it. You want a different call sign? Pitch it to me, and I'll see what I can do. It's like a nickname, though. Sometimes you don't get to pick the one you like."

"That sucks."

Several of the mercenaries stayed at the office while the rest formed up around Jess and Sandra. The Rainforest guards wisely got out of the way when they saw them coming.

Harry was in a conference room in the basement of the security building with one of his guys and several Rainforest types. He had a satellite view of what looked like a college campus up on the screen. He paused what he was saying when she came in. "Jess, I hope you're feeling better."

"I'm riding the tiger." She picked out the most senior-looking Rainforest guy and held out her hand. "Jessica Cook."

"John Cradock, chief of Rainforest security operations."

Part of her felt sorry for him, but the rest wanted to slap him for hiring traitors. "I'm sorry you lost some people."

He grunted as though someone had punched him in the stomach. "I'm sorry one of them turned on you. That's on me."

The large man gestured to the screen. "We're planning on returning the favor. Mister Rogers—the elder—told me about the change in organizational structure. The younger Mister Rogers is in command of these operations going forward. As a minority stakeholder, you'll have input too."

Harry gestured toward the chair beside him. "Have a seat, and I'll fill you in."

Jess sat down while the mercenaries took up places against the wall. "Did you sign the contract? I signed mine just before I came down."

"Not yet." He pulled out his tablet. "Let's get that out of the way so this is official. Done. It's off to my father. God help me."

He pointed to the screen. "That's BenCorp headquarters in the US. My mother's flagship company."

She leaned forward and examined it closely. "Is this a retaliatory raid? Do we have time for that?"

"We always have time for payback. In this case, though, it actually has some relevance." He touched the controls and brought up the image of a skinny man. "Meet Vincent Cruz. He used to work for my mother as the assistant IT manager of BenCorp."

"Used to?"

Harry nodded. "Right up until the moment she found out he was spying for my father. Now he's almost certainly a prisoner. He was supposedly in the process of stealing a trove of classified information that he never had a chance to turn over, including detailed plans for the facility where they built the reactor. We need them, so we need him."

Jess could only imagine the trouble the man was in. "He must've stood to gain a lot of money to cross people like Kathleen Bennett. She doesn't even know me, and yet she's tried to kill me several times. How can I help?"

"Honestly, you can't," Cradock said. "This is a straightforward security operation. Having you along would be a major distraction. With the damage here at the port, it might be best if you worked on getting ready to launch the fuel and reactor once we get them."

She agreed with the basic sentiment. The last thing she wanted was another gunfight. "Do we have the fuel?"

"Not yet, but we will. The militants won't be able to hold onto the facility. I'm taking care of that operation while Harry gets the data on the Paris facility. Then he'll lead his people there to get the reactor."

"It'll need to go into orbit as soon as we get it back here," Harry said. "We don't want to give them a chance to strike back before we can boost it."

Jess considered the two assaults and their timing. "With one pad out of operation, we can only do launches on two. We could fuel one of the lifters and carry it over to pad three. When the reactor arrives, we'll load it and fire it off. I figure maybe an hour, if we're on the bounce. You'll need me in Paris."

Harry didn't look pleased at that news. "Why?"

"Because it's a nuclear reactor. You need a skilled engineer in case they've made it operational. Based on what I've seen of the design, we could move it locally even while it's running, but flying it in that configuration is out of the question.

"Worst case, we'd need to power it down, disassemble it, and fly it out a few days later. That would require a secluded area that no one could find for three days. Hopefully, it won't come to that."

"It better not," Harry said. "The French will lock the country down as soon as they know its missing. We need to get clear before they realize what we took."

"The laws of physics and thermodynamics are outside my control," she said. "I also need to be at the factory in Africa, once you have it locked down."

"That's not happening," Harry said bluntly. "The area is overrun by fanatics. The fuel extraction will almost certainly be under fire."

She shrugged. "Then you probably won't get the fuel."

Harry and Cradock glanced at one another. "And why is that?" the Rainforest security man ventured.

"Because it's locked down in an area where the militants aren't looking for it. Only a few people were ever on the access list. They died when the militants took over the factory. The computers are isolated, so it's too late to add anyone else. I'm on the list already."

"Crap," Harry said. "Give me a minute to think about this."

Her tablet chimed. She looked at the incoming message. "Your father just signed the contract. We're committed now."

"Yea." The young mercenary's tone indicated anything but excitement. "You can go, but you're not going in until they've suppressed the enemy. You land, open up the storage area, and get the hell back out of there. The security teams will extract the fuel. You got that? I want you in and gone before the militants can strike back."

"No argument from me. I'm tired of getting shot at."

"And Sandra takes a team in with you. If she says it's too hot, she'll abort your portion of the mission. You got that, Sandra?"

"Orders received," the sniper said.

Jess was both relieved and annoyed by the exchange. Somehow, she suspected her life would never go quite the way she expected from this point forward.

* * *

ONCE JESS and her team had left, Cradock gave Harry a searching look. "Are you sure that's the best idea? We need her for the reactor."

"Then make sure the facility is locked down. Hit it with everything you have, clean it out fast, and get clear."

Harry stood. "My people and I need to get moving. I need you to get us out of here without advertising it. My mother obviously has eyes on what we're doing. I don't want her to know we're coming."

"How about you make a big show of boarding some cargo planes bound for the Middle East?"

"And then what?"

The security guy grinned. "Then we play a shell game. Swap them out for other planes going to the US for high-tech equipment. We just lost a fueling station. We need those parts."

Harry liked the plan. It played into the events his mother had caused.

"So long as no one knows, we can work with that. Military equipment is more difficult to get into the US, so we'll need some help on that end. France too."

"I'll work something out," Cradock said. "The US is the more difficult of the two. You can buy heavy weapons on almost any street corner in Paris these days."

"Okay." Harry stood. "Let's get this in motion."

18

Clayton spent the next several hours getting things in order. Harry was heading to the US, his other teams were diverting to Paris, and Jessica Cook was on her way to the factory in northern Africa.

Her mission would kick off first. The ruckus might give Harry an opening to get into the BenCorp facilities. Clayton had a few more people on his payroll that could provide some kind of cover, but the less they took for granted, the better.

Where were they keeping his spy, and where was the pilfered data? Hopefully, the man had secreted it somewhere they could get to it. They wouldn't know that until they had him.

His ex-wife's chief of security was a real sweetheart. Rumors swirled around the man's penchant for torturing people. If he had Cruz, odds were good the man was in whatever dungeon the sadist had constructed.

And that just might be the right place to look first. Kathleen was a terrible person, but he doubted she let her security chief torture people in her office building. The man probably had a private facility for his personal amusements. One where the screaming wouldn't disturb the neighbors.

Clayton smiled. Time to see if he could locate it.

* * *

Kathleen Bennett examined the book closely. The cover looked like leather, but it wasn't natural. It had a slickness that spoke to something artificial. The pages were definitely synthetic. The lettering didn't look like anything she'd ever seen before.

The tools were a combination of modern and other. They didn't look like any alloy she was familiar with, but that would come out in the lab report.

It wasn't much. She'd expected significantly more from a direct intervention. Dammit. They had a spaceship in the jungle. Surely, they had more than this to examine.

She glared at her son. "This can't be everything."

He shrugged. "It's all they had in their makeshift lab. Your man in the hotel said that the permanent facility wasn't ready yet."

"Why would Clayton call Harry's people in? Not for guarding the spaceship. They've buried the site in Rainforest security people. What are we missing?"

"Maybe the mystery is right under your nose, Mother. He's on a spaceport, paying Harry to protect a space engineer. Perhaps the secret is in orbit right over our heads."

She made a derisive noise. "The space hotel? Don't be any more of an idiot than you have to be. He's welcome to pour money down the drain on that project."

"Are you certain it's what you think it is? The old bastard is sharp enough with the rest of his business ventures. Could the space hotel be a cover for something else?"

She considered that. "A weapon's platform? There's no way. All of the leading nations are keeping an eye on nukes. The little power plant he has up there is barely strong enough to keep the lights on.

"Besides, I paid to have the construction monitored from a telescope in Hawaii. They watched it for months. There's no place to hide missiles."

"You asked the question," he said. "If my answer doesn't satisfy you, perhaps you should look elsewhere."

"Go figure out where your brother is," she snarled. "If he's going to get even, I want to know where to double the guard."

She dismissed her son from her mind as soon as he was out the door and picked up the phone. She'd rouse her staff and figure out if anything was going on in orbit, just in case.

* * *

GETTING into the US proved to be anticlimactic. The plane flying Harry and his people in landed in Texas, and the inspector never even looked inside. It lifted off and was in Chicago two hours before the sun rose.

They'd spent the entire trip gathering intel and rejecting plans. The security chief, Donald Reynolds, lived in company housing to one side of the facility. His home was large and somewhat separated from the rest, but it was inside the perimeter.

The man himself had an unsavory reputation and a criminal record. His rap sheet looked like the guidebook to a serial killer. Animal torture and mutilation, assault of the elderly, and the police suspected he'd had a hand in the disappearance of a high school classmate.

Those run-ins with the law stopped once BenCorp hired him. Apparently he'd found someone willing to use his talents and provide a cover for his hobbies. He wished he could say that surprised him, but it didn't.

The team exited the plane once it landed at a smaller airport near Chicago and piled into an unmarked van. It took them to a disused warehouse about half a mile from the target. Two men who didn't give their names were waiting for them.

The larger one, a black man with closely trimmed hair and a diamond stud in one ear, gestured toward a number of boxes stacked neatly on the floor. "You'll find weapons and electronics there. The plane will be ready to take off the moment you get back to the airfield. Good hunting."

Harry helped his people unpack the boxes. The selection was a little sparse on the weapons front but more than he'd expected to have available in the US. The police would freak if they had any idea of what was in the warehouse. He made sure everyone had burner cells, just in case.

Jeremy Gonzales went over the electronics. "This is good stuff. Top of the line. If we can get past the perimeter fence, I can get into the house."

"And how do we slip past the live guards and electronic security?"

"With these." Jeremy held up some jumpsuits. "They minimize IR radiation. I can get us through the exterior fences. We time the patrols and slip in right after one passes. The monitors will see something but probably mark it as an artifact of the team that just went by."

"And if they don't?"

The Hispanic man grinned. "Then we better not take our sweet time. The guards will circle back and check the area again. By then, we'd better be gone."

Harry liked the audacity of the plan. "That's entry. Next up, we need to breach the target residence. You can bet that he'll have top-of-the-line intrusion detection. Once inside, we have to locate Cruz and get him out. Preferably without making a big scene. We still have to retrieve the data, if possible. Then we exit stage left, possibly with everyone on alert and hunting us."

Rex hefted a rifle with a grenade launcher. "That's where I come in. I can make a ruckus in a different area and draw their attention. If you need me, then they're already aware of you. It won't matter if I blow something up."

Harry examined the communications gear. It was similar to what he normally used. Encrypted burst transmissions. Anyone hearing it would think it was static. Unless, of course, they had the very best equipment and were on the lookout for strange signals.

"Okay. Gear up, and we'll make entry in thirty minutes. We need to be in the target house by dawn. We'll plan on exterior guards and a very short window of opportunity. Keep communication to a minimum."

* * *

JESS SLEPT through the flight to northern Africa. She blearily stared out the window as the aircraft touched down. She was almost awake by the time they pulled up to a hangar. Two other large aircraft sat nearby.

Cradock's people exited first, and many went inside the hangar. One of them gave a high sign.

Sandra started down the stairs. "That's the all clear. Let's get in there and get this show on the road."

People crowded the hangar, all of them dressed in desert camouflage and heavily armed. Cradock's people were gearing up from open crates.

The senior security man gestured for Jess to join him at a table. Several other young security types stood around. The map in front of them showed the manufacturing plant.

"Where's the fuel stored?" Sandra asked.

She pointed to one of the barracks. "Under here. The cover story was that the building had bad pipes. They kept it locked during the plant's operational run. The rear wall butts up against the plant where the finished product came out. Trusted personnel moved the fuel into the secure facility and shipped out water in its place."

One of the younger men spoke up. "Why the switch? Why not really ship the fuel back to Mexico when it was finished?"

Jess had asked that very question when she'd found out what they were doing. "The station everyone expected doesn't need this kind of fuel. If they'd shipped it back then, there was a significantly higher chance of someone seeing something they shouldn't.

"The cover story for this plant is that it was creating heavy water for research. Enough was on hand to verify the contents shipped to the test site in Italy. The first few barrels actually held heavy water. The rest came from a tap. No one ever checked past what they saw."

Sandra grunted. "Clever. Only the government here fell, and this became a lawless state. Now a warlord runs things. He probably looked the facility over and decided that he didn't need something like that. Besides, a little common sense would tell someone that heavy water is pretty useless by itself.

"Which explains the militants taking over. Common sense isn't their strong suit. Do we have any idea how many hostiles we're talking about?"

"We sent a drone over the area an hour ago. IR shows a good number of people scattered throughout the buildings. Including the target."

"What's the plan?"

Sandra leaned over the map. "We have helicopters inbound to pick us up. The militants have sentries out, but our scouts will take them down as soon as we're on approach. We'll drop in right on top of them. A few rockets into each of the other buildings will take out the majority of the hostiles.

"Our main team clears the barracks while the rest of the buildings burn. After they call the all clear, Jess comes in to open the vault. We verify the fuel is present, and she evacuates while we start loading the bins into cargo helicopters. Total mission time should be less than half an hour.

"And then we get her out of country before anyone starts getting nervous.

We've got a private jet fueled and ready to go in another hangar. We'll return straight here and head to France."

The rest of the mission planning went quickly. The helicopters arrived, and the armed strike teams were on their way. The helicopter Jess rode in with Sandra's group headed in the same direction but more slowly.

Her chopper was an older cargo model fitted with door guns. Jess had flown similar craft a number of times. Earning her pilot's license was a proud moment for her, and flying was fun, as well as being useful in getting equipment to remote areas.

The helicopter crested a low hill, and she saw the fuel facility burning. They landed without any fanfare, and the mercenaries hustled her into the barracks.

The whole area smelled of gunpowder, fire, and death. A number of bodies lay scattered about. They all seemed to be men. Based on the number of weapons lying around, they'd fought back. Armed security people had a number of women and children crowded into a corner of the barracks. They were crying and screaming, of course.

Jess had limited sympathy for them. She'd seen plenty of video where men just like their husbands and fathers had done inhuman things. These people were here because they'd thought they could build a weapon. That made them fair game.

The bathroom was foul. She gagged from the stench but forced herself to the showers. Someone had ripped the tile down in one area, probably so they could sell the pipes.

She pointed to a blank cinder-block wall. "This has to come down. There's a lift behind it."

They pulled back, and a few charges shattered the wall. The lift behind it was operational and took a group of them down to the lower level. A massive vault just outside the lift door yielded to her palm print.

Bins filled the storeroom. Jess opened one and examined the fuel pellets. They were sealed and looked good.

"All of these need to go. Without the factory, we won't be making any more fuel in the foreseeable future."

"Is that it?" Sandra asked. "Then let's get the hell out of here. The clock is ticking."

The trip back out of the building to the helicopter went much more quickly. As did the flight. Gunners kept a close lookout for other aircraft as they flew toward their ride out.

They landed outside another hangar. Sandra's team dismounted and formed up around her. They made it halfway to the large doors before a number of trucks burst onto the airfield and raced toward them at high speed.

19

Harry and his team watched the security patrols for half an hour before they slipped in. They didn't linger. Their caution proved wise when the enemy patrol they were using as cover circled back around. Someone had seen something.

The guards searched for a bit and then went on their way, likely convinced they'd been the victim of a false reading. Rex slipped away as soon as they were clear.

Harry's team made good time to the executive neighborhood where Reynolds lived. They stayed out of sight as much as possible, but they had to skulk across several roads along the way.

The house that they'd identified wasn't as extravagant as the rest in the area, but it had privacy in abundance. Set back into a forested area, it afforded the occupant a lot of isolation.

They scouted the trees, convinced they'd find both live guards and automated alarms. They found all that and more. It seemed the paranoid bastard was so worried about people slipping up on him that he'd planted antipersonnel mines.

If someone actually blew themselves up, Harry could only imagine how his mother would attempt to spin the situation to the police. Gas leak? Maybe. In any case, it would take a lot of money to hush the authorities up. He'd wager she had no idea what her security chief was doing to make himself feel safe at night.

It took them significantly longer to scout the way in than he'd planned for. The sun was up by the time they'd evaded the IR tripwires and motion sensors leading up to the grove where the house sat.

Two men patrolled the yard. He'd be taking a chance when running for the house, but Harry liked the second-floor balcony as an entry point. It would hide them from casual view while they broke in and bypassed the alarm.

The man of the hour left as they were discussing how to best evade the yard patrol. They used the distraction of him walking out to an SUV to make it to the house. By the time Reynolds drove away, they were on the patio and scaling the exterior of the house.

The large balcony had a hot tub and a nice barbecue grill. It also had enough room for them to crouch down while the patrol walked below.

Jeremy worked the alarm slowly. This wasn't the time to take chances. Only once he was certain that he'd disabled the sensors did they pick the lock and open the door leading into the man's bedroom. There were no signs of a woman's presence. Or a second man, for that matter.

That made sense. If you were torturing people in your basement, you didn't want comments from the peanut gallery.

Jeremy pried the security keypad open carefully. "This is homegrown. It may take me a few minutes to hack into it."

"But you can, right?" Harry asked.

"Probably. Especially with access to the panel. Here we go. A computer port. That's helpful."

The slender man pulled a tablet out of his pack and ran a cable to the jack. "I'm running some codes to get past the login. Unless he's fiendishly clever, it shouldn't take more than sixty seconds."

It took three times that long.

"Got it. I've isolated the house from sending status changes. We can shut everything down, and it'll look like it's still on to everyone else."

"Do it."

A few moments later, Jeremy unplugged his tablet. "We're good. I have it linked to my gear wirelessly. If I need to make any other changes, I can do it on the fly."

They spread out and searched the top floor. Harry spent a few minutes in the man's home office while the team cleared everything else. A set of monitors showed the yard and several spots in the forest. Reynolds had helpfully labeled the mine controls. The switch was in the off position.

Harry found a safe behind a painting, but he didn't have time to spend cracking it. He wouldn't count Jeremy out on that point, but that wasn't their mission. Unless, of course, the data they needed was inside it. Only the client could tell them if it was still in play.

He called Jeremy in to start copying files off the man's computer. Why waste the opportunity?

The security wizard ignored the ports and opened the machine. "It'll be faster if I plug right into the drive. While it's working, I'll plant a chip on the board. Even if he swaps out the drives later, I might be able to access it remotely."

"Come down when you've got it going. We can clear the first floor while you work. Then we head for the basement."

It turned out that the torture room wasn't in the basement. In the place where a normal house had a garage, Reynolds had a prison. The central portion was, as expected, a table with lots of straps and racks of tools one might see during the Middle Ages.

There were two narrow cells with excellent views of all the action. Both had occupants.

Harry didn't recognize the woman in the first cell. She wasn't in shape to tell him anything, either. Reynolds had strangled her.

Her sightless eyes stared at the ceiling from a face etched with terror and hopelessness. A zip tie bit into her neck, and the torn skin around it told him that she'd been very much aware when Reynolds killed her. Based on the smell and bloating, she'd been gone for over a day.

Perhaps her body was a message to Vincent Cruz. He could hardly miss her from his cell.

The IT specialist looked to be in significantly better shape, though he wasn't unscathed. The bastard had pulled out some of the man's fingernails, broken a few fingers, and beaten him.

Cruz stared at them hopelessly. He probably thought they were there to take him out and do more nasty things to him.

"Mister Cruz," Harry said, "we're here to get you out. Where are the keys to the cell?"

The other man blinked. "What?"

"If you want to leave, now is the time to tell me how to open the door."

That got the man's attention. He stood abruptly. "Thank God. The keys are on a hook under the table."

It only took Harry a moment to find them and open the cell. "Time is limited. Did you manage to hide the data that Mister Rogers paid you to get?"

Cruz suddenly shrank back. "How do I know this isn't a trick? You just want me to tell you where it is, and you'll kill me!"

That was something they'd planned for. "You have a code word from our employer. Infinity. We're for real."

The other man sagged. "Thank God," he repeated. "I didn't tell them where the drive is. I knew they'd kill me as soon as I did. It's safe."

"Is it on the BenCorp campus? We don't exactly have an all-access pass."

"It's in the cafeteria computer. I hacked it and then 'fixed it' as a favor to the guy who runs the place. I didn't connect the drive, so you have to go after it. I didn't want them to be able to sniff it out over the network."

That would make things more difficult. The cafeteria wasn't in the headquarters building, but it was right next door to it. Somehow, they needed to sneak into the heart of enemy territory and retrieve it without raising the alarm.

His radio came to life. "Liberty Six, Hacker. We have a vehicle on the road. I think Reynolds is on his way back. He's in a hurry. We might have triggered something."

* * *

KATHLEEN BENNETT HAD FUMED about the situation all night. Her people had come in early and worked hard on double-checking what they knew about the space hotel project.

They didn't have any spies working on it, though she'd had a man there early on. He'd seen nothing out of the ordinary, and she'd found another area of her ex-husband's business empire where he could do her more good. Or so she'd thought.

Someone had arranged for a telescope to give the orbiting project another look. She saw nothing that could hide a weapons platform. It had been another wild goose chase.

Just before dawn, she'd sent everyone home to clean up and to come back fresh after breaking their fast. They were already hard at work on what she considered plan B.

This time she wouldn't let Nathan anywhere near it. This project required a fine hand and lightning execution. Donald Reynolds would head up the operation. He wouldn't fail her.

She smiled. Her ex-husband would be screaming in frustration before the day was out. He only thought he knew what pain was. He'd learn his error the hard way.

* * *

SANDRA TOOK one look at the speeding vehicles and pushed Jess back toward the helicopter. "Move! It's an ambush!"

Someone in the back of one of the trucks opened fire on the helicopter with a large machine gun. Bullets smashed into the fuselage, and the pilot slumped over. The burst also cut down the copilot, who'd gotten out to check something. One of the door gunners returned fire, and the hostile truck rolled, throwing a man high into the air. He bounced when he hit the ground and lay still.

Jess reversed course and opened the copilot's door. "Get in!"

"You can fly?" Sandra shouted as she piled into the back with her team and the downed copilot.

"Well enough to get the hell out of here!"

As soon as the team was inside the aircraft, Jess opened the throttle and pulled up on the collective. The rotors bit into the air, and the helicopter rose, far too slowly for her taste. As soon as she could, she pushed the cyclic forward and began building speed away from their attackers.

The sound of bullets slamming into the fuselage made her wince. She increased their speed even further and put a hangar between them and the trucks.

"Turn left," Sandra shouted. "I need to lay down some covering fire."

Jess pushed her left pedal in, skewing the helicopter somewhat to the left as it flew. As the copilot sat on the left side of the aircraft, she had a good view of Sandra shooting the living crap out of the trucks and the men trying to kill them.

One glance convinced her the pilot was dead. Yet another memory she'd be reliving at night.

The engine still sounded good, and a check of the caution and warning lights showed no problems. The burst that had killed the pilot had taken out the radio, though. If that was all they'd lost, they were damned lucky.

The firing stopped as she crossed the airfield fence. She took her hands off the controls long enough to strap in. Sandra handed her one of the headsets from in back. The noise level immediately dropped.

"You're a woman of many talents," Sandra said over the intercom. "How did you learn to fly a helicopter?"

"Equipment needs to be moved all the time. It seemed like a handy skill to have in my toolbox. We're lucky this is an older cargo chopper. I might not have been able to figure out something more modern."

"You know Mister Scott could fly a helicopter, right? You're stuck with that call sign now, Scotty."

"That was Mister Sulu, but fine. There are worse things in life. The radio is toast. We need to warn the rest of the team away from the landing field. It'll be swarming with nasty people before they get there."

Sandra leaned in over Jess's shoulder and stared out the blood-spattered canopy. "Land on that hill over there, and I'll make a call on my sat phone. We can get that poor bastard out of the other seat and into the back too."

Jess brought the helicopter down on the hilltop, slowed the engine to idle, and looked around. There was dust behind them, but she judged they'd have some time before their pursuers could catch up. Besides, the hill wasn't on a road.

Two men opened the pilot's door and pulled the body out. She rejected the idea of changing seats. Not that it really mattered. Blood covered the entire cockpit. It looked like a scene from a Paul E. Cooley horror novel.

"Get me a rag to clean the canopy," she shouted into the back.

One of the mercenaries handed her a white cloth and a canteen. That would have to do.

It worked well enough. By the time Sandra hung up and climbed into the blood-soaked pilot's seat, Jess could see everything she needed to. "I called and warned them off. The new plan is to fly out to a container ship in the Med. He'll text me the GPS coordinates. Do we have enough fuel for that?"

"It depends on where in the Med we're talking about. Probably. I've never landed on a ship before."

Sandra grinned at her. "Considering the things you've done this week, I'll put my money on you pulling it off with panache. Let's get the hell out of here before someone else starts shooting at us."

20

H arry grabbed Cruz by the arm and hustled him back up the stairs. They'd have to deal with the on-site security and the men in the vehicle. With luck, they could evade them long enough to get off the grounds with the client.

"Speed it up, Jeremy. Take the drive. We're leaving now."

He made a snap decision and dug into his pack as he called Rex over the radio. "Scout, Liberty Six. Turns out, we'll be creating the distraction for you. Can you get into the main cafeteria and steal a drive from the computer? It'll be the one not connected to anything."

"Scout here. Copy. What kind of distraction will you be providing?"

"You'll know it. Liberty Six out."

Reynold's vehicle slid to a halt outside, throwing gravel everywhere. He and the driver leapt out with their guns at the ready.

Yep, they must've triggered some kind of silent alarm. Time for the diversion.

Harry reached over to the minefield controls and switched them on. "Fire in the hole." He selected them all and pressed the red button.

Reynolds had a lot more mines out there than Harry had expected. The noise almost rivaled the Mayan pyramid coming down.

It turned out there was a mine under the area where the SUV had stopped too. It tossed the vehicle into the air when the fuel tank detonated. All the windows on that side of the house shattered, and the house alarm went off. Harry felt like he was in an action movie.

As soon as things finished crashing to the ground, his people headed for the balcony. The driver opened fire, and they cut him down. Reynolds wasn't anywhere in sight. Maybe he was under the burning SUV. Or maybe he was just faster than his man at finding cover.

A crash downstairs told him the guards had broken in. Time to exit stage left. He grabbed a charge and set the timer for one minute. He dropped it onto the floor inside the bedroom and made tracks.

Even with an injured client, they were on the ground in seconds. They almost made it to the trees before someone fired on them from the balcony. Harry returned the favor, and the man went down. He saw someone else in the room right before the explosive charge went off and blew that corner of the house to splinters.

To say that explosions and gunfire got the BenCorp security people excited was something of an understatement. His team made it through the woods and carjacked a woman in a minivan. He left her tied up on the side of the road. He felt bad about that, but they needed her vehicle.

He stripped down to his black T-shirt. Once everyone had hunched down out of sight, he drove sedately away from the chaos. He even waved at several security cars as they flew past.

Once he reached the fence line, Harry gunned the minivan across the field and rammed the barrier. It was designed to slow people from getting in, not escaping, so they bounced over it. Security would know where they were now, but he couldn't do anything about that.

It took only a couple of minutes to get back to the warehouse. The number of sirens he heard in the distance told him that they'd caused quite the scene. His mother wouldn't like having to explain exactly what had happened back there.

Harry shooed the team toward the van that had brought them from the airport. "Back into civilian clothing. Leave anything incriminating in the minivan. Take Cruz and get going. I'll meet you at the plane when I get Rex."

They didn't want to leave him, but a cordon would go around the general area before too long. They needed to get clear. A couple of guys had a lot better chance of escaping unnoticed than a full combat team. Harry kept a pistol for defense and the smallest explosive charge he had.

The cases and equipment were gone. The unnamed men had removed anything his people hadn't used. The only sign they'd been there was the stolen minivan. It almost certainly had some of their DNA inside. The fastest and easiest solution was to burn it.

It only took a moment to put the explosive charge on the gas tank and set it for twenty minutes. He grabbed the poor woman's belongings and put them in a reusable shopping bag he found in the back. She was doing her part to save the environment. Good for her.

He put his camo with the others' discarded clothing and took a snapshot of the license plate. He'd do what he could to make up for the woman's rough treatment later. The police cars that went shooting by paid him no attention as he walked away from the warehouse.

Once he was clear, he called Rex on his cell. "Scout, Liberty Six. Status."

"Hey, man. I'm a little busy right now. Mind if I call you back in five?"

"Give me a direction to head."

"Try north."

"Copy."

He'd need another vehicle to get them clear in a hurry. Harry didn't feel like carjacking someone else, though. This was Chicago. They might shoot first.

That's when he spotted the motorcycle behind the drycleaners. A casual touch showed it hadn't been there long. Hotwiring it was a quick proposition. Another expense for his father to pay when this was all over. He put the carjacked woman's personal belongings into the saddlebags

Harry put one of the helmets on, started the bike, and took off casually. It probably wouldn't be long before the owner noticed it was gone, so Rex needed to hurry the hell up. With all the police in the area, they'd connect a stolen vehicle to the explosions fast.

A few minutes later, he parked out of sight and called Rex again. His scout answered on the first ring.

"There you are. I got you a hoagie. Where are we meeting?"

"Can you talk?"

"Not really."

"I'm on a motorcycle behind an office building." He gave Rex the address. "I can be out front when you get here if you give me an ETA."

Rex passed the address on to someone else. "We're just going out the gate. Man, there are cops and firetrucks everywhere. I hope it wasn't terrorism. I hate terrorists. I'll be there in a couple of minutes. Later."

Harry waited three minutes and drove around front. Rex was just getting out of a car. A pretty girl said something to him before driving off with a smile. He'd ditched his camo for executive wear. Where the hell had he found a suit?

His scout waved at the woman and walked over to him. He had a white bag in his hand. "The drive's in the bag with the hoagie. Man, you caused a shit storm."

"It's a gift. Give me the drive, and you can have the sandwich."

"Sounds like a fair trade. I hope we come back this way someday. My ride seemed nice. Invited me out for coffee. She's single."

Harry tucked the drive into the saddlebags. "How do you do that?"

"It's my superpower. Did you get Cruz out?"

"Sure did. Let's scram before the owner of the motorcycle gets everyone in an uproar. Put your helmet on so that the traffic cameras don't get our faces."

He pulled into traffic and headed away from the BenCorp headquarters. The police will probably be very interested in the torture chamber and murdered woman. His mother would be furious.

It was turning out to be a good day.

* * *

JESS FLEW low to stay off any curious radars, and they reached the cargo ship just as the sun was beginning to set. Someone had cleared the bow, giving them enough space to land. A number of choppers from the raid circled and waited their turn. One was unloading bins as she joined the rest flying around the ship.

One of the other helicopters pulled up beside her, and the pilot got her attention. He pointed at her and held up his index finger. She took that to mean she was next up for landing.

As soon as the cargo chopper took off, she cautiously approached the deck. A man waved two glow sticks at her. He had one in each hand and used them to guide her right down to the landing spot. When he crossed them in front of his legs, she heaved a sigh of relief, let the helicopter settle, and slowed the engine to idle.

A man in a flight suit and helmet helped her out and took her spot. He lifted off as soon as everyone was clear.

Sandra pulled her along as they followed a crewman to the tall control deck. One of Cradock's men was standing there waiting for them.

"The warlord took out the jet's crew and the guards we left behind," he said grimly. "I'll make him a special project in the very near future. I'm glad you managed to get clear, and I'm sorry about your flight crew. It was damned lucky you could fly."

She felt a little hollow at his words. "It's been a rough few days. What's the plan now?"

"The ship docks in Italy early tomorrow morning. We'll get the fuel moved to a cargo plane and on its way by dawn. You'll meet Harry in Paris tomorrow."

"My passport won't have a valid entry stamp. Won't someone freak out?"

The security man shook his head. "I'll get you stamped when we dock. The same woman who'll get our cargo through will make sure you don't have any issues." He looked at his watch. "You should clean up and get some sleep. Things are going to be happening fast from now on."

"They've been coming fast and furious for a while," she muttered. "A shower sounds good, though."

"The captain is loaning you his quarters. If you'll follow this young man, he'll get you there."

A boy with curly black hair and bright eyes led them through a confusing maze of corridors and ladders. He bowed a little and opened the metal door for her.

Sandra went in and cleared the room. It was small but neat. The bathroom was actually clean.

"Give me your clothes, and I'll see if I can get you something that fits," Sandra said.

Jess stripped down to her underwear and discovered that her phone had a couple of missed calls and one voicemail.

Two decades ago, before cell service and wireless became ubiquitous, she wouldn't have reception on a freighter at sea. Now everything was a hotspot. Progress was wonderful, sometimes.

She played the message. It was from Rachel Powell.

"Miss Cook, I just wanted to let you know that we've identified the language. It's the lettering used in the Voynich Manuscript. No one has managed to translate it. Call me for details as soon as you get this." She left a number.

"I better call her and find out what this means." She passed her bloody clothes on to Sandra.

"Lock the hatch behind me, and don't open it for anyone else. Two of our men are in the corridor. And remember, nothing classified over an unsecured line. The NSA monitors everything." The mercenary let herself out.

Jess locked the hatch and made the call.

"Doctor Powell. Jess Cook. I just got your message." She did a little math in her head and realized it must be night in Mexico. "I'm sorry for calling so late."

The other woman's voice held no hint of sleep. "I'm still up writing a report on the book for Mister Rogers. Have you ever heard of the Voynich Manuscript?"

"No. Please give me a brief rundown. And remember we're on a commercial line."

"I'll keep that in mind. The Voynich Manuscript is a handwritten codex from sometime between 1404 and 1438. They verified that time frame by carbon dating the vellum. They named the folio after Wilfrid Voynich, a Polish book dealer who bought it in 1912.

"Some of the pages are missing, but around 240 are still in the same collection. The manuscript is at Yale University."

Jess considered that. The book they'd found was from centuries earlier, and it wasn't written on vellum. "You said that no one has been able to crack the meaning of the manuscript?"

"That's correct. Scholars have proposed a number of origin theories. Everything from aliens to it being a complex code. Even people at the NSA have made runs at it. The use of the letters is internally consistent, but the meaning has eluded everyone. Most of the pages have illustrations of unknown plants and medieval figures."

The engineer snorted. "Well, if the NSA can't crack it, I doubt we will, either. Unless we can find a Rosetta Stone."

"To be fair, the NSA looked at it in the 1950s," Powell said. "A supercomputer might be able to crack the meaning."

"You said that there were only 240 pages left. Does that mean that there were more originally?"

"That's correct. Someone removed a number of pages and probably sold them. They're almost certainly in the hands of private collectors at this point. There's a subculture of wealthy people that want to own objects of historical and artistic significance without any intention of ever allowing them to see the light of day." Her tone indicated strong disapproval.

"Is there any chance that you can find out who the owners of these missing pages might be?"

"I'll make some calls, but I don't think I'll have any luck. These people are quite secretive."

"Do the best you can. Let me know if you get lucky."

Jess hung up and padded into the bathroom. A hot shower might make her feel clean again.

21

K athleen Bennett was ready to kill someone. Specifically, her ex-husband. She'd have added her security chief to the list if he hadn't died in the explosion that wrecked his house. The police and FBI were overrunning her headquarters, asking the kind of questions no sane human being wanted to answer.

She might've been able to cover this up as some kind of gas explosion if Donald hadn't installed a minefield. Really? That was insane.

They'd already put out the fire and found several bodies, including one in a cell. For a few minutes, she'd deluded herself into believing the body might be that of the traitor, but her man in the police department told her it was a woman.

No matter how this played out, she'd look like an idiot or worse. Why, no Mister Federal Agent, I have no idea how my head of security smuggled all those land mines onto my facility. He was torturing and murdering people, you say? Oh dear.

With the way this was going, they'd find a bunch of unmarked graves in the woods.

She sighed. Of course they would. Where else would that homicidal idiot hide the people he killed for sport? Could things get any worse?

As if on cue, Nathan came in and closed the door. "Well, things are certainly exciting this morning. Are you ready to let me kill Harry now?"

"We don't know it was your brother."

"Do you think it was the tooth fairy? It was Harry. He and father conspired to do this to you. Are you going to bend over and take it?"

The urge to reach into her desk for the pistol she kept handy was strong. "Don't you dare speak to me like that, boy. I can blame your death on Donald."

"Please. If you want payback, I'm the person to make that happen. Say the word, and I'll go make them suffer."

It wasn't as though she had much choice now. With Donald gone, Nathan was her best chance of pulling off her planned revenge. God help her.

"If you fail me, I'll put a price on your head so big that you'll never get a moment's peace. This has to go exactly according to plan. The timing is critical. Is that clear enough for you?"

"I'm not a moron," he sneered. "Of course I'll succeed. Other than the girl, I've never failed you."

Kathleen brought a map up on her screen and explained what she wanted done.

* * *

Jess had just finished showering when she got another call. The number wasn't familiar to her.

"Hello?"

"Jess, this is Harry. Everything came out fine. We're in the air."

A bit of tension that she hadn't been consciously aware of drained away. "Thank God. Did you rescue the man?"

"We did. My father's people have the drive. They'll assess its contents while we're in the air. How'd your thing go?"

He was being circumspect because of the NSA. She really had to struggle to keep that in mind.

"It was a little more exciting than I'd imagined it would be, but we got it. I have more information about the book too." She explained the Voynich Manuscript to him.

"That's pretty odd. The Europeans didn't know about the Mayans until almost a hundred years later."

She grabbed her tablet. "I'm sending you some images. Check out the plants in the original manuscript."

After a minute, he spoke. "I've seen something like this before. On the mission before we met. There were pages like this in the office."

"Are you sure? These things look like a lot of other manuscripts of the time, except for the unknown language and unrecognizable plants."

"I'm almost certain. I didn't look closely enough to recognize the lettering, but the style of illustrations is spot on. I didn't recognize the plants, but I'm not a botanist."

"How many pages were there?" she asked.

"I had other things on my mind. A dozen? Maybe twice that."

She grinned, even though he couldn't see her. "We need to get them. Or at least pictures of them."

"No way. That bastard's security is going to be super tight."

"He doesn't have to know I'm connected with that."

"So, you just waltz in and say, 'Hi, I heard through the grapevine that you had these secret manuscript pages,' and he lets you in for a peek? I think not. Besides, when would you do this? The schedule is tight from here on."

"We had a change in plans too. We're on a ship about to dock in Italy. I can do this and still beat you to France."

She started pacing. "Harry, you don't understand how important this might be. Even the NSA couldn't crack the damned thing. We need those pages. It won't take your mother long to figure out the connection. Do you want to take the chance she might get these pages before we do?"

He sighed. "Sandra has to sign off on your plan. Please be careful. If it's too dangerous, walk away."

"Don't worry about a thing. I won't take any unnecessary chances."

* * *

HARRY CALLED Cradock on an encrypted line. He was already in Paris. He really needed to get an encrypted phone to Jess. The security man sounded just as displeased at Jess's plan as Harry was. "Dammit. Someone almost shot her at the airport. Does the woman have a death wish?"

"Shot? What happened? Tell me everything."

He listened to how the warlord had almost killed everyone on Jess's helicopter, and how she'd managed to escape. And now she wanted to go play James Bond. It made his teeth ache.

Maybe he needed to focus on the things he could control. "When does the fuel leave for Mexico?"

"In about six hours, once we dock and transship it to a cargo plane. Look, it will take a while before we have the data to plan for stealing the reactor. Get some sleep. Call me once you wake up. We should be able to make final plans by then."

"Get Jess an encrypted phone, and try to get some sleep," Harry said. "Text me the number."

Harry hung up, but getting to sleep was hard. He kept imagining all the things that could go wrong with Jess's mission. And he couldn't do a thing about it.

Well, that wasn't quite true. He dialed his father's number. Maybe the old bastard could talk some sense into the crazy engineer before she got herself killed.

* * *

JESS DRESSED while Sandra stared at her as though she were crazy. "You want to do what?"

"Break back into the house you rescued the little girl from earlier this week."

"That's what I thought you said. And Harry signed off on this?"

"Reluctantly. This is important. He'll get the assault on the reactor plant set up while we make this happen."

The mercenary shook her head. "We observed the target for more than a week last time. We knew how the guards behaved and what the routine was. This time, we'd be going in blind after we stirred them up like a hornet's nest. It's crazy."

Jess didn't disagree. Yet, what choice did they have? If they passed up the opportunity, they might be up in space for months before they could try again. The forces of darkness could find out about the manuscript pages and take them.

"Don't you do this kind of thing under urgent circumstances?"

"Urgent is a child in danger of harm," Sandra said. "Getting your hands on some papers isn't in the same league."

The mercenary sighed. "You're talking about a daytime incursion. That means the help will be awake and alert. The police too. We need to get into the office and get the papers, or at least take a close look at them. Going in shooting isn't the right answer."

"Who's the man in question?" Jess asked. "What do we know about him?"

"Alessio Romano. He's a bigshot in local politics. A judge. Word is that he's also connected to the mob."

"Is his art on the shady side?"

The mercenary shrugged. "I have no idea. That wasn't part of the mission parameters."

The phone Sandra was holding rang. She held it out to Jess. "This is your new encrypted phone. Use it from now on."

Jess took it and answered the call.

"Hello?"

"Jess," Clayton said. "I just got off the phone with Harry. He tells me you're on your way to see a man in Italy about some illicit art."

"That's true, though I'm kind of hoping he doesn't find out we were ever there."

"I'm somewhat familiar with the gentleman in question. He and I have had some dealings in the past. I may be able to make an introduction between the two of you, if you're willing to employ a little subterfuge."

She knew Sandra wouldn't like that, but she was willing to take a few chances. "What do you have in mind?"

"I have a security firm in Rome. Romano has hired them to upgrade his systems. I can get the man in charge to provide you a cover while you examine the building. You'd need to interface with someone knowledgeable about security, but with the right equipment, that shouldn't be a problem."

Jess smiled. "That sounds relatively straightforward. Thank you."

"Your target is a man used to dealing with the seamier side of society," he warned. "He's already been stung, and he's looking to make someone pay. If he thinks you're playing him, he'll turn on you. Trust me when I say that would be a terrible outcome."

Jess didn't want that. She really didn't want it. "A security consultant can get into every room in the house. If I can transmit the images out to someone else, they can tell me what I need to know through an earbud."

"All very true, but if he gets wise, you'll be in very dire straits."

"How long would it take to get everything we need into place?"

"I can have a man in the area by the time you get there. He'll have everything you need. The company needs to confirm that Romano will see you, but I expect he's quite eager to close the holes in his security as soon as possible. Is your guard going to buy off on this plan?"

Jess looked at Sandra. "I can make that happen."

* * *

CLAYTON HUNG UP. Jess's plan worried him. Project Liberty absolutely needed her to be hale and whole. Should he really enable her like this? Perhaps Harry had been right to ask him to stop her. Were these pages really as important as she thought?

He sighed. Probably. He'd make the calls. He finished just before his assistant buzzed.

"Pardon the interruption, but you have a call from the security man in Guatemala on the encrypted line. It sounded quite urgent."

"Put him through."

The light for the other line lit up, and he pressed it. "Rogers."

The first sound he heard was a long burst of automatic gunfire from very close to the receiver. "Mister Rogers, we're under heavy attack! They swarmed in from nowhere, and they're pushing us back. We can't hold onto the site with the underground chamber."

"Get to safety," Clayton said. "I'll call the federal police and get you support."

"I'd hurry if I were you." Another burst of gunfire sounded and then an explosion. The line went dead.

He hoped the caller hadn't gone dead too. He looked up a number and called his man in the Guatemalan government.

Clayton hadn't expected something this bold. It had to be Nathan. He couldn't imagine how the little shit expected to steal a buried spaceship before reinforcements arrived, but the boy obviously believed he could do it. If he got away with the theft, it changed the game.

22

Harry woke halfway through the flight to Paris to the news that Nathan was trying to steal the spaceship. The plan was audacious. A true international incident. His brother might have to fight it out with the Guatemalan military or police.

Well, there wasn't anything he could do about it. At least his father hadn't told Jess. He'd been concerned that the events would throw her off her con. That was about the first thing he completely agreed with his father on.

They'd begun delving into the data drive, and Harry now had detailed plans for the facility in Paris. He spent the next few hours going over them with his team on the plane. Cradock linked in via secure com.

The place was just as tough as Harry had expected. The sewers were indeed a trap for the unwary. The general plan they finally agreed on felt too much like the raid on his mother's headquarters for his comfort. A lot of it came down to taking bold risks.

The major difference in this case was that they'd have a lot more hardware. Including planes to get them on-site very quickly. Those came courtesy of his father. He had a group of cutting-edge military transports in France for an airshow.

The stealth on them was so good that they were making a few extra test runs for the French military over the next few days. The potential buyers wanted to see the planes break contact, which was perfect for Harry's strike team.

If the planes carrying his people could slip away from the test area, they could deliver Harry onto his mother's facility with devastating surprise before going back to play with the French Air Force.

One bit of good news was that they'd packed the reactor. The test wasn't going to be in Paris after all. His mother's plan was to ship it out to the US before the supposed demonstration. Apparently, the security team probing the sewers had spooked them.

At least that meant they didn't need to have Jess underfoot. They could grab the reactor while she was taking care of business in Italy. Then she could fly to Mexico on her own. They'd meet there, and she could oversee the loading of the reactor into the lifter.

Finally, something was going their way.

* * *

JESS SLEPT until the ship docked. The time zone change had her body confused, but she'd been in that situation before. Sleep cured most of the trouble, given enough time.

Cradock's man hurried them past a woman who stamped their passports. Jess suspected that their entry wouldn't appear anywhere official. Which, considering the things they planned to do, was probably for the best.

The team took vans and set off before dawn. They met the man who'd coordinate with her on security matters for breakfast about an hour away from Romano's villa.

Paolo Sorrentino was an unprepossessing guy with classic Italian features. He laid some gear on the table as he sipped his cappuccino. "They tell me these are state-of-the-art spying devices. Even a close search shouldn't turn them up. Unless of course, someone looks inside your ear." His English was excellent, with just a hint of his native Italian.

Jess picked up the earbud. It looked like a little torpedo with some silicone around the back. "It doesn't have anything to grab onto. How do I get it out when we're done?"

"A small hook will catch the flesh-toned exterior. Without a grip, it's much harder to see. It has a small microphone that allows you to hear as well as you normally would. It's quite clever."

Jess picked up the glasses next. Classy wire frames. She'd expected ugly plastic. A quick check showed the lenses had no prescription. A good thing, since her vision was perfect. She wondered what they'd have done if she'd needed glasses of her own. Probably contacts.

There wasn't any indication of a camera, no matter where she looked.

"Okay, I give up. Where is the lens?"

"It's inside one of the nose pads."

She examined them more closely. "Now I see it. That's a good design. And there's no chance that he'll detect it sending a signal?"

Paolo grinned boyishly. "I'll load an app onto your mobile phone, and it will communicate over an encrypted wireless frequency. Even though you don't know it, your phone is always pinging the towers. That will disguise the signal. The phone will record video, even if you go into an area of the building where the coverage is spotty. When you come back out, it will sync up with the base unit."

"That sounds a little worrying. What if he asks me something I don't know while we have no connection?"

"I'll be with you. The plan is for us to examine everything as a team. I'm the primary security specialist, and you are my beautiful American assistant. The camera will keep your security team apprised of your personal situation at all times."

That was reassuring. Jess wouldn't have to bluff her way through a job she knew very little about. The sniper could feed her some thoughts so she didn't sound like an idiot, if need be.

Sandra pocketed the gear as the waitress came over to deliver their food. The mercenary waited until they were alone again to speak.

"The estate is big. He has a number of vulnerable approaches to the house itself. He was lax in his personal security. He didn't even turn the alarm system on. Honestly, you'd be shocked how many people shoot themselves in the foot by ignoring the most basic precautions."

Paolo dug into his food with gusto. "This is excellent. I was up early, and fast food is a national tragedy."

Jess couldn't argue with that.

"When is he expecting us?"

He checked his watch. "I told him we'd be there in about ninety minutes. We should finish up and be on our way."

She glanced at Sandra. "Where will you be?"

"There's an unoccupied house nearby. We'll set up inside the woods there. All it'll take to get to you is hopping over a stone wall and running through some trees. I figure three minutes, tops. If I get worried, I'll get the team moving early."

They finished breakfast and got on the road. Just outside the town where Romano lived, she moved to Paolo's car. They'd go in separately, just in case someone was watching traffic.

The estate looked imposing. The tall wall and imposing iron gate would've kept her out. The armed men just inside were an added incentive to behave.

Paolo rolled down his window and said something in Italian to one of the men. A brief exchange resulted in the gate opening. It shut with ominous finality behind them as they drove into the lion's den.

They were committed now.

* * *

HARRY'S PLANE landed on schedule, and Cradock picked them up. They drove to a different part of the airfield and directly into a large hangar holding four sleek planes.

They didn't look like transports. They looked like something out of a movie, all aggressive lines and angles. That was probably to help defeat the radar. Based on the engine configuration, Harry thought they were probably capable of vertical takeoffs and landings.

He didn't know much about planes, but they looked badass.

"The pilots are in on the plan," Cradock said, "but not the ground crew. We'll have a meeting with everyone to plan things, but keep mum on the details even out here. You never know who's a spy."

Harry couldn't agree more. French prisons were better than many others he'd risked over the years, but he'd rather avoid the experience.

He walked under one of the wings. "Is it VTOL? How good is the stealth? How many people can each hold? And realistically, what are the chances you can really evade the French radar?"

Cradock smiled. "These are fully VTOL-capable and can switch modes quickly in the air. Each one can hold two of your teams. As for the stealth, it's good.

"We have two modes. One is passive, which is what the French are buying. One is active, which we're keeping to ourselves. We'll give them a taste of what these planes can really do when these babies drop off their screens."

Harry shook his head. "I'm surprised the US is letting you sell these things to anyone other than them."

"The American government doesn't know about the active mode. With the way they've gutted the military, they can't afford them anyway. Rainforest is a true international company, incorporated through a country that doesn't care who we sell to, so long as they get their taxes. We don't need the US government's permission to do squat."

That bothered Harry, but it wasn't his fight. The American government had done this to themselves. The incredible polarization in politics meant only the most extreme politicians got into office. Nationally, the liberals had occupied the White House for the last three decades. The Senate bounced back and forth, depending on which party had more seats up for grabs, and the penny-pinching, socially stunted conservatives had a lock on the House.

That meant nothing of import happened to address the country's woes. The debt was out of control, inflation was through the roof, and any country that felt froggy could push the formerly great nation around like a schoolyard bully. Only international terrorism was able to bridge the gap, and even it never got the attention it deserved.

France was teetering on the edge of collapse. Selling them these planes wouldn't help. They needed to take their country back from the people willing to burn it down. He doubted they had the will to save themselves.

Well, that wasn't his problem. Once the country fell, these planes wouldn't be a worry anymore. The fanatics couldn't fly them.

"Have all my teams arrived?"

Cradock nodded. "They're scattered around the area, but they're here. We'll pull them in once you're ready to lay out the grand plan. We can get eight teams into the target building with four teams to cover your withdrawal. The reactor is supposedly loaded into a container.

"Word is that it's scheduled to leave early tomorrow morning. We'll probably be able to get you there right after dark tonight. That means security will be lighter than normal. They want more people on duty for the move tomorrow, so some people have the day off to rest up."

That worked. Harry gave the planes one last appreciative look. Maybe he could buy one for his company. It would sure make some jobs easier.

"Call in the teams. It's time to get this rolling."

* * *

NATHAN WATCHED the excavation with satisfaction. The earthmovers had cleared the area around the underground chamber with astonishing speed. The goal was to open the room below to the air without dropping debris on the spacecraft.

That had sounded impossible to him until an expert explained how it worked. Teams would go in through the side tunnel he'd seen the woman use. They'd fire stabilizers into the roof. A lot of them. The choppers would act in unison to lift the roof off. Then they'd lift the spaceship up on the slings the team was putting into place.

"We're ready to lift the roof, sir," the excavation boss said.

A glance at his watch confirmed that they were ahead of schedule. "Excellent. Proceed."

The local government had failed miserably at sending help to his father's guards. Most of them were dead. His men were pursuing the rest through the jungle. His mother had sown massive confusion in the Guatemalan government. No one would stop him.

Nathan held his breath as the choppers lifted the roof. The stonework was amazing. It broke into a billion pieces when they dropped it off to the side.

The spaceship looked a little worse for wear in the bright sunlight, but that hardly mattered. The limitless wealth it promised was all he cared about. That and sticking it to his father and brother.

It took them another few minutes to hitch the slings. They'd made an educated guess at the weight. Two choppers should be able to lift it.

In fact, it came up so easily that he made the decision to try one helicopter alone. That would greatly simplify the move.

It worked.

The spaceship headed out on one last journey. Several armed helicopters accompanied it on its way toward international waters and the ship that would carry it back to the US. He had fighter jets that would screen any inquisitive military presence.

He'd disguised them with Honduran markings. He could only imagine what kind of trouble that would cause. He might even be able to get some business out of the ensuing troubles.

Once it was away, he sent his people in. "Pick up every single bit of that ship. Leave nothing. Then plant the explosives. Father can waste his time digging it up to find nothing."

23

J ess tamped her jitters down as Paolo drove the car slowly up the drive. There were a lot of guards on the grounds. A man with some kind of rifle was just visible on the roof.

"Yeah, I sure hope Sandra doesn't have to come in after us," she said to the Italian. "I'm not sure she could manage it."

"You know I can hear you, right?" Sandra's voice said in her earbud.

Jess laughed a little. "I forgot. Are you seeing all this?"

"I sure am. Don't worry. We can get you out if push comes to shove."

The man himself met them at the front door. She could tell it was Romano because his morbidly obese form matched the description Harry had given her. He was almost a cartoon of a human being. To say that he looked ludicrous in a tailored suit was an understatement.

The initial conversation was in Italian, but Paolo switched to English after a moment. "And this is my assistant, Jessica. She's fresh from our American branch and doesn't speak Italian."

The large mobster held out a meaty hand for her. It was sickeningly damp. She resisted the urge to wipe her hand on her pants when she reclaimed it.

"Welcome to Italy, Jessica," Romano said in a deep, rumbly voice. "If the two of you come inside, I will explain the situation. One of my assistants will accompany you on a tour of the building, of course."

Obviously. He wouldn't be making any long trips along the grounds. Stairs must be a challenge.

And, as it turned out, not a worry. He had an elevator.

A man in coveralls was painting the wall beside the staircase. Whoever had done the repair work hadn't done such a terrific job. Jess could still see a few dimples. Bullet holes, she imagined. That would be an ugly reminder to the mobster of past failures.

Romano pulled a key from his vest and unlocked one of the doors near the end of the hall. It opened into an office. Her heart leapt in her chest. They might be able to get what they needed right up front. That would be a wonderful break.

Jess examined the Egyptian figurines in one of the cases as Romano sat behind his large desk. "This is a wonderful collection. Forgive me for asking, but did someone try to steal them?"

"No," Romano said with a snarl. "The bastards kidnapped my daughter and took her to America. My ex-wife, an unfit woman with the morals of an alley cat, paid someone to take her. I want this house to be a vault before I bring her back."

Paolo nodded. "Of course. We'll do everything in our power to make certain that she's safe here. Do you know how they obtained entrance to your property?"

Jess walked from case to case, slowly moving toward the one she most wanted to see.

"They came over a wall in the dead of night. They used darts to knock out my guards and myself. I shot several of them, but they overwhelmed me. The man outside is fixing the bullet holes I made. The guards who failed were severely punished."

"Bullshit," Sandra said in her ear. "Harry shot him in the ass before he even got his pistol out of the nightstand. One of the guards shot the wall when we darted him."

The pieces Jess was seeing were good. Some of the paintings looked like authentic Renaissance masters. She wondered if Romano had stolen them. Or paid someone who had. She couldn't see him climbing through a window in the dead of night.

Paolo made sympathetic noises. "Was the home alarm activated before the intrusion?"

"No. The idiots never turned it on. The intruders made their way in through the patio. The interior guards were no match for them, either. Pathetic. You must look at every door and window, scan every wall. I want no weakness left when you finish. Money is no object, but don't think to cheat me. I will know."

Jess stepped in front of the low case that held the pages. They were definitely from the Voynich Manuscript. The lettering was unmistakable.

She listened to Romano drone on with half an ear as she scanned them one by one, looking for any sign that might help them decode the book.

Her heart sang when she found something on the next-to-last page. It was only a few lines at the bottom, but there was the strange alien script set beside something that looked like Italian. Or perhaps an older variant of what became Italian. She wasn't a linguistics expert.

Maddeningly, the page after it had just a few lines at the top. What she needed to see was on the back of the pages, and they were under locked glass.

Somehow, she had to get this case open.

* * *

IT TOOK a few hours to gather the team in another hangar. Harry led the briefing, showing them where they'd be landing, where in the building they'd be going, and running through the timeline for the assault.

The building schematics were a tremendous help. He knew which floor had the loading dock, where his mother stationed her security teams, and which paths might make for the fastest ingress.

The reactor was supposedly in a container, which meant the only means of transportation was a big rig. He had several people that could drive one, so they were ready.

Only a few roads allowed commercial traffic of that size. A cargo container was tall. If he picked the wrong street, a bridge might give them an unpleasant surprise. And, only the very largest cargo planes could even carry the damned thing. Those factors limited his options for extraction.

"Cradock, what are we doing for transport to Mexico? That'll dictate where we have to take this thing."

The large man grinned. "You'll like this. We're going to steal your mother's transport plane too. It's on the ground at Charles De Gaul. Once you guys are committed, my team will liberate the plane. We'll fly it to the regional airport nearest the facility and be waiting for you. With all the hullabaloo, we'll be halfway across the ocean before they notice the plane is gone."

Harry liked it. "How do we keep them from using traffic cameras to determine our path? Once we're moving, we'll stick out like a sore thumb."

"I've arranged to have half a dozen legitimate cargo containers being moved around the area about the time you leave. All through local businesses that won't be traced back to us. You'll get lost in the rush."

"Good enough." Harry checked his watch. "Let's go talk to the pilots. Please get everyone that isn't cleared out of the other hangar."

"On it."

Harry and his team leaders took a van with dark windows to the first hangar when they got the all clear. Once the main doors to the hangar closed, he stepped out.

Four men in flight suits waited beside the planes. "The copilots are in the aircraft getting them ready," Cradock said. "Everyone has already been briefed on the plan."

One of the pilots, a tall man with a buzz cut, stuck out his hand. "Mister Rogers, I'm John McCarthy, formerly a lieutenant colonel in the US Marines. Call me Black Jack. I'm the flight leader. I need to say I'm damned impressed with your bravery. Damned impressed."

Harry smiled and gave him a firm handshake. "Then I've probably underestimated how scary this is going to be. Thanks for your service, sir."

"Hell, I've heard about some of the things you did in the sandbox, so thank you for *your* service. Time is short, so let me run you through the flight plan.

"We'll lift off in half an hour and run a series of engagements with the frogs. Excuse me, the French Air Force. The plan is to break contact and let them find us again half a dozen times."

The pilot patted the side of one of the aircraft. "At that point, we go active and ditch them. By the time they cry uncle, we'll have you delivered onto the roof of the target building. The bad guys won't know we're coming until the first plane—mine—drops you on the roof."

He gave Harry a smug look. "That ought to scare the living shit outta them. Everyone in that building will know we've arrived, and your clock starts ticking.

"Make no mistake, we're going in hot, and I expect you to unass my aircraft in an expeditious manner. Then you need to clear the LZ because the next plane is right behind me. Once we drop all of you, we circle back to pick up our hosts. Questions?"

The military speak for exiting the jet made him smile. "Are you sure you can break contact?"

He gave Harry a disbelieving look. "Seriously? They're French. That means we'll need to work extra hard to keep them from giving up before we're ready."

* * *

JESS TURNED BACK toward the men. "These are really interesting. Is there a chance I could look at one more closely?"

The fat man gave her a disapproving scowl. "You are not here to ooh and aah over my art collection. I've never understood why Americans are so pushy. My man will take you to examine the house and grounds. Good day."

Paolo stood and gave the man a half bow. "Thank you for your time."

Another man opened the door, and they filed out behind him. "Shall we start with the first floor?" he asked.

Jess fell back a little. "Dammit. If he'd have just been a little more accommodating, we could've been home free," she murmured.

"Don't get all tore up about it," Sandra said. "You saw enough to know there's something worthwhile. That was Italian, right?"

"It sure looked like it. If I can get that one page flipped over, we might be able to unlock enough to make some headway. The author obviously knew something of both languages."

"Don't get carried away and blow this," Sandra said. "You've already expressed an interest in the pages. You can't get back in there without him getting the wrong idea."

"Maybe I can slip away. Get in while everyone else is busy."

"Bad idea. Really bad idea. Don't even try it. Am I clear?"

Jess sighed. "Crystal clear."

They made their way through the ground floor. Jess added to the conversation when Paolo prompted her as she looked at everything. She wanted as complete a visual record as possible.

Once they'd made the rounds below, the man led them toward the patio. "Next we can look at the grounds."

Paolo frowned. "We should examine the upper floors before we make the rounds outside."

"According to the weather report, there will be rain in an hour. It would be best to look at things in the light, don't you think?"

"I have a wonderful suggestion," Romano said from the doorway leading toward the elevator. Jess hadn't seen him there. He moved quietly for such a large man.

"Why don't you take your time examining the grounds while I escort your associate on a tour above? I'll be certain to show her everything she needs to see."

"Did he really just say that?" Sandra demanded. "Hell, no. Do not go anywhere alone with this sleazeball."

Jess smiled at Romano. "That sounds like a wonderful idea."

* * *

HARRY and the men from his best two teams, now called Team One for convenience, strapped into the back of the lead plane before the ground crew opened the hangar and towed the jet out. Takeoff was smooth and easy. He wore a headset to listen as the mock war games took place. The French pilots sounded competent enough.

He mentally went back over the plan. He wanted to play out all the worst outcomes he could think of. Walking into a prepared enemy scared him the most. If his mother's people were ready for them, they might all die in that building.

About twenty minutes before the planned assault time, Black Jack called him on the private channel. "We're almost ready to break away. I got word from your large friend that the distraction group is setting off a couple of alarms in the sewage tunnels. Not enough to make them sure an attack is coming, but maybe enough to relocate some of their people to be ready for one. Your other teams are staged to provide an escape corridor for you and the package."

"Copy that, Colonel. Good luck on breaking contact."

"If you keep insulting me like that, I'm not going to buy you any drinks later."

Harry laughed.

Right on schedule, the planes dove for the deck. "Active countermeasures activated," Colonel McCarthy said. "Everyone form up on me."

The French pilots had lost the Rainforest jets before, so they didn't sound too upset. Of course, they'd always reacquired them quickly.

By the time the formation was approaching the BenCorp facility, the French controllers were getting a little frantic.

"You're sixty seconds from drop," Black Jack said. "Good luck."

"Thanks, Colonel," Harry said. "See you for that drink soon."

He hung up the headset and stood. "Thirty seconds. Stand in the door."

The red light in the rear started blinking. Harry led his people to stand under it. The plane slowed, and his knees flexed to take up the pressure as the rear ramp lowered. Parking lots and buildings seemed to be sliding quickly by right below him.

The engines went full VTOL, and a rooftop appeared only a few feet away. When the momentum was almost gone, Harry ran down the ramp as the jet thundered behind him. As soon as the last man cleared, the jet reoriented and lifted like a giant bird of prey, vanishing into the darkness.

He could already hear the next jet coming in. "Go!"

His people ran for the roof access as the second jet came barreling in out of the darkness to offload more of his people. It was damned impressive. He'd buy two if he could afford them.

"Alarm off, door open," Jeremy said.

Harry followed them in. Now he'd find out if their plans had a chance in hell of working. They charged down the stairs with their weapons up and hunting for targets.

24

Romano led Jess back to his private elevator. "Please pardon me if I sounded brusque earlier. Times such as these try a man's soul. Allow me to make up for my boorish behavior. Perhaps a glass of wine? I assure you my cellar is quite good."

"That sounds lovely. Thank you."

"Don't trust this guy," Sandra said through Jess's earbud. "He's the kind to slip something in your drink."

Jess couldn't respond, but she'd already considered that. How would Romano explain any sudden issues she developed to Paolo? There was no telling. She'd figure out how to stop him as she went.

He once more escorted her into his office. "Perhaps you should take another look around while I pour for us." His insincere and oily smile cemented the thought that he had something in mind.

Her brain raced. "I shouldn't drink while I'm working."

"What can one glass harm? I insist."

Jess went over to the case with the manuscript pages, taking her glasses off and holding them so that Sandra could see behind her.

"Yeah, he's looking at you and acting all sly. He's putting something into your glass. Don't drink it. I'm moving the team up to his property line."

She put her glasses back on and looked at the manuscript pages again. If she ever wanted to see them, she needed to figure out how to turn this situation around. And she'd like to avoid even the thought of this bastard doping and raping her.

Romano stepped up beside her and handed her a glass of red wine. "These are beautiful, are they not? My grandfather bought them after the Second World War. Well, during it, really. No one can read them, but they look pretty."

He smiled at her. "Drink. I must know what you think of the vintage."

Jess faked taking a sip, hoping that mere contact with her lips wouldn't let the drugs into her system. "Mmm. I'm no expert, but it's good. Would you mind if I take a closer look at one of the pages?"

The fat man considered her request and then nodded. "For just a moment. These are very old, so do not touch them." He set his wineglass on a nearby case and dug out his keys.

She wiped the rim of her glass clean of lipstick and set it down beside his while he focused on the lock. She picked up his drink and took a sip, putting her mark on the glass.

The wine was actually quite good. Fruity with a hint of something earthier.

Romano raised the lid and stepped back. "You can place your glass on the other case. I don't want to risk you spilling anything on these valuable artifacts."

Jess watched with a smile as he picked her old glass up and took a sip. Karma was a bitch.

* * *

IT ONLY TOOK a few floors for Harry to realize that they'd completely surprised his mother's forces. If they'd been lying in wait, he'd have seen them already. Even now, the rest of his teams were spreading through the building, heading for the strong points.

No alarms rang out. Had they not heard the jets? Did they mistake them for something else? He didn't know, but he wasn't going to complain.

Jeremy had bypassed the systems at the roof door. As long as they didn't use the elevators—which would've been stupid—the security teams would only see them if they were monitoring the upper floors.

Or when Team Two hit the security center.

Team Two peeled off when they got to the appropriate floor. The rest of them continued down. Automatic weapons firing in controlled bursts told him the moment his men attacked. Then the alarms went off.

They reached the ground floor in a rush. The stairwell opened into the center of the building. Rex moved out with teams three and four. They'd keep the enemy forces from getting back into the building.

Harry took his team to the interior loading dock and dove for cover when the security guards started shooting. He fired off a long burst to pin the enemy down as his men came in behind him.

The container was still where he expected it to be, thank God, already loaded and ready to move. Everyone had orders to avoid shooting the nuclear reactor, but some of the BenCorp security people decided to hide behind it. That delayed his men from securing the room.

A bullet ricocheted off the concrete beside him. He ducked lower. "Get those bastards."

One by one, the enemy fell to their fire. He tallied his men as soon as the area was secure. Two wounded, one seriously. The medic saw to them as Harry assessed the container. They'd locked it, but a bolt cutter fixed that.

The doors opened smoothly, and he saw the reactor, safely disassembled and stored inside. The radioactive fuel sources were in a massive lead case. It was all here.

He checked the shipping container for bullet holes but found none. A wave of relief washed over him. His mother's people had already hitched the big rig to the container. He climbed into the passenger seat as one of their trained drivers took the wheel.

His team opened the doors leading outside and got into a brief firefight with some security guards. These had come in SUVs. Perfect.

"Take the vehicles, and make sure the gate is clear. We'll be right behind you. Rex, is everything secure?"

"Right and tight, boss. We're planting the charges now. This will more than make up for the hotel bombing. I think the whole building might come down. We'll be ready to move out in five minutes."

"Don't be late. I don't want you pinned down by any reinforcements. We're leaving now."

"Drive safe, and don't rush. That's when accidents happen."

Harry laughed. "Copy that."

His exterior teams had already secured the gate. They raised the arm and waved him through. He gave them a salute. One of the SUVs rushed ahead to scout traffic while the rest settled in around the big rig.

It was early evening, so traffic wasn't as light as he wished. Still, that was a good thing. They merged with the cars leaving the industrial area without the slightest ripple.

* * *

NATHAN WATCHED the helicopter lower the spaceship into the freighter's hold with more than a hint of unease. If something went wrong, his mother would blame him. He breathed a sigh of relief when the load was down and secure.

The helicopter moved away from the ship, and the crew began securing the new cargo. It would take a while to get it to the US, but this ship was one among many on the international shipping lanes. His father wouldn't find it before they had the spaceship safely to port.

He called his mother as soon as they closed the hatch and started moving.

"Mother, everything went according to plan. We have it."

"I need you to gather your people and head for France. Someone—hell, probably your damned brother—just stole my new reactor. They blew up the building. Sound familiar?"

Nathan cursed. "I thought you had it secure. Weren't you moving it early?"

"I was," she said bitterly. "Tomorrow morning, local time. He got there just before the extra security. The police are tearing up the city, but how much do you want to bet they never find it? Incompetent bastards."

"And by the time I get there, it'll be long gone. Where will he take it?"

"How the hell should I know?"

Nathan reviewed what he knew of his father's holdings. The old bastard had a lot of them in Great Britain. Of course, the reactor would be to its destination by the time he found out where that was.

"I'll direct my teams to London. If you get any more intelligence before we get there, call me."

He hung up and called for the helicopter to come back. He'd catch the first commercial flight.

He looked over the spaceship one last time before he headed up to the main deck. No matter how this played out, they'd still won. Let his father have the damned reactor. They could always build another one. This baby would give them so much more.

* * *

JESS CLOSELY EXAMINED the pages she suspected of having Italian. Her fingers itched to pick it up and look at the reverse.

"Come," Romano said. "Have some more wine."

He just wouldn't let it be, the sleazy bastard.

She took up her glass with a smile. "Don't let yours go to waste, either. We can drink up and have another glass."

The fat man smiled and took a large drink. When she did the same, he matched her until both glasses were empty. Perfect.

"That was too good to gulp," she said with a laugh that wasn't at all fake. "More, please."

"That was slick," Sandra said in her ear. "Real slick. Now play him until the drugs take effect. As fat as he is, it probably won't knock him out for long."

Romano virtually swaggered over to pour them fresh glasses. "You're very lucky, you know. Many Americans never get a chance to see how the rest of the world lives. And even when they do, they look down their noses. That's no way to take in the history and greatness of Europe."

She raised an eyebrow and sipped her fresh wine. "Really? I suppose that's true to some degree, though I'm not sure the arrogance is solely ours. So, your grandfather bought those during the Second World War? Not from the Germans, I hope."

"Of course. Who else was selling stolen art?"

Romano blinked in apparent surprise at his answer. "I mean... no, of course not. Everything was legal and above board. I don't know what came over me. My sense of humor can be somewhat odd."

Sandra laughed. "It sounds like the drug makes him more compliant. Let it take hold, and we'll really get him on the record."

Jess nodded at what he'd said. "I understand. Has this villa been in your family for a long time?"

"In one form or another, my family has owned this property since the Dark Ages. It was originally a monastery. We bought it from the church and tore down the old buildings."

She asked him about the area for a few minutes as the man became drowsier. Once he seemed fully in the grasp of the drug, she decided to test him.

"What did you put into the wine?"

"A designer concoction that will make you more suggestable and interfere with your memory of the next few hours. It's completely undetectable."

Her stomach roiled at the thought of how many women he'd done this to.

"Did you use this on the American woman you married?"

"Of course. The damned condom broke, and she got pregnant. I used the drug again to get her to sign a prenuptial agreement. I couldn't have her taking half my money when I dumped her."

The bastard. "So you tricked her into signing away her rights? Is that how you got control of your daughter?"

"No." His eyes were glassy now. "I never anticipated wanting the child, so I didn't specify her in the agreement. When the harpy sued me for custody, I had some of my men break into her house and take the child. She's mine. Blood of my blood. I'll kill the bitch when the time comes to take my girl back."

"Not if I have anything to say about it," Jess muttered. It was time to get him to confess to doing this before.

"Have you drugged other women?"

He laughed. "Of course. All the time. Sluts. Deep inside, they want it. Some try to get me arrested or sue me, but there's never any proof."

"Has anyone sued you falsely?"

"No. Isn't that funny? They all told the truth, but no one could prove a single thing. My friends in the judiciary dismissed the cases. I'm a judge, you know."

"And I hear you're in the mob too. What terrible things have you done?"

He began listing a spree of horror. Killings, embezzlement, drugs, and more. He mentioned enough names to implicate plenty of other people. She made sure to ask where they'd buried the bodies and where to find any evidence of the crimes.

"You need to wrap this up," Sandra said.

Jess agreed. "Mister Romano, you tried to do something terrible to me. Give me the pages from the Voynich Manuscript to make up for it. Write out a receipt transferring their ownership to Humanity Unlimited. Make sure it's legal."

He wrote out a receipt and signed it.

"You know this is just as sketchy as that prenup he forced his ex-wife to sign," Sandra said. "It'll never hold up in court."

"Then he can sue me for them," she said firmly. "Maybe the irony will give the bastard a heart attack."

Jess folded the receipt and put it into her jacket. She gestured toward the case at the end of the room. "I'll need a briefcase to carry the manuscript pages. Please pack them carefully for me."

He took a briefcase made of fine Italian leather from a cabinet and lay it on the case beside the manuscript pages. He found some latex gloves and began tugging them on.

Jess made certain she had a good view. "Put them face down, please."

He complied, and she watched the previously unseen pages as they appeared. The back of the one she suspected might have more data was better than she'd hoped. Two columns of script filled it, one in Italian and the other in the strange lettering. If anything was the Rosetta Stone, this was it.

She closed the briefcase and had Romano give her the combination.

"You've done very well. Would a second dose of the drug harm a person?"

"Probably not," he said.

"Good. Make another one."

She watched him pull a packet out from the desk, empty it into his glass, and fill it with wine.

"Drink up," she said. "Call your people. Tell them you're sending me back down and you don't need to speak with Paolo. Then go to bed. You've had a busy day, and you want to get a good night's sleep. I'm not sure if it works this way, but you'll only remember you had a good time once you wake up."

Once he'd called for someone to come get her and retired to his bedroom, she spoke aloud. "Sandra, I'm on my way out. I'll find Paolo, and we'll meet you at the house next door. I think we should make tracks back to Rome. We can cut out the video of the confession and send it to someone trustworthy. The police will come for him before he wakes up."

"Have I ever mentioned that you're my hero?" the mercenary asked.

"Well, you are. Now get the hell out of there before something goes wrong."

Jess grabbed the briefcase, corked the wine, and took it too. It was the least the bastard could do.

25

Harry worried all the way back to Mexico. He expected to have a military jet of some kind show up to herd the stolen cargo plane to another landing spot as soon as he got close to the spaceport.

Two jets did show up, but they were obviously of Rainforest manufacture. They escorted the plane in without incident. His father stood waiting as he and his men climbed out of the plane and stretched.

"Well done, Harry. Well done. Jess's flight lands in ten minutes. She'll be just in time to get the reactor transported to pad three and begin loading. I don't know if I'll relax until it's in space."

"How long will it take to get it installed once the lifter gets it up there?"

"I believe she said twelve hours, but that seems like too short a timeframe."

That did seem optimistic. "How about the fuel?"

His father smiled. "Two loads are already in orbit. They tell me that the remainder will take two additional launches. Then we resume personnel and supply missions. We should be able to wrap those sometime tomorrow."

"So, about the time you get your primary power supply online, you'll be ready to leave? That sounds like good timing. Mother will figure everything out before too much longer. I wouldn't put it past her to try and shoot the station down."

"Wouldn't that make for some ugly headlines?" His father grimaced. "I can't believe they managed to steal the crashed spaceship. Dammit. I'm certain they moved it offshore, but I probably won't be able to figure out which ship it's on before they get it somewhere. So much technology lost."

"If you can figure it out, I'll go get it back."

His father gave him an odd look. "That might be challenging from orbit. You're going with Jess, aren't you?"

Harry felt his eyebrows rise. "What would I do up there? I'm not an astronaut."

"You don't want to walk on the surface of Mars?"

"Exactly how are you planning on doing that? I can see visiting asteroids, but without small craft, how do you visit something like Mars?"

"With the increases in efficiency, the reusable lifters will do. A number of them will stay with the ship. Fuel is available in space too. Phobos, the larger of Mars's moons, is very much like a D-class asteroid and probably has water inside. A lot of it.

"Eventually, we can use the high carbon content to create a beanstalk. That's a long tether that goes out beyond geosynchronous orbit and uses elevators to move people and cargo from the surface to a station in orbit."

"Are you serious?" Harry asked. "You'll build a space elevator?"

His father nodded. "Yes. The gravity is much weaker on Mars. That means the carbon nanotube cables would be much shorter and slimmer. A number of scientists and science-fiction authors have explored the subject. I intend to explore the reality."

He shook his head. That sounded almost as impressive as exploring the solar system.

"Back to the subject," his father said. "You could be one of the first humans to walk the surface of another planet. As one of the owners, perhaps even right behind Jess."

"You're not going?"

The older man shook his head regretfully. "Alas, no. I'm far too old for that kind of nonsense. Besides, I have a covert war to fight here on Earth. Once the ship leaves orbit, everyone is going to go mad. Your mother in particular, but also the various governments that see they've missed the boat. I foresee a number of attempts to nationalize the company. My work will be to keep that from happening."

The noise of another plane landing announced Jess's arrival. Harry considered the offer. Did he want to go? His work on Earth was satisfying, but this was a once-in-a-lifetime opportunity. What could he contribute once they were in space?

Admittedly, going with Jess had its appeal. He'd grown quite fond of her in the last few days.

The airplane taxied up to park beside the cargo plane. A motorized stair positioned itself, and the passengers started making their way down. Jess was in the lead with Sandra right behind her.

The blond engineer came up to him with a huge grin on her face and grabbed him in a tight hug. "We did it! We got the reactor and the papers. That'll show your mother."

His indecision vanished as he held her in his arms. He knew his body was making a hasty call, but he was willing to see what happened. He felt a little more alone when she pulled back.

"I'm sorry to burst your bubble, but we didn't get our way in everything. Nathan stole the buried spaceship."

Her face fell a little. "Dammit. Well, maybe we can find another one. One in better condition."

She turned to his father. "Did the fuel make it up?"

"Half of it has. The other half is loading now. It will launch just before the reactor does."

"Excellent! I need to start moving the reactor. Excuse me."

The two men watched her run to where they were unloading the cargo container. His father spoke after a moment. "How can any project with her at the helm fail? She's like a tornado."

Harry hadn't agreed with his father so completely in years.

* * *

NATHAN'S PHONE WOKE HIM. Even at cruising altitude, there was no escaping his mother. All passenger aircraft had satellite links these days. The other first-class passengers glared at him, but he ignored them and answered the call.

"Hello, Mother. Have you located your property?"

"The bastard stole my plane. With all the confusion, no one noticed the pilots had disappeared. The French police found them locked up in a hangar at a regional airport."

That made things more complex. With an aircraft, the reactor could be anywhere in the world.

"Do you have a transponder on the plane?"

"They disabled it, but that doesn't matter. My spy at the Yucatán Spaceport said they landed there just a few minutes ago. Turn around, and get back there as soon as you can."

He rubbed his face and checked their location. The plane was almost ready to land at Heathrow. "You know all my assets are landing in London, right? It will take at least a couple of hours to get on our way back. Figure half a day to get to Mexico to begin planning a mission. Why the hell did they take it there? To slip it across the US border?"

"I have no idea. My man is keeping an eye on the situation. Stop complaining, and get your ass in gear. I want that reactor back in my hands before they get it somewhere we can't recover it." She hung up before he could respond.

Working for his mother was becoming a chore. Nathan turned his phone off when the flight attendant told the first-class passengers to do so. He'd call his men as soon as he landed. There was just enough time to get a decent meal while they refueled. He'd order something for his men, and they'd eat on the flight back to Mexico.

* * *

JESS FRETTED while loading the reactor on the lifter. There was no room for error. One mistake and the whole project could go up in flames.

She'd planned on an hour to load, but the painstaking process took almost ninety minutes. With that high-stress task done, Jess retreated to the control center for pad three.

Harry was already there, waiting. He handed her a bag.

"What's this?" she asked. It smelled good.

"A meatball sub."

"It can wait until they fire this thing into orbit."

"And then you'll say you can wait until it docks. Or some other milestone. Eat the damned sandwich. I have a glass of tea too."

It was easier to eat than argue. She sat at one of the empty consoles and looked at the main screen. The countdown clock showed only a few minutes until launch. Her first bite brought her hunger to life. The sub was delicious.

"I hear you got the pages," Harry said as he took a seat. "Congratulations. Sandra said you kicked some ass too."

"The police arrested Romano a few hours after I left," she said smugly. "And I forwarded the edited video to his ex-wife through Sandra. She's going to get a chunk of his fortune for her daughter, I think. Once the prenup is voided, she'll be in a good position to take over the bastard's assets."

Harry grinned. "Remind me never to get on your bad side. Did the papers have everything you needed?"

"I'll know once Doctor Powell takes a look, but I think they might. It looked like it had a long segment of medieval Italian and the unknown language. That might be enough to figure most of it out."

"My father asked if I was going on this mission," he said. "What do you think?"

She looked at him in surprise. "Well, of course you are. You think this is all for physicists and pilots? You'd be exploring where no man—or woman—has ever gone before."

"He said we might be going down to Mars, and that as an owner of Humanity Unlimited, I could be one of the first few people to step onto an alien world. Behind you, of course. As the senior owner present, you should go first. I hope you come up with something suitably historic to say by then."

Jess froze with her sandwich halfway to her mouth. "Oh shit!"

"I'd seriously recommend something classier."

She swatted him. "You know what I mean. Me? The first human on Mars? Are you serious?"

"Why not? Though, to be fair, you might not be. Aliens, you know. They might have been there before us."

That was true. "Yes, but I'd be the first modern human. Wow. No pressure."

The flight director called out. "Jess, we're about to launch."

She rose to her feet and stepped over to his console. The timer was down to fifteen seconds. She watched it slowly drop to zero. The engines ignited right on schedule, and the lifter rose from the pad.

In less than a minute, it was lost to sight. Ten minutes later, it was safely in orbit. It would dock in four hours.

Then the real fun started.

* * *

CLAYTON LOOKED up when his assistant knocked on his door. "Sir, the courier is here, and you have a call."

"Who is it?"

"Your ex-wife."

That surprised him. He'd lost count of the number of knives they'd planted in one another over the years, yet she'd never called him about any of the incidents. Not even to gloat when she'd won.

"Keep her on hold. If she wants to talk to me, she can wait for me to finish my business. Send the courier in."

His assistant ushered in a young woman in a casual suit with a flat package. He closed the door behind her.

"Set it on the desk, and I'll sign for it," Clayton said.

The papers were straightforward, and he had the woman on her way in only a few minutes. Alone with the package, he spent a few minutes carefully opening it. They'd protected the contents very well, just as he'd asked. The old pages of the Voynich Manuscript had cost him a significant amount of money. Yale hadn't wanted to give them up, but they could use the funds he'd offered for so many other projects. And the endowment hadn't hurt, either.

Clayton didn't know if the pages themselves would provide any extra clues, but he doubted that anyone had analyzed them rigorously since they'd been stored away. They might contain any number of undiscovered secrets.

Doctor Powell could examine them with the newly acquired pages. Well, she could once she and her associate had set up shop in orbit. They were going along, of course. The odds were very good the explorers would find new artifacts in space, and Clayton wanted them preserved correctly.

Then he answered his ex-wife's call. "Sorry to keep you waiting, Kathleen. Business, you know."

"The wait only makes me more determined to hurt you," she said. "What the hell are you doing, Clayton? You stole a nuclear reactor from me and shot it into orbit."

"And you stole an ancient spacecraft from me. You also killed dozens of people and blew up my hotel."

"Which you got even for when you destroyed my research facility. Drop the *faux* outrage."

He shook his head. She'd never understand the difference between them. Or realize that she was a monster. "What do you want to talk about, Kathleen?"

"To tell you the kid gloves are off. You and Harry aren't on the safe list anymore. Keep looking over your shoulder, dear. One day, Nathan will be there, and you'll die."

"You can't believe how little that actually matters to me. Send whomever you like. I'll return them to you in a body bag."

He hung up the phone and pressed the buzzer. His assistant answered at once. "Sir?"

"I want security around the spaceport tripled. No one gets onto the launch pads or into this hotel without being cleared."

He stared out the window. Phase one was almost complete. If he could just hold things together for a while longer, he'd take all the marbles.

26

Harry made time to talk with Rex, Sandra, and Jeremy. The rest of his people were coordinating with the Rainforest security people to keep things sane while the last of the launches were taking place.

The four of them wedged themselves into a booth at the hotel restaurant. It was deserted. He got right to the point. "I wanted to let you know that I'm going up to the station."

All of them stared at him. Rex finally spoke. "Look, I know I told you to stay close to your lady friend, but that might be a little too much commitment. Stalkerish, even."

Sandra smacked Rex on the back of the head. "Sexist jerk. That sounds exciting, Harry. Maybe you'll miss all the fallout of the theft, if you'll forgive the pun."

"I might be able to miss all that and more," he said. "Before I talk about it, I wanted to make you three an offer. You're the best people I have, and I want to keep you with me. I'd pay very good money if you'd join me."

Jeremy grinned. "In space? Hell, yeah!"

Harry smiled and shook his head. "Not so fast. There's a lot more to this situation than you know. Let me lay it all out for you."

He spent the next ten minutes explaining the whole space station being a spaceship surprise and the alien tech. That kept them quiet for a while.

Sandra was the first to speak. "So, you want us to leave the Earth and fly to Mars. Why?"

"Because I want people I can trust at my back."

Rex nodded slowly. "Sure. Hey, I wasn't doing anything for the next few months anyway."

Sandra and Jeremy also agreed.

With their buy in, he relaxed. "Great. There's room on the lifter for all of us. With luck, the last of the supplies will be on the ship tomorrow."

Harry looked at his watch. "You have enough time to pack a bag. They'll provide everything ordinary, so limit yourselves to personal items and luxuries. Meet me in the lobby in two hours."

* * *

JESS ALREADY HAD her personal belongings on the ship, so she stuffed her bag with coffee, tea, and chocolate. They were going into deep space. There was no such thing as too much caffeine or chocolate.

Even though she shouldn't take it into space, she put her pistols, holsters, and spare magazines in the bag too. A few discreet inquiries with her guards got her a few boxes of ammunition. She'd turn them over to the ship's captain. Maybe. She might just keep them close until they were safely away from Earth.

Once she'd stuffed her bag to the limit, she went down to the lobby. The bag was heavy enough to make her feel like a pack mule.

The other elevator opened, and Harry walked out with Sandra, Rex, and the security guy at his back. Jeremy, that was his name.

She waved. "Hey. You guys excited about going into space?"

Harry shrugged. "Excited might not be the word I'd choose, but I'm ready to go. What happens next?"

"A van will pick us up in a few minutes and drive us to pad one. We'll get into suits and board the lifter. Once we're all aboard, they'll launch when the station is at the right point in orbit. About an hour from now."

Sandra hefted her bag. "Where do we check in our baggage?"

"They'll put it in the back of the passenger cabin when we board the lifter."

The elevator opened again, and Clayton Rogers strolled out. "Ah, good. I was afraid I might miss you."

He extended his hand to Jess. "My deepest congratulations on the magnificent engineering marvel you've helped design and build. This achievement will see humanity finally leave this planet for good. I couldn't be prouder to be a part of such a grand venture. You'll keep me up to date on everything you find?"

She shook his hand firmly. "Of course I will. This is a wonderful adventure. Thank you for allowing me to be part of it."

The older man turned his attention to his son. "I know you don't trust or approve of me, but that doesn't matter. You're helping to do something important. Keep her safe, and enjoy the ride."

Harry took his father's hand. "Don't make me regret this."

The van pulled up out front. "Our ride is here," Jess said. "Let's mount up."

The trip out to the pad took longer than she'd expected. Security stopped them twice, comparing the passenger's faces to something on their security tablets. They searched the bags and scanned everyone with detection wands.

She expected trouble about her weaponry, but the man in charge of the checkpoint made a short call and put everything back. Clayton had cleared them to take weapons up with them.

The launch pad towered over the area where the van stopped. A protected door led them into the concrete base. The changing room wasn't large, but a partition separated it in two for modesty.

Jess stripped down to her underwear and put on a ship's jumpsuit in light blue. Once Sandra was ready, Jess picked up her freshly bagged clothes and led the mercenary through the door into the suit room. The three men were already on the other side.

Technicians fitted them into suits in short order. Gone were the days of bulky, hard to wear vacuum gear. These were relatively light and flexible. Not as much as the rotted suits in the crashed ship had been, but much easier to wear than twenty years ago. The helmets were clear composite. They'd be able to communicate through built-in radios.

They went up the elevator one at a time. A technician on the upper level escorted her into the lifter, helped her secure her gear, and strapped her in. Even though she'd been on a number of flights, she still got the safety lecture. She listened intently and reviewed it in her mind once the man left for the next passenger.

The two pilots were going through their checklists. The passenger cabin had three seats side by side and four rows. She didn't know the other passengers but waved anyway.

They strapped Harry in beside her, and she had him switch to a private channel once he was settled in. "I'm so excited. This is really it."

"At least you have some idea of what we're getting into. Tell me about the ship. How many people does she carry?"

"More than you might think possible. The torus has three levels with the floors arranged so that our feet point outward. They rotate twice a minute, giving the outermost level 95 percent of Earth's gravity. The innermost level is about 85 percent."

He looked impressed. "How many people are aboard?"

She smiled. "Get ready to have your mind blown. The torus supports about 2,500 people, with plenty of space left for manufacturing, research, and cargo. It's a mobile colony. We've been sneaking them up over the last six months as the ship came online."

Harry looked a little stunned. "Considering how much the first international space station cost to house just six crew members, my father invested a lot more into this project than I thought possible. Even considering how he's lowered the launch costs. I was thinking fifty or a hundred people, max."

"We need a lot of people. We're planning on dropping off three mining outposts. They'll have a lot of work to do. They'll be building stations similar to the ship for long-term colonies at some point.

"We have habitat plans that would support more than half a million people in one massive space station. They'll be building one like that in Mars orbit once we get to mining Deimos and Phobos."

He shook his head. "That's staggering."

"Your father thought big. He wants to get mankind off Earth in a permanent way. Imagine colonies around Venus and Mars. The asteroid belt. Jupiter and beyond. Ultimately, millions of people. Even billions at some far-off future date. The planet that gave mankind birth would no longer limit us."

The pilot turned in his seat and spoke over their radios. "Welcome aboard. I'm Lenny Kawasaki, and I'll be your pilot today. We hit the burners in about ten minutes. Once we reach orbit, we'll have another three and a half hours to get to our destination. Thanks for flying with us, and we hope you'll choose Humanity Unlimited for all your orbital launch needs."

Harry seemed disinclined to talk, so Jess settled back and meditated. The engine ignition caught her a little off guard, shaking her and then pressing her back into her acceleration couch firmly.

The boost to orbit took just over ten minutes. They didn't have windows, but the small screen above the pilot's cubby showed the view. It was breathtaking.

Once the engines shut off, they were in microgravity. Basically, they floated. The pilot allowed them to unbuckle once the lifter was on course. Jess decided to stay where she was.

Watching the mercenaries figure out how to move around was fun, though. They were surprisingly adept at it, though they had a tendency to overshoot their marks.

The fun and games kept them from being bored while Jess reviewed the data dump from the ship. They'd unloaded the reactor and had it roughly in place. She'd see to the final connections once she was on board, but she was satisfied with the work that her people had done so far.

* * *

HARRY PLAYED AROUND for a while and then buckled back in to watch Sandra, Rex, and Jeremy. The sniper was trying to figure out how to compensate for zero gravity when she tossed a Ping-Pong ball toward a small basket someone had taped to the far wall.

Apparently, this was a fun game for everyone. They'd try to get the motions just right and mostly fail miserably.

"This is more complex than it looks," Sandra said after a while. "I'll figure it out, though. I wonder how a shooter does her business without gravity. The recoil would shove her hard enough to screw up her aim. And the slug might penetrate the hull."

"They might not have weapons in space," Harry said.

She stared at him for a moment and laughed. "Stop trolling me. Of course they have weapons in space."

Rex held onto the back of one of the chairs. "Maybe it uses compressed air and frangible rounds."

That made some sense, Harry decided. Overpenetration would be a bad thing in space. "Most of the ship has gravity, just not as much as you'd expect. It would mean knowing how to shoot in every level and being able to compensate correctly the first time. That could be fun."

"But the central area doesn't have gravity, right?" Sandra asked. "I bet I could manage something, but it'll take time to develop the right skills and tactics to secure the whole ship. I know what I'll be doing most of the trip out. Chasing Rex around."

"Just what I'd been hoping you'd say."

"You are such a pervert."

The big scout laughed. "Hardly that. It's all natural."

"I want to get a good look at their systems," Jeremy said. "They must be seriously advanced."

Jess tapped Harry on the shoulder. "We're almost there. Check the screen."

Harry watched the small dot grow into a ship on the screen. The lack of reference points made it hard to tell the size until they got close. Liberty Station was huge.

The shaft the torus rotated around was shorter than he'd expected, and he couldn't see any sign of the engines Jess had spoken of. Four massive spokes connected the rotating torus to the spine, helping it rotate majestically. The torus was thicker than he'd imagined, too, but there were thousands of people in there.

Three long arms projected from the ship above the torus. He suspected there was a fourth that he couldn't see because of the ship itself. One looked like a dock. He could see two lifters attached to it. That gave him a new sense of scale. The station was even bigger than he'd thought.

One of the remaining arms held a solar array. The other held three large disks that looked ready to drop. Maybe the mining equipment Jess had mentioned.

As they came around the station, he saw a similar set of disks on the far side of the ship on the last arm. He'd have to ask about them when they had time.

A smaller disk, about a third the size of the torus but just as thick, sat on the top of the station. It was rotating in the opposite direction from the torus. The ship looked amazing.

"We dock at the end of the arm to the left," Jess said. "We'll get off in zero gravity and unload the cargo they brought up. You guys can settle in and take a tour of the ship while I get the reactor installed. By this time tomorrow, we'll have left Earth—and our troubles—behind."

27

Jess fidgeted during the approach. In space, ships and people moved slowly and carefully. The lifter edged close to the docking arm and allowed the clamps to lock it down.

The pilot instructed everyone to stay in their seats until someone came to get them, unless they were zero-G certified. Which she was.

She unbuckled, spun over her seat, and launched herself to the handhold beside the personnel lock. She opened a cubby, retrieved a line, and went back for Harry.

"You can get out of the suit now. They'll pack it away for you."

Jess helped him get his suit off and then stripped off her own. She folded them and strapped them into their seats.

She held up the line. "Let me hook us up. Until they're satisfied that you can maneuver on your own, you'll need to be paired up with someone who can keep you from hurting yourself or others in microgravity."

"Does that take long?"

"That depends on the person. I think you'll take to it quickly. Sandra too. Rex, well, maybe by the time we get to Mars."

"Hey," he said mildly.

She laughed. "I'm sure you'll do fine. Okay, use your hands to gently push on the chair and send yourself toward the handholds. I'll be right there with you."

Harry shoved off with too much force but not as badly as some she'd seen. He also tumbled in the air because he was off balance. She let him hit because it wouldn't hurt him, and it would teach him a lesson.

He looked chagrined. "That didn't go so well."

"You'll pick it up. You ever go scuba diving?"

"Sure. Is this like that?"

"Only in that you had no idea what you were doing before it all clicked into place in your head. This will be the same. Everyone gets the hang of it eventually."

She led him through the airlock. A pair of attendants was just arriving to bring the new crew on board. "I'm certified," Jess said. "I've got this one."

The ship's air smelled different from the lifter. A shade more metallic but not as stuffy. It definitely wasn't like natural air, but it was good enough.

Planting her feet on the hull, she grabbed his belt. "Hold still. We could use handholds, but I'm in a hurry."

One light push sent them floating the direction she wanted. She was pleased to see that she'd accounted for his mass fairly well. They'd only miss her point of aim by a few feet.

They drifted with deceptive slowness, and she stopped them at the hub. She pulled them around the corner into the spine. The spokes to the torus were only a short distance away.

Unlike the rest of the spine, the torus's hub rotated. So, each spoke made a trip around the spine twice each minute. That took some getting used to.

It had also taken a tremendous amount of engineering to account for the edges. The spine was inside the moving hub so that conduits, pipes, and supports could run along the entire length of the ship. The junction with the spokes could even seal if there was an explosive decompression.

Jess got Harry to the hub. "See how the ladders have arrows?" she asked. "That's direction of travel. It's awkward to run into someone going the other direction. If you do, the person in the wrong has to back up.

"There are also elevators. We built the doors into the spokes since the cars can't come all the way into the hub. We cinch cargoes into the hub and match speeds. It's a bit complicated, but it greatly simplifies boosting the ship."

"Seems straightforward enough. We're in zero-G. That changes as we go down, right?"

"Right, though we don't use up and down. Too confusing. Going toward the torus is outward and going toward the spine is inward. In the torus, the direction of rotation is spinward. The other is antispinward."

He considered that. "How do you know which is which?"

Jess smiled. "You can feel the rotation. I'll show you. Come on."

She moved ahead of him. "Always keep one hand on a handhold until you're certified. Then you can do this." She lightly shoved off and coasted above the handholds. After a dozen feet, she stopped herself. It would ruin her image of competence if the line yanked her up short.

When the centrifugal force grew strong enough, they switched directions, and it felt as though they were climbing down a ladder. The pull grew stronger with every rung until they came out in the innermost torus level.

Jess unhitched the line and put it into a cubby with others just like it. "Let's get you settled in, and I'll be off."

She led him down the corridor. "See how it curves up in each direction? It always makes me think of hamsters in their exercise wheels. And plenty of people get their exercise in just that way. Walk long enough, and you'll get back to where you started."

"You said we could tell which direction we're spinning. How?"

She stopped. "Close your eyes. Turn in the direction that feels like you're moving toward."

He paused and turned to spinward. "That's weird."

"Your inner ear knows when you're moving, even if your eyes tell you you're not. Also, check this out. Do you have a coin in your pocket?" It usually took a while before people stopped carrying money around with them.

"Probably." He found one and held it out to her.

"Drop it."

He let it go, and it fell to the deck but not in a straight line. The coin fell in a curve, angling toward antispinward.

"Whoa!" he said, grabbing the coin and doing it again. "What the hell?"

"That's the Coriolis Effect. We're rotating, but the coin is falling directly away from the spine. As we move, that direction changes from our perspective. So, the falling object curves. If you toss a ball, you'll have to deal with the same physics. It'll seriously screw up your basketball game."

"And shooting. Sandra will be extremely dismayed."

Jess laughed. "We don't have any shooting ranges, so that won't be a problem. You'll get used to it after a while. Come on."

She led him to a cross corridor and down to her room. "I'm here. I reserved the room across for you. We assigned the others rooms on this corridor. Your personal gear will arrive once they start unloading the lifter."

"People get single-occupancy rooms in space?"

"They do when we have enough to go around. The rooms are small compared to those on Earth, but they're large enough. I really need to go look at the reactor, so you'll have to hang here for a bit. Someone will be along to give you a real tour shortly."

She grabbed him by the shoulder. "Welcome to space, Harry."

* * *

HARRY GAVE his new home a short walk-through while he waited for his guide. He'd expected the room to be something like a cruise ship cabin, but it was more like a small apartment. He had a living room, a kitchenette, a bedroom, a bathroom, and a spare room that he could use for anything he wanted, he supposed.

The bed was a queen and already made. Built-in dressers and closets had basic supplies like new underwear and ship suits like the one he wore. The ones in his closet already had his last name on the breast. A quick check showed that the bathroom had basic supplies as well.

The kitchenette had a microwave to heat things up and a small oven to bake. The two-element stovetop would suffice for his cooking skills. A small fridge stood ready but was empty.

A buzz at the door announced he had a visitor. A short Asian man with silver oak leaves on the shoulders of his jumpsuit smiled at him and extended a hand. "Mister Rogers, welcome aboard. I'm Captain Lee, the commanding officer of Liberty Station."

Harry shook the man's hand. "Captain, it's a pleasure to meet you, but I'm sure you're a very busy man. You don't need to show me around."

"It's no problem at all. I needed a break, so I thought I'd give you a tour of the ship's common areas and then have dinner. I realize it's after lunchtime down at the spaceport, but we run on GMT up here. Have you looked around your quarters? I hope they're acceptable."

"They're bigger than I expected, actually. So is this whole ship. She's amazing."

The officer grinned. "Yes, she is. Come on, and we'll stroll down to the public section of the torus. Your bag should be on your bed when you get back from lunch."

"Is there a lock for the door?"

"No. Where would someone take a stolen object? We don't use money directly on the ship. Everyone gets their pay electronically, and purchases come out of those accounts at the public stores. Meals are part of the pay so no charge there."

They walked back to the main corridor and then headed antispinward. Harry nodded and smiled politely at the people they passed. "What about secure areas of the ship, like the bridge and engineering?"

"Those are locked. Only authorized personnel can access them. The control consoles are locked as well."

They passed out of the housing section and into what looked like a park. Harry stopped and stared in amazement. There was grass on the ground and small trees under a large opaque dome. The lights seemed to be about the same color as the sun.

"This is one of our habitat zones," Lee said, smiling at Harry's bemused expression. "We have other areas for growing food hydroponically, but places like this let the crew have a taste of home."

"I'm surprised you don't have a view of space here. Radiation?"

The officer shook his head. "Not exactly. We have a powerful magnetic field that will protect the ship once we leave Earth's orbit. Impact shields and water surround each hull. Micrometeorites are a concern, as well as cosmic radiation that might be too energetic for the magnetic field to stop. There *are* a few viewing areas, but we thought the habitat zone wasn't the right place for them. We'll look at one before we stop off in the cafeteria."

Harry mulled that over. "I saw my cabin had a kitchenette. If there's a cafeteria, what use is it?"

"Want to watch something on the screen while you snack on some chips and dip? Maybe make a grilled cheese sandwich or an intimate dinner? That's why we put one in every set of quarters. Feel free to use it or not, as you like."

He saw movement in one of the trees. Something was up there. An orange cat walked out on a limb and stared haughtily down at them. It crouched and leapt to another branch, seemingly accounting for the Coriolis Effect with ease.

"You have cats," he said, surprised. "Do you have pests?"

"Not that I'm aware of. The screening process was good enough to make sure we didn't get rodents or insects. Vacuum does wonders for that. No, we have some cats and dogs as common pets. They're all domesticated and friendly.

"We have several crewmen dedicated to seeing to their health and wellbeing. Given how quickly they breed, we should be able to start allowing private pets in a few years."

The area next to the park was similar to a mall, with all kinds of stores. Many of the people were dressed casually. Harry was glad he'd brought some of his regular clothes.

Lee gestured around them. "You can buy any number of personal items in these stores. They're charged to your account."

"How do they know who I am?"

"That's a good question. We'll get you set up with a chip in your palm. The ship will know who you are and be able to track you anywhere inside the hull. That's partly for safety. We don't want someone wandering into a dangerous section of the ship."

"It's also a security feature," Harry said approvingly. "You know if someone enters an area they aren't cleared for."

"True enough," the captain agreed. "That isn't the reason for them, though. We've vetted every member of this crew thoroughly. The cafeteria is just ahead, but let's go see the observation level first."

That required a detour to the edge of the habitat area. A short set of stairs led them up to an airlock. The doors stood open, and he could see a wide room with a clear ceiling. The central spine of the ship was directly overhead and shone brightly in the sun. The Earth occupied one side of the view and seemed to spin quickly.

"It's beautiful," Harry said. "I think I'd get a little dizzy if I had to watch it all the time."

Lee laughed. "Most people feel that way at first, but the mind adjusts just as well as the body. The micrometeorite protection for this area is under the deck. If you're ever here and this section loses pressure, there are hoods and oxygen canisters in the lockers against the wall. Keep calm, put one on, and go to the lock. It has two doors, so you can get back into the habitable area."

Harry pointed at the section of the spine facing toward the Earth. "Those are the engines? They don't look the part."

"Appearances can be deceiving. The hull there is on hinged arms. When the time comes to boost, it opens like a flower. And, once we reach a new orbit, the hull closes, and we can use the equipment mounted there. We get the best of both worlds."

Harry watched the universe turn for a few minutes in silence. This made him feel almost insignificant. The entire Earth could vanish, and the rest of the galaxy wouldn't notice.

"What's the plan going forward?" he eventually asked.

"We're still bringing the last of the crew and supplies aboard. We have another dozen lifters coming. Once the new reactor is online and our current one is playing backup, we'll disassemble the solar array and put it into storage. That will give us six docking points for the lifters.

"Once the last of them has unloaded, we'll rotate the ship so the engines are in line with our orbit around the Earth and start boosting. We'll break orbit on a course for the comet Miss Cook found the coordinates for."

"How long will it take us to get there?"

"It's not all that far away, so about five days. We'll boost to a speed somewhat faster than its speed and coast into the same orbit. Then we'll decelerate to match its speed."

Harry took one last look at the Earth. "I can only imagine how that's going to freak them out down there."

"No doubt," Lee agreed. "I'm afraid it's time to go get some food. I have to get back to the emergency bridge. We're using it to monitor the reactor installation. We'll have plenty of time to get to know one another as we head to Mars."

Harry followed the captain out, but he couldn't tear his eyes away from the glory of the view until it was out of sight. This would be an amazing trip.

28

"**D**on't move it so quickly!" Jess said.

Chief Engineer Ray Proudfoot gave her a look. "Jess, take a breath. I promise I won't slam the radioactive material into the reactor."

"Sorry. It's been that kind of week. Just go extra slowly."

She watched him resume moving the manipulator arm that held the fuel. He inserted it into the reactor and locked it in place. She double-checked the work and nodded. "Good. Really good. Thanks."

A nuclear reactor wasn't like a light switch. She couldn't just press a button and have power. She had to bring it online in stages. It would take about six hours to get the reactor to full output, but they didn't need that kind of power on a spaceship. They'd wanted the unit for its portability and longevity. For their purposes, one-quarter output was more than good enough. It would take them two hours to get it up to that.

Step by step, she and her team walked through the process. In an hour, the reactor had taken over supplying power to the ship from the weaker unit that the UN had approved. That anemic reactor would make a good backup, but it couldn't do more than keep the lights on. They'd need twice the power to generate the protective magnetic field and fire the engines.

"Power output at 25 percent," the chief engineer said at last. "Lock it down. Great job, everyone."

Jess relaxed a little. The hardest part was over. At least until they fired the main engines.

She headed for the hatch. "I'm going to the emergency bridge. Let me know if you see any unusual readings."

"Relax," he said. "I have everything under control. Go get something to eat and maybe have a glass of wine. You're wound up pretty tight."

"I will. I even brought a fresh bottle of wine. I hope it made the trip okay."

She left the power center and made her way forward in the spine to the emergency bridge. Her chip allowed her access to every portion of the ship, so all she had to do was wave her palm in front of the reader, and the hatch slid open.

The emergency bridge wasn't very big, but it was close to the reactor room. The large screen up front took up the most space. It showed the Earth spinning below the ship. Four angled control panels allowed the officers to monitor various parts of Liberty Station. Several observation chairs could fold down from the rear bulkhead.

They were almost ready to shift operations to the control deck. That would be a big improvement since it had gravity. This one would now be reserved for unforeseen crises.

Lee glanced up as she came in. "I see the new reactor is providing power. Well done, Jess. All systems are in the green, and we'll be ready to break orbit tomorrow morning. There are ten lifters still in the queue. The next two will lift in half an hour. The launch windows are ninety minutes apart. Once they dock, we'll unload them.

"We'll get a good night's sleep while that happens and be on our way shortly after breakfast." He looked pleased. "It's hard to believe we made it."

She took a slow breath and shook her head. "I'm not counting on that until we're away. If things look good, I'm getting something to eat and having a glass of wine."

"Have two. Good night, Jess."

"Good night, Captain."

It only took a few minutes to get to her room. She hesitated and then buzzed on Harry's door.

She smiled when he opened it. "Good. You haven't gone to sleep. I wanted to see if you were up for dinner."

"Sure. We'll have to go to the cafeteria, though. I don't have anything to fix."

"We can go to my place. I have some steak. And wine. I brought a fresh bottle. Did you get your gear?"

"Yup." He stepped into the hall. "I've put everything away, and I've been scanning the entertainment channels. You've got the full spectrum up here. I'm especially impressed with the sports lineup."

Jess opened her door and led him inside. "We get the feed straight from the commercial satellites. Some of the channels will continue once we get going. The transmitter that we'll be communicating with has a lot of bandwidth. The library is fairly extensive when it comes to movies too. One of the benefits of Rainforest being the leading provider of streaming entertainment."

She found her freshly acquired bottle of wine and opened it to breathe. "We got the power online. We're almost ready to go. How are Sandra and the rest getting along?"

He followed her to the kitchenette. "Pretty good. They're off exploring."

"Why didn't you join them?"

"I'll do that tomorrow. I wanted to review what my people back on Earth have found out. There's still no sign of Nathan, but my mother swore revenge. We need to be on our toes."

Jess put two steaks into the oven. "They can't even get to us up here. I hope. I can't wait to watch the news channels when they notice we're leaving. It will be awesome!"

Harry didn't seem convinced. "I'm not resting easily until this is over. Can I toss the salad?"

It would be a tight fit in the kitchenette, but she didn't mind. "Be my guest."

* * *

NATHAN MET the paid weasel outside the spaceport. Security was tight, so it was easier for the man to come to him. They'd broken into a small warehouse. It looked disused, so he'd taken the chance. It was large enough for his team to assemble.

The cadaverous man looked nervous as he walked in under guard. "Mister Bennett, I can't be gone long."

"You can be gone as long as I say. My mother tells me they took our reactor to the space station. I want you to tell me how I can get it back."

"Impossible. If it's up there, it can't be retrieved."

He punched the man in the gut, smiling as he folded and retched.

"You don't tell me what's possible. You take my instructions and make them happen. How can we commandeer one of the lifters and get to the space station? Once we get up there, no bunch of scientists is going to stop me from doing what I want."

"You don't understand. That's impos—"

Nathan slapped him. Hard. "I'm getting tired of your excuses. I understand the spaceport is at a heightened state of security. Figure out how to get my men past it to one of the pads. Tonight."

The man rubbed his face. He was sweating heavily. "Security is exceptionally tight, Mister Bennett. It will take me several hours to see what options we have. Perhaps if you waited a while for things to calm down, it would prove simpler to get you up there. It's not like a space station is going anywhere."

"Not that I need to explain myself to you, but I might be able to steal it back if they haven't installed it. You have four hours to get back to me. Go!"

It took almost the full four hours for the man to return. He shook like a leaf, so Nathan was prepared just to shoot him, but the man had a plan.

"They're still loading personnel and supplies. There are four launches left on tonight's schedule. Two lift off within the next hour, so I can't get you into the secure area before they go up. One of the last two is a personnel launch. It will need to be that one.

"Security examines each vehicle going to the pad area closely, but I've discovered an old service tunnel that isn't used anymore. It goes past both perimeters."

The man took a deep breath. "You can't just walk in and hijack the lifter. The pilot can tell the control center something is wrong in so many ways that you'd never notice. The weapons need to go into bags. They're stored in the cabin. Once the lifter docks on the station, you can take action. Not before. You have to pretend to be the real crew until then."

Nathan could work with that. "How will you get us into the spaceport?"

"Through the employee entrance. I brought paperwork for you. There's a bus outside. You're new hires, already vetted by me. Once I get you in, you have to pay me off. They'll know I helped you in."

"Of course. You'll get everything you're owed and more. Get my team where it needs to go, and I'll make the call."

The bus ride was stressful, but the paperwork got a dozen of his men past the guards. The spy drove them to a run-down area of the spaceport and stopped beside a decrepit warehouse. They made their way inside.

The man gestured toward concrete steps leading down into the darkness. "The stairs go to an old access tunnel. It exits in a building much like this one." He handed Nathan a hand-drawn map. "Go west several blocks from the exit, and you'll find the main thoroughfare. A bus with people is going past there in half an hour on the way to pad one. The pad crew won't check ID."

"Is that all I need to know?" Nathan asked.

"Yes."

Nathan smiled. "Excellent." He drew his knife and stabbed the idiot in the throat. He wiped the blade on the man's jacket and sheathed it as the fool writhed on the floor, drowning in his own blood. "Say hello to all the other suckers when you get to hell."

His team fell in behind him as they made their way into the tunnel. It was nasty but not as bad as the jungle had been. Rats and roaches he could handle.

With the security lockdown, there weren't any people wandering around the area where the tunnel led. His people were able to find the target road without any problem. They set up an ambush and waited. If this really was the last flight of the night, he couldn't afford to miss it.

He heard the bus coming about the time he expected and stepped out into the road. He held up his hand with authority as it turned the corner.

It slowed to a stop, and the driver stared at him in confusion. "We already passed the screening zone. What now?"

Nathan aimed his pistol at the man and grinned. "Now you raise your hands. If you reach for that radio, I'll shoot you dead."

That got everyone in a terrified but cooperative mood. His men rushed the bus and started pulling people off. The driver and twelve passengers. They herded them back to the warehouse and returned alone. His father's people wouldn't find the bodies until long after this was over.

They drove to the pad and parked. Nathan pointed to one of his men.

"Drive the bus to a different area and go back out the way we came. Tell the rest of the men to head back to the US. You're done here."

The preparation crew didn't realize anything was wrong and got them all fitted into spacesuits. They helpfully loaded the bags laden with weapons and explosives into the lifter and strapped his men down.

One of the pilots—a woman—turned toward them. "Welcome aboard. We're the last personnel flight to Liberty Station. They must've saved the best for last. We'll launch in ten minutes and dock in four hours. Sit back and relax."

Nathan did exactly that after launch. He fell asleep. All this flying around was catching up with him.

He woke when the lifter was settling into its dock with a thump. The pilot again turned and held up a hand. "No moving around until you have an escort, unless you're zero-G certified. Welcome to Liberty Station."

The weapons were just a few feet away, so Nathan unbuckled and pushed himself toward them. He missed by a wider margin than he'd imagined possible and hit hard.

"Sir? Are you okay?" the pilot asked. "You need to stay still."

Nathan opened the door and grabbed one of the bags. It didn't matter which. They all had weapons. He pulled a pistol from inside and surprised the pilot with it just as she got to him.

"Don't move," he said. "You at the controls. Touch anything and she dies now, and you'll be right behind her."

It only took them a moment to subdue the pilots, remove their helmets, and tie them to chairs in the passenger compartment. Their escorts opened the airlock just as they finished. They took one look inside and fled. Several of his men fired at them and missed. No matter.

"Two of you stay here and keep our ride secure. The rest of you, bring our gear. It's time for some payback."

29

"Harry! Wake up!"

He woke abruptly and blinked at Jess. She was standing over his bed. "What?"

"We're under attack!"

That got him moving. He threw the covers back and grabbed a fresh set of coveralls from his closet. He briefly thanked God that he didn't sleep in the raw. "Tell me."

"Someone hijacked a lifter," Jess said, her hands gripped into a ball in front of her. "It has to be your brother. He's here."

He put his shoes on and grabbed a pistol belt out of the lowest drawer. "What's he doing?"

"We don't know. The captain called me. One of the pilots was talking with them, and they heard enough to realize what was going on before he cut off. They shot at men inside the ship."

Harry slid a pistol into the holster and grabbed his extra magazines. "Do we know where they are?" He grabbed a backup pistol and clipped the holster to the rear of his belt.

"In the spine. Maybe he's after the reactor."

"Can they take it?" He headed for the door. Time to wake his team.

Jess followed along behind him. "No. It would take days to cool off enough to remove. But he likes blowing things up. He could destroy the ship if he wanted to. One bomb would turn it into a radioactive wreck."

Sandra was just down the corridor, so he pounded on her door. He explained the situation in a few words as soon as she opened it.

The sniper cursed and headed for her bedroom. She'd gather the rest of the team.

He focused on Jess. "What about security? Surely this ship has people trained to defend it."

She wrung her hands. "I don't think they ever expected someone to get an armed group on the ship. The command team is on the emergency bridge. Nathan has to go right past it to get to the reactor room."

"I need to talk to them right now."

Jess took him into her quarters and picked up a regular-looking phone from a holder beside the couch. She dialed a number and handed it to him.

He heard it ring once before it picked up. "We're a little busy, Jess." It was Captain Lee.

"This is Harry Rogers, Captain. I need your security team to gather at Jess's room with everything they have."

"That won't be much. Tasers only. We never expected an armed incursion like this. Since the pilot reported a full load of passengers, there must be a dozen of them. I don't know how many they left in the lifter, but we can't fight something like that easily."

"Where are they?" Harry asked as his people arrived at the door, heavily armed.

"They're in the main corridor heading toward the emergency bridge, reactor room, and engineering. I've ordered the other areas to evacuate and lock down, but these men can probably force the doors. I told the incoming cargo lifter to stay clear, and I'm rousing the other pilots now."

Harry decided not to wait for the security forces. Tasers wouldn't be of much use. "Send the pilots along with the security people. I assume you have a real weapon on the bridge. Try to hold them off for as long as you can. We're coming."

He looked at Jess after he hung up. "Take the remaining lifters, if you can. Get them away from the ship. Nathan isn't suicidal. If he has no ride home, he won't blow up the ship."

Once she nodded, he headed for the corridor. Sandra, Rex, and Jeremy were waiting. "Let's go end this once and for all."

* * *

NATHAN HELD BACK when they blew the locked hatch to the emergency bridge. A good thing, since someone inside opened fire and hit the first two men through the door. The next two spun out of control as soon as they opened fire. They must've hit the bastard, though. The firing stopped.

He looked in and saw more destruction and blood than he'd hoped for. He needed people with authority, and he needed them alive. This had seemed like the perfect place to look, since they'd marked it so prominently and it was on the way to the engineering spaces.

Three of the men in the room were floating uncontrolled and bloody. Some of the control panels were smoking, and the main screen was dark with a number of holes in it.

The captain of the station was easily identifiable with his silver oak leaves, but he wouldn't be useful. Dead men rarely were.

One of the others was similarly dead, one badly wounded. A fourth man had his hands up.

Nathan shot the wounded man. A mistake, as he spun out of control until someone grabbed him.

Once he'd righted himself, he glared at the remaining crewman. "You've made things harder than they needed to be. Where's the reactor you stole?"

"In the reactor room," the man said, obviously terrified. His name tag gave Nathan a name.

"Williams, you'll want to be more specific than that if you want to live. Where's the room?"

"Aft of here on the main corridor."

"Good. Bring him," he said to one of his men.

The captain's aim had been good. The two men he shot were dead. Nathan's incursion party was down to eight.

Two of his men struggled to move the prisoner slowly through the zero gravity. All of them struggled, truthfully.

The reactor room was clearly marked. Nathan pointed his pistol at the man's head. "Open it."

Williams held his palm over the plate beside the door, and the hatch slid open. Expecting more gunfire, Nathan sent his men in first.

The room was unoccupied. "Where is the crew that belongs here?" Nathan demanded.

"The captain ordered them to run."

Nathan grunted. Effective and inconvenient. He didn't know anything about nuclear reactors, but this one looked like it was operating. That couldn't be good for his plan to steal it back.

"What is the status of the reactor?"

"They brought it online last night," the prisoner said.

No, stealing it back wasn't an option. There were probably more of them than he had bullets too. Eventually, they'd overpower him and his men. Mother wasn't going to be happy.

He shot Williams in the head, making sure to grab something as a brace first. The blood spatter in zero-G was impressive.

"Plant the explosives."

* * *

JESS RALLIED the security people and led them into one of the spokes. It let out into the main corridor of the spine, which was a dangerous place, but there were access panels leading to some of the maintenance crawl spaces. They were tight, but safe, methods of getting close to the docking arms.

She'd sent pilots to get the craft on the opposite arm free. Several others remained with her party to get the rest, if they could. A dozen meters of vacuum was as good as being on the other side of the planet.

Jess had brought her pistol and was steeling herself to the probability she'd need to use it. Those bastards had hostages. Of course, if she did, the lifter would almost certainly lose pressure. They'd need to act fast.

Once they were close to the compromised docking bay, she peered out from an access panel. The airlock to the hijacked lifter was open, and no one was in sight. There were several crates secured to the deck. They'd provide a little cover once the security team exited the crawl space.

She turned to the man behind her. "Spread out once I go in. I won't lie. Some of us will probably get shot, but we can't let them have a way off this ship or everyone dies."

He nodded grimly. "We're behind you."

Jess looked at the pilots. "You get the other lifters clear." She floated to the crates. She'd only just arrived when a man came out from the lifter's airlock. The security man pulled the access panel closed behind her while the intruder was looking up the arm.

The mercenary scanned the compartment and floated there, blocking her way into the lifter. If he stayed, there was no possibility of getting in quietly. She'd have to shoot him, and that would warn any of his compatriots still inside.

She quietly took one of the bullets from her spare magazine, estimated the angle she'd have to toss it to hit near the arm, and gave it a light push.

The bullet floated slowly enough that it didn't grab the eye. It bounced off the bulkhead beside the arm. The sound of metal on metal got the guy's attention. He made a clumsy jump to one of the crates close to the airlock and peered around it.

Jess pushed off and sailed across the docking bay toward the airlock. She hoped she didn't have to shoot him, because that would send her tumbling in some unexpected direction.

She touched down beside the lock as softly as she could and slipped inside. He wouldn't be able to see her if he looked back now. This was the time to act.

"Everything okay, Zack?"

Jess guessed which direction that voice had come from and slapped the airlock controls. The hatch behind her slid shut and locked. That gave the guy some warning, but he wasn't expecting her to come out shooting.

Because it was insane. Her first shot missed him, and he opened fire on her. The loud whistling sound told her that she'd probably shot one of the viewports up front. If it failed catastrophically, she'd die quickly and horribly.

His bullets tore into the side of the lifter. Some of the ricochets must've went back into the cabin because someone screamed.

Jess jumped for the first seat and shot the mercenary center mass. He grunted and fired until his weapon ran out. Jess bounced off the bulkhead, grabbed a pipe, and shot the man until he stopped moving.

The sound of leaking air came from all around her. Someone was pounding on the airlock. Probably the other mercenary.

One of the pilots slumped in the acceleration couch they'd tied him to while the other struggled to free herself. "He's hit. We need to get out of here and give him first aid."

She untied the woman. "I'll look at him. Disengage the docking clamps, and get us away from the ship."

"We're leaking air, and one of the ports is cracked. You don't have a suit. If it blows, you're dead."

"I'll make do. Hurry."

Jess examined the pilot's wounds while the woman put her helmet on and climbed into the cockpit. The man was in bad shape. Really bad. She had to get him out of his suit to treat him, and that meant the dropping atmospheric pressure would kill him. A no-win scenario.

"We're free," the pilot said. "The cargo lifter is holding position just ahead of us. We're at 60 percent pressure and falling fast. You don't have more than a couple of minutes."

Jess racked her brain for a plan.

* * *

HARRY FOUND someone to lead them to the reactor room. Once he knew they could find it on their own, he sent the guide away. Speakers had begun a kind of hooting alarm. A recorded voice advised people to seek shelter in their quarters and prepare for possible decompression. He hoped that wasn't a reality.

Sandra got as close to the central corridor as she could and used a compact mirror to peer around the corner. "Four armed men in the hall, two looking in each direction. They're wearing pressure suits with the helmets hinged back. None of them is your brother. He must be inside the reactor room."

"I like those odds," Rex said. "We can pin the bastard down. Then we take him out."

"Without damaging the reactor?" Harry wasn't sure how that would work out. Still, he didn't have a better plan. "You sure you can shoot straight without gravity?"

The sniper grinned at him. "Oh yeah. That just means no drop. The trick will be dealing with the recoil. It also means the bastards will miss those critical first few shots."

Harry sighed. Time to act. "How do you want to do this?"

She readied her combat rifle. "You three hold onto me and the ladder. I'll pop up like a jack-in-the-box and let them have a piece of my mind."

It took a moment to figure out how to do that. "Go," he said.

The sniper raised herself and fired. Her whole body jerked back. The three of them kept her from flying loose. She fired again just as the enemy shot back with a fully automatic burst.

Sandra didn't flinch even though Harry heard bullets bouncing off the bulkheads. She fired twice more. "They're coming this way! Back up!"

They released her and retreated up the spoke until they found cover. Harry grabbed a pipe, aimed his pistol, and shot at the men pouring fire at them. It took a minute, but their limited experience in low gravity carried the day.

They cautiously went back toward the spine and looked out. He counted six bodies floating there. A noise from one of the other spokes drew his attention.

Two men were rushing down it. One of them looked like Nathan.

He sent the others to check the bodies. He didn't want someone to ambush them by playing possum. The enemy was dead or dying.

"The reactor room is clear," Rex said. "Of people anyway. I think they planted a booby trap."

"Jeremy, see what you can do."

"Let me tie off Rex's leg first," the security specialist said.

A glance back showed that the scout had taken a round.

"I've cut myself worse shaving," Rex said. "Get in there. I'll handle this."

Harry had no choice but to trust them to do their jobs. "Sandra, take that spoke and cut them off. We'll box them in between us."

Sandra dove down her spoke, and he headed for the one his brother had taken. A scream sounded from inside it. One that cut short abruptly.

He peered around the corner and saw one of the men was almost to the other end of the spoke, climbing down the ladder as fast as he could. A form was sprawled in the corridor below him.

The torus looked as though it was over his head, but he knew from experience that the perspective was false. If someone pushed themselves too hastily, they'd find themselves falling. One of the men had obviously missed that until it was too late.

He wished he could believe it was his brother, but that would be too lucky.

Harry took aim and fired at the fleeing man with slow deliberation. The Coriolis Effect screwed him up, and none of his shots found their mark. He hoped none of the bullets went all the way through the outer decks. If they had, someone would need to find them and patch the leaks.

His brother fired a salute back at him, grabbed the body, and dragged it out of sight.

Dammit.

30

Nathan stripped his man of ammo and explosives. If he couldn't get back to the lifter, they wouldn't make much of a difference, but he'd gotten out of worse predicaments in his life. He'd started toward the lifter but spotted several men with weapons waiting for him and reversed course. There was no way they'd make it to the lifter under fire with their lack of zero-G experience.

There weren't any convenient hostages where he was now, so he ran. The corridors all looked alike. They had to have escape pods of some kind in case of a serious emergency. Like, for example, a reactor explosion.

He was out of sight from the ladder when he heard someone jump down. Probably his asshole brother. He needed to lose him fast.

The corridor opened up into a wide area with trees and grass. If he hadn't been running for his life, he'd have gaped. Instead, he bolted across it and spotted a sign over a nearby side corridor that read Viewing Room. He didn't know if that also held a way out, but he'd try it.

Nathan bolted down the featureless corridor and up the stairs. He stared at the space station rotating over his head for a moment. It was a lot bigger than he'd expected.

There wasn't any time for this. He started looking for escape pods. There were many access panels, but none of them was large enough for a person.

"Throw down the weapons."

He looked back the way he'd come, and there his brother stood, hiding behind the hatch with his pistol aimed and ready.

Nathan sighed and dropped the rifle. "Well, it seems as though you have me."

"Kick it over. Hands on your head and keep them there."

A light kick sent the rifle about halfway to the hatch. His brother gave him the stink eye but came in slowly. He was ready to shoot, but Nathan bet the weird rotation would make him miss. All he needed was one chance.

When Harry was almost to the rifle, Nathan threw himself aside. His brother fired and missed, giving Nathan enough time to get a grip on a grenade he'd had behind him and pull the ring.

"I'd stop right there unless you want to go up in a bright flash. Put the pistol down. Who's holding all the cards now, big brother?" Nathan gloated.

* * *

JESS TRIED to staunch the flow of blood, but the pilot stopped breathing. She closed her eyes for a moment and then headed for the cockpit. "He's gone. Can the other lifter dock with this one?"

The woman sighed. "Dammit. You don't have time for them to decide to trust us. There's an emergency suit in the airlock and enough air to put it on."

Jess climbed into the lock and shut the hatch. It didn't have an exterior viewport, but she could see into the ship. She knew when the shadows became as sharp as knives that the interior was in vacuum.

She opened the valve marked Emergency Air, and a reassuring hiss began. It didn't last long, but she wasn't as dizzy. The locker right next to the nozzle had suits that were exactly like the one she'd worn on the trip up.

It took her a few minutes to get one on and make sure the air was feeding correctly. She reversed the airflow and brought the airlock down to vacuum. Only then did she open the interior door.

The pilot looked over at her as she sat down. "The other pilots don't know if they can trust us, so we're all waiting for word from the station. The reserve watch officers are in the main control center. Apparently, there's still at least one hostile aboard, and they rigged the reactor with explosives."

"This week just keeps getting better," Jess said bitterly. "Can you turn us toward the station?"

She prayed as the lifter reoriented itself, and they began waiting.

* * *

HARRY CONSIDERED HIS OPTIONS. If he let Nathan out of this room, more people would die. Was he willing to let that happen?

No.

"If you let that go, you'll kill yourself," he said. "Your ego won't let you commit suicide."

"Then I'll have to trust fate." His brother tossed the grenade at Harry and dove away.

Harry threw himself forward, swatted the grenade back at Nathan, and rolled as he hit the deck. He looked away as it went off.

The blast smashed him into the wall and knocked many of the storage areas open. He grabbed for one as the clear ceiling gave way. The air chuffed out into space, dragging him with it, and he missed his grip.

Several hoods flew past him, and he managed to snag one. He quashed the panic threatening to overtake him and read the instructions. Seconds later, he had it on, and he was breathing canned, nasty, wonderful air.

Nathan was tumbling near him, struggling to get his helmet on. It looked as though they'd both be flying off into the darkness of space.

Well, screw that. Harry drew his backup pistol, lined up on his brother's head, and pulled the trigger.

Which sent him spinning wildly. He had no idea if he'd hit the asshole.

He watched helplessly as he tumbled past the spine and flew out into space.

* * *

JESS SAW the flash from the torus and gasped. "Something exploded! It wasn't the reactor."

The pilot leaned forward. "That looks like one of the observation bubbles. People watch the ship from the inner ones and space from the outer ones. I wonder why it blew."

Something flashed near the spine. Jess frowned. "That looked like a gun. Can we move closer?"

"So someone can shoot at us?"

"I doubt they'll be in any condition to use a weapon by the time we get there, but if that was a friend, we need to see if we can rescue them."

The pilot brought the lifter to life and moved in. "Based on the angle, they probably missed the spine. We'll circle around to the other side and see if we can spot them."

Jess scanned the darkness and spotted a series of shots. "There! Someone is shooting. Maybe they're trying to get back to the ship."

"We'll go slowly so they don't try to shoot us," the pilot said as she refined their course.

The lifter had radar, but that wasn't any use in finding a person in space. The pilot did three passes and spotted something on the last one. "There. That's a person."

Jess saw the tumbling body. She couldn't tell if it was male or female at this distance.

The pilot nudged the lifter around in front of the body. "Go open the outer airlock door. Use one of the lines to secure yourself. You don't want to get separated from the lifter."

"Got it." Jess grabbed one of the lines, made her way into the airlock, and secured herself. Then she opened the outer airlock door.

A man was spinning wildly about ten meters away. He was coming toward the airlock slowly.

"He's almost here," she said to the pilot.

"I'll catch him in the airlock. Don't let him hit your helmet. Hold him while you close the outer hatch. Pressurize and see if you can revive him."

"He's wearing some kind of hood. He might still be alive."

Jess grabbed the man's arm and stopped his rotation. It was a good thing she'd secured herself. She pulled him in, closed the exterior hatch, and started the air flowing.

Only then did she get him turned around. "Harry!"

He looked a little rough, but he was awake and smiling. The air pressure rose high enough that she could hear him. "I'm a big fan of your timing."

"Are you okay?" She scanned what she could see of him. His left leg had a large splotch of blood, but otherwise he seemed uninjured.

"I think I caught a piece of shrapnel, but I'll live. That beats what's happening to Nathan as we speak."

The pilot called over the radio. "How is he?"

"Hurt, but alive. We need to get him back on the ship."

"The docking bay is clear. I'm taking us in now. Stay there."

Jess returned her attention to Harry. "Your brother was with you?"

Harry nodded. "He blew out the observation bubble. We both went flying. I took a shot at him, but that worked out spectacularly badly. He was wearing a suit."

"Hopefully, he's flying off into space and dies a horrible death," she snarled. "We're heading back to the ship. I heard something about explosives."

"Nathan rigged the reactor. Jeremy and Rex are trying to disarm the charges. I need to get back there as soon as I can."

She couldn't see outside, but she felt the lifter dock.

"You can exit the airlock," the pilot said.

Jess opened the outer hatch and sagged in relief when the members of the security team were waiting for them. They'd captured the mercenary and tied him to a crate, where he glared at everyone.

Harry ripped off his hood. "Get me to the reactor room. And have someone tie that guy up and bring him along. We can guard him better there."

She grabbed Harry and shoved off down the arm. Perhaps a little faster than was wise, but she managed to keep them from bouncing off anything.

They made the corner and sailed past the bridge. The mercenaries had blown the hatch open, and she had a glimpse of blood inside. The thought of Captain Lee and the others being dead infuriated her. First Abel Valdez and now Lee. Two close friends. Would she ever stop losing people to these bastards?

There were several people gathered outside the reactor room. She used them to stop their forward momentum. "Sorry!"

Harry grabbed the handhold and rushed into the room. She followed, hoping desperately that he could save them all.

* * *

THE FIRST THING Harry saw when he came in was Jeremy working on a bomb. "Tell me you have this," he said as he came to rest beside the man.

"It's a tough one, boss," his security man said. "It's got all kinds of redundancy and antitampering features. The timer gives us less than five minutes, and this is only one of six."

That didn't sound good. "We need to evacuate the ship."

Jess shook her head. "Even with the escape pods, I don't know that we'll get everyone off."

"If the damned things didn't have motion sensors, we could get rid of them," Rex said.

"How does a motion sensor work in zero-G?" Jess asked. "It should've caused the bomb to detonate right away."

Jeremy stared at her for a moment and dug back into the bomb. "It has to be a dummy. We can move them."

Harry grabbed Jess's shoulder. "Where's the nearest escape pod?"

"Grab the bombs and follow me."

Sandra came in then. "All of the intruders are accounted for, except Nathan. One is alive and the rest dead. Where did your brother go?"

"Into space," Harry said. "Take charge of the prisoner."

He and the others took the six bombs and followed Jess to an elevator. It took them to the exterior level of the torus. A long row of escape-pod hatches was marked in red on the floor.

She flipped open a recessed control and opened the hatch. It slid sideways into the deck, revealing another hatch. This one also opened at her touch.

The escape pod looked like it could hold a couple of dozen people. Harry climbed in and secured the bombs to the walls. They had less than a minute to go.

He scrambled out. "Launch it."

Jess reached out, grabbed the prisoner, and yanked him over the opening. He fell in with a wail before Harry could react.

The blond engineer hit the controls, and both hatches slid shut. A thump vibrated the deck as the pod ejected.

"Why did you do that?" he asked softly.

Jess defiantly stuck her chin out. "That bastard helped kill my friends and tried to commit mass murder. He had it coming."

Harry couldn't disagree with her logic. "The people in Geneva probably wouldn't approve."

"Then let's not tell them."

The deck shuddered, almost knocking them off their feet. Harry hadn't expected to feel the explosion in the vacuum of space. The pod must've detonated fairly close to the station, or the blast was larger than he'd imagined.

He helped steady Jess. "We need to get a status on the ship. And to call my father and see what we do now. We've lost the command crew."

She nodded. "Let's get to the bridge."

It was located at the front of the ship. The room had six spacious consoles and a large screen. Two men and two women manned the controls. The gravity here was less than in the torus, only about Mars normal.

One of the women stood. "Mister Rogers. Miss Cook. I'm Lindsay Waller. Liberty Station's reserve pilot."

Harry gestured toward the screen. "Did the bombs go off? What's the condition of the ship?"

"The bombs exploded short of the atmosphere," the pilot said. "The ship is in good shape. The emergency bridge is wrecked, but other than the blown-out observation port, a lot of leaks to plug, the damaged lifter, and the two ejected escape pods, everything is fine."

Harry looked at Jess. "Two pods. We only used one." He returned his gaze to the pilot. "Who ejected on the second?"

She shrugged. "We've accounted for everyone. Maybe it was a malfunction?"

He cursed under his breath. "It never worked out that way in the movies, and it probably isn't true now. Dammit. My brother somehow survived me blowing him into space. He escaped."

31

Nathan stared out over the waves from the hatch of the escape pod and enjoyed the strong salty smell of the ocean. His idiot brother had almost killed him, but he'd overcome everything. Luck was his bitch. The bombs he'd planted should've already destroyed the station. Victory was his.

He hoped he wasn't too far from civilization. In any case, his sat phone should be able to get him a lift.

His mother answered after a few rings. "Nathan?"

"Alive and well, Mother. We couldn't retrieve the reactor, but I planted explosives on the space station. You should've seen it blow up by now."

"Something exploded in orbit, but the station is still there. Maybe you only damaged it. That could be good enough, I suppose. Where are you?"

"In the middle of some ocean. I can give you GPS coordinates. I need a pickup." He recited his location.

"I'll send someone," she said. "This war with your father is only starting. I want you back here as soon as possible."

She hung up without another word. Nathan climbed back into the escape pod. There had to be something to eat in here somewhere.

* * *

CLAYTON LISTENED to his son explain the events from orbit with a mixed sense of anger and relief. It could've been so much worse.

"I obviously failed in providing enough security," he said at last. "I needed a heavily armed cadre of troops there to protect the station."

His son shrugged. "It was hard to imagine this happening. What about the people who were supposed to be on that lifter?"

"Dead. We found them in an old warehouse. It had a tunnel right under the security cordon. I have people searching every building for more. We also found one of my executives with his throat cut. Probably the leak."

"That sucks," Harry said. "The engineer said the ship is fit to boost. We still have the reserve pilot. The captain and primary pilot died on the bridge."

Clayton shook his head. "That won't do. I'll find someone else who can learn to pilot the ship. Call your people. We have two lifters held in reserve. That's two dozen more security people. Have them pack whatever weapons you think you'll need. Hell, pack things you don't think you'll need. You should be prepared if anything like this happens again."

Jess leaned over Harry's shoulder. "We should've put weapons on the hull. It'll take us a few days to replace the panels in the observation room, but we can do that while in flight. I'd really like to break orbit as soon as possible."

Clayton couldn't agree more. "I have the lifters under heavy guard. No one will be using them without authorization. The only other ways into orbit are the spaceports in China and India. I'll warn both of them."

He checked his screen. "Let me make a few calls. We'll launch as soon as we can. Get things ready on your end." He terminated the connection.

That had been entirely too close for his comfort. He needed to get the ship on its way before something else went wrong. He picked up his phone and called his assistant.

* * *

TEN NERVE-RACKING HOURS LATER, the last two lifters docked with the station. Harry had spoken with his people on the ships, so he was certain there wouldn't be any trouble. He still had all four trained fighters on hand to welcome them. Armed to the teeth.

He relaxed when his people came out of the hatches. The addition of two dozen of his men and women took the edge off his anxiety. They'd keep one of these lifters to replace the damaged one. They'd already jettisoned it. The pilots that had just brought them up would go back down in the remaining one.

Harry knew one of the new pilot trainees. Lieutenant Colonel "Black Jack" McCarthy. The tall man floated out of the lifter with a huge grin. "Mama always wanted her boy to be an astronaut."

He pulled the pilot over to a crate and shook his hand. "We're glad to have you with us, Colonel. The crew will get your stuff into your new quarters while we break orbit. I don't want to give my mother or brother another chance to screw us up."

By the time they made it to the bridge, the departing lifter was undocking. The one that had been holding position was ready to reattach to the ship.

He introduced McCarthy to Waller. The two pilots immediately started talking shop.

While that was going on, Harry commandeered a station and called his father. It was night, but he knew he was waiting for them to get on their way.

Harry was surprised when he only got audio. "Is your screen broken?" he asked.

"I'm on my jet, but not in my office. Mexico might get a little warm for me once everyone discovers I've been building a spaceship. I have a little island nation that's considering electing me president for life. In exchange for a very substantial payment and jobs at the new spaceport I plan on building there, of course. It's recognized as a nation by the UN, so that might give me some cover."

"Are you expecting a lot of trouble?"

His father laughed. "Oh, hell yes. The UN will hold endless hearings. Every gasbag on the planet will call for my head on a platter and demand that I bring the ship back at once. The US government is going to have a conniption. Things will be very exciting. I'm sure that they'll attempt to nationalize all my holdings. That won't stop me, but the fight will be long and glorious."

"Good luck, then. Captain Waller tells me that we're about ready to break orbit."

"She's only the command pilot and, while competent at that task, has no leadership experience. I think you would be best suited to that role."

Harry stared at the display in confusion. "Me? I don't know the first thing about running this ship."

"And you don't need to. You know how to lead. The subject-matter experts can handle the details for you. Learn as you go, just like Colonel McCarthy. Right now, everyone needs a confident, steady hand at the helm. That's you.

"Miss Cook will be your second. She knows every aspect of Liberty Station. She can teach you about it while you show her how to be a leader."

He looked over at Jess. She was staring at some readouts on one of the other consoles. "I think she's already learning that. Fine. We'll break orbit in fifteen minutes or so."

"Allow me to wish you the very best of luck. Humanity is counting on you. I'll keep you up to speed on events here as they unfold."

Harry ended the call and walked over to Jess.

She looked up. "We're ready. Both lifters are docked, and the engines are uncovered and ready to fire."

"My father thinks I should assume command of the ship. What do you think?"

Jess beamed. "That's the best news I've heard all day."

"Then let me bring you down. He said you should be my second in command."

"Me? Is he smoking crack?"

Harry laughed. "Doubtful. He just thinks that you'd make a good counterbalance. You know the ship better than anyone else, and I've seen how decisive you can be."

"That wasn't me being decisive. That was me being impulsive. I'm not leadership material."

"And I'm not trained to run a spaceship. We'll both have to learn as we go. Are you ready?"

Jess took a deep breath. "Ready, Captain."

"Just Harry, please."

He returned to his console. "How can I speak to everyone on the ship?" he asked Waller.

She reached past him and tapped the controls. "Hit the green button to activate the speakers. Hit it again to close them."

He smiled at her. "Thanks. As I just told Miss Cook, my father has appointed me as the captain of Liberty Station. I'm sorry if that steps on your toes."

The woman held her hands up. "I'm a pilot, third in line for flying the ship. I have enough on my plate becoming the command pilot. You can gladly have the sleepless nights."

"Tell me that in a month."

He touched the button. A chime sounded from the speakers overhead. "Attention, everyone. This is Harry Rogers. You don't know me, but after the terrible events that took Captain Lee from us, I'm assuming command. Miss Jessica Cook will be my second."

Harry paused a moment to allow that to sink in. "We're going out to explore the solar system. There are many things that you don't know yet, but I'll be talking with all the section leaders as soon as possible. You deserve to know what we're looking for and what we hope to find.

"For the moment, just accept that this is the most exciting and important voyage of exploration humanity has ever undertaken, bar none. If we find what we hope to find, you'll be helping to free mankind to explore the universe.

"Think about that as we get under way. We're breaking orbit in ten minutes. Do whatever you need to do to get ready. Inform your supervisors if there's a problem. Rogers out."

He touched the button again to shut off the speakers. "Ten minutes, pilot."

She looked at her console. "Orbital mechanics being what they are, I can work with that. We'll start out slow and build thrust as we come into the best course. Just as a heads up, if you'd waited twenty minutes to say that, we'd have been on the wrong side of the planet and would've needed to wait."

Harry felt a little chagrined. "I've obviously watched too much television. Let me rephrase. When would be the optimal time to break orbit?"

She turned in her seat. "Just over fifteen minutes."

"Go with that."

"Aye, sir. Rotating the ship to bring the engines into the correct position for burn."

* * *

JESS WATCHED the countdown clock until it hit zero. She'd been in communication with Ray Proudfoot for the last five minutes, and everything was ready. Right on the mark, the engines began firing.

The fuel pellets dropped one at a time into the fusion chamber, and intense magnetic fields crushed them until they ignited. The thrust from each burst wasn't massive, but one after the other, they got the ship moving. The ship slowly began rising into a higher orbit. The consoles and seats rotated until they found a balance between the thrust and the centrifugal force.

They'd continue to burn for several passes around the Earth before they escaped its gravity. The fusion burn would be visible below. She wondered how long it would be before anyone noticed they were leaving.

* * *

THE RINGING PHONE woke Kathleen Bennett from a sound sleep. No one called her at night unless something was terribly wrong.

"Bennett," she said groggily.

"I'm sorry for waking you so late, ma'am," her assistant said. "Something serious has come up regarding the space station. It's leaving."

"What? Is it falling out of orbit?"

"No, ma'am. It has some kind of thruster that we couldn't see. It's firing now. The astronomer you paid to keep an eye on it feels certain that it's leaving Earth orbit. It's not a space station. It's a spaceship."

She sat bolt upright. "Is my son back?"

"Yes, ma'am. He arrived an hour ago and went to bed."

"Wake him. I want a full team in my office in twenty minutes."

Kathleen hung up and began dressing hurriedly. She didn't know how they'd missed this, but she knew what it meant. Her ex-husband was going to wherever that crashed ship had come from. She was certain of it.

She wouldn't let him steal a march on her. Somehow, she needed to get in front of this.

* * *

JOSH QUEEN, the secretary of state for the United States of America, woke at the first ring of his phone.

"Yes?"

"I'm sorry to disturb you, sir. Something has happened." The man outlined the events in orbit.

Queen sat up and slowly nodded. "The president will need to know about this first thing. Contact the owners of this station and demand to know what they think they're doing. I want details on my desk in an hour.

"And, Paul, don't let them push you around. This is a direct threat to the United States of America. I don't care who they think they are, no one secretly builds something like this in orbit around our planet. They might have nuclear weapons. They'll answer to us directly or suffer the consequences."

He rose, looked at the clock, and started getting dressed. Today would be long and difficult. At best, someone had built an unauthorized spaceship, duping the American government. At worst, they were threatening the stability of the greatest nation on earth.

He couldn't allow that to stand.

* * *

WANT to get updates from Terry about new books and other general nonsense going on in his life? He promises there will be cats. Go to TerryMixon.com/Mailing-List and sign up.

DID YOU ENJOY THIS BOOK? Please leave a review on Amazon. It only takes a minute to dash off a few words and that kind of thing helps Terry make a living as a writer and gets you new books faster.

WANT the next book in this series? Grab *Freedom Express* today or buy any of Terry's other books, which are listed on the next page.

VISIT TERRY's Patreon page to find out how to get cool rewards and an early look at what he's working on at Patreon.com/TerryMixon.

FREEDOM EXPRESS

BOOK TWO

Harry Rogers made it onto the first manned mission to Mars. Well, the first one since the unknown others hid their ship under that Mayan pyramid.

He hopes to find priceless relics of an ancient civilization. Too bad his diabolical family wants them, too.

The revelations threaten to set the world ablaze. Those who unlock the long-buried secrets first inherit the galaxy.

1

———

Harry Rogers watched the extinct comet grow slowly larger on *Liberty Station*'s main screen with something approaching awe. Not because they'd managed such a feat, but that he found himself somehow intimately involved with the project at all.

A week ago, he'd been in Italy, planning the rescue of a kidnapped child from her scumbag biological father. He hadn't even heard of *Liberty Station*, much less guessed that it wasn't an orbital hotel. If someone had told him it was humanity's first interplanetary spaceship, he'd have laughed his ass off.

Since then, he'd circled the globe to save a beautiful woman named Jess Cook and found out that aliens had once visited Earth and uplifted humans. At least that's what he and Jess thought had taken place.

Perhaps they'd figure out a few answers to their myriad questions on the unassuming mass of rock slowly rotating before them. The extinct comet had a designation, but he couldn't remember it. They'd taken to calling it the city of gold. Not in the literal sense, but in the hope they'd find treasure of a different sort there.

"What's our ETA to orbit, Lindsay?" he asked *Liberty Station*'s command pilot.

Lindsay Waller half-turned away from her console to face him. "We'll match speed in twenty-three minutes, Harry. No orbit, though. We'll be about a kilometer away from it."

"Thanks. I'm still getting used to this space-pirate thing."

Lindsay gave him a look of mild disapproval. "We're not space pirates, Harry. You're actually the commanding officer of this ship, believe it or not."

"Oh, I think he believes it," Jess Cook said as she walked in. "He just refuses to act like an adult about it."

"That's a base libel," he said with a tone of false dignity.

"No, it's not. It's slander. Libel is something in writing." Jess sat down at the engineering console. "The reactor is still working perfectly. I wanted to give it a thorough diagnostic since it's been almost a week. If something goes wrong, we'll have a long walk home. I have to say, they really designed it well. I think it's going to keep trucking longer than the ship is rated for."

"I'll pass my compliments on to my mother, if she decides to chat before shooting at me next time we meet. I'm sure she'll be pleased. Maybe she can use that in the brochure."

They'd stolen the prototype nuclear reactor right out from under his scheming mother's nose. Slickly planned, he had to admit. It had been his father's idea, which caused him no small amount of annoyance. At least he'd had to redo the plan to make it work. That was something.

Still, Jess had a point. It wasn't as if they had any spare parts. It would be a lot better to spot a problem before something broke.

"What about the alien power supply?" he asked. "Could we use it?"

The crashed ship they'd found near the Mayan pyramid had still been turned on. Jess—against all common sense—had taken the blue cube that powered it before they fled his murderous brother, Nathan.

Well, he supposed it hadn't been such a bad idea. The asshole had stolen the ship.

It annoyed Harry to no end that Nathan had escaped *Liberty Station*. At least they'd gotten rid of the bombs he'd left behind.

Jess shook her head. "I've been examining it in the lab, but it's still holding tight to its mysteries. Without the cradle it came from, I'm not seeing how it transmits energy. Of course, the reverse will hopefully be true for your mother. That crashed ship won't tell her how the cube generated power. Even if she manages to cram a reactor into its hull, it still won't fly."

"That's not an assumption we can safely make. Eventually, she'll strip the drives out of that thing and mate them with another of these nuclear reactors. Then she'll come after us."

Jess looked unconvinced. "She's in a lot of trouble. The police are looking into her dead chief of security and his hobby of torturing and killing people. And then there's the aftermath of your raid on her lab in Paris. You blew up the building where she made the reactor. No, she won't be after us anytime soon."

He admired her somewhat naive optimism. In fact, he liked a great many things about the plucky woman. But, history had taught him never to count on his enemies doing what he wanted. After all, they were the enemy.

* * *

KATHLEEN BENNETT STALKED into the secret laboratory she kept for special projects. It was still in Chicago, but it wasn't on the BenCorp campus. She'd buried it so deep under layers of deception that she doubted anyone would ever connect it to her. With all the ruckus, that turned out to be a blessing.

She'd put in a full day at the office, dealing with the police and the FBI. It had been infuriating and exhausting. Now it was late evening, and she could finally focus on this.

The vessel carrying the crashed alien ship had arrived last night, and as much as she'd wanted to see what all her blood and treasure had paid for, she needed to allow the scientists time to unload it and make an initial assessment.

Her mood couldn't possibly be worse, and she had to remind herself that she needed to exercise restraint. No ripping people's heads off—no matter how royally they deserved it.

One of the subjects of her ire was watching the wrecked ship from an enclosed office above the lab floor. She came here to get briefings from her senior science staff. The last person she wanted to see there today was her son.

"Nathan," she said coolly. "I thought you were working on other matters."

He turned away from the glass and smiled. She could see his father in his eyes. That didn't improve her mood one bit. Clayton was on her shit list too. In fact, she'd cheerfully exterminate all males in the bloodline.

"Mother, you're looking radiant today." His tone held a hint of mockery just under the surface. He just couldn't help himself. All her restraint vanished in an instant.

"You let that damned space station get away and lost every single member of your newest team in the process," she said harshly. "I told you that I didn't want to see your face, yet here you are, testing the limits of my patience. Aren't you supposed to be figuring out how to kill your father?"

Nathan shrugged indifferently. "Things are too hot in that corner of the world. Not only is his security on high alert, but the US Navy surrounded his new island getaway with a carrier battle group. The only flight allowed in was for some UN bigwig.

"So, I decided to come back here and see how this situation has developed. If I can't kill my father, I'd like to make some gains on figuring out how to kill my brother."

As much as she wanted to disagree with his assessment, he'd hit all the high points. Oh, except for the police still crawling all over her campus. Thankfully, her lawyers had stymied their desire to search every building. What did they expect? That her dead chief of security had hidden even more bodies in them? Probably.

As if the seventeen they'd already dug up in the woods around his house weren't enough.

And those bodies had brought in the FBI, which was another entirely unwelcome experience. Those bastards had been trying to get access to her secrets for decades. Now they thought they had carte blanche to do as they pleased.

Her legal eagles had been less successful on that front, but they'd kept the nosey bastards out of the most sensitive areas by having a friendly judge quash the overly broad subpoenas on national security grounds. Thankfully, they didn't even know they needed to look in this building.

If they had any idea what she had hidden here, they'd go absolutely apeshit. A real-life Area 51. Complete with a spaceship. One that had supposedly crashed when the Mayans were a going concern.

Oh yes. The FBI would lock everything down and shuffle them all off to some secret prison if they had even the slightest suspicion of what she possessed.

Kathleen stepped up beside her son and stared down at the wreck. At one time, it must've been fairly sleek, in a boxy sort of way. It looked like a cargo container with wings.

"And what have you found out since you've been here?"

"Your people are still taking pictures of the inside. Father and Harry didn't get anything useful from it, though. The engineers think they've found where the battery would've gone. It's missing, so the thing is an expensive paperweight."

She shook her head. "Sometimes I despair. What makes you think your brother didn't take it? He had the opportunity. Or better yet, the woman you failed to kidnap for me. Twice. No, three times. We mustn't forget your magnificent foray onto their spaceship. I'm sure she was there somewhere."

"I'm sure because I saw their lab. We took everything in it. And I only had her in my sights twice. She's proven to be unexpectedly resourceful."

"So I've heard. How's your rear healing up?"

The one bright spot in this was that she'd never tire of reminding her son that an untrained woman had shot him in the ass. That never got old.

His gaze narrowed. "It's healing well, thank you. As I said, she's a lot more than your scant intelligence briefing indicated. And now she's as far out of our reach as if she'd gone to another planet. Almost literally, in fact."

It annoyed her no end that her husband had built a spaceship right under her nose. One that had once belonged to her. Dammit.

Leaving aside the fact that she'd milked the government dry on "cost overruns" and "falling behind schedule," she'd sold the subpar skeleton to the Russians. They'd passed it on to her damned ex-husband.

She'd caught wind of his plan to make it into a space hotel. He'd rambled on about that pie-in-the-sky vision while they'd still been a couple. Idiocy, she'd called it. She'd told herself that he was welcome to waste his money on it when she'd uncovered his purchase.

Her spies hung around the orbital construction site long enough to make sure that was what he was really building before moving on to other parts of his business. She needed to know about projects that mattered, after all.

That had been a mistake. By the time she'd realized that Clayton was building a spaceship, he'd already stolen her nuclear reactor prototype and smuggled it up to orbit. Him and her oldest son, Harry. Nathan failed to stop them, and it had left Earth on what certainly looked like a quick trip to Mars.

Once, she'd have been unimpressed, but the ship on the floor below highlighted her folly. They were looking for more technology. The aliens might have gone elsewhere in the system. Perhaps there was an undiscovered base waiting on Mars.

Something they'd found had clued them in to a specific location. Probably the damned book.

That was the one useful thing Nathan had recovered from Clayton's hotel at the Yucatán Spaceport before he'd blown it up. Her experts had determined it bore marked similarity to something called the Voynich Manuscript. Only the unknown author had penned those papers five centuries after the Mayans had buried the spaceship.

There were scanned pages of the manuscript all over the internet. Thankfully, since her ex-husband had bought the original. The damned thing was probably on the spaceship too. Yale University had traded it for a substantial endowment. As if they didn't make enough money already. Those places were a whole other kind of scam.

With her luck, there was some secret message written on them in an alien version of invisible ink.

Clayton had been ahead of her every step of the way. He'd played her like a sucker. Now she had to show him that he'd made a terrible mistake.

"I've been thinking about how we can capitalize on this situation before it becomes public knowledge," she said. "I have a new mission for you."

Nathan raised an eyebrow. "I do hope it's more fruitful than your most recent endeavors."

"Since it mostly relies on people other than you, I have some confidence it will succeed. Still, you have a part to play in this. My sources tell me that your lady friend made a stopover in Italy on the way to steal my reactor. Whatever she was doing, it got one of their local mob kingpins in trouble with the law. I want to know what she was after."

"Why don't you have your local contacts find out?"

She wondered how she could've failed so badly in raising him. "Because I don't want even more people to know what we're doing, idiot. I'm always looking to keep my secrets more tightly concealed. Stop pissing me off and get moving."

* * *

JOSH QUEEN, the secretary of state for the United States of America, stepped out of his plane and onto the island of Nauru.

The bright sunlight came from high overhead, baking the tarmac. He recognized at a glance that the man he'd come to see hadn't bothered to come in person. That made him boil on the inside, but he kept his face pleasant. It wouldn't do to tip his hand too early.

As it was, it had taken him almost a week to arrange a meeting with the old bastard. After the farce of an election the islanders had held, naming Clayton Rogers president, he'd told the US Navy to bugger off when they'd tried to isolate him. And he'd gotten the UN to back him.

Only the United Nations General Assembly, to be sure, but that carried weight with the public. Especially since the United Nations Security Council had been nothing more than a deadlocked joke for decades. The US, Russia, and China never agreed on anything anymore.

The other permanent members were a bunch of clucking chickens. Little more than noise. France would collapse any day now, overrun by Islamic fanatics.

That was the correct title for them, even though the US refused to call them that. Great Britain was under a state of siege. At this point, it was a fifty-fifty guess on who would blow up the Channel Tunnel first: the terrorists or the British government. He personally had money on the terrorists.

And why was Russia still even a member? After their economy collapsed again, they couldn't even feed themselves. Their military was so weak that Iran pushed them around.

As for the nonpermanent members of the council, who cared?

China, on the other hand, was a real military power. It was arguably stronger than the US at this point, though the Americans would never admit it. Unfortunately, both of them knew how the cards were stacked. US might was shrinking as they fell under the economic thrall of the Asian bastards.

The small delegation awaiting him seemed to be a mix of islanders and Rogers's executives. One of the latter stepped forward and extended his hand. "Mister Secretary. Welcome to Nauru. I'm Jacob Thomas, vice president of island operations. The president sends his regrets, but he was unable to put off a very important meeting."

Screw it.

"Well, that's refreshingly blunt and as insulting as hell. Might I inquire who might be more important to meet than the secretary of state of the United States of America?"

If the man was intimidated, it didn't show. "A delegation from the United Nations led by the secretary general. He came to personally provide certification that the world government acknowledges the sovereignty of our nation."

The man was trying to piss him off. "As we both know, the United Nations isn't a government at all. And it certainly doesn't tell the US what to do. You've got a lot of balls talking trash like that when we have a task group waiting to come in and free these people from the economic slavery you're about to put them under. We won't stand for that."

"You won't? Interesting. I wonder what President Duan thinks about that?"

Queen narrowed his eyes. That could only be President Duan Xiaoying of China. "And what does she have to do with this?"

"She's graciously extended the protection of her navy over us while we get on our feet," the man said. "There's a task group of her ships on the way as we speak. I suspect she'd take a dim view of any unwarranted aggression after her government recognized Mister Rogers as the rightful president of this wonderful nation."

"Are you threatening my country?"

"I was just about to ask you the same thing."

Queen took a deep breath. It didn't matter who supported this little pissant of a country. He'd squash them like bugs if they didn't reverse course. And if China wanted to make an issue of this, perhaps it was time to bloody their noses too.

"I think I've heard as much of your posturing as I care to. If you'd like me to go back into my plane and leave, I can do that. At which point, I'll call the admiral in command of this carrier group and tell him to start operations. I bet the Chinese back down in the end. They certainly will if we're in control when they get here and you're all on your way to Guantánamo.

"So, stop pissing me off and take me to see your boss. Now."

2

Jess watched the extinct comet as *Liberty Station* settled into place beside it. It wasn't much to look at. The surface was dark enough to make it difficult to see, even from only a kilometer away. It filled an arc of sky fifty-three degrees across, so the lack of stars in that area was a lot more noticeable.

Maybe once the lifters got into place, their lights would make it more visible. Probably not, but you never knew.

Which was as good a reminder as she was going to get that she needed to head for the docking area, or her ride would leave without her.

Well, okay, they probably wouldn't. She was the executive officer, after all. They'd give her crap, though. Good-natured crap, but crap nonetheless. So, it was time to get a move on.

Harry had decided to send three lifters. One would make a series of close passes, using radar and lasers to map the surface. The second would watch the third land for samples and maintain an overwatch.

Colonel John McCarthy had used that term. He was on that second lifter to familiarize himself with flying it. Based on what Harry had described to her of his skills in a jet, he'd probably make a kickass small-craft pilot.

By chance, the pilot of her lifter was someone Jess knew. She'd met Brenda Alvarez on the unfortunate day that Nathan Bennett had tried to blow up *Liberty Station*. The woman's copilot had died while Jess tried in vain to save him.

Those terrible events had been less than a week ago, but the other woman seemed to be recovering. At least she put on a good face.

"Hey, Jess," she said from the pilot's cubby. "Remember this rock is just a little bitty thing. Don't get all excited and jump right off it."

While she didn't know how much gravity the comet had, the engineers had warned her that she could indeed jump right off the damned thing. Everyone exiting the lifter would have beacons and thrusters on their suits, just in case. They'd also stay linked by ropes as much as possible.

Jess was zero-G certified and more than capable of leading any part of this mission. She'd do her best to avoid any embarrassing blunders.

"Don't worry about me," she told the woman as she pulled herself up to the copilot's couch. She waved at the team of geologists that were already strapped into the passenger compartment. "What's the basic plan?"

"We let the comet rotate under us and get a good look before we go down. If we see something interesting, we call back to the ship and let Harry know. Then we approach slowly and explore. If we don't see anything unusual, we pick a likely spot and go down for samples. What are you expecting to find? Other than aliens."

Harry had told the entire crew what the stakes were on this mission. Everyone knew about the high-technology humans they'd discovered in Guatemala. They had the ship's communications array locked down so word of any finds didn't spread.

That hadn't stopped the news services on Earth from guessing what *Liberty Station* was doing. They were all over the map too. They focused on Mars for the most part, but some of the guesses were remarkably close.

The tabloids were the most amusing. Of course, aliens were high on their list of favored topics. Based on what they were speculating, you'd think Edgar Rice Burroughs was right about what was on the Red Planet. Maybe they should make a transmission in the clear calling the planet Barsoom to spin them up.

Of course, these days everyone knew that Mars was an uninhabitable, frozen wasteland with only a trace of atmosphere. That didn't stop the rags from publishing their drivel.

When she complained to Harry, he laughed and told her to look up the Flat Earth Society. Point taken.

No one back on Earth knew that they'd stopped at an extinct comet yet. Someone would figure it out before long. There were undoubtedly a lot of smart people watching them.

Based on some of the radio messages they'd received since their departure, not everyone was happy to see them on their way. The US had been first up, instructing them to turn their butts around and hustle back to orbit.

China and India had been right behind the US, warning *Liberty Station* away from Mars. None of the three nations had made any direct threats, but it was obvious none of them was happy with the new player in the space race. Which was kind of amusing, since the US had nothing to do with space anymore.

Harry had decided to leave dealing with the Earthlings to his father. A bit of a cop-out, in her opinion, but it certainly made their lives easier.

Once the various players figured out where they were, she knew the speculation would turn to asteroid mining. And they'd be right, as far as that went. The ship had three mining setups, but they wouldn't use any of them here.

The comet was on the fast track out of the inner system. They only had a few days before they needed to start slowing down for Mars orbit.

If they'd been able to mine something like this comet, the payoff would have been volatiles and organics. Water was an example of the former and carbon the latter. The scientists and engineers working for Humanity Unlimited—of which she and Harry were partners with his father—had developed several promising processes to extract those kinds of things. They could then create oxygen and fuel. Eventually, many other things.

They'd chosen to come here not for the mining potential, but because the comet had shown up in a map left by one of the space-traveling humans. That meant it might have something much more important than recoverable resources. Maybe the remains of a preexisting mining complex or even a base of some kind.

She felt optimistic. In space, any relics would still be in great shape.

Brenda turned to the team in the passenger compartment. "Helmets on, boys and girls. We just received permission to launch. Who wants to go on a field trip?"

Everyone said, "me!" and then laughed.

Jess locked her helmet down and made sure her straps were tight. This was going to be fun.

* * *

Clayton Rogers waited in his new office for the second official delegation of the day. As offices went, it was a bit small for his taste. And a bit plain, but time had been short. His moving company would soon see his old office packed and relocated.

Assuming the warplanes circling the island let them in.

The view of Nauru from his office window was less than inspiring. It had once been home to massive phosphorous strip mines, and the scars still showed. On the land and on the people.

The government buildings sat next to the airport, but he'd decided that he wanted to be inside the ring road. He needed to be at the heart of the island. So, he'd taken over an office in one of the mining buildings until they could construct a modern headquarters for Humanity Unlimited and Nauru.

There weren't many people on the island. Only about ten thousand. The country's GDP was less than $40 million American. That was a far cry from what each man and woman had earned back when outside corporations were stripping their island of its resources.

The natives were of Micronesian stock. An astounding number of them were obese, and almost half of the population had diabetes. That was one of the things he intended to fix.

With today's medical technology, there was no excuse for it. There were treatments that were more effective than insulin. They just cost money.

The cost to convince a majority of the major families to sell their sovereignty to him wasn't that much, really. Not compared to the amount he'd already spent.

Those few billion dollars had gained him not only an island to build a new spaceport that he completely controlled but also the protection of being a nation unto himself. Diplomatic immunity was very useful. Especially when the second most powerful nation on Earth was pissed at you.

The door to his office opened, and his assistant stuck his head in. "Secretary Queen is here to see you, Mister President."

"Send him in."

Clayton turned away from the work he kept planning outside the window behind his desk and faced the trouble walking in his door. He'd met Queen before at various government functions over the years. His people had a thick dossier on him, so Clayton had a good idea of what the man would do under certain stimuli.

He saw the welcome party at the airport had managed to wave a red cape in the man's face. Queen stormed into the office with steam almost literally rising from his ears. Good. Angry men made mistakes. Misjudged people. Missed things.

Queen stopped in front of the desk, glaring at Clayton. "Mister President."

The slight emphasis he put on Clayton's new title told him the man didn't think very much of it. That was fine. Neither did Clayton. It was a means to an end.

"Mister Secretary," Clayton said serenely. "Might I offer you some refreshment? Or even lunch? I see that the afternoon is upon us."

"I'd rather get this over with."

Clayton sent his man back out of the office and sat down behind his desk. "Then let's get to it."

A petty man would have put an uncomfortable chair in front of the desk to make a point of how unwelcome the other man was. Not Clayton. He put a luxurious and most comfortable seat there. The impression he wanted to send wasn't so overt.

He watched Queen sit. The man was somewhat surprised by the comfort of the chair when he'd expected something completely different. The people at the airport had made him unwelcome, but the seat sent the opposite message. Putting him even further off his game.

That didn't keep Queen quiet for long. "Let me start off by saying you have a lot of gall. You've been dodging me for almost a week. Five long days where I've only gotten more pissed off. That wasn't wise."

Clayton shrugged. "I had a number of pressing matters that had to be dealt with, Mister Secretary."

The younger man's expression soured. "So I heard. Do you really think China can protect you if the United States decides to act?"

The threats had come even sooner than Clayton had expected.

"Speaking bluntly, yes," Clayton said. "The United States isn't the military power it used to be. Your navy is a third the size it was thirty years ago. You've cut the army in half and virtually eliminated the marines. Your technological edge is a fond memory.

"Your allies are either fighting for their lives against Islamic extremists or circling the two of you to see what parts they can tear off if you start fighting. No, you don't dare challenge China directly."

He held up a finger before Queen could speak. "And before you trot out that threat of using force to unseat me, I think you'd best be warned that I have potent weapons on this island that would make that most painful."

Queen laughed. "China might be a threat, but you're not. I don't care what kind of high-tech weapons you have waiting, we can take you."

"If you chose to, yes, I'm sure you could. Unfortunately for you, my weapons are words and images. You see, I invited the press to come along with the UN delegation. Even as we speak, they're getting a tour of the island and seeing the damage that's been done here. And getting the complete rundown on how I'm going to help these poor people."

"What?"

Clayton smiled. "Public relations, man. Surely you've heard of it. Not only am I compensating every person on this island generously for the sale of a worthless rock, but each is also gaining a new career, should they want it, and the best health care money can buy. Some have chosen to relocate to other places, true, but most of the people have decided to stay.

"The reporters are getting the story on how their lives are being improved. Told by the very people themselves. They're quite happy with the arrangements, I assure you. Is that the image the United States wants to send the world? Of them crushing these people under their military heels?"

Queen sat back and gave Clayton a long look. "What kind of game are you playing?"

"The kind where I get to keep my marbles. Let's cut to the chase, Mister Secretary. You don't give a rat's ass about these people. We're both men of influence looking to protect what's ours, so I understand how you feel. People are a means to an end, much like money or power. What are you actually looking to change in this situation and why?"

The other man considered him for a while before he responded. "Very well. Your spaceship is of grave concern to my government. Leaving aside the fact that we authorized no such construction, my experts tell me that to move that quickly you'd need to have a substantially more powerful reactor than was allowed to be transported into orbit. You've used nuclear power for that ship's propulsion."

"I see," Clayton said. "Let's address that concern first then, shall we? Yes. *Liberty Station* has a true nuclear reactor. Not a large one, but not that pissant little thing the UN approved. So what? Space is brimming with deadly radiation. Where do you think the fuel for the reactor came from in the first place?"

"There are rules for a reason, Mister Rogers. If we allowed everyone to do as they pleased, it would be anarchy. There's an international treaty prohibiting nuclear power in space and shipping weapons of the same nature there. What's to say you haven't violated the latter rule if you scoff at the first?"

That nuclear power treaty was a fairly recent one, ratified only a decade ago. There had already been a treaty about the weapons but not reactors. It made the rules on weapons even clearer, though.

The major world players didn't want to expand their destructive arsenal into space. Something Clayton actually agreed with, though he was sure they would ignore it soon enough. If they hadn't already. So, perhaps it was more accurate to say that they didn't want to see their enemies with weapons of mass destruction in space.

"I'd offer you my word that I have not, but that seems unlikely to satisfy you," Clayton said. "And I'll thank you to use my title, Mister Secretary. Let's mind our p's and q's."

"I'm not here to be lectured by the likes of you, Rogers. I really couldn't care less about your tender sensibilities. I suggest you listen up. If you don't want your commercial empire seized, you'll pay close attention. Turn your ship around and bring it home. The UN will send up an inspection team and remove the illegal reactor. The fines will be heavy, I'm sure, but better than the alternative."

"And if I refuse?"

"Then I impound everything you own that isn't on this island."

"Go ahead. Make the call. I'll wait."

The other man blinked in surprise. "Excuse me? Have you lost your mind?"

Clayton smiled. "It might seem like it, but no. First, let's address that little reactor. I shipped it into space, guilty as charged.

"One problem. I'm not a signatory to that treaty. I was a private citizen at the time. And Nauru never signed it either, so I'm still in the clear on that."

Queen surged to his feet. "Don't even try to play games with me, Rogers. Mexico is a signatory, and your spaceport is in their territory."

"They had no idea what I intended. In any case, if you want to go after someone, shouldn't it be them, then?

"No, Mister Secretary, I don't think you'll be able to tag me with that. Especially since I asked the UN secretary general about the legalities of that treaty. The UN, it seems, concurs with my opinion."

"The UN is a building full of blowhards that couldn't tie their own shoes without taking a bribe," Queen sneered. "Is that what you did? Bribe them?"

Clayton leaned back in his seat. It creaked in a satisfying manner. "Bribery is such a harsh word. I prefer to think of it as a fee. A substantial one, I'll grant you, but just the price of doing business."

"Don't think the opinion of those corrupt bastards means one thing to me or the United States of America," Queen snarled. "You either comply with my instructions or you won't have a pot to piss in."

Clayton stood slowly. "That brings to mind the other work I've been doing over the last week. Perhaps you're curious why the Chinese are so friendly with me. They were initially quite angry about this entire situation. Now they've recognized my government and are coming to protect us from the 'imperialist dogs' of the US Navy. Quite the change, isn't it?"

That derailed Queen's train of thought. "You bribed them too? They can't stop us from seizing everything you or your companies own. Rainforest has many operations in the United States. That's going to hurt."

"True enough," Clayton admitted. "Only it won't be me you're hurting. I sold everything to the Chinese. Other than my now-flush bank accounts—which are in countries that won't play ball with the US, by the way—everything I own sits on this twenty-one-square-kilometer island. Except for *Liberty Station*, of course. And she's outside your jurisdiction too. Space is just the same as international waters, I believe."

Queen stood there with his mouth working, but no words came out.

"Now, Mister Secretary, I suggest you take some time to collect your thoughts and consult with your country. I believe that's the correct phrase, isn't it? We don't have to be enemies, but I'm not your whipping boy.

"I wasn't joking about the Chinese sending a naval task force. Nauru signed a defense pact with them a few days ago. And we're a lot closer to China than to the US. I think it would be in all our interests to take a deep breath and step back from the edge of this cliff."

Queen took a long, deep breath, just as Clayton had advised. "I see. This does change the complexity of the situation somewhat."

"It does," Clayton said amicably. "Rather than get angry, perhaps you'd allow my chef to prepare us something interesting. The people here have some amazing dishes. We can eat, and I'll tell you about what *Liberty Station* is up to and how it could be beneficial to the US. I'll give you a clue. Asteroid mining."

That part was true enough, if not the full story, and those sorts of things made the best red herrings. Queen would have his mind on all the complexities of asteroid mining and the incredible wealth in space. So much so that he wouldn't see the real mission the ship was carrying out.

Clayton allowed himself a smile. Diplomacy wasn't just for nations. And sometimes the biggest players weren't used to operating at their highest potential. Queen was a bully and a piker. By the time he realized there was anything more to the situation, it would be far, far too late for him to do anything about it.

3

"We're starting to get some surface scans back."

Harry looked up from the dinner he'd decided to eat at his console and examined the main screen. They had a rotating object with the same rough shape as the comet on display. Unlike the real one, the model was light gray and was only beginning to get some elevation shading.

He'd seen video from the surface. It was darker than the devil's armpit. Even with the lifter's lights playing over the surface, it still drank in the illumination.

Radar and laser rangefinders, on the other hand, were working just fine. The lasers got them precise elevations, and the radar penetrated the surface to look for things they couldn't see. Like any hidden bases or old mining shafts.

He'd been disappointed when he'd heard how shallow the initial readings would be. The radar wouldn't map the entire interior of the comet. Far from it. Still, this should be enough to find anything obvious or only marginally hidden.

"How long to map the entire surface?" he asked.

"A few hours," Lindsay said. "Though the spin will bring most of it into view in less than an hour. Then the lifter has to go hit the areas that aren't rotating the way we want."

A chime on his console drew his attention. It was Jess. He opened the channel.

"Talk to me, Liberty Five."

"I think these military names are silly. Who's spying on us up here? Can't you just call me Jess? It was good enough for Kirk and Spock."

"You're a civilian through and through. What can I do for you, Jess?"

"I just thought you'd like to know we've sunk a few test holes, and I have excellent news. This isn't an extinct comet after all. It's a dormant one."

"And the difference is?" he asked.

"The difference, my martial friend, is that under a few centimeters of hard surface, there are plenty of volatiles and organics. We'll have to take the samples back to the ship to get a breakdown."

"That's good news, but isn't this thing on its way out of the solar system?"

"That *is* a problem," she admitted. "It'll be past Mars before we could even set up shop. I figure we have roughly three more days before *Liberty Station* needs to start decelerating for Mars orbit. Then this comet just keeps rolling right out of the system. It's not going to be a source of fuel for us, but it makes for good science. There are plenty of similar specimens near Mars and Earth. What have you found?"

"That the surface of that thing isn't so conducive to seeing anything. We're mapping and looking for anomalies, but that might take a couple of hours."

Lindsay cleared her throat. "Good timing, Harry. We just spotted one of those aforementioned anomalies. It's almost on the other side of the comet from Jess's team."

"I heard that," Jess said. "What is it?"

"Some kind of surface structure, I think. The lines are too regular to be natural."

Harry grinned. "Jackpot! Jess, I'm going to grab a lifter and head that way. I'll pick you up."

"Roger, wilco, and all that. See you in a few minutes."

It took longer than a few minutes to get a team together. This time, he had Sandra Dean, Jeremy Gonzales, Leann Branson, and Rex Jamison from his special-operations team with him. They'd be on hand to deal with any trouble.

He also had Doctors Rachel Powell and Paulette Young. They were the restoration specialists his father had hired to preserve anything they found. They'd been working on the language the others had used.

The ship's chief engineer, Ray Proudfoot, had slipped in at the last second. Harry wasn't going to complain.

Their lifter detached from *Liberty Station* and made the trip in just a few minutes to where Jess was waiting. She boarded and strapped in next to him. Neither of them removed their helmets.

"Any more detail on what you've found?" she asked.

"Not really. The subsurface readings are a little cloudy. There might be an open area under the structure, but they can't be sure."

"Do you really think it's a base or mining facility?"

He shrugged. "I'm not going to prejudge. Whatever it is, we'll know in a few minutes."

The lifter made short work of circling the comet. Harry spotted the unnatural lines of the target as they were settling in and the lifters lights played over it.

It was a cross between a dome and a rectangular building. It wasn't very tall and had a number of flat triangular panels fitted together. Definitely artificial, and it looked intact.

"Holy shit," Jess whispered. "We've really found something."

"Looks like. All right, everyone. Listen up. We're treating this as a potentially hostile entry. Don't touch anything and be wary of booby traps. If someone opens fire on you, light them up. Clear?"

His team quickly confirmed it was.

"Do you really think we're going to get into a shootout on a comet that hasn't been visited in hundreds of years?" Jess asked.

"Not really, no." Harry unstrapped and held onto the back of his seat. "But if the unexpected happens, we'll be ready."

She sighed. "I suppose I can't blame you. Our luck with this hasn't been the best. Everyone, link up your lines. I don't want someone getting all excited and jumping off into deep space. That would be embarrassing for all of us. And be ready for any use of those pistols to send you flying. Use them only as a last resort and brace yourselves."

Jess was the resident expert on zero-G operations, so Harry deferred to her leadership in getting everyone out of the lifter. Frankly, he couldn't imagine anyone being up here. The others had abandoned this facility long ago.

Harry had seen pictures of the Apollo astronauts walking on the moon. This was nothing like that. The comet didn't have enough gravity to pull them down very well, so they used their suit's thrusters to behave as though they were working outside the ship in flight. Honestly, this was about the same.

The structure had an obvious entrance. Two of them, actually. A large one that certainly looked big enough to allow the crashed ship they'd found to pass through, and a smaller one that seemed suitable for people. Both doors were flat and rectangular, standing at ground level.

"We'll check out the personnel lock first," he said.

They floated over to it as a group. It was made of the same metal as the crashed ship. The wall panels seemed to be the same makeup as the comet's crust. He supposed they'd used local materials as much as possible.

The hatch was just like the one on the crashed ship, except it seemed geared to going down instead of sideways. He found the dimple where the key they'd found would fit. He pulled it carefully from a pouch at his waist. The chief engineer had attached a line to it for him, so even if he let it go, it would stay right there with him.

Harry slid the key into the lock until it clicked. The hatch came to life and slid down into the comet, revealing an airlock very similar to the one on the crashed ship.

"They still have power," Jess said. "That's a very good sign."

"Rex, you and Sandra take the lead," he said. "Cycle inside and call us back with a status. If for any reason you can't reach us, come back out."

"Copy that," his scout said. "Come on, Sandra. Time to make the donuts."

"Really?" Sandra asked. "That's what you have to say on an important occasion like this?" The sniper sounded disgusted.

"What would you like me to say?" Rex asked as he went into the lock. "This is one small step for man and that chick that came with him?"

"You're going to pay for that."

The two of them were still bickering as the airlock cycled. Since Harry could still hear them, he knew the building wasn't blocking their signals.

"Are they always like that?" Jess asked.

"You have no idea."

The two inside went silent, their bickering ending abruptly. That wasn't natural.

"You two okay?" he asked.

"Yeah," Sandra said. "The inside door is open now, and something unexpected happened. As soon as the airlock closed, something pulled us down to the floor. It feels like we have normal gravity in here. I'd have expected there to be air, but it's still reading as a vacuum."

"Holy cow," Jess said reverently. "Artificial gravity. Do you have any idea of the implications this has?"

"Not a clue," Harry admitted. "And it doesn't matter right now. We're exploring a potentially hostile area. We can celebrate once we're sure it's safe."

"It looks clear in here, Liberty Six," Rex said. "The personnel lock leads to a short corridor beside what looks like a hangar. There's a clear window looking into it. There's no ship there, but it's the right size for the one we found."

"Pity," Jess said. "It would've been nice to find one intact."

"True," Harry agreed. "Rex and Sandra, does it seem safe?"

"Come on in," Sandra said. "The water's fine."

"And you were giving me shit about my little speech?" Rex asked, starting the two of them off again.

Harry led the rest of them into the airlock and took the key with him. Honestly, that seemed like a crappy way to get into and out of things. There had to be something they didn't understand about opening these doors. Some kind of remote manner of accessing them.

A fine layer of dust covered everything in the interior of the building. It didn't show any footprints beside their own. The room on the other side of the glass did look like a hangar. Racks of containers and bins covered the wall beside the larger door. It reminded Harry of a garage.

They'd have to examine it at some point, but he was more interested in what else the building contained.

The short hallway ended at another door. This one had a button they could press. He mentally shrugged and pressed it.

The door slid open, revealing what certainly appeared to be an elevator. The panel beside the door had twelve buttons with alien characters beside them.

He recognized them as numerals from the book. The restoration specialists had been hard at work cracking the language used in the Voynich Manuscript and the book. They still had a ways to go, but some things were becoming clear, based on their last report.

"These are numbers, right?" he asked, just to be sure.

Paulette Young nodded. "We've figured that much out. They used a base-twelve system. That's going to be hard to get our heads around, but it's a more efficient system. Richer."

"So, the question now is, do we work our way down one level at a time or go for broke?"

Jess reached past him and pressed the button for level ten. "Let's live dangerously."

The doors slid closed with slow finality.

* * *

NATHAN BENNETT MADE his way through customs and looked for his driver. He spotted the man negligently leaning against a late-model black sedan and holding a sign with Nathan's name on it. Misspelled, of course.

The man barely moved when Nathan dropped his bag in front of him.

"Signor Bennett?" the man asked with a strong Italian accent.

"No, I'm Leo Tolstoy."

"Sorry, not your car."

Nathan counted slowly to ten. "Yes, I'm Bennett."

The man frowned. "Why didn't you say so?"

"Take my damned bag, and let's get going. I've been up for hours and have people to meet. And breakfast. I'm hungry."

Mother's private jet had taken him across the Atlantic quickly. It was just after eight in the morning here, though his body thought it was almost 1 AM.

"Of course." The man picked up Nathan's bag and negligently tossed it into the trunk. He didn't bother to open the door for his passenger. He'd better not expect much of a tip.

"Where to, signore?"

"Regina Coeli prison. I need to see a man."

The driver put the car in gear and pulled out of the airport. He seemed unconcerned as other drivers cut him off and, in two cases, almost smashed into the front of the car. Nathan had forgotten how insane Italian traffic was.

The driver's curses at the other maniacs seemed pro forma. As if he was required to yell at them, but his heart really wasn't in it.

"Who are you going to see, signore?" the man asked.

Nathan considered telling him to bugger off but decided it didn't matter.

"Alessio Romano."

The driver perked up a little. "The judge? Ah, now there, signore, is a story."

"Why don't you tell me? I like stories."

"Of course. The judge, he has friends that do bad things. He is very wealthy. Well, more like he *was* wealthy. He gave a lot of his money to his daughter."

"And this matters to me how?"

"Ah! Because he swore he did no such thing. He said some woman drugged him and made him give it up! And the police, they found drugs. The woman, she was there. Her voice was on a recording the police in Rome received where Romano confessed to drugging and raping women. Big scandal."

Nathan smiled. It was always gratifying to see someone else screw up worse than him. "Is that all?"

The driver shook his head. "No. The woman, he says she stole papers from him. Art."

That sounded odd. "What kind of art?"

"Manuscript pages. Like those in old books."

Nathan sat bolt upright. Those sounded suspiciously like what his mother had been griping about. "With strange writing no one can read and pictures of plants that don't exist?"

The man grinned. "Yes! Exactly! How did you know?"

"That's not important. How long until we get to the prison?"

"I will check." He pulled out his cell phone and called someone. They spoke briefly for a few moments before he hung up. "There is a problem."

Of course there was. "What kind of problem? Some kind of accident?"

"The judge, well, he has killed himself. Or someone who didn't want him talking made it look like it. But there is a positive side to this."

"I can't imagine what that would be."

The driver pulled to the side of the road and stopped. He turned in his seat before Nathan could say anything and pointed an automatic at him. He held the pistol in what looked like a competent manner.

"It's good for me that you can explain what those manuscript pages mean and who the woman was," the driver said, his accent much less noticeable now. "Alessio might have been a fat pig, but his death leaves a gap in our ranks. Someone will pay for that. What you need to worry about, Mister Bennett, is convincing me to start looking for someone else to bother. I suggest you do so promptly. I'd hate to have to shoot off parts of you to make you talk."

4

Queen sat in a fury as his plane headed back to Washington, DC. How dare that bastard speak like that to the United States of America? Preening and thinking himself invulnerable because the Chinese were running to help him. Rogers thought the US was whipped. That he'd sent them packing.

Well, that wasn't going to happen.

Oh, Queen would let it look as though he was backing down, but that was just for show. He needed time to plan a better attack strategy. The Chinese wouldn't risk nuclear war over Clayton Rogers. And they damned sure weren't taking over a multibillion-dollar company like Rainforest.

That was the first step, he decided. He'd call the regulators, and they'd freeze those accounts. There were laws about the ownership of American megacorporations. And if there weren't, Congress would quickly correct that deficiency. Let the Chinese scream.

Then he'd talk over this asteroid-mining scheme with his science advisers. It had to be a scam. He wanted to know who Rogers thought he was going to bilk. The only ones that robbed the American people were their own government.

The president—of America, not some Podunk little island—had instructed him to take the lead on this. Election season was just around the corner, and he didn't want this blowing up in his face. If things went well, he'd hinted that there was a very good possibility that he'd need a new vice president.

Of course, if things went poorly, Queen would become the fall guy.

Either way, no one could publicly thumb their noses at the US. Not the Chinese and not Clayton Rogers.

And if the talk about mining the asteroids was as lucrative as Rogers had bragged, the US was going to get its share of the pie. Queen hadn't missed that whole bit about space being international waters. Rogers thought that he could laugh off the taxes he owed on hundreds of billions of dollars.

That wasn't going to happen, either.

While the amended space treaty allowed for commercial mining, everyone knew that it meant under the auspices of a major government contract. No, it didn't spell that out, but private companies didn't do things in space. Not since that bloodsucking leech Kathleen Bennett had screwed the US space program and Congress had called her bluff.

The Chinese had to be thinking about that money. Otherwise, why cover for the old bastard? They wanted all those riches in space for themselves.

Queen was plugged into the intelligence services as well as any of the senior leaders in the US, and better than most. He knew the bastards were falling behind the Indians in their "race to Mars."

That had to gall them. Losing out to the people that owned every technical support line in the world.

Well, no matter what they had in mind, he'd figure out a way to play them against one another.

The one angle he didn't know how to corner was that ship. The US had given up on space. Hell, that ship was the skeleton of what was supposed to have been the next international space station. The US should've been a major player in that. And they would've been, if Bennett hadn't screwed them.

If only he could turn back time.

He sat up a bit straighter. Maybe he *could* turn back the clock. It was time for a side trip to Chicago.

A wide smile stole onto his face, and he reached for his phone. Time to make some people very, *very* unhappy.

* * *

JESS COULDN'T TELL how quickly the elevator was moving, but it took a while to get to the lowest floor. Long enough for everyone to grow more than a bit nervous. Her suit clock said that it took just over two minutes.

The doors slid open on a wonder. The elevator had stopped in the center of a spherical room that was at least a hundred meters across.

A short walkway led from the elevator to the craziest thing she'd ever seen. Stairs leading in six different directions. Machinery and other things covered the entire surface, whether that was over their heads or under their feet. Or off to the sides. It was all very disorienting. It was like one of those mind-bending paintings.

Harry led the way out, cautiously putting one foot in front of the other until he reached the junction of the stairs. Soft light came from nowhere but illuminated everything. It was all very natural. It looked like sunlight, or at least light made to be in the same frequencies.

"What the hell is this place?" Rex asked.

"A power center," Ray Proudfoot said. "I can see several of those glowing cubes."

While that might be part of it, Jess was certain there was more to the room. She spotted several clusters of control consoles similar to the ones on the crashed ship.

"I think this is the center of the comet," she said. "We took the elevator down until we were in the middle. They must be using artificial gravity to keep everything where it's supposed to be. That's probably how this works." She gestured at the odd stairs with the last sentence.

Jess stepped onto the hoop and started walking forward. Her orientation changed, but the gravity always seemed to be below her. In a few moments, she was standing with her head pointing toward the others' feet.

"Well," Sandra said. "That's creepy. How the hell could someone design something like that? It makes my brain hurt."

"The design seems pretty straightforward," Proudfoot said. "If you have artificial gravity. We could make a much more efficient layout inside *Liberty Station* if we had this kind of tech. It would mean we could fit a lot more people and cargo inside."

"Not without the crew staging a mutiny," Rex said. "This is messed up."

Jess had to agree with him. "In any case, if we'd designed *Liberty Station* with that kind of technology in mind, we could work around the human factor and have a much more efficient ship. That's true."

She started down the closest set of stairs. As above, a layer of dust covered everything. With the lights and gravity on, she wondered why there was no air. Surely, that had to be intentional.

By the time she reached the floor, she felt almost normal. Unless she allowed her eyes to follow the curve of the floor up. The rest of them came down behind her. At the floor level, the special-operations people stepped out front again.

"What do you want to look at first?" Sandra asked.

"The power unit ahead of us," Proudfoot said. "Now that I'm closer, I can see that the cube is bigger than the one you recovered, but I want to see by how much."

Quite a bit, it turned out. The cube from the crashed ship was only about ten centimeters along each edge. This one was more like sixty centimeters. She could only guess at how much power that represented. A lot.

The equipment seemed generally like what she remembered from the ship. So, these were probably some kind of distribution centers for the rest of the comet. Why did it need so much power?

"I found something," Sandra said.

Jess looked over at the other woman. She was peering past the power unit. It only took a few steps to join her.

Lying behind the unit was the desiccated body of a woman. She wore a gold jumpsuit with patches similar to what the man under the Mayan pyramid had on his shirt.

She lay sprawled on her back with her limbs twisted around her. The hilt of what was obviously a knife protruded from her chest.

* * *

NATHAN KEPT his hands still on his lap. "If this is a robbery, allow me to suggest that you've picked the wrong man."

The driver grinned. "Actually, you picked me, signore. And this is no robbery. We're going to take a trip, you and I. To see a very important man with many questions about the events you are investigating.

"I suggest you cooperate. If my employer is satisfied with your answers, you can go on your way. If not… well, let's just hope you're a smarter man than that."

Another sedan pulled up behind them, and two large men climbed out. Their demeanor and build suggested they were hired muscle.

"Get out of the car very slowly," the driver said. "My associates will search you for any weapons you might have slipped past the monitors at the airport. Once they do that, they'll put you back inside this car, and we will go see my employer. You're not going to give us any trouble, are you, Signor Bennett?"

"Do I look crazy?"

One of the goons opened the door and gestured for Nathan to climb out. His associate pulled his coat back enough for the holstered pistol to show. He rested his hand on his belt near it.

Nathan exited the vehicle slowly, keeping his hands in plain view. He stepped to the left, putting the goon nearest him between himself and the driver. The open door would also be an impediment to the man with the gun in his hand.

Then he struck, smashing his fist into the goon's face and ducking low under the return swing. His hand shot out, finding a gun on the man's belt right where his friend's was, and claiming the automatic for himself.

The other goon had his pistol out and was shouting something in Italian. Stupid. Nathan put two rounds into the man's head, eliminating the threat.

The live goon was quicker on the uptake than his friend. He slammed his fist down on Nathan's arm, sending the appropriated gun flying.

That hurt like hell, but Nathan didn't have time to bitch about it. He reached behind him with his uninjured hand and drew the knife he'd recovered from his carry-on luggage at the airport from its concealed sheath.

He heard the passenger door of the sedan open and knew the driver was coming to his compatriot's aid. He had to finish this quickly. A knife against a gun made for poor odds.

The goon was bigger than Nathan was but slower. Nathan could use that to his advantage. He lunged at the man's face, slashing for his eyes. That guaranteed a response. No one ignored an attack that might blind them.

When the man leaned away from the steel and brought his arms up to block, Nathan dropped to his knees, jammed the blade into the man's groin, and rotated the knife so that the man's insides became puree. The goon lost all interest in the fight and fell to the ground, trying to hold himself together.

That took the second man out of the fight but left the armed driver.

Nathan spotted his fallen pistol just off to his left, but going after it would expose him to the driver's fire.

"You are quite the fighter, Signor Bennett," the driver said. "But there are many other men on the way. You cannot win. Surrender now, and we can forget this ever happened."

Nathan grinned. "As if that's how mob justice works. You'll talk nice and then kill me slowly. I think I'll pass. Oh, if you'd asked my mother, she'd have told you that I'm both crazy and an idiot. Only the first is true."

He picked up a handy pebble on the roadside and tossed it toward the rear of the sedan as he crouched lower. The stone didn't make much noise, but the driver would be listening very closely for Nathan to make his move. It wouldn't fool him, but it would lead his eyes in the wrong direction for one critical moment.

Nathan sprang toward the front of the sedan, cocking his arm back and throwing his knife at the driver as soon as the man came into view. The man had turned just a little toward the rear of the car, as expected.

The bastard was good, though. He spotted Nathan right away and pivoted back while leaning to the side to dodge the thrown knife.

The man's movement and Nathan's somewhat awkward throw meant the blade sank into the driver's thigh instead of his gut, but that worked well enough.

Nathan hit the ground and rolled, snatching up his appropriated pistol and exchanging shots with the driver. His hit, the other man's didn't.

Less than thirty seconds after the three men sprang their ambush, the fight was over. Nathan climbed to his feet and kicked the driver's pistol away from his hand. The other man lay sprawled on the ground beside the front of the sedan, bleeding from half a dozen wounds.

The man gasped for air, already dying. "You are... quite... the fighter... Signor Bennett. That... will not... save you."

"We'll see who it saves," Nathan said. He raised the pistol and shot the man between his eyes.

A few steps brought him around to where the live goon was dragging himself toward his partner and that man's fallen gun. Another shot ended his pain too.

The road here wasn't the most active, but several cars had driven by. It was time to get out of the area before some idiot with a cell phone caught a picture of him.

He grabbed all the weapons and retrieved his knife. No telling what had fingerprints on it. He also took their wallets and phones. Something in them would lead him to people with the information he needed.

Nathan climbed behind the wheel of the sedan he'd been a passenger in and drove slowly away from the dead men. Well, at least this trip wouldn't be as boring as he'd expected.

5

Harry sent the special-operations team to search the rest of the level. Once they were gone, he stood beside Jess and stared at the woman who'd been dead for longer than his country had existed.

"This obviously happened a long time ago," he told Jess. "I suppose those bodies in the back of that spaceship didn't die in the crash. There was some kind of fighting."

The blonde engineer knelt beside the body. "I'm no forensics expert, but I agree this happened a long time ago. Maybe about the time our Mayan friends met the crashed man. Look at her shoulder. She has the same patch he did. That links them together."

The image on the patch was of a stylized tree surrounded by alien text. Now that he could get a decent look at it, Harry recognized it as an oak. The preservationists would need to decipher the text, if they hadn't already done so from Jess's picture.

"In the military, that would mean they were in the same unit or served aboard the same ship," he said. "She's not in a spacesuit, so there was atmosphere when the attack took place. One more mystery about these people."

He stood and looked around. "These people built to last, though. These machines have been operating for hundreds of years without anyone maintaining them. That says a lot about their skills in that arena."

Considering how the woman had died, perhaps that was a poor choice of words.

"Jess, you need to head up a team to explore this base quickly and recover as many things as you can. This hunk of rock and ice is on the fast track out of the inner system. We can't afford to dawdle."

She straightened and wiped her gloves on the outside of her suit. She hadn't even touched the dead woman, so it had to be an unconscious gesture.

"This comet is moving at roughly seventy kilometers per second. That means about ten days from Earth's orbit to Mars. We're damned lucky it was passing near Earth when we needed it to be, or everyone back home would know exactly what we're up to.

"We have three days max, if we use a lot of deceleration to break away from the comet. If we don't stop, that starts a lot of questions back on Earth. Is that really what we want to do?

"We can catch up to it at any time with *Liberty Station*'s drives. Though, I'll admit it won't be a quick trip by the time it reaches aphelion, the farthest point it gets from the sun. Our best guess is that its orbital period is about a thousand years."

"That makes sense," he said. "That would have it somewhere near Earth when that ship crashed near the Mayan pyramid. How long would it take to get to its farthest distance?"

"It'll continue to slow down until it's barely moving at the farthest point. Eris's orbit takes it anywhere from almost forty AU out to just short of one hundred. It passed aphelion in 1977 and is still pretty far out.

"Eris isn't the most distant object we know about, either. They've discovered a number of trans-Neptunian objects in the last few decades. V774104, for example. It's about half the size of Pluto and sits at 103 AU."

"What's an AU?" he asked.

"An astronomical unit. That's roughly the distance the Earth orbits the sun. 150 million kilometers. With the drives on this ship, we can catch up to it, if we have to. It might take months, or perhaps even years if we wait long enough, but the entire solar system is within reach of humanity now. Move over Kirk and Spock, we're coming."

Harry shook his head, amused in spite of himself. She was so geeky. What else could one expect from an orbital engineer?

"We'll make that call based on what we find," he said. "That's why you need to do an inventory as quickly as possible. At the very least, I want pictures of everything. Gather up any loose items in a central location so we can take them with us."

"You realize this is really a job for Doctor Crockett and his archaeological associates, right? And he's going to want to document everything. And I mean *everything*."

That was true. Clayton Rogers had sent Doctor Michael Crockett and his wife, Sierra, for just this kind of find. They and their tech wizard, Emily Adams, should be running the show.

"I'll have them sent over as soon as I get back to the ship," he said. "I need to have a conversation with my father about this as soon as possible."

"Is that safe? I know he can transmit whatever he wants to us from his satellites. No one can intercept outbound transmissions. NASA might have been able to at one time, but they abandoned all their robotic probes. Inbound transmissions are different, aren't they?"

"They are," he admitted. "He and I worked out a method so that I could give him a basic rundown even with other eyes and ears paying close attention."

Harry looked down at the woman's body. "I need to send the doctor over to remove any bodies too. We'll want to study them in the medical bay. They might have any number of unknown pathogens, so we have to treat them as hazardous. A long-lived virus that we don't have resistance to could exterminate life on Earth."

"Don't you think that's being a little overly dramatic? Wouldn't the Mayans have all died when they met the man from the crashed ship?"

"Do you want to take a chance? Look what happened with smallpox and the Native Americans. The Europeans were lucky it wasn't a two-way street. Think the black plague and then up the death toll by however many billion people we have on Earth."

That obviously gave her pause. She made a show of shuddering. "That's horrible. Okay, I'll ride herd on the Crocketts and make sure we sterilize everything. Do you think a thousand years in a vacuum is enough?"

"We can't count on it. Treat everything as if it were contaminated. We brought UV equipment. I'll send that over too. And I know this goes without saying, but be careful. This equipment is still operational. We don't want to start something we can't stop."

"What about computers? Shouldn't we recover any data we can?"

"I doubt our media is compatible. If you find any data storage devices, make sure to get readers that go with them. And I'm serious. Be careful. And don't stay up too late. It's only a few hours to midnight."

He left her to it and headed back toward the elevator. Once he was back on *Liberty Station*, he'd call his father. They were running the ship on Nauru time, so he'd get the pleasure of getting the old bastard out of bed.

* * *

CLAYTON WAS JUST GETTING ready for bed when his son called. He headed right back to his office. The communications lag was significant, so this would be short on back and forth, though he'd stay as long as he had to.

The initial message was solely so that he could be ready for the data dump. Coming in from space, there was no way *Liberty Station* could narrow the beam to the point they wouldn't have curious little ears listening in.

That meant they could be certain that the NSA, CIA, DIA, FSB, MSS, MI6, and every other intelligence agency on the planet would be working to crack the code.

And that didn't take people like his dear Kathleen into account. Any number of multinational companies would want to know what Humanity Unlimited was up to.

With that kind of attention, there was no way they could keep any normal transmission safe. It might take a while, but someone would crack the code, no matter how heavily encrypted it was.

So, they'd decided to use that to their advantage.

He brought up the video from Harry on his private screen. His son sat on the bridge of *Liberty Station*. The bottom right corner of the video had a time stamp running in it. That would prove key in deciphering the hidden message later.

They'd encrypted this message too, but only to levels consistent with the normally secretive operations that companies like his conducted. The NSA would crack it in short order.

"Dad, we're about halfway to Mars. Everything is working well. All ship's systems are in the green. We're anticipating deceleration in about seventy hours. That will put us in Mars orbit in five days.

"I'm including a stream of the ship's telemetry, so expect a transmission with the agreed upon cypher. I'll let you know more once we get closer to Mars. I have that flag you sent along ready to plant. That should piss Mom off.

"I'm not expecting a return transmission, so goodnight."

The video terminated.

Clayton smiled. The flag reference meant they'd found something interesting. Good.

He brought up the first and last frames of the transmission. The two time stamps together would determine which one-time pad this data dump would use.

One-time pads were an old-fashioned way of sending secure messages. They might be cracked, but it wouldn't help with any future messages because they'd never use the code again.

A stream of data began flowing in. They'd encrypted it as heavily as possible. Clayton ignored it. It was a red herring. The data was gibberish. Anyone clever enough to crack the key to it wouldn't be able to make sense of it. They'd waste an incredible amount of computer time on it.

The true hidden message was in the carrier wave of the transmission. To "hide" the messages, *Liberty Station* was transmitting on thousands of channels at the same time. Bursts here and there, all sending some kind of signal.

It wouldn't take the various spy agencies long to zero in on the one they wanted. They could then ignore the rest of the noise.

Only the noise was the message. They'd based the cypher on rapidly shifting channels and differing lengths of time on each one. And not just one channel at a time, but many. Once the computer peeled that data from the rest, the cypher would reorder them. They were useless in the wrong order. They'd also been coming in since the first message started.

Once the computers reordered the pieces of data, a one-time quantum cryptographic key would get to work on the packets. Only then would the message become clear.

It was as damned close to unbreakable as the best experts in the field could make it.

That didn't mean it was secure forever. Someone would eventually catch on to the hidden aspect of the transmissions and start putting it together. That might take years. Or decades.

The transmission went on long after the message was complete. Another way to confuse eavesdroppers.

He was relieved that it had worked, frankly. That would've just been his luck if he got a garbled, meaningless transmission after all that work.

Harry's face reappeared on the screen, this time without the timer.

"We rendezvoused with the comet right on schedule and scanned the surface. That's still going on, but we found an intact base with the power still on. It's sizable, so we need to make a decision. We only have three days to examine it before we break off for Mars. If we stay longer, people will start asking questions.

"But, if we leave, it will take a long time before we can come back. The orbital period on this comet is a thousand years. Almost all of that will be in the outer system. I'd suggest we leave a team to work on it, but they might be trapped here if something goes wrong. Even if everything went perfectly, it would take a long, long time to get to them once their work was complete."

He stared out of the screen at Clayton. "I'm inclined to go with that option, but I need to hear what you think before I make a decision."

He raised a finger. "And don't think you can tell me what to do, Mister Majority Shareholder. I'm the man on the scene, and I'll do what seems best. I just want to know what you think before Jess and I make the final decision.

"But, since you'll be dealing with the fallout if this goes public, you deserve to have a say. I've attached the initial video footage. Be warned, we found five bodies. We haven't searched the entire facility, so I expect that number to rise. They all died by violence, so something terrible happened out here about the time that ship crashed."

Harry leaned toward the camera. "No matter what you end up deciding, this find is the biggest thing that has ever happened to humanity. The technological knowledge it brings is incalculable. It looks as though you'll be making back all that money you've invested. Have fun counting it."

The transmission terminated abruptly.

His son had the worst expectations of him. With reason, admittedly. The money would be very welcome, and he'd enjoy counting it immensely. One of life's little pleasures.

That said, he had plans for what to do in space to free humanity from the bonds of Earth. If this sped them up or made the outcome more likely, that was worth far more to him than diving into a pool filled with money like Scrooge McDuck.

Clayton called his assistant and ordered food. He was going to be here long into the night watching the videos of the find again and again, making detailed notes for himself and for the teams on *Liberty Station*. Only once they'd discussed every aspect of what they'd found would he make a recommendation.

Hopefully, events here on Earth wouldn't distract him.

6

B eing somewhat paranoid, Nathan took the sedan to the nearest city and set it on fire. He'd already disposed of most of his luggage. He then slipped into a tourist group. Their bus became his transportation, and their hotel became his lodgings.

Of course, that meant he spent all day touring the city with his carry-on bag. It was now late in the evening, and he was exhausted.

The place wasn't upscale. They never even asked to see his passport. A little extra cash—of which he had a fair amount from the dead men—smoothed everything.

He made a side trip to the closest bar, where he pilfered a cell phone from a woman who'd drunk far more than she should have around cads like himself. He made a call to his newest team leader and ordered him to send men from their operation in France.

The idiot suggested there were closer people in Rome. While true, Nathan could be certain that any local muscle worth the name was part of the organized crime families. Not so helpful when those bastards wanted to put the hurt on one Nathan Bennett.

He scrubbed the call from the phone logs and put it back into the woman's purse. She'd be none the wiser come morning.

He slept with one eye open, as the saying went, but had no problems. He found his support team right where he'd ordered them to go after he had breakfast. He took the phone they'd brought for him and called his mother.

"What's this I'm hearing about some kind of gangland shooting?" she asked.

"Good morning to you too, Mother. I did sleep well. Thank you."

"Don't be an ass. Was that you?"

"Technically, it was them. It seems that woman you wanted stole some manuscript pages from the mobster. Based on what the man kidnapping me said, they sound like pages from the Voynich Manuscript."

His mother cursed. "How the devil did she even know they existed? From what I've read about the man, I doubt it was public knowledge. She certainly didn't have the contacts to be aware of them. Clayton, perhaps. What are the chances of getting more information from the man?"

"Which one? The jailed mobster killed by his associates to make sure he didn't tell any more tales or the kidnapper who died of his wounds in the gunfight?"

"Can you be involved in any project where you don't kill everyone?"

"Certainly. The spaceship project. Though, to be fair, that wasn't for lack of trying."

She sighed. "Well, now that you've got the police *and* the mob up in arms, what are you planning to do to get the information?"

"I've called in backup from Paris. We'll turn this around. Someone has copies of these documents. Pictures, perhaps. It's just a matter of finding them. I'll also touch base with the criminal element and make it clear to them that they chose their target poorly. If they have the documents, or a lead to them, I'll find it."

"Do try to keep the body count to a minimum. I don't need another Donald moment. I can just see someone from the State Department coming to harass me over your killing spree."

He smiled. "Aw. You really do care."

His mother hung up without another word.

Nathan pocketed the phone and found the leader of his makeshift team. He handed him the dead men's identification. "I want you to find out who these men worked for. Quietly. Get as much information about that person as possible. Also, look into the dead man from the prison. We'll want to make a little side trip to wherever he kept his valuables."

* * *

JOSH QUEEN SHOWED up in Chicago unannounced early the next morning. He'd learned a long time ago that you never gave opponents any warning. Kathleen Bennett didn't know she was his opponent. That changed today.

He'd had his staff dig into her as soon as he'd left her ex-husband's island. My, hadn't *that* made for interesting reading.

The FBI and local police were all over her. Apparently, her chief of security liked torturing and killing people. That had blown up in her face—literally—last week. Coincidentally, right around the same time as Clayton Roger's spaceship took flight.

Since coincidence was bullshit, the two events were somehow connected. So, the fabricated story that he'd intended to hold over her head became real. She was involved in the spaceship events. Somehow.

That was good. It meant she knew something about what was going on. The trick would be getting her to tell him.

He made a few calls as they were landing and arranged to have the FBI assist him in this matter. They hadn't received the warmest of welcomes at BenCorp, so he could count on them making a nice wall of unfriendly faces to have at his back.

The lead investigator met him at the airport. That was a neat trick, since Queen had only gotten word that he'd help fifteen minutes ago.

The man looked like a walking cadaver, all pale, loose skin, and gangly limbs. His tailor had fitted his suit masterfully, but that only made him look like a zombie with good sartorial taste.

His appearance probably helped him solve cases, even if only by intimidating the criminals. His closure rate was quite enviable. And the attorney general said he had a hard-on for Kathleen Bennett.

Queen extended his hand as the other man approached. "Special Agent in Charge Arthur Pembroke? I'm Josh Queen. Thank you for being unexpectedly prompt. I do hope that you didn't break the sound barrier on my behalf."

The man smiled grimly. "I was actually here following up on a tip, Mister Secretary. Director Bradford told me to extend every courtesy. What can the FBI assist you with today?"

"Kathleen Bennett. Specifically, evidence has come to light that she might be involved in some national security issues. I'm going to confront her about them, and I'd like to have you there with me. I understand she's stymied your attempts to search her facility from top to bottom. Has she given you a reason for that?"

The agent gestured toward a black SUV of the type favored by the FBI. "Why don't we start toward the campus while we talk? As a matter of fact, she used the argument you just mentioned. National security. Also industrial trade secrets and other business-related arguments.

"That's been mostly effective. A federal judge only granted us access to a small fraction of the facility. He seems to feel the chances the security chief hid bodies in classified areas is low. I agree with him, sadly."

"You do? Then why ask for it?" Queen slid into the passenger seat of the SUV and buckled in.

Pembroke climbed behind the steering wheel and started the vehicle. "If you ask for as much as you can get, then you might get as much as you need. I'm looking for proof that she's tied into her security chief's little hobby."

Queen felt his eyebrows rise. "*Really?* You think the head of one of the largest multinational corporations in the world was party to torture and murder. What led you down that rabbit hole?"

They pulled out of the airport and headed into the city. The FBI agent drove with all the assurance of a trained driver. He skillfully dodged around careless motorists and the slow with casual ease. Queen watched a woman in the car next to them applying her makeup as she drove. She almost struck a fat man juggling a burger, fries, and a large drink at the crosswalk.

Thank God he didn't have to get out into traffic much.

Pembroke zipped through it all without blinking an eye. "Reynolds couldn't have smuggled dozens of people onto that campus and into his house without someone knowing about it. And that doesn't even begin to cover planting a minefield around the damned place. We've confirmed at least sixty detonations. We have to proceed slowly, because not all of them went off. We've found two that failed to detonate."

"That's a lot of bombs," Queen admitted. "I assume these were actual mines, as in military ordinance."

"They were. At least the ones the bomb squad excavated safely were. Not US made, thank God. Russian. Which probably explains why they failed to go bang. It makes me wonder what we haven't found yet. Oh yeah. She's involved in this, at least as far as turning a blind eye.

"And that's not all. Somebody shot the company guards at his house. Ballistics says with military-grade small arms. They've already ruled out all the weapons recovered at the scene. Also, someone carjacked an employee and drove her minivan over the fence on the way out. While the security teams were heading the other direction. They got away clean."

Queen shook his head. "Was this a scene from a summer blockbuster I missed? Who are these new players?"

"I have no idea. Chicago PD found the van in an abandoned warehouse not far from the BenCorp campus. Someone burned it up good. We won't be getting any evidence out of what's left. Half an hour after the fire, someone stole a motorcycle. It turned up here at the airport.

"That leads me to believe someone raided the facility. Specifically, they attacked the head of security. They had to be after something specific. And I want to know what it was."

That gave Queen a lot to consider. He'd intended to use Bennett as a pawn in his conflict with Rogers, but it now seemed as though she was actually a combatant. If her chief of security was a casualty, that meant she knew a lot more about what was going on with that spaceship than he'd originally expected.

And, there was the explosion at the spaceport. Both explosions, actually. The one that destroyed a fuel dump and the second that almost brought down a hotel. Roger's company blamed both of those attacks on terrorism.

In these perilous times, those explanations had held up. Until now.

There were unconfirmed reports that there was an explosion in space, somewhere near the spaceship, before it departed so hastily. Tie this together with the attack on the BenCorp facility outside Paris, and this might actually be an honest-to-God corporate war.

* * *

"As an archaeologist, you make a passable engineer," Doctor Michael Crockett said. "I don't know which movie you used as a basis for your expectations, but I'm leaning toward one of the Indiana Jones films. I can only hope it isn't the one about the aliens and crystal skull."

Jess couldn't help smiling just a little. The large man had a certain way about him that made it difficult to take offense.

Of course, she was a little tired. They'd been at this for over a full day now. It was two in the morning, and she was running out of steam.

He had a right to be in an uproar, she supposed. She was treating this important site with a lot of disrespect.

"Which aspect of my performance are you objecting to, Doctor?"

"Call me Michael. Everything! We need to stop everyone and document everything where it currently sits. Then, we can start a closer examination in selected areas, but nothing is to be moved without proper care." He stared over her shoulder. "You there! Put that back!"

A glance showed one of the engineers from *Liberty Station* had picked up something from the floor and was about to put it into a bag.

Jess planted herself between the archaeologist and the unfortunate engineer. "You do realize that we're pulling out of this facility in less than three days, right? And we've already used one of them."

"Three days? Are you insane? This excavation will take years. These people are going to destroy irreplaceable artifacts and historical information. This simply will not do."

"Michael," the man's wife, Sierra, said. "Are you expecting her to control the laws of physics?"

He turned toward his wife and somehow managed to huff inside his spacesuit. "Of course not, but we can't come in here with a back loader and haul everything out. It's… sacrilege."

"Tell me how to stop time, and I'll listen," Jess said. "Everyone is being as careful as they can. They're taking pictures and making note of where everything came from. If something looks fragile, they'll call you or the preservationists.

"While it's *possible* we'll leave a team here, I think that's very unlikely. We don't have time to treat this with the reverence you want. I'm sorry."

He sighed. "Well, I suppose I should be grateful you didn't blow the whole thing up."

"One stupid pyramid and you're tainted forever," Jess muttered. "It wasn't even me! Hell, it wasn't even Harry. It was his crazy brother."

Sierra took her husband's arm. "We have an area on the next level up where the crew is bringing artifacts. Emily is already there. We should go help her."

The archaeologist threw his arms up theatrically. "Fine! But I want to go on record as saying this is a bad idea. When history judges us, I want my voice heard loud and clear!

"Emily is bringing the digital scanner. I want everyone to leave things alone until we scan each room. Then we can see how it was originally in high resolution. I'm afraid I must insist."

Jess raised her hands in surrender. "So long as it doesn't take too much time, I'll do what you suggest. I promise we'll be careful."

She watched the two of them head for the stairs with more than a hint of bemusement. And some sympathy. This wasn't how she preferred to operate, either.

"Jess, we found something," a male voice said.

"Who are you and where are you?"

"Sorry. It's Ray Proudfoot. Look up."

She tilted her head back and saw a suited figure waving from the hemisphere overhead. "Man, I hate this design. I'll be right there. What is it?"

"It looks like a power control station. I think. All the power cubes seem to be connected to it, anyway."

Jess trudged around the hollow sphere until she stood beside *Liberty Station*'s chief engineer. The console he was looking at bore a striking resemblance to the one in the crashed ship. The slick glass of the dark touchscreens wrapped a full two hundred seventy degrees around the chair and so did the screen perched above it.

"Damn, this looks nice."

He nodded. "See the cables around back? They lead off to all the power substations. Well, them and a bunch of other machines that we haven't managed to figure out yet. How did the one you found before work?"

She sat awkwardly in the seat. "The touchscreens came to life when I ran my hand along the surface to clear the dust. I'm not sure it will work from inside a suit. It might need something warm and hand-like."

A smear in the dust gave her the idea that he'd already tried that. Unsuccessfully, it appeared.

"What's the surface temperature in here?" she asked.

"Cold. Not absolute zero, but I wouldn't touch anything with your bare hands. That would be almost as bad as licking a flagpole in winter."

She cocked her head and gave him a look. "That sounds like the voice of experience."

"No comment. But beer was involved."

"Well, that explains everything. Let me try something."

The spacesuits had bulky mitts, but the wearer could swap them out for other equipment that required fine manipulation. The suit pressure wouldn't leak out of the arm while the change was taking place.

She didn't intend to do anything stupid, but the colder temperature might allow the console to read her hand without actually touching it. If not, no harm.

Jess disconnected the mitt on her right hand and pulled it off. This wasn't the first time she'd done so in a true vacuum, so she knew it was safe. All those stories about bodies exploding without pressure or freezing immediately were wrong.

The human skin did an admirable job of keeping all the squishy bits inside. Even the eyes were fine in the short term. Certainly long enough for someone to asphyxiate, which would be what killed you in an explosive decompression.

The vacuum was also a virtually perfect insulator. So long as she didn't touch something a couple of hundred degrees colder than zero, she'd be fine.

She brought her hand slowly closer to the console until it lit up. She was still a good few centimeters from the surface, so it was sensitive. It would probably require a touch if the temperature was normal. For safety, it should require an actual touch even to activate. The builders probably hadn't considered that it might get this cold.

Once the controls were active, she pulled her hand back and scanned the brightly lit console. It wasn't like the pilot's controls she'd seen before, so a power control board wasn't out of the question.

The monitors showed interior views of the comet. Some in this room, based on the people moving around in the images. Others were dark. Perhaps rooms they hadn't seen. It was possible the lights didn't come up until someone was there to need them.

"Look at the icons on the right side of the console," Ray said.

She turned and looked at them. These were ones she could make a guess at. One that looked like a lightning bolt was highlighted. There were others that seemed to represent other needs. Water might be life support. Or maybe supplies. One looked like a little spaceship.

Maybe that was a map of the comet or something to do with their surroundings.

Jess knew she shouldn't touch them, but time was very short. She lowered her hand close to the spaceship icon, and it lit up. The controls reconfigured to something much more like the ones on the crashed ship. A lot simpler in layout but recognizable.

The monitor showed a map of the solar system. The comet was a gold diamond on its way toward passing Mars's orbit. There were other colored icons scattered around the system.

"Do those icons mean other installations?" she asked.

"Damned if I know," Ray said. "We should take pictures."

Jess slid her hand back into her mitt and stepped out of the way while Ray used his suit camera to take images of everything.

"Looks like these people went just about everywhere. There's nothing on Mercury, but there's something on Venus. And just about every bit of real estate out from there. It seems as though Earth and the moon might have more than one. It's hard to tell at this kind of resolution. I wonder if we can get a close-up."

He reached out and touched Earth. Nothing happened.

"It must not like my mitt."

"Or it doesn't expand any further." She shooed him out of the way and took her mitt back off. The Earth-Moon system grew slightly larger as she brought her hand close to it, and a red circle appeared around it.

"I wonder what the hell that means?" she asked. "Let me try something stupid."

She touched the screen with the back of her knuckle. The cold was painful, but she pulled her hand back before it had more than a moment to register.

The Earth-Moon system expanded to take up the entire left side of the monitor. Both globes rotated moderately quickly. The maps were good, which made sense. This comet had been active only a thousand years ago. The Earth hadn't changed on a geological level in that time.

There were six red triangles scattered across the Earth's surface. One in France, one somewhere in the Middle East, one in China, one in Africa, one in New Zealand, and one in South America. Not Guatemala, she noted.

"Hmm. There are a few places on Earth they were interested in." She looked over at the Moon. "One location on the Moon. That's the far side somewhere near the North Pole, I think."

Ray leaned in and looked at the icons. "Might be. At the very least, these people were all over the damned system. Now they're gone. Kind of spooky."

A tap away from Earth brought the image back out to showing the entire system. "There's something on Mars, but I'm curious about the outer system. The Mayan art showed something way out past Eris."

She saw that on the map, but there was a smaller dot much closer to Pluto. She touched it with the back of her knuckle, and it expanded a little, but it just stayed an icon. She couldn't tell anything about it.

It had a greenish circle around it. That meant something, she was sure. She pressed her knuckle against it again, hoping she'd just failed to get it to enlarge.

The circle started flashing, and alien text appeared beside it.

"Uh-oh."

"Okay," Ray said. "Playtime just ended. We need to get the doctors up here to tell us what that says. And we should probably stop screwing around with equipment we don't understand."

The flashing of the circle sped up, and then it changed color to gold. The writing changed.

Hopefully, that didn't mean something bad.

7

K athleen Bennett felt like screaming when her assistant told her the walking dead was back.

"Which part of 'call my attorney' does that idiot not understand? Park him and call legal. I want them here to document this harassment. Then they can have a contest to see who can write the most legal papers to bury the bastard with."

She said that with more relish than she should have, but he was running neck and neck with her son for the Moron of the Year award. She didn't even care that he'd undoubtedly heard every word she'd just said.

"He's not alone, ma'am. He has someone from the State Department with him."

"I don't care if he has the president with him," she snarled. "They can wait."

Kathleen cut the line and leaned back in her padded chair. What could some State Department flunky want? Was this about Paris? Well, that wasn't her damned fault.

In the end, they'd blamed the attack on those ISIS loons. Why not? The bastards had no qualms about blowing up buildings and killing people. They could take the hit for this too. Karma was a bitch.

She'd considered blaming her ex-husband but rejected the idea. After all, even though that was true, it would start a chain of uncomfortable questions that might lead back to her possession of the crashed ship.

As far as she knew, no one could connect her to Guatemala. Nathan might be a psychopath, but he was thorough. No witnesses survived that could identify him or what they'd taken.

He'd killed the general workers and left them to rot in the jungle. Those too valuable to dispose of had come back here to work on the project. They didn't know what happened to their friends, of course.

The head of BenCorp's legal department came into her office with several of his henchmen at his heels. She filled them in on what her assistant had said and parked them against the wall. Then she told her assistant to send the bastards in.

That walking corpse Pembroke smiled smugly at her. The man with him looked vaguely familiar. Maybe she'd seen him at some Washington party.

"This is getting tiresome, Agent Pembroke," she said flatly. "I think I've made my position as clear as humanly possible. You don't get to see what we have in the other buildings. You'll just have to take our word that we didn't find any bodies or secret journals."

"Your rocky relationship with honesty compels me to doubt that, but I'm not here to argue with you about it. The appeals court will come to a decision before long. One I have every expectation will allow me unfettered access to these buildings.

"I'm actually here as an interagency favor. The State Department would like a few words with you."

The other man smiled on cue. "Mrs. Bennett, we've met, but I don't believe we've ever been formally introduced. Josh Queen."

That poked her memory and sent a chill down her spine. "I thought you looked familiar, Mister Secretary. Though I have to confess to some confusion about what could bring a cabinet secretary to my office."

She shifted her eyes to the FBI agent. "Especially in the company of someone I see as hostile."

"I prefer to think of Agent Pembroke as the stick to my carrot. There have been a series of disturbing events that the United States is watching with grave concern. Unless I'm mistaken, you and your company are tied up with them far more intimately than most people suspect."

His smile widened. "Most aren't even aware of the scope of what I'm talking about, but I'll wager you understand. Either we can discuss these matters in front of your lawyers and Agent Pembroke, thus making this all on the record, or we can speak privately.

"Personally, I think a quiet chat would be far more productive, but a public spectacle would be fabulously entertaining. It all depends on what you want to do."

* * *

A CHIME WOKE Harry from a sound sleep. He rolled into a sitting position and slapped the accept button on the desk beside his bed. Years of working dangerous situations made the transition to wakefulness proceed quickly. "Go."

"Harry, this is the bridge. I'm seeing something unusual on the comet. I think our sensors might be screwed up."

"Well, I'm not exactly much help when it comes to tech. What are you seeing?"

He rose to his feet and started getting dressed. If this was nothing, he could go back to bed. If it was trouble, seconds might matter. The clock said he'd only been asleep a short while.

"The comet is moving. Not just in its orbit, but the scanners say it's speeding up."

"Call me old fashioned, but I prefer my planetary bodies to coast along. Get the engineers to start checking the equipment. Has anyone called the team on the comet?"

"We don't have a reliable relay that can carry transmissions into the base. They have a transmitter unit, but it isn't operational yet. We've just been passing messages with lifters."

"I'm on my way. Have one of the lifters primed for immediate transit, just in case. Are there any over there right now?"

"Negative. We've wrapped the surface scans, so there aren't even any in orbit. The one that's normally on site came back to get more oxygen canisters."

He slid his boots on. "Have them expedite. We'll want to find out what's happening in there as soon as possible. Rogers out."

It only took a few minutes to get to the bridge, but he could feel the tension was higher when he walked through the door. "Give me a status."

Lindsay Waller had joined the third-shift pilot. She looked up from the console, her expression a mixture of concern and befuddlement. "It's not the instruments. The damned thing *is* picking up speed."

He sat down at his console and examined the main screen. Things still looked relatively the same as when he'd left to get dinner.

"What's your projection?"

"Bad," she said. "I've already adjusted our speed to match several times. We're on continuous thrust now just to keep pace. Harry, we're up to 80 percent thrust and climbing."

"How long can we maintain contact?"

"Half an hour, if it doesn't decide to up the ante."

That wasn't much time. "How many people are over there?"

"Almost three hundred. We had a deadline, so the extra bodies were getting more work done in that short window."

They couldn't move everyone in half an hour. The lifters normally carried a dozen passengers. In an emergency—which this was—they could stuff three times that number aboard briefly. There physically wasn't room for more people in vacuum suits. And with no airlock they could dock with, everyone *had* to wear suits.

That meant they could rescue 216 people. Worse, that meant they couldn't save almost a hundred others.

Or maybe they could.

"First things first. I want all the lifters ready to fly. Load them up with life support, food, water, and critical supplies. If this doesn't work, we need to give the people left on that comet the best chance to survive."

"Already in motion," Lindsay said. "I did the math. I tasked one lifter for a mining setup. They can get a lot more water than they need from the comet itself. Fuel too. If we get them all off, we've only lost the mining gear."

He nodded. "Good thinking. I want Jess on the radio as soon as the first lifter gets there."

That initial lifter broke away from *Liberty Station* ten minutes later. It made the trip quickly and settled down outside the base. Five minutes later, the rest were on their way with everything they could scavenge.

"Incoming transmission from Jess," Lindsay said.

Jess appeared on the main screen. She was sitting at the copilot's station on the lifter with her helmet off. "What's wrong?"

"The comet is accelerating," Harry said. "It has to have some kind of drive system. It's almost outpacing us. You need to evacuate."

"Dammit! We were looking at some equipment. I must have activated it. We can try to turn it off."

He shook his head. "Time is *very* short. The lifters are on the way with consumables and critical equipment, but they can't carry everyone."

"That's not a problem. The gravity here is so light that we can jump off the surface if we have to. You can use the beacons to pick people up. I'm more concerned about this thing getting away from us."

"It's not worth anyone's life. Maybe we can catch it when it comes back into the system."

She shook her head. "That might never happen. I'll ask for volunteers to stay with me and try to turn the thrusters off. We couldn't lay claim to something like this before, because international treaties say we can't claim real estate, but that just changed. It's moving. That makes this a ship. It's salvage, and I'm not giving up our claim."

He bit back the first words that wanted to come out of his mouth. "And if you can't stop it? You'll all die slowly."

"Then I better stop it. We've unloaded the supplies, and we're loading people now."

"This is insane," he said.

"Only if it doesn't work. Wish me luck."

* * *

CLAYTON WOKE when his phone rang and sat up groggily. It was three in the morning. "Yes?"

"Sir, we need you in the war room."

His assistant wasn't in the habit of summoning him in the middle of the night, so something was wrong. "I'll be right there. Coffee and an egg sandwich, please."

"Yes, sir. Thank you."

He dressed quickly and headed for the office they'd dubbed the "war room." They'd outfitted it with all the most advanced communications equipment and the computers required to decipher transmissions from *Liberty Station*. His staff was all there.

"What's happening?"

"We received a message from your son. He said to wake you. A data stream started coming in after that, but I felt it best to leave the decryption to you."

Clayton nodded. "That's fine. Let's see what he has to say."

The decryption of the video only took a few minutes. Understanding the incredible facts his son had laid out took a lot longer.

The comet could move. What a marvel that was. Particularly after all this time.

On the downside, anyone would be able to spot the change if Harry continued his pursuit. They'd gone to a lot of trouble to mask the comet. If they made a scene chasing after it, that would only serve to draw attention to it.

Luckily, his son wasn't an idiot. He'd rescued every person he could from the base and was picking up the few that had jumped to safety. The final lifter had only barely made it there with the mining package. Another five minutes and even the fast craft couldn't have caught it. *Liberty Station* was already decelerating for Mars.

The situation might remain unnoticed. That far from Earth, things were vague. The ship's precise location was always somewhat fluid. As long as it didn't take too long, the people here would be none the wiser.

The comet, on the other hand, might cause a lot of attention if people were watching it. Natural bodies did not speed up. And any large telescope on the planet might note the unusual position of the damned thing.

Or no one might. There was no way to tell. The only thing they could control was avoiding drawing undue attention to the situation.

Jessica Cook had decided to stay on the comet and attempt to turn off the engines. She'd kept three dozen volunteers with her, and two lifters. He only hoped she hadn't doomed herself to a protracted and lonely death.

8

Without waiting for an invitation, Queen sat in one of the comfortable chairs set against the wall. He knew how unsettling that was to most people.

"Without knowing what you mean," Kathleen Bennett said, "I'm unsure how to respond. Perhaps you could give me some context."

Queen widened his professional smile. "A pattern has emerged linking many purportedly separate events over the last week together. I've come to discuss them with you and decide if you are an enemy of this nation."

He watched how she responded to his charges. This should be very illuminating.

"An enemy of the US? Hardly. It would be simpler to discuss this in private. I can always throw you out later. Besides, the less time Agent Pembroke spends in my office, the lower the cleaning bill. Everyone, get out."

Queen looked over at the FBI agent. "For the record, I think you brighten the room right up. If I think it needs airing out, rest assured I'll call you right away."

The FBI man inclined his head. "I stand ready to serve, Mister Secretary. Call me anytime."

The lawyers left with disapproving scowls. Bennett's assistant closed the door behind Pembroke, leaving the two of them alone.

"Well, Mister Secretary," she said. "You certainly know how to make an entrance. Would you care for some refreshments before we begin?"

He rose to his feet. "Certainly. I see you have an admirably stocked bar. What would you like, Mrs. Bennett?"

"At eight in the morning?"

"The sun is over the yardarm somewhere."

"Surprise me."

He examined the bottles on the bar before opening the cabinet above it. "Ah, what have we here? A nice dusty bottle of... fifty-year-old single malt. This will do splendidly."

He set out two glasses and poured several fingers of amber. "I won't soil it with ice. There's no need to be sacrilegious."

Queen offered her the choice of tumblers before resuming his seat and sipping his drink. As he'd suspected, it was excellent.

"Splendid," he said. "I think the explosion at your chief of security's house was part of a larger series of events that I'd like to understand more clearly."

She didn't react at all. "What larger events are we talking about?"

He smiled and shook a finger at her. "Don't be coy, Mrs. Bennett! You're engaged in a corporate war with your husband, aren't you?

"The attack on your facility in Paris and the one here, the attack on the Yucatán Spaceport and Clayton Rogers's hotel. The mysterious explosion near his space hotel turned spaceship. There's even an attack on a jihadi camp in Africa to consider."

She frowned. "I hadn't heard about that last one. I don't have anything there worth attacking. The place is a disaster. In any case, I'm not certain why this is of interest to the State Department."

He widened his eyes in a mock show of concern. "Surely the State Department should be concerned when a prestigious company such as yours is attacked by a man intent on becoming his own nation."

"I don't care to have the government stick its nose into my business. My ex-husband and I have differing views on a great many things, but that's one opinion we share. It was a large part of what drew us together in the first place."

"Not love? That's disappointing."

"I suppose it's rude to tell a high government official not to be an idiot, but do try," she said after sipping her own drink. "I'm told the attack on the Paris facility was insurgents. France is in almost as bad a shape as North Africa and the Middle East, you know. They've allowed so many refugees in and failed to force them to assimilate. Now the jihadis are almost strong enough to take the City of Light away from them.

"Which is a tragedy on many levels. Mine is not the first target of a terrorist attack there, nor even the largest. Anyone with half a brain is getting the hell out of that place as fast as they can. Why should I blame my ex-husband for something that's obviously the result of frothing fundamentalists?"

Queen inclined his head. "All of what you say about Paris is unfortunately true. It's regrettable and deplorable that not a week goes by without an attack somewhere in Europe. You'd be horrified to know how many plots we've foiled over here.

"Not that I'd say so publicly, of course, but the conservatives' knee-jerk rejection of barring refugees from that area into the United States may have slowed the progression of attacks here. It doesn't make them right, you understand, but even a stopped clock is correct twice a day."

He let that hang there for a few moments. "I don't believe in coincidence. The only question in my mind is who to go after to get the answers I need. The way I see it, you can either tell me what's going on and I take my frustration out on your ex-husband, or I find out the truth for myself and punish the one I can still get my hands on.

"I can make one call to my close friend, the attorney general, and get the FBI the search warrant they're looking for. What do you think they'll find if they dig deeply enough?"

Queen smiled. "Which way do you want to play this, Mrs. Bennett?"

* * *

JESS WANTED to scratch her nose, but the clear helmet of her suit made that impossible. Ignoring an irritating itch was the hardest thing about working for long periods in vacuum. And she'd been in it for more hours than she cared to contemplate.

Ray Proudfoot and his people had found a suitable room on a nearby level they could block off with a portable airlock. There were heaters and chillers that could make the room tolerable.

Harry and *Liberty Station* had already begun decelerating for Mars. The extra speed they'd generated keeping up with the runaway comet bumped up their arrival time by almost two full days.

Nothing they'd picked up from Earth indicated anyone there was aware of the comet speeding away from where it should be. That was good.

With a ship named *Liberty Station*, it didn't seem too much of a jump to call the comet *Freedom Express*. It was certainly on a nonstop route.

Doctors Young and Powell had stayed with her small team of raving lunatics. That was good, since they were the only hope she had of deciphering the text on the screen. Nothing they'd tried had changed their course or acceleration in the slightest.

Paulette Young had the most experience with the translation efforts, such as they were. So she was running what they saw next to the new destination on the screen through the computers to see what they said.

Damned little, unfortunately.

"A number of the words don't have direct translations, I'm afraid," the woman said. "At least not yet. The best I can figure is the part that says 'destination unavoidable,' though I'm pretty sure it means the destination is locked in. The rest we don't have a frame of reference."

"We need a larger sample size of these kinds of terms and more certainty in what they mean. Once we have that, we can keep grinding away on the specifics and at least get a sense for what they mean."

Jess was afraid of that. "How long might that take?"

The other woman shrugged, though it was hard to see inside her suit. "Damned if I know. Weeks? Months? Hopefully, not years."

"If it takes weeks, we'll be at our destination. Less if this thing keeps increasing the rate of acceleration."

The sun's gravity would normally slow the comet as it raced out of the inner system. By the time it reached the outer system, it would be crawling along. Not this time.

Not only was their speed increasing, but the rate at which the comet ship was accelerating was going up too. It was the equivalent of a car accelerating but the driver still having more accelerator to push. As she sped up, she could still press harder on the pedal and speed the car even further.

Jess suspected the comet's body was what was keeping it from just dropping the hammer. Too much acceleration might fracture the thing into pieces. That would be very bad for the people inside it, so there was probably a safety mechanism.

"Well, even if it isn't helpful for us in this situation, surely you have some of the Voynich Manuscript and the dead guy's diary translated. What can you tell me about them?"

"The translation of the Voynich Manuscript is somewhat more straightforward, but the addition of the second translation, from Old Italian to English, and accounting for inconsistencies due to the lack of complete fluency on the part of the author, has been making that more difficult."

"Lack of fluency in which language?" Jess asked.

"Italian, I think. The translation on those few pages between the unknown language and Italian seem to have been an exercise. His or her grasp of Old Italian was not complete, I suspect.

"The parts we've been able to convert to Old Italian and then to English seem to be a listing of plants and some of their properties. The naked people aren't explained, so I suspect they serve to distract anyone who might otherwise be overly curious about the unknown text. Most people in that day and time wouldn't be able to read, so they could be told a fanciful story about the pictures."

That wasn't very useful. A listing of imaginary plants didn't help anyone.

"What about the diary?"

"We're making some progress, but we thought we had more time. There are large areas of the text that are difficult to translate. The man's handwriting is inconsistent and more than a bit sloppy." She said that last with a tone of disapproval.

Jess wished the news was better, but she had to admit she hadn't expected anything else. "That has to be the priority for you two. Keep crunching the data you have, and we'll bring anything we find in written form to you to add to the list.

"The words on the piloting screen are the most important, but it would be nice to get out of these suits. To do that, we need to figure out the life-support controls."

The other woman nodded. "We'll give it everything we have. The larger the sample size, the more likely we are to have a breakthrough. I'll keep you informed."

Jess watched the other woman walk away. This task seemed impossible, but they'd make it work. They had to.

* * *

Nathan looked over the initial intelligence his men had gathered. The three dead mobsters were exactly who their IDs claimed. Two were nothing more than muscle. The third one—the driver—was somewhat higher in the food chain.

Vincenzo Battaglia had been the equivalent of a frontline manager in the mob. Not one of the little fish, but not so far removed from them. He reported to Luca Russo. That man controlled a district here in Rome and was definitely not a small-time hood.

With the killings so fresh, the mob was hunting them, so getting to the man would be challenging. Nathan had a few people trying to pin down where he was so they could assess how difficult that would be.

Meanwhile, he'd located the executor for the estate of the dead prison mobster, Alessio Romano. She was a lawyer, of course.

Vanessa Messina. She'd know where his belongings were located and probably had some idea where any images of the papers were stored.

She worked for one of the most prestigious firms in Rome. Getting in to see her was out of the question. She was a mob lawyer. She'd scream for help the moment he showed up.

Instead, he sat in the back of a van, watching her building. She lived in an apartment close by her office, so the odds were that she walked.

Miss Messina must not have been a hard worker. She strolled out of her office just after four in the afternoon. She headed down the sidewalk with a confident strut.

Nathan got out of the van and slipped into the crowd behind her. This would not be a quiet snatch and run, but he'd verified this area didn't have any damned cameras to record events. Other than those in the crowd itself. He'd have to make sure it happened quickly to avoid ending up on the internet.

His men had stolen two vans. One to use for the brazen, daylight kidnapping, and the other for a more sedate getaway. It wouldn't do for some traffic camera to lead the police right back to them.

As for the strike, he saw the perfect opportunity coming up. The traffic lights were going to catch her on this side of the street but near the front of the crowd. He signaled his team to start moving.

When the light turned red and everyone stopped, he pulled a stun gun from his jacket pocket and stuck it into the small of her back. The noise was quite distinctive, but in the press of people, they'd have difficulty telling where it came from.

The lawyer slumped with a choked cry, but he wrapped his arm around her waist, supporting her. The van made a right-hand turn, and the door slid open. Nathan casually jumped inside with the woman, and they were gone.

"They're calling the police as we speak," he said as he cuffed the stunned woman. "Get us to the other van right away."

He spent the trip to their new ride searching her closely for weapons. The last woman he'd tried to kidnap had been full of unpleasant surprises. Other than some pepper spray in her purse, she had nothing dangerous.

Unless one counted those fingernails. Though those could be a weapon of passion, he supposed.

Some duct tape across her mouth completed her abduction. The van pulled into an alley and drove to where a second van awaited them. Switching everyone over to the new vehicle only took a moment.

They quickly doused the first van with gas and tossed in a time-delayed flare. Then they were on their way back the same direction they'd come.

He dropped his jacket in the back of the van and on top of her. That would keep anyone from recognizing it or seeing her. He slid a ball cap on and swapped his sunglasses for the mirrored kind. That changed his appearance enough to avoid issues.

The police were on the ball. It hadn't been five minutes, but two men on foot were talking animatedly to several pedestrians. They all seemed to be using their hands to help describe him. Several were pointing in the direction the van had disappeared.

Nathan smiled and enjoyed the architecture as they drove through the city and toward their new accommodations. It was about time something had gone his way.

9

K athleen stared at the smug little bastard. Queen was used to getting his way, to bullying people. It was time for him to learn a few hard truths.

"If you'd done your research into me or my ex-husband, you'd know we don't just take abuse. We fight. I hate that bastard with every fiber of my being and I'd like nothing better than to throw him under the bus, but not under these conditions.

"And I won't let you sit in my office like you own it, drinking my whisky, and thinking you have me over a barrel. Get out. And don't come back without a warrant."

The expression on Queen's face was almost comical. "Excuse me? I don't know why you think you can talk to me that way, but you're sorely mistaken. The US government has far more power over companies like yours than you seem to realize. A few phone calls from me, and you'll be under a microscope."

"Make your calls from outside my property. And when you put me under the microscope, expect to need a proctoscopy to find my lawyer's boot. The public is already primed to be watching for government corruption, and I'll see that they have all the proof they need that you're unfairly targeting me to get back at my ex-husband."

She rose to her feet. "Get the hell out of my office. Now."

He eyed her for a moment, drank the rest of his whisky, and set the glass on her desk. "In the State Department, we've had to deal with declarations of war a few times. It never turns out well for the bastards that think they can win against us."

"That was back in the days where the US meant something. We haven't fought a war since before you were born, much less won one. Generations of spineless drones like you have eroded this country's will. You don't scare me."

"We'll speak again, then. And next time I won't be generous in how we play. See you soon, Mrs. Bennett."

She waited until he was out of her office to sit down and shake a little. Not with fear, but with rage. The nerve of that smarmy little bastard. If he'd given her half a chance, she might have served Clayton up like a roast pig.

Well, probably not. There was entirely too much danger of their secrets spilling into the open if she did that.

If he pushed things, he was in for a rude surprise. She recorded everything that happened in her office. Then she erased the parts that wouldn't look good if subpoenaed. He'd made enough threats to suffer if she leaked them to the press. With everything that had happened in the last few weeks, she could probably spin it so she came out the victim.

Worst case, he turned up the heat. So what? The amount of money she'd lose paled in comparison to what the alien technology could make for her.

And that was just the cash. The tech opened new opportunities. Clayton had bought an island nation to move into the political ring. Queen hadn't said much more than that, but she had her spies. He'd sold Rainforest and his other holdings to the Chinese for good money and their support. Now the US had no leverage over him at all.

The Chinese, on the other hand, might prove a problem for him later, if played correctly.

Or was this a deeper game than she was giving Clayton credit for? Was this his chance to buy out the Chinese space program? They were in a race to Mars that they'd just lost. Did they really have the gumption to push forward in the face of being second place? Or third?

Rather than worrying about Queen, perhaps she should be securing her own way into space. After all, just having the crashed ship did her no good if Clayton's minions were sweeping the table. She needed to get after them as soon as possible.

If he was in bed with the Chinese, perhaps it was time for her to consider how to co-opt India.

She picked up her phone and waited for her assistant to answer.

"Get me the head of the Indian space program on the phone. And no, I don't care what time it is over there."

* * *

QUEEN STALKED out of the building and over to the SUV where Pembroke waited. The FBI agent smiled. "That was quick. I'll assume things didn't go as planned."

"You could say that," he said, trying hard to keep a snarl out of his voice. He dug a twenty out of his wallet and handed it to the FBI agent. "I'll admit I didn't expect her to throw me out of her office, particularly when I offered to let Clayton Rogers be the heavy. But, no. She's a lot stronger willed than I gave her credit for."

"So, what now? Or is that something above my pay grade?"

He smiled at the agent. "I'm willing to give you some hints. Unlike her ex-husband, her property is mainly still inside the US. I'm going to start court proceedings to see she loses a big chunk of it. She doesn't get to play for free.

"But that's only payback for her rebuffing me. What I really need to do is discover what her secret is. She's hiding something. That has to be the reason for her intransigence. There's more going on between her and her ex-husband than meets the eye, and I want to know what it is."

"Could it tie into my investigation? If so, I can always use more pressure to get the answers."

Queen considered that. "I believe the attack here was part of the general conflict between Kathleen Bennett and Clayton Rogers. The security man's penchant for torturing and killing people? Probably not."

"But you can't be sure," Pembroke said. "Why not feed me more information and get me the leeway to dig deeper? I want to see her brought down, and if the ex is tied up in it, I'll bring him down too."

The thought of that made Queen's inner child happy. Pembroke was a straight arrow. In diplomatic circles, that was a disadvantage. For law enforcement, not so much. He was a blunt instrument, and that looked like the perfect tool for the job.

He held out his hand to the agent. "I think we can work together, Special Agent in Charge Pembroke. Trust me, what these people are doing will blow your mind and chill you to the bone when the implications sink in.

"Let me make another call to the attorney general's office. Then we can start taking this whole corrupt web down."

* * *

CLAYTON SKIMMED the footage from inside the spaceship that Jess Cook was calling *Freedom Express*. Astounding. Simply astounding.

And game changing. As Jess had guessed, international law treated space the same as international waters. An abandoned vessel was salvage. The catch was they had to claim it before it was theirs. Also, the process was not one that allowed for much privacy. They'd need to make a claim in a court with standing.

In this case, probably Australia. Though New Zealand was a strong second choice. It, after all, had the strange icon on the South Island. Based on when humans had arrived in New Zealand, the aliens had set up this base on a deserted island. That probably meant something, and it was up to him to figure it out.

The US Navy had departed after the first Chinese vessels had arrived. That meant that Clayton could make a trip to Australia or New Zealand without too much difficulty.

The call he'd made to an old friend in Australia yesterday had gotten him a conversation with the Department of Foreign Affairs and Trade. Since the UN recognized Nauru, the woman had agreed that an embassy was a good idea and assured Clayton that they would honor his diplomatic immunity while he came over to discuss the matter in person.

Astonishingly, he hadn't even needed to spend money to make it happen.

He'd want to do the same in New Zealand, China, and probably Japan as soon as practical. The other nations in the general area would need to wait for events to catch up. He'd also have to decide on who to make his ambassador.

His assistant had gathered the people to assist him in this project. The man had chosen a woman with dual Australian and New Zealand citizenship to head the team. Penny Cash.

She met Clayton at his plane, sharply dressed and wide-awake despite the hour. "Mister Rogers. It's a pleasure." His ear pegged her delightful accent as significantly more New Zealander than Australian.

"Miss Cash. I don't suppose you're related to Johnny?"

Her smile told him she'd heard that one before. With a name like Penny Cash, she'd probably heard any number of failed attempts at humor over the years.

"No, sir. But you can blame my father for my first name. He thought he was being funny, and my mother was too distracted with giving birth to stop him. Poor impulse control and lack of subtlety, my father. Big heart, though. Named John, by the way, and a big fan of Johnny. He was an American serviceman when he met my mother."

Clayton settled them at the front of his private jet. "I apologize for my foray into bad jokes. Your mother was a New Zealander?"

"Yes. She happened to be in Australia when I was born, so I'm a dual citizen and have a number of contacts in both countries. As a New Zealander, that isn't strictly required, but it helps avoid some of the rivalry. I know people at the local and national level."

He waited until the plane took off to order an early breakfast. She joined him.

The flight to the capital of Australia was a bit more than four thousand kilometers, so they had a few hours to work with. They'd be landing early in the morning.

That was fine, of course. He had an excellent Murphy bed in his office, and the seats out here reclined fully. Everyone would be ready to get moving once they hit the ground.

"Now, before we begin, I have some paperwork for you. All standard. I've already vetted you to within a centimeter of your life, so this is just covering the bases."

He handed her a very tight nondisclosure agreement.

She read the first few lines. "I've already signed one of these."

"This is for much more confidential information. It's the price of doing business, I'm afraid. I need to know that my deepest secrets are safe with you."

Penny read every single word. Three times. Only then did she sign it.

"That is by far the most stringent nondisclosure agreement I've ever seen. I'm surprised there wasn't a clause about my firstborn son."

"Page three. You must have missed it."

She smiled. "What's this really about?"

The flight attendant, a young man with a sterling smile, delivered their meals right then, so he held off on starting that explanation until they'd both sampled their food and sent him on his way.

Clayton took a bite of his breakfast. Perfect, as always. His chef knew just how he liked everything after all this time.

"The full story will take some time," he said, "but the portion we're concerned with leads me to Australia to file a claim on an abandoned vessel. Or New Zealand, if you feel that makes more sense. An abandoned space vessel, actually."

She raised an eyebrow, but only gestured for him to continue with her fork.

"It all started when I was a young man and decided that I wanted to see people in space, but the real meat of this story only happened a few weeks ago in Guatemala. You see, I sent my son Harry off..."

That story and the questions it generated would take them early into the morning, he was sure, but this was the first time he'd been able to tell it to anyone. And he loved a good story.

10

Nathan was pleased to see his prisoner waking up just after they arrived at their new quarters. He'd set up shop in a rented—under an assumed name—villa on the hills outside Rome. One with a commanding view of all the approaching roads and excellent routes to escape any problems.

Out of an overabundance of caution, he'd secured the woman to a chair. Ankles tied to the legs, a rope around her waist like a seat belt, her hands tied behind her and her arms also tied to the chairback, and a rope around her neck that would choke her if she tried to lunge.

It was ridiculous, really. He was definitely overcompensating for past traumas. But he didn't take the restraints off her.

He wondered if she'd try to scream when she realized her situation. Some did, some didn't. Honestly, there was no guessing. It didn't matter, or he'd have gagged her.

Vanessa Messina's sudden tensing told him she'd awoken to her peril. Her breathing changed but no screams. Mildly disappointing.

Nathan grabbed a straight-backed chair and set it down in front of her, backward. He straddled the seat and looked into her attractive face from only a few feet away. "Welcome back. I hope you enjoyed your midday nap, because it's time to get back to work."

"Do you know who I work for?" Her tone was a mixture of fear and anger.

"I'll assume you don't mean the law firm. Yes, you work for the mob. I'm quite aware of them. In fact, it's one of the reasons I paid you this unorthodox call."

"They'll kill you. Let me go and I'll ask them to spare your life. Otherwise, they'll slit your throat and dump your body in the ocean."

He smiled. "Very melodramatic. And a little late. They tried to kill me already. That didn't turn out so well for three of them. And unless you'd like to share a similar fate, I suggest you consider cooperating with me.

"Do so and you'll walk away from this unfortunate misunderstanding in one piece. That won't be true if I have to induce you to cooperate. So, I suggest you forget attorney-client privilege."

She considered him for a moment. "What do you want to know? Some secrets are worth my life."

"Thankfully, my questions have nothing to do with your mob boss's crime secrets. Let them murder, rape, steal, and deal drugs to their hearts' content. I want to know about the Romano estate. I know you're sorting it out. And no, I don't care one bit that his friends had him murdered. In their shoes, I'd have done the same. I just care about his property."

She cocked her head. "Why?"

Nathan gave her his best boyish grin. "I know, right? You never saw that coming. In fact, your mob associates didn't, either. That's why we have this little problem. One that I'll clear up very soon, I promise."

She seemed to think about it for a few moments and then shrugged. "I can't think of anything in his properties that his former associates would care about. They've already recovered anything incriminating. I'll cooperate unless what you're looking for would be a problem to them."

He leaned forward, his arms crossed over the back of his chair. "There! That wasn't so difficult. I'm concerned about his art collection. Specifically, some manuscript pages."

She frowned. "The ones he claimed the unknown woman stole from him? Right before she made him dictate his drug-addled and completely fictitious list of crimes?"

"As a lawyer, I'm sure you have to qualify things like that. I know those crimes were real, and I don't care. That's a problem between you and the Italian authorities. The papers are my only concern. I'll assume he didn't bother insuring them officially. That's standard for... off the book purchases... shall we say?"

She gave Nathan a thin smile. "Mister Romano self-insured them, yes. They weren't illegal, by any means, but he preferred to keep his art objects private."

"I completely understand."

And he did. He had a similar collection that would shock his detractors. Most people thought he could only appreciate felt paintings of dogs playing poker, but he actually liked cityscapes. He'd bought a wide selection for his home and had others he couldn't acquire stolen for him.

"Now, the question I have for you is simple. Did he have images of the pages?"

"Of course. If they were ever stolen, he'd need them to verify they were authentic when the police recovered them."

Irony, there. Nathan was certain a number of works in the man's collection were stolen. Perhaps even a significantly larger percentage than in Nathan's.

"Where did Mister Romano keep these pictures?"

"With our office, but I don't have them now. The police took them as part of their investigation. I'd be happy to ask for them back for you."

He was sure she would.

"Are the local police in Rome investigating this case, or the national authorities?"

"The national ones, of course. The Guardia di Finanza. Rome doesn't have jurisdiction on many of the alleged crimes that are being investigated."

"Who is the lead officer in this case?"

"Angelo Basile."

He turned to one of the men. "Get me a dossier on him right away. Then we'll start formulating a plan to get what we need."

"Are you going to release me now?" she asked warily.

Nathan smiled at her. "Not just yet. Once I have what I want and don't have to worry about the police, you'll walk away in one piece as promised. In the meanwhile, I must insist you enjoy our hospitality."

He rose to his feet and gestured for the man watching the door to come in. "Let's help Miss Messina to her new quarters. Since she has nothing but time on her hands, I might as well entertain her privately."

She didn't like the sound of that, and for good reason.

He'd taken the liberty of installing some tie-down points around her bed. Another thing he had a lot of experience with. It wouldn't do for one of his lady friends to bite him while he showed her precisely how little control she had over her own body. If she was as entertaining as he thought, he might even let her live.

Of course, he'd have to send her back to Paris. There was no way he'd allow her to walk away a free woman. Not after the things he was going to do to her.

* * *

HARRY WENT over everything they had about *Freedom Express* and wanted to bang his head on the console. They had images of almost every compartment now, and there were a lot of them. As one might expect from a kilometer-thick body, that left a lot of room for people to put things.

The interior control and power center wasn't even the most interesting compartment, to his thinking. That had to be the vast jungle on the fourth level. It reminded him of the Genesis Cave in the *Star Trek* movie. The original series, not any of the idiotic attempts at rekindling it. And don't even get him started on *Star Wars*.

If they hadn't let the air out and the temperature hadn't fallen to almost nothing, it might still be going. Who knew? The rest of the power was still running.

Nothing Jess or her people had tried was unlocking the drives or changing their course. It seemed they were on a one-way trip out of the solar system. At their current acceleration, they'd pass Jupiter before he settled into Mars orbit.

And speaking of Mars, he needed to decide what they were going to do when they got there. Admittedly, his heart wasn't into it. He was worried about Jess and his other people. Still, he had to put on a good show.

Obviously, they'd want to see what was at the area where the aliens had marked their map of Mars. And, it was certainly an obvious choice. Olympus Mons. The tallest place on the planet. A volcano so impressive that one couldn't see the edge of the lava shield from the summit because of the curvature of the planet.

The resolution on the images he had were too low to tell what part of the mountain might be so important. The orbiting satellites had certainly mapped the entire planet thoroughly before NASA abandoned them.

Nothing jumped out as artificial. If it had, every alien contact nutjob would've been screaming. Of course, it turned out they were right after all.

Except for the probing. That was never right.

Honestly, without examining the possibilities on the mountain firsthand, he'd be very nervous trying to land. Yet, the climb to check from ground level would be brutal, even at gravity roughly a third that of Earth.

The atmosphere was almost all carbon dioxide and so thin that even the most impressive dust storm would be like standing in a light breeze. The temperature might get comfortable during the day, but it was astonishingly cold at night.

They had pressurized habitats for use down there. The engineers had planned well. They just hadn't known they'd need to put them on the side of a mountain. There were plateaus that would be wide enough, if they could set a lifter down on them.

He called the bridge.

Lindsay answered. "Yeah, boss?"

"You said you'd already launched some new satellites toward Mars. When will we get the fresh data from them?"

"Hang on." She tapped her console. "It looks like they're set to enter orbit in about an hour. We have six altogether. I think we'll only leave a couple in Mars orbit for long-term mapping, but they wanted enough to get a lot of details fast."

"That makes sense," he said, leaning back. "I'm looking at the data we have now. It's pretty good. How much better is the new gear?"

Lindsay grinned. "You'll like this. One of your father's companies—the same one that builds the military jets—won the contract to provide the NSA and CIA with their latest-generation spy satellites.

"The units we have are built to the same specifications, only bigger and with finer resolution. Since we didn't have to launch them on a rocket, we weren't constrained by size or aerodynamics. These things are long and wide, built for space."

"That sounds good, but what does it translate to?"

"I have no idea. Maybe you can see a wart on a Martian's butt. I'd ask Jess or Ray, but they're probably asleep, now that they have an area they can pressurize. We'll know soon enough."

That was certainly true. "Put one of the satellites in geosynchronous orbit over Olympus Mons. I want to target it on the mountain for detailed shots of any area we like. That's priority one."

She nodded. "Will do. I'll look at the current vectors and get things adjusted. For a lightweight like Mars, the geosynchronous orbit won't be nearly as high as it is on Earth. That should make for even more detailed images."

"That would be good. Get the rest mapping the planet in close detail. I want an interactive map that I can zoom down and see those proverbial Martian butts."

"Roger that. It'll probably take several days to get the equator done and start spreading toward the poles. We'll have to put one bird in a polar orbit. Once things are going, I'll have a better idea on how long this will take."

"Sounds good. I'll grab something to eat and join you shortly."

He made his way down to the cafeteria closest to the bridge for breakfast. The temptation to stay locked up in his office working on this was strong, but the crew needed to see him regularly. To feel his confidence. That's how leadership worked. Even when the leader felt out of his depth.

Harry spent more time there than he'd planned, but the crew was visibly more relaxed after some of them stopped to chat with him. They needed to feel as though everything was going to be okay. Even if they didn't come right out and ask him about it.

Once he finished, he made his way to the bridge. Lindsay was looking at a globe of Mars on the screen. He stopped beside the pilot's console.

"Is that live?"

"Relatively speaking. We're not too far off, so the time delay is down to less than two minutes. That's the image from the geosynchronous satellite over Olympus Mons. It performed just as expected and came online perfectly."

Harry could see the massive mountain spread across the image. "What about the other birds?"

"They're entering their orbits now. Basically, they're in place, but we're still tweaking the final details with the thrusters. The high-resolution images should be coming in soon."

He found the mapping data on his console and examined the volcano. It was shaped like a circus tent spread across hundreds of kilometers. The edges rose from the surrounding surface by up to eight kilometers.

That gradually increased until the caldera was almost two-dozen kilometers higher. The massive shield of lava was so heavy that it caused the crust to sag, creating an angular depression around its base almost two kilometers deep.

That was impressive.

It was so large that someone on the summit wouldn't be able to see anything except for the volcano. And someone on the planet couldn't take in the full picture of Olympus Mons, either. It was just too huge.

Harry drilled down as far as the image allowed him and discovered that even from the distance it was orbiting, the spy satellite could see a hell of a lot and in significantly more detail than he'd expected. He wouldn't have been able to read a license plate on Earth, but he could have seen the make and model of the car.

Scanning the entire mountain was going to prove time consuming. He'd send the data back to his father and let him add people and computers to the job. It still might take them weeks to find what they were looking for.

"Virtually the entire volcano would make a good landing area," Lindsay said. "The slope is only about five degrees until you get to the central area. And there you could land inside the caldera. Though, fair warning, the atmospheric pressure up there is very thin, even for Mars."

"How thin?"

"The surface of Mars is less than 1 percent of the pressure on Earth at sea level. Up there, it's only 12 percent of Mars standard."

He nodded. "Yeah, that's pretty thin. I suppose we can forget about all those stories where we humans could get around on Mars with just additional oxygen."

"No," she said. "I think you can rule that right out."

He brought the caldera up on his screen. There were several overlapping craters. "It does look solid. If we have to land an exploratory party, that might be the place to do it. How long since it was active?"

She checked her console. "My data entry for it says about 150 million years. I think we're probably safe for the short-term."

He laughed. "And the long-term. I doubt anything down there is still active."

"I wouldn't count on that. This entry says that the volcano might still be a going concern. It was created by a hot spot, like the one in Yellowstone. Only Mars doesn't have moving tectonic plates, so it just sits down there."

"How far down?"

"This says they think the magma chamber is about thirty-two kilometers under the caldera floor. The calderas are sixty to eighty kilometers across and 3.2 kilometers deep." She looked at a different part of her console. "We're getting our first low pass now, Harry. I'm targeting the caldera."

The images started coming in, and the computer quickly sorted them correctly. Now he could see a Martian's butt. Or read a license plate. The resolution was good enough to see stones on the surface of the caldera.

"I set the computer to scan the images for anything that seems unusual," Lindsay said. "It came right back with something. I'm putting it on-screen."

An image of what looked like the caldera floor appeared. It was a section right up against the wall. Harry couldn't quite make out what it was, but there was something there. A rockfall, maybe.

"Can we enhance any of the images?" he asked.

"Some. The software has some default settings for that. A trained person could probably do a better job, though."

"Let's start with what we can do ourselves. I think it might be a rockfall. I'd like to get a better look at it. It might mean we need to pick a different landing area."

The section of the image in question popped up on the main screen. Lindsay highlighted it, and the computer went to work.

Image enhancement had to do with colors, shadows, and sharpness. That whole business on the TV shows where they took grainy images and sharpened them so they could see things was bull. The detail had to be there to begin with. At least mostly.

The computer lightened parts of the image, and it became clear he was looking at a large pile of rocks that had slid down from above.

Part of it was too regular, though. He could just make out something with the same basic outline as the rear of the crashed ship on Earth sticking out from under the pile.

It wasn't an avalanche. It was a crash site.

11

Jess woke, groggy and unsure of where she was. She sat up and blinked at the people moving around her. Ah. Now she remembered. She was in the area they'd pressurized on *Freedom Express*.

Getting the large compartment ready for occupation had taken long enough that everyone had to change the air supplies in their suits twice. They'd gotten things set up just in time. The suits were reaching their limits on storing bodily wastes. That would've been messy to clean up.

The large room had been for storage, they thought. At least there had been a few crates stacked off to one side. They were gone now, taken somewhere else to examine.

Harry had sent over equipment designed for field use on Mars, so it worked here too. After a fashion.

The cots were designed to support a person in weak gravity, so they were a bit uncomfortable at a full G, but she'd slept on worse. The portable toilets worked well enough, as did the kitchen.

The room had plenty of space for all three dozen of them to stay in relative privacy. They'd hung a curtain between where the men and women slept. That was good enough.

They'd set aside one corner of the room for examining their finds and for the computers. Doctors Young and Powell would work there.

Jess rose to her feet and stretched. The water recycler was more than efficient enough to allow showers, thank God. She took one when her turn came and then got dressed for the day. She'd slept more than twelve hours. She'd needed it.

She took her reconstituted breakfast over to where the restoration specialists were already hard at work.

"Morning, ladies. I hope you have good news for me."

Rachel Powell looked up from her screen. "Some. The man watching the pilot's console indicated we passed Jupiter's orbit while you were sleeping. Congratulations on leading the first ship out of the inner system."

"I don't know if it counts when we did't have a choice in the matter. What about the controls. Anything?"

The other woman shook her head. "The language is still a barrier. We need to find more translated works."

Paulette Young gestured toward the table where she was working. "The crates they found in this room were filled with medieval manuscripts. We're scanning them and preserving them as best we can.

"We hope there are translations on one of these systems. If we can just increase the sample size, I'm sure we'll be able to make some kind of difference."

"I didn't think we had access to their computers," Jess said.

The preservationist shrugged. "You'll have to ask Ray about that. He seems to think he's making progress."

"I'll check once I've made my rounds. Surely, these computers have some kind of useful data on them. We just have to find it. Any other interesting information?"

"We have piles of small equipment," Rachel said. "Ray examined them and seemed interested in a few. Nothing big."

Jess was disappointed but not surprised. This was going to be a long haul. They'd be at their destination before they found anything useful, she suspected. She only hoped this thing came to a stop when it got there.

She finished her bland breakfast and headed for the airlock. They'd fitted some racks for the suits beside it, and one of the techs was on hand to verify everything was good before anyone went into the vacuum.

Suiting up took about twenty minutes. Reaching the core another ten.

That's what they'd decided to call the central chamber. The core. It was at the center of the comet, so that only made sense.

She found Ray Proudfoot at the main control console. He was looking at a screen that wasn't familiar to her.

"Morning, Ray," she said, peering past his shoulder. "What's this?"

"I think I found the primary life-support controls. The screen is split between an overview of all the systems, individual controls, and a map of the ship."

"That sounds useful. What's what?"

He pointed to an image of a stick figure standing on the floor. "This is the gravity controls, I think. When I touch it, I get a screen that has the entire globe on the left. I can touch that, and it seems to select an area. I get bars I can move. I have someone in the area now. I was about to see if I was correct."

"Well, don't let me stop you."

"We're on channel six. Rex, you ready?"

The special-ops scout answered him. "Ready. Try not to squish me to paste. The ladies don't like paste."

He'd stayed with Jess's team to provide what security he could. She was grateful to have him.

Ray touched the bar with his knuckle and slid it down a little. "Anything?"

"Yeah. It does feel a little lighter."

"Okay, I'm taking it all the way down," Ray said. He slid the bar slowly to the side.

"Yep. I'm in zero-G. Give me a minute to get myself back into some kind of proper position before you crank it back up."

"Roger that."

Jess was impressed. That was the first ship's system they'd manage to identify and control. "Good work, Ray. So, you can control single areas. What about the ship as a whole?"

"There's this sphere at the top of the display. If I select it, all the areas light up. I didn't want to screw with it right now, though. You ready to get heavy, Rex?"

"Ready."

The chief engineer slid the bar back up to full. An icon that looked like a clock with one hand appeared beside it.

"That's new," Ray muttered. "How you doing, Rex?"

"Back at normal weight, I think."

"Hang tight. I have something else I might want to test. Shout out if anything changes."

"Roger."

Ray touched the dial, and it expanded. There was a solid line from the center of the dial to the twelve o'clock position. The gray fill came out to about three o'clock.

"I think this might let me take things up a bit more," Ray said. "I'll move this slowly."

He touched the dial and dragged the line down to the six o'clock position. "How now brown cow?"

"Ooof. Heavy. I feel like I have a full pack on. Well, maybe a bit more. Possibly double my weight. How high does that thing go?"

"If the scale is true, four Gs."

"Let me sit down for this. I don't want to fall and crack my helmet. I'm ready."

The engineer ran it all the way up. "Rex?"

"Man, I need to lose some weight. Yeah, this could be about four times normal. I'd sure as hell have trouble walking."

"Okay. I'm taking it back down to normal."

Ray ran the dial back down to one G, and a tap dismissed the dial to the background. "You good?"

"Yep," Rex said. "I'm back to my normal weight. Any idea how this crap works?"

"Not a clue. Stand by. I'm going to look at a few other screens."

"Nice," Jess said. "What other stuff do you have?"

The engineer left the gravity controls and went to a different screen. It seemed to show a lot of systems at a high level. Almost all were purple.

Three were orange. One had an icon that looked like a wave, one had a cloud, and the last had a symbol that resembled a thermometer, she thought.

"I wish we knew what the colors meant," Ray said. "I'm betting orange means something bad, but I'm not sure about purple. Is that good or bad?"

She shrugged. "We'll figure it out."

"I think these two are air and water. This last one is temperature. The systems that someone shut down after murdering their friends."

They'd recovered twenty-six bodies. The ones in the core had gone back over to *Liberty Station*. They'd laid the rest out in the area where the small ship parked.

"Well, then," she said. "By all means, let's get the air turned back on."

Ray selected what he thought was the air, and she saw the bar was all the way at the bottom. He tried to draw it up, but the bar stubbornly refused to move.

"Maybe something in the system is still broken," he said.

"Or maybe it's because the area is still open to the rest of the ship," she said. "Look at the globe."

Rather than highlighting a single room like on the gravity screen, this time a fairly significant area on that deck was marked.

"That might be it," Ray said. "Rex, I'm going to have you close some doors."

It took almost half an hour to close off all access to the area. Then when Ray tried to move the controls, they worked.

"I'm hearing something," Rex said. "I think air might be flowing into the area. One of your guys is here with an analyzer. He says the mix is good, but the pressure is light."

They waited for the pressure to stabilize, and then Ray brought the bar all the way up. Another icon appeared, but it wasn't a dial. More like an on-off switch.

"I'm going to mess with this some more," Ray said. "What does it look like now?"

"The pressure is about good for sea level. The mixture is good too. It's warming up but too cold to take off a helmet."

"Don't do that," Jess said. "We need to give the air a lot more testing before any of us breathes it. What if it has biologicals in it? We don't need any diseases."

Ray moved back to the temperature monitor and saw that it was online. It must've activated with the air. With the two of them up, he found a way to drag the icons together and have both screens up at the same time.

"Score!" he said. "Let's add the water." Moments later, he had them all up.

He touched the icon and again saw an on-off switch. "I'm going to flip a switch. Hang on."

Ray flipped the switch, and a whole array of indicators appeared. "Hello. What have we here?"

Jess saw over his shoulder that the top of the screen had three stick figures. One was the same as on the gravity screen, the second was taller and the lengths of the arms and legs were longer, and the third was short and squat. The normal one was lit.

The chief engineer reached out and touched the thin stick figure. The levels of the bars changed. Some went up, some went down. The gravity went down to what looked like 60 percent.

"Hello," Rex said. "The gravity went down some. And the tech says the air pressure is dropping. The composition is changing too."

"Presets," Jess said. "There are presets for humans and two others. Aliens?"

"Could be," Ray said. "I'm trying the other one, Rex. This guy looks stout, so be careful of the weight change."

He touched the squat figure, and the gravity shot high. Maybe three Gs. The atmosphere became a lot thicker too.

"Thanks for the warning," Rex said. "That was quite a step."

In the end, they had three separate settings that certainly looked as though they belonged to three separate sets of beings. The squat biped's atmosphere was thick and high in oxygen, but breathable. Like an oxygen bar.

They brought the isolated section back over to human normal and let it sit for a while. It took almost an hour for the temperature to get to normal and for the teams they had in place to do what checks they could. As far as the lab could tell, there were no biologicals in the air. It should be safe.

They'd have to trust it at some point. Their bottled air wasn't going to last forever. They could replace it with the mining gear, but that would take time and work. It would be better if the ship could take care of itself.

Next, Ray set out to bring the entire ship back up to pressure. That took longer, but at the end of the day, he was successful. They all stripped out of their suits and got to have some air that actually smelled natural.

Jess wasn't sure how they'd managed that, but she'd take it. It would make searching the rest of the ship easier and speed the process. *Freedom Express* was back in business.

* * *

JOSH QUEEN WOKE the next morning to some good news. The attorney general had decided that the space station sale had defrauded the government. The Justice Department was working with the SEC to void it. They'd have to take all due care, because Bennett would certainly contest everything in court.

Assuming they were ultimately successful, that left BenCorp on the hook for a lot of money, but Bennett wouldn't be going it alone. The end buyer—Humanity Unlimited—would need to return the US government's property. And if they didn't, well, that would lead to other measures to enforce the seizure of stolen property.

Of course, the other nations that had been part of the ISS2 program complicated the ownership claim, but they could settle their differences later.

The false narrative that Clayton Rogers had sold everything he owned outside of Humanity Unlimited to the Chinese was the first thing that Queen was going to see to. There was no way he'd allow that to stand.

He arrived at his office ten minutes late. His staff was already hard at work. His assistant—a woman named Gina Tanner—appeared at his side as he walked into his office.

"It seems Clayton Rogers is in Australia. He's meeting with several high government officials, and they've declared he has diplomatic immunity. I asked in case you wanted them to arrest him."

"That would've been too easy," Queen said with a sigh. "No, we're going to have to work harder for this one. I had an early morning conversation with the attorney general. That spaceship is the property of the US government. He's going to start legal proceedings.

"I want you to make contact with our partners in the ISS2 program and make them aware of our position. Offer them money or other favors to get their transfer of title. Don't take no for an answer."

The former international partners wouldn't stand up to the US on something like this. Besides, they'd receive two payments for the same property. They'd like that. It might almost make up for their original loss.

"There's one other thing," Gina said. "Someone from NASA has been calling since early this morning. He said he needed to speak with you about *Liberty Station*. He left his name and a callback number, if you want them."

Queen took the proffered slip of paper. Doctor Paul Scott.

"I'll see what he has to say. Keep me informed on the other items we discussed."

He made his way into his office and logged into his computer. A quick check of the name told him that Doctor Scott was an astronomer at the Palomar Observatory. The number they had on file was the same as on the slip of paper.

What the hell. He dialed the number, expecting the man to have gone to bed hours ago.

"Hello."

"Doctor Scott? Josh Queen here. I understand you were trying to reach me earlier."

"Thank God. I was afraid that woman was telling me she'd pass my messages along and then trash them. I don't know if you know who I am or what I do, but I'm involved with some research at the Palomar Observatory."

"Of course, Doctor. I checked you out. Don't keep me in suspense. What's going on?"

"Were you aware that the spaceship they're calling *Liberty Station* had matched course with an extinct comet?"

That sharpened Queen's interest. "No. Tell me more."

"It's a long-period body with a catalog number for a name. Completely uninteresting, except for the fact that it was between Earth and Mars on its outbound leg when they left Earth orbit. We don't have firm data on it, but based on its current speed, it will make it all the way out past Pluto before it starts its way back in."

"Okay. So they're the first people to visit a dead comet. And this is important because?"

"The comet is *gone*. We've been peeking at the ship between scheduled observation times on other projects. We'd wrap up one, move to take a look at the ship and comet, and then move on to the next scheduled sighting of whatever some university wanted to look at. We looked at them at 3:43 AM, and the ship was decelerating. There was no sign of the comet."

Queen tried to get his mind around what the man was saying. "Are you telling me they took the comet with them?"

"No. It's far too large for that. Something close to a kilometer in diameter. Far bigger than that ship. What I'm saying is that the comet is no longer in its predicted orbit."

The man said that last as though it was supposed to clear the whole matter up. Queen obviously needed a translator.

"Forgive me, Doctor Scott. It's early, and my mind isn't snapping to what you're saying. How could a comet that large just disappear?"

"That's precisely the thing. It can't. Not without changing course or speed. Something natural bodies do not do without exterior influence."

Queen sat up as it sank in. "They did something to the comet. They made it change course. They have a way to move large bodies like that around the solar system. That's what you're saying?"

"That or they blew it into pieces small enough that we're not able to locate them. Perhaps if they drilled into the core of the comet and planted a nuclear device down there."

The explosion theory sounded more likely. Queen couldn't believe they had some other space drive that was even more effective than the one they'd built into the old ISS2. And that meant he'd been right to be afraid of what they were doing.

Clayton Rogers had weaponized his ship. He'd taken nukes into space despite all the treaties forbidding it. And he no doubt meant to hold it over their heads.

The job of stopping him just became critically important.

12

Clayton was pleased with the work they'd done today. It was almost midnight, but they'd only just finished the last meeting. Rather than return to their hotel, he'd decided to spend the night in his new embassy building.

That afforded him the right to have heavily armed guards in attendance around the compound without the Australian government raising a fuss. In fact, their police patrolled outside the grounds in significant numbers, making certain that it wouldn't be easy for anyone to slip inside.

He'd arranged for that by paying off-duty officers to take officially sanctioned overtime work. And for funding direct pay to their department to cover for a number of additional officers to make up the difference.

Money well spent, if it kept some CIA kill squad out of his hair.

Some of Harry's people provided interior security. They came with the highest of recommendations, and Clayton made certain that they had everything they needed and more.

Men just like them were forming the core of Nauru's new military forces. All trained in the very best schools that the US government could provide, back before they gutted the military. Nauru would never challenge a major power, but if they could make it painful enough, well, that would make certain people think twice before starting a fight.

The people of Nauru had volunteered in surprising numbers. It exposed his biases, he supposed. He was an American, and he hadn't expected the laid-back islanders to show such a martial spirit.

Yet, they'd come willing to learn and work. Not only for the military but also for the nascent space program. He had plans to make the center of the island an even bigger commercial spaceport than the one he'd built in the Yucatán.

Rather than being made up of tapped-out phosphorus mines, the island would now become a clearinghouse for valuable minerals mined in space. The tariffs on the import of his products were low, but it would fund not only the spaceport but getting these people back on their feet and into space.

Clayton hadn't considered that before, but he knew it would happen. These men and women would venture into space and make their own claims one day. He'd see that they had the tools to make it happen.

Rather than be a mostly forgotten people languishing in poverty, they'd become the next generation of explorers. Seeking out the far corners of the solar system and making it their own. Good for them and good for him.

France had decided against buying Clayton's military jets, so he'd sold them to the government of Nauru at cost. He'd also sold the production facilities to Humanity Unlimited, along with other critical infrastructure and intellectual property that he wasn't going to give away.

They'd already moved the critical components and people to the island. The knowledge and skilled workers could be making new lifters for the spaceport in a very short time. And, perhaps spacecraft at some point.

Those jets now made for a very formidable air power. Other weapons systems that he manufactured formed a shore defense that could sink hostile ships, if need be. Antiair guns and missiles would make attack by jet an unpleasant experience as well.

All under the watchful eyes of the Chinese patrolling the waters offshore.

His erstwhile allies would eventually decide he wasn't worth the trouble. They'd most likely attempt to take him over themselves when it became worthwhile. They just didn't know what he was doing, yet.

Once they realized he was mining in space and the value of the ores became clear, they'd make a move to clip his wings.

His job now was to balance potential foes against one another to protect himself and his people while he built infrastructure. Considering the flaws they all had, that shouldn't be too difficult.

The Chinese owned the spaceport in Mexico, at least until the US forced the Mexican government to renege on the deal and pass ownership to them. That would happen, he was certain.

The US had scrapped all their facilities and would want to get people back into space as quickly as possible. They'd sold everything in Florida to commercial enterprises who'd then gone bankrupt. The gantries, buildings, and control centers had all collapsed over the last two decades. Or been cut up and sold for scrap. The people with the know-how had retired long ago or moved on to companies that appreciated their talents.

On their own, it would take the US a long while to build a modern spaceport. So, they'd steal one.

When he'd built the facility, he'd designed everything important so that he could destroy it easily, if he had to. Shaped charges hidden in all the critical areas. His security team would have ruined everything for any invader.

Clayton had told the Chinese all about those measures. His people had noted the Chinese technicians carefully removing the devices before they'd finished the handover. The Chinese seemed to feel they were safe from that sort of thing. It only went to prove there were idiots in every corner of the globe.

A rap at the door to his room drew his attention. It opened to reveal Miss Cash.

"He's here."

Clayton finished his drink and rose to his feet. "Excellent."

Their late-night guest was waiting for them in a small conference room. He stood and extended his hand. "It's a pleasure to meet you, President Rogers."

It was interesting to note how his accent differed from Miss Cash's New Zealand lilt. Clayton had been unaware there was some animosity between the two peoples until today. He'd seen how some people reacted to her and had had to rip a few heads off. Verbally, of course.

He'd need to inquire about the specific details at some point. For now, all that mattered was that everyone be professional. Of Miss Cash, he had no doubts. She'd proven herself thoroughly capable.

"The pleasure is mine, Mister Crabtree. Miss Cash tells me that you have some experience as a solicitor in marine-salvage litigation."

The man nodded as he resumed his seat. "Been doing it all my life. My father too. We can trace our work history as a family all the way back to the Admiralty courts. So, yeah. Me and my extended family are the best there is at this kind of thing."

Clayton sat on the other side of the table with Miss Cash. He poured himself some water. "That's excellent news. I'm afraid what I'm doing is going to put your encyclopedic knowledge to the test. We're doing something that has never been done before."

The man smiled, his expression doubtful. "We've done everything I can think of. You'd have to go pretty far out to find something that hasn't been worked on by my family."

Clayton nodded. "Very well. Miss Cash has paid your retainer, and you've signed the nondisclosure agreements. Let's cut right to the chase. You've no doubt heard that I have a spaceship on its way to Mars. Well, they found a nonterrestrial space vessel adrift up there and are engaged in salvaging it."

The man had started to pour himself a glass of water and promptly spilled it on the table. He hastily set the pitcher down and grabbed a handy towel to start soaking up the mess. "Excuse me, but did you say nonterrestrial? As in alien?"

Clayton smiled. "I did, though it's not certain what the providence is. There are human bodies on board, but our doctor indicates they've been dead for about a thousand years."

"I... see. And this has to do with marine salvage how?"

"This is where that new territory comes in," Penny said. "Space is considered international waters by treaty and law. So, finding this ship is in many ways the same as finding an unknown ship at sea."

The man slowly nodded. "I'll have to put in the research time to verify that's true, but let's assume for the moment that it is. If you found an abandoned ship at sea, the law doesn't allow you to claim outright ownership. That's a myth.

"The courts will determine what amounts the true owner has to pay for saving the vessel. In cases where the true owner can't be determined, it may be that the government of the owner may lay claim. That happens all the time with historical wrecks.

"And that's not all. This sounds like a high-order salvage, but it has to meet several criteria. The property must be in peril, the salvagers must be rendering voluntary service, and you have to be successful in saving the vessel in whole or in part."

Clayton nodded. "The research I'd already done hinted at that. Let's discuss peril. Are we talking immediate danger of loss of the vessel?"

The solicitor shook his head. "Not at all, though the peril has to be real. It can be something that might take a while to happen."

"The ship's engines came on once our people boarded it. It might have been something they did, but they're not sure. We evacuated almost everyone because it's headed out where we can't easily rescue them.

"In point of fact, it's already crossed the orbit of Jupiter and is on the fast track to the very outer edge of the solar system with three dozen of my people on board trying to bring it to a halt before it's lost forever. Along with themselves."

"Well, I'd certainly say that counts as meeting the first two items. And, I suppose if they can't get back with it, a salvage claim is a moot point, isn't it?"

"Indeed. We're planning for this to be successful, and I suggest that we count on them making it back with the ship. If need be, we can send *Liberty Station* after them. That would take a while, but so long as they stop somewhere in this solar system, we can do it."

"Right," Crabtree said. "Then we've got a lot of detail to fill in before I make our first appearance in court to file this. Even though the salvage isn't complete, we'll want to be ready to make a claim the moment it is. And for our purposes, that includes when you get it back on course into the system."

He shook his head and pulled out a legal pad. "My sister is never going to believe this one."

* * *

NATHAN PUT in an appearance just after noon. He'd enjoyed an early morning visit with the delectable Vanessa Messina and a private lunch. Both had been delicious in their own way. She had fire. He was going to enjoy breaking her when he had the luxury of time.

She'd be almost as much fun as Miss Cook, when he finally captured her. Maybe he could keep them both as a set.

The lunch on the patio overlooking the hills below had relaxed him. He was ready to make this happen now.

Most people would be intimidated to learn that they needed evidence from the police. Not Nathan. And particularly not in Italy.

The corruption here was legendary. Money could get him as much access as he wanted. Particularly in a group as underpaid as the police. Someone was always unhappy seeing how the criminal half lived.

His team leader had made a few calls overnight and located a source for the documents. The thing about evidence, the police needed to see it to make use of it. That meant it was vulnerable to leaks.

If he'd wanted it destroyed or a physical object removed, that would be a different matter. The controls on evidence might be difficult and expensive to overcome. A copy or picture? Well, that should be simple enough.

As everyone knew, skullduggery took place in the dead of night and deep in the shadows. So, he'd pick up the evidence in broad daylight where anyone could see them.

He'd use cutouts, of course. If the contact had been more trusting, he could have wired the money and had him send the data to an anonymous email account.

Unfortunately, the man knew watchdogs monitored the accounts of police for unusual activity. So cash was a better deal for him. He could put it away and spend it as needed with no one the wiser.

Ah well. That was sometimes the price of doing business.

They'd do the swap at dinnertime. He'd have one of his men meet the man at a public location. The man could see the cash, but he couldn't leave until Nathan's man verified what he had to offer. Otherwise, he'd never get out of the area alive.

Nathan wasn't going to be completely out of the picture, though. He'd be in a café just across the street. He liked seeing things as they happened.

They showed up an hour and a half early to make sure no one else was watching the meeting place. Everyone that came by got a look from his people.

None of them smelled like cops. And since they had no reason to suspect someone would want copies of the images, there would be no reason to send the kind of talent that could slip in without smelling like pork.

The contact showed up a few minutes early. Probably doing some scouting of his own. He scanned everyone in the area and spotted Nathan's man. He was the one with the bright-yellow handkerchief on the table.

Nathan focused on his earbud as he sipped his tea. The man quickly confirmed that he was the one with the data. He wanted to see the money.

They'd planned for that, so Nathan's man slid the briefcase partway across the table. It had the agreed amount inside. His man only let the other guy open it wide enough to see. He didn't want everyone gawking.

The informant nodded. He reached into his jacket and pulled out a large manila envelope. That wasn't according to plan.

Nathan keyed his radio. "Look alive. Something is wrong. Be ready to evacuate."

"What the hell is this?" Nathan's man asked. "You were supposed to bring me a data stick."

"I couldn't put the other papers on a data stick," the informant said. "You wanted all the weird writing. Well, they hadn't scanned everything yet. Don't worry! I made sure nobody saw me take them. With all the crap they're going through, it'll be weeks before someone misses it. And even then, they'll just think it was misfiled."

Nathan saw something out of the corner of his eye and turned his head a bit. A woman behind him and to the side was dropping money on the table. Her jacket was open just enough for him to see the gun on her hip and the badge on her belt.

That by itself meant nothing. Cops had to eat. The wire running up to her ear is what told him things were in the toilet. Others would be moving into place right now to block them in and arrest everyone.

"Code blue," he said.

His man pushed the case across to the idiot and grabbed the envelope. He turned and went inside the café quickly and without a word.

That brought police closing in from every direction. Jesus, they'd been all around them. These were pros too. Nathan counted six men and women. There would be others cutting off the likely escape routes.

All Nathan had were lemons. It was time to make lemonade.

13

It took close to their maximum acceleration to slow *Liberty Station* for orbital insertion. To say that it was a tense time was something of an understatement. If anything went wrong, they'd make a huge skid mark on the Red Planet.

Thankfully, nothing went wrong. All those hard hours of training paid off in spades. They slid into orbit without a bobble.

It took a few hours before they were in a stable position over Olympus Mons, but that was worthwhile too. The large telescope on the station had an even better resolution than the spy satellites.

He called his senior people together in his office. It was after midnight by then, but they were all too excited to call it a day.

Lindsay looked exhausted but amped. John "Black Jack" McCarthy, the pilot's understudy, was a sea of calm. Being an ex-marine fighter pilot, that wasn't a surprise.

Sandra Dean, his team sniper and now commander of *Liberty Station*'s security, looked as though she'd just woken up. "I assume we're orbiting Mars," she said, pouring herself some coffee. "Is there a reason we couldn't arrive in the daylight? Metaphorically speaking."

"That's just how the cookie crumbled," Lindsay said. "It's daylight down on the planet, though not yet inside the caldera. That comes in about an hour."

Harry nodded. He'd already confirmed those times. "Which is why we're getting up early. Or late. Whatever you like. There's something inside the caldera that I want to see in the daylight. We spotted what looks like a crashed ship."

Black Jack shook his head. "Man, these people are pissing me off."

He raised an eyebrow at the marine pilot. "How's that?"

"Every place they go, they crash land. That sounds kind of incompetent."

Harry laughed. "I see your point. Sooner or later, we'll find an intact bird for you to look at."

He turned to the others. "I want to get a team together in the next half hour. Our primary lifter pilot is prepping right now. We'll go down and take a good look at what's there. We'll only have about seven hours of light, based on the location of the crash, so we want to be as efficient as we can."

Sandra nodded. "This place was marked for a reason. Probably not because of the crash. There's a base of some kind down there. We're going to have to find it and see what kind of shape it's in."

"Anything we find might help Jess get control of her runaway locomotive," Harry said. "We'll take along some geologists and everything we need for a camp. If we find something worth exploring, I want to have a base camp. So, time is short. Get ready to go."

Half an hour later, they'd all gathered in the lifter. Black Jack sat up front with the command pilot while the rest of them strapped in. Harry had taken a few minutes to go to the observation level and watch the Red Planet beneath them. It was awe-inspiring.

The lifter detached from the ship right on schedule and drifted down toward the planet. Atmospheric entry was a lot rougher than he'd expected, considering how thin the atmosphere was.

The lifter had to make a short turn to come back over Olympus Mons, but it was a lot more manageable in flight by then. If he hadn't known they were over the system's largest volcano, he'd never have guessed. It looked like the rest of Mars.

Except for the caldera. It was amazingly huge.

The lifter sailed over the lip of the nested calderas and banked toward the crash site. The floor of the depression looked flat from orbit, but up close, it was a lot rougher. There were cracks, ridges, lumps, and boulders. Debris covered the ground.

Luckily, his father's engineers had designed the lifter to set down in rough terrain. "I see a good spot off to our left," the pilot said. "It looks to be less than five hundred meters from the crash. I won't say it'll be an easy walk, but it looks doable. Hang on."

The lifter slowed and hovered over the landing zone. The pilot lit the thrusters hard, jerking them up and blowing loose debris away. That made sense.

They did that three times before the pilot slowly settled to the ground and shut the thrusters off. "We're down and secure," the pilot said. "Welcome to Mars, everyone."

They all cheered and began unstrapping.

Sandra poked him in the shoulder. "I hope you've given this some thought."

He frowned. "What?"

She shook her head and clucked sadly. "You're about to be the first human being from Earth to step onto another planet. This is a big deal, Harry. You'd better have some heavy words to lay down for all the kids back home. 'One small step for man. One giant leap for mankind.' You remember that, right?"

Neil Armstrong was a hero. Harry, not so much. He'd stumbled into this. Almost literally. "I think Armstrong actually said, 'One small step for *a* man,' or at least he meant to. Yeah, give me a second to think about this."

It actually took them a good ten minutes before the pilot said it was cool enough outside for them to exit. They'd be using a winch to lower the personnel down from the airlock. The cargo, too, but that was a different part of the lifter.

Harry's mind raced as they secured him to the cradle. He could see across the basin. Well, not completely across it. The most distant walls were more than fifty kilometers away, even if they were more than three kilometers tall. Reddish dirt dominated everything.

The lifter's telescoping landing legs had cameras there for the pilot to make sure everything was clear. They'd catch him with Mars spread out behind him as he touched down. The time to put up or shut up was here.

He took the manual controls and lowered himself down until he was just above the planet's surface. He stopped the winch there and took a deep breath.

One slap and his quick release opened, dropping him to the surface, where he bounded forward. He prayed to God that he didn't trip over something.

"Today Mars. Tomorrow the universe. Humanity unlimited!"

* * *

KATHLEEN HAD JUST WALKED into her office when her private phone rang. It was Nathan.

"Please, tell me you didn't blow up the Colosseum."

"Have no fear, Mother. All the historically important sites are safe. I can't say everything went off without a hitch, but we had more success than I expected. I bribed a cop to get a copy of the manuscript pages. They're on the way via high-security courier."

She smiled coldly. Finally, something was going her way.

"Why a courier?"

"The idiot we bribed attracted more than his fair share of attention. It turns out there were more papers than Father's little bit managed to retrieve."

Kathleen leaned back in her chair. "Explain that."

"The pages she stole were not the only ones Romano owned. These new ones look like notes the author made to himself. Several dozen pages, some of them badly faded or stained. A mixture of the strange language and Italian. Some Latin, too, I think.

"And that's not all. There's a map. It looks like somewhere in France. I think that makes this pretty damned important. There was also something that looks like a data stick, but it doesn't fit any computer I know of. The courier left before I found it in the bottom of the envelope. I can get it to you later."

"Excellent work. I assume you got away cleanly."

"We're still in Rome. With the police swarming, we'll probably stay for a day or two. Besides, I have some unfinished business."

She really didn't want to know what it was this time. With Nathan, it might be a woman or a killing. Or both.

"Fine, as long as this doesn't blow back on me. Call when you get to Paris. Send digital images of the papers, both old and new."

"I'll get them off to you within the hour."

Kathleen hung up without responding. Her experts working on the book might be able to crack the code with this new material. Otherwise, it was proving impossible. They could see the patterns, but it wasn't making sense. Gibberish.

Now it was time to see if her assistant had wrangled the conversation she wanted with the Indian space officials.

Her private phone rang again. "Bennett."

"Mrs. Bennett, this is Ethan Wagner. I was wondering if you could make time to come by."

Wagner was the senior scientist studying the wreck. If he wanted her there, they'd made some kind of breakthrough.

"Look for me in an hour, Doctor."

It would take that long to be sure she'd lost the tail the FBI had on her. What they expected to find, she didn't know. Perhaps they hoped she'd lead them to another trove of bodies.

Rather than take her car, she climbed into the back of a panel van with the BenCorp logo in the parking garage. There were hundreds of them running all around the campus. Another one wouldn't draw any undue attention.

She still had the driver take a roundabout path into Chicago. He dropped her in another parking garage near a major hotel. A vehicle from the secret site picked her up, and they made it there without any complications.

Wagner was waiting for her in the lobby. Sweat covered the short man's bald head. It always did, no matter what the temperature was.

She followed him into the secure section of the building. The hard-eyed men guarding the doors not only examined their ID cards, but also took retinal scans. She'd been here often enough that they undoubtedly knew who she was, but that didn't stop them from verifying her identity.

Paranoia of which she heartily approved.

They ended up on the floor where his team was dissecting the wreck. The scientist only spoke once they were safely inside the area. "We've managed to crack the power requirements and have the ship's consoles online."

"Really? That's *excellent* news. How did you manage that without understanding the language?"

"We cheated. There's a secondary console in the aft section. Not much of one, but enough to experiment on. We isolated it and started feeding it low power levels and looking at how it responded.

"Once it reached a certain threshold, it came on enough to have data on the screen. Not much, but enough to tell us we were getting closer. One of my people wondered if it was telling us how the power needed to change.

"We modulated the voltage and amperage and watched the response. That let us compare what we were feeding it to the writing on the inputs. We made some educated guesses and pegged it closely enough for the console to come online and show the data its designers meant for it to display. With that as a guide, we did the same for the main control console. And here we are."

She nodded judiciously. "Very clever, Doctor. Very clever. That gets us one step closer to plumbing the secrets hidden in the ship. What about the drives?"

"Those have power requirements too. Ridiculously large ones, if I'm supposed to believe the numbers. I'm not certain I'd trust them. If our calculations were correct, it would take the output of a nuclear reactor to move this vessel. From a cube ten centimeters on a side. I'm not certain I believe that."

Kathleen gestured at the spaceship. "Yet here it is. I have people working on upgrading the prototype for my minireactor. Perhaps it will do the job. It won't fit in a small area like that. Or in the crashed ship, for that matter. Show me the main console."

They'd cleaned out the inside of the ship since the last time she'd been there. Now everything gleamed. And the body bags were gone.

She sat at one of the forward couches. "How does this work?"

"The console comes alive when you touch it. We don't know any of the controls, so we've been very cautious about exploring it."

A touch brought the console to life, along with the screen above it. It displayed the lab in very high resolution. The controls looked like something out of a science-fiction movie.

"If this vehicle is designed like anything we have, it has a record of where it's been. Perhaps even a log. I want those found. We've had a breakthrough on the language, so we might be able to start deciphering all this very soon. If we're lucky."

"That would be wonderful," the scientist said. "I'm certain there's so much we could learn here. The propulsion system must be very powerful."

She turned in her seat to face him. "Do you have any ideas on how it might work?"

"Well, it's not a reaction-based system. No fuel. My guess is that it manipulates the curvature of space."

"I'm not certain that I follow. How will that move a ship?"

His expression told her he was trying to find words small enough to explain a complex idea while not offending her.

"Just spit it out, Wagner. I'm not going to rip your head off."

"Of course. You see, gravity is an effect of mass distorting space. Imagine setting a bowling ball on a mattress. The ball presses into the mattress, and there is a divot. If I put something near it, that second object will roll into the depressed area. That is actually how gravity works. Roughly."

Not what she'd expected, but she didn't need to know that kind of thing. "Fine. I'll accept that as true since you say so. How would this ship move?"

"What if it can create a curve in space wherever it wants? Above it, say. Then the ship would rise. In effect, it would fall upward. Increase the curvature, and the ship would fall in whatever direction even faster. We believe that is what these drives are designed to do, though we have no idea how they work."

That was going to take a while to get her head around. She could use the technology in other ways, she was sure, but they'd actually have to reverse engineer it. That wasn't going to happen overnight.

It was time to move on. "You've done well. Keep working on it. As we make strides in the language, we'll keep you in the loop. Pass what you've done on to the linguistics people. It might help them to know what the power requirements translated to in reality."

He inclined his head. "Yes, ma'am."

Kathleen headed to the area where they'd taken the bodies. It looked very much like the morgues one saw on the television shows. And the anthropologist running the show looked like a mortician. Tall, gaunt, and humorless.

She walked into the area outside the lab and went through the clean-room procedures. He'd explained the reason for it quite forcefully. These bodies might have pathogens that could kill billions.

Kathleen had few scruples, but global extermination was something she'd prefer to avoid. Now, if they could isolate some strains that they could tailor to other uses, that was different. There were whole groups of people on the planet they'd all be better off without.

Once she was fully suited, she let herself in. The color codes on the arms of the suits told her who was who, so she knew which one was Doctor Damion Grey. He was standing over the mummified corpse of one of the unfortunates. He'd laid the body out on a stainless-steel table and cut it open like in an autopsy. Perhaps the comparison she'd made earlier wasn't so far off.

"Doctor Grey."

"Wait."

She knew better than to force the issue. It looked as though he was using a pair of tongs to dig around for something.

"Aha! There you are."

He pulled out the pliers. Covered in dried gore was something artificial. A dart?

"What is that?"

He half-turned toward her. "Mrs. Bennett. This is the cause of death, unless I miss my guess. All of the bodies had a number of these in their vital organs."

She leaned in close and examined the object. "It's a dart. I can see little fins and a point."

"Indeed. I'd call this a flechette. There's no sign of chemical propellant on the rest, so I'm envisioning a magnetic weapon. Something that gets them moving at high speed without pushing them up the barrel."

"I see. What else can you tell me about these people?"

"Have my reports gone astray? I'll have a word with my administrative assistant."

She'd gotten them, all right. They'd just been difficult to understand. "I'm not a professional in your field, Doctor. I want the rundown of what we know in layman's terms."

He blinked at her. "Ah. Of course. I see my mistake. I should've included an executive summary." He gestured at the man on the table. She knew the body was male because they hadn't bothered to leave the corpse any dignity whatsoever.

"This is subject three. A male of approximately forty years of age. He was in good health when he died rather abruptly. We recovered three flechettes from his torso already, and I'm sure there are half a dozen more in there."

Kathleen considered the dead man. "Can you estimate how long ago he died?"

"Based on carbon dating, I'd wager somewhere in the range of 800 to 1,200 years."

She cocked her head. "That's an unexpectedly wide range, Doctor. I thought carbon dating was a lot more specific."

"It usually is, however this man came from space. We don't know what variances his unusual environment introduced. If he were from Earth, I'd pin his time of death at just over a thousand years. That meshes well with the location of the body, time-wise. For scientific purposes, I'll leave the uncertainty factor in place until we know more."

Kathleen nodded. "And the others?"

"Another male and a female. The second male was younger. No later than his midteens. Possibly a little younger. The woman was in her late thirties. We've run genetic testing, and the DNA verifies the female is the younger male's biological mother. This gentleman is the father, so I suspect they were a family unit."

"And someone felt the need to execute them. Interesting. I wonder if we'll ever know the reason they were killed."

"Perhaps. I've turned their personal effects over to your lab people. The boy had what looks remarkably like a modern cell phone. It might have any number of interesting things hidden inside it."

With what the engineering team had discovered, that might actually prove helpful.

"Excellent work. Tell me, Doctor. Are they completely human?"

He frowned at her. "Of course they are."

"You say that like it was inevitable. They come from a technologically advanced, space-faring society. None of them came from Earth, so you'll forgive me if I wonder whether they aren't from a different evolution entirely."

"Mrs. Bennett, you are a brilliant woman in your field. You'll have to trust me that there is no possibility whatsoever that these people came from another planet. They are as tied to Mother Earth as we are. Theories of parallel evolution are the ravings of fools.

"Not only is their DNA exactly what I'd expect for a modern human, but the genetic markers allow me to make a fairly good guess at where these people originated from."

"Modern as in from our time frame?" she asked.

He shook his head. "Modern as in the last 150,000 years or so. Physically, humans have been pretty much as you see us since then. These subjects came from somewhere in central Europe. I'd wager the northern part of Italy. With access to a large genetics database, I could probably find people related to them today."

That was somewhat unsettling. Yet, the location tied into the papers they'd recovered. "How did they get into space?"

"Therein lies the mystery. If you'll excuse me, I'll see if I can't do my part to figure it out."

"One more thing," she said. "Have you found any pathogens we should be concerned about?"

Grey shook his head. "As near as I can determine, they don't have anything that isn't common on Earth today. We're only maintaining these suits out of an abundance of caution. I'm fairly sure we're safe from any superbugs."

"Thank you, Doctor. Keep me informed. With executive summaries."

"Of course." He turned back to his work as though she'd vanished.

She took her time with the decontamination procedures. The basic information they were getting confused her. Who were these people, and why were they no longer in evidence? Better yet, who had given them this technology and why?

14

"Ambassador Chen is here, Mister Secretary."

Queen looked up from his computer screen. "Send him in."

He rose from behind his desk and came out to meet the man who spoke for China. Chen was muscular for an Asian man, in Queen's experience, though short. He obviously lifted weights. A lot of them.

The man's massive build hid a keen mind, though. Queen knew he'd fooled others, to their chagrin. Chen wouldn't be one of them.

"Thanks for coming to see me on such short notice, Mister Ambassador. Can I get you anything? My chef is quite good."

"Thank you, no, Mister Secretary." His voice came out as a deep rumble, but his English was almost perfect. "Your message sounded quite urgent."

"It is. Please have a seat, and I'll get right to the point."

Queen resumed his seat behind his desk. "As you probably already guessed, we need to speak of Clayton Rogers."

Chen nodded. "I suspected as much. I believe my government has already made itself clear, though. We recognize his election as president of Nauru, and he is a head of state. The United Nations has also certified the election as free and fair. A term you Americans believe you invented and a yardstick you use to beat everyone else with."

"Hardly free or fair," Queen said. "He paid each and every man, woman, and child on that island a bribe to elect him to a position that no longer has any kind of term limits. A choice they will regret, I assure you."

The other man made a show of considering that. "I see. And that's different from American democracy in that your party provides expensive programs to lure many voters to support you. That also seems like bribery to me. No offense, of course. Just making a comparison."

"We both know there are no similarities there. We help the poor. We give them a hand so they can one day support themselves. Rogers literally handed them a stack of cash."

"I've often wondered if that would be more effective here in the US," Chen mused. "The numbers I've seen indicate that if you took the money meant for the poor and just gave it to them, it would be in the range of hundreds of thousands of dollars per person per year. And it would eliminate the inefficient bureaucracy Americans complain about so often. Is that not what you call a win-win situation?"

Queen reined in his temper. "We're getting off subject. Before I start reminding you about how terrible your own bureaucracy is, allow me to get back on point. The United States is unwilling to stand by and see this international criminal use diplomatic immunity to escape the punishment for his crimes."

Chen's eyes widened slightly. "International criminal? Have you brought charges in the international court? I believe only the United States wants to see the man punished."

"Don't play word games with me. After all, he fooled you too. Have you been following his progress?"

"His spacecraft?" Chen's expression soured. "Yes. He reached Mars last night. They have already landed a small craft and claimed the planet for themselves. Now that, I grant you, is a violation of international treaties."

"He did *what?*"

Chen smiled. "You obviously haven't seen the video they beamed back to Earth. It's quite illuminating."

Queen tamped down his rage. The bastards! The unmitigated gall of these people.

"Just another example of their character. In any case, these people have not only violated that one treaty. We have evidence they took weapons of mass destruction into space. They stopped at an extinct comet and destroyed it with a nuclear weapon."

He slid a data stick across the desk. "We expect you'll want to verify everything on that, but the data should allow you to identify the comet. You can confirm that it is gone now. Blown to bits."

Chen took the stick and slid it into his jacket. "Those are troubling charges. If true, they will bear thinking about."

"It's also come to our attention that he smuggled a nuclear reactor into orbit in contravention of international treaty. I have no doubt the ongoing investigation will reveal other crimes.

"The bottom line is that it is the position of my government that the original sale of the ISS2 space station to his company was part of a fraudulent scheme to defraud American taxpayers of billions of dollars. We will reclaim possession of our property."

Chen smiled. "So, you intend to take ownership of that vessel? An interesting ploy, but you do not control the international courts. A ruling in America means spit when levied against another country. Unless, of course, you can seize the property in America."

It was Queen's turn to smile. "Ah, about that. We intend to invalidate every sale of property he made to your country. Stolen property, you see. Rainforest was obviously complicit in these crimes. And those other purchases you made? I wouldn't expect them to remain in your hands for very long, if I were you.

"In fact, I've already spoken to the Mexican ambassador about the spaceport. They went in early this morning to take possession on our behalf. I'm shocked you haven't heard."

"You take great liberties with my country," Chen said, his voice cold. "Large talk from an inferior military power. We will not stand idly by while you steal from us."

Queen was in his element now. "Will China go to war to protect one man? You made a bad call. His money is in your banks. Seize it and we can all walk away from this without harm."

He knew Rogers had already slipped his cash to other holdings. Well, that wasn't his problem.

Chen stood slowly. "The acts you consider will carry grave consequences. We will defend the property of our state and our people with force, if need be. You should consult with your government before you push us to the point of proving the inferiority of the American military. Good day, Mister Secretary."

Queen watched him leave with satisfaction. This was all talk. China wouldn't go to war over Rogers and some property.

Still, it might be worthwhile to have a talk with the secretary of defense. Moving forces down to Mexico to hold onto the spaceport would make things more certain. And naval units. They had enough of them stuck in port due to budget constraints. Let those people go earn their pay.

* * *

It took Nathan and his people several hours to be certain they'd escaped cleanly and more time for him to send the data to his mother, so that put him into evening rush hour by the time all was said and done.

His primary mission here was a success, so he should be able just to slip out of the country. Under other circumstances, he would. Only he still hadn't gotten even for the mob trying to kill him.

They needed to understand that some people were not on their list of targets. By the time he finished with them, they'd certainly get the message.

His team was just down the street from a business used by the man who'd ordered Nathan's kidnapping. It was still a busy time of day, so they probably felt secure in there. The search teams the mob had sent out hadn't had much luck. That had to be frustrating.

Nathan's group was armed and armored for a full frontal assault. In and out. Just a few minutes and they'd be on the road. He'd return to the villa, and they'd depart directly from there. He didn't want to leave his new toy, after all.

The driver pulled out of traffic and stopped in the loading zone. Two men got out and blocked the flow of pedestrians. They'd taken the time to make up vests that looked like they belonged to law enforcement, so the people backed off.

When the time came that the real police wanted descriptions, there would be nothing to identify them. Neat and clean, in his opinion.

The rest of the team hit the front door hard and fast. A portable battering ram reduced it to splinters. They shouted that they were the police in Italian. Poorly accented Italian, to be sure, but that produced the desired effect of giving them the initiative.

He'd ordered the men to let anyone that seemed harmless to flee, but not if they had any doubts. The customers in the front of the store did the smart thing and dropped to the floor. The mobsters went for guns.

They were woefully outclassed.

When his men broke into the back of the store, they used grenades to clear the rooms. An informant had already told them where Luca Russo's office was. He was there. They'd made sure of that. A message needed ears to hear it.

His guards died hard, but die they did. He tossed a stun grenade through the shattered door, and they rushed in. The mobster was on the floor but fired on them anyway.

Thank goodness for body armor. A slug caught Nathan in the chest but did him no lasting harm. He stomped on the mob boss's hand, breaking bones and dislodging the weapon.

"You shouldn't have targeted me," Nathan said conversationally. "Tell me you understand or I'll just kill you now."

"I understand," the man grated. "Get it over with."

"Ah, you misunderstand. I'm not going to kill you. I'm going to let you live so my message gets to your bosses. Don't screw with me or mine. Ever."

He grinned. "But, there *is* a price for attacking me. You'll live, but I'm going to hurt you *real bad.*"

He shot the man in both kneecaps. And while he was writhing and screaming, he pinned the man's undamaged hand under his boot and ruined it too. Now the mobster couldn't walk or handle things. He sure hoped that the mob had good disability benefits.

"Time to go," he said.

They withdrew the way they'd come, killing a few more men rushing to the scene. He let his men handle that while he tossed white-phosphorous grenades into the rooms as they passed. He wondered if the man would get out before the building burned down. Nathan hoped so, but only after some nasty burns.

The van was waiting for them. He could hear sirens in the distance as they slammed the doors and took off. He'd picked a ubiquitous color for the stolen vehicle. It wouldn't get a second look.

It only needed to work until they got to the second vehicle. After all, why change a plan that worked?

The police flew past them as they cleared the area. The vehicle change went off without a hitch. A phosphorous grenade made sure it was burning merrily by the time they were gone. The fire department here was really getting a workout.

The trip back to the villa was quiet, but the place was in an uproar when they arrived. His second team was out in force, scouring the grounds.

"What's happening?" he asked as they arrived.

"That bitch got loose," one of the men said. "She stabbed François in the jewels and got out of the house."

The idiots. He'd told them to leave her alone.

"Forget her. Gather everything important. Anything that could identify us. You have five minutes."

He recovered everything from his room and made a pass through to follow up on everyone else. Once they finished scouring the house, he used the last of the phosphorous grenades to set it on fire. He made sure to leave one on his bed. They'd get no DNA evidence from him.

As they drove away from the second fire of the day, he wondered if they'd label him a serial arsonist. Ah well. And he'd miss the little bit. She'd been *so* amusing. Maybe he'd come back some day and find her.

On the down low, of course. She'd no doubt make an accusation of rape against him. It had happened before. He'd have plenty of witnesses to say he'd left Italy the same day he'd arrived.

Nothing would stick to him. It never did.

15

J ess slept fitfully and woke foggy. Only after breakfast and an extra dose of coffee was she really awake. It was hard to get any sleep when things were changing so rapidly. Which sucked, since she was usually a morning person.

She wasn't sure how it was possible, but their speed had grown incredibly high, and the rate of that acceleration just kept edging up. They'd already passed the orbit of Saturn and would handily beat her guess that they'd reach the strange object that they were rushing toward in a week.

At this rate, they'd get there in another day. Faster, if they didn't start slowing down soon. If they didn't stop, they'd exit the solar system a day or so later and be into interstellar space.

Doctors Powell and Young were waiting for her as soon as she reached the core. The two women looked almost giddy.

"Tell me the truth," Jess demanded. "You found chocolate."

Rachael Powell laughed. "Not quite *that* good but close. We found a library. Those crates in the dorm compartment had a ton of old books and scrolls. A historical treasure trove."

"And that's not all we found," Paulette Young said. "There's another compartment with even more, and it had a console with electronic versions. It took most of the night, but we figured out how to open them. Best of all, we know how to link them to the paper versions."

Rachael nodded. "It was something like the Dewy Decimal System. Once we found the corresponding book in electronic form, we discovered that it wasn't just scanned, it was translated into the alien language."

Jess blinked. "So, you can read it?"

"We're working on something right now. We have optical scanners, and we'll try to superimpose what we think a word means over it. Programs like that existed as far back as twenty years ago. You could get something in a different language on your phone screen in real time and get a very rough translation. It actually changed the words you were seeing.

"We'll try to do the same thing. Unknown words will be in a different color or something. As we make progress, we can refine the translations."

"That sounds wonderful," Jess said. "What kind of time frame are you thinking?"

"Hours for the first iteration," Rachel said. "It probably won't work that well. We're modifying a program on one of the crew's phones. Violating all kinds of copyright, I'm sure. So, we're starting from a platform that we know works."

"The bad part is that we're working in the dark," Paulette said. "We won't really know if some subtle interpretation changes the meaning. We can translate what we know back to Old Italian, but we're not really fluent there, either. It's going to be rough."

Jess nodded. "And the technical terms probably won't translate at all. Or not well. How will you handle that?"

"If you think a word means something, we'll add it to the database. We can always fix it as we go if we're wrong."

"That sounds great!" Jess said. "Ladies, you might just have saved our lives. Have you slept?"

She knew from the way they looked at one another that they hadn't. "Go get a few hours of shut-eye. Then hit this fresh. At this point, speed is not the critical factor. Accuracy is. And you'll be more prone to error if you're tired. Scoot."

Once they were gone, Jess looked around for Michael Crockett. She didn't find him, but she did find his wife. Sierra was cataloging various small objects on a tablet.

She looked up and smiled at Jess. "Good morning."

"Morning. I wanted to ask your husband a question, but you might be the better choice. We've found some old books and scrolls. They need to be safely categorized and preserved. Doctors Powell and Young found them and didn't have concerns about their condition, but I figure if I don't tell your husband he'll…"

"Have a cow? Probably." Sierra smiled. "I'd look for him in Emily's room. They had some things to discuss but should be done by now."

Unlike Jess and about half of the others, the Crocketts and Emily Adams had decided to move into the original crew quarters. It felt a little creepy to Jess, but that wasn't her problem.

"That's good. I need to talk with her too. The doctors have hit on a way to use a phone program to do translating for us, but they don't really have the computer background that Emily does. She should probably take the lead on that."

Sierra nodded. "She's a whiz at computers and programming. And a damned fine artist too. Not that that's relevant for this, but still."

"That might help in ways we can't see yet. Thanks."

Jess made her way to the adjoining cabins and tried to remember which was which. She shrugged and knocked on one. Michael Crockett's muffled voice came through the door. Jess thought he said come in, so she opened the door.

Just in time to see a partially clad Emily run into the bathroom. She'd obviously picked the wrong room. "I'm sorry. I thought Doctor Crockett was here and told me to come in."

"Actually, I said to hang on a minute," Michael Crockett said as he came out of the bathroom, putting his shirt on.

Jess stood there with her mouth halfway open, not sure exactly what to say.

* * *

CLAYTON AND PENNY CASH arrived in New Zealand at 9 AM local. They landed at the International terminal at the Queenstown Airport. The scenic view on approach was one of the most beautiful he'd ever seen.

Penny got them out of the airport and into a car quickly and smoothly. In just minutes, they were driving. His driver watched the roads while the two of them sat in the back and watched the beautiful countryside and Lake Wakatipu slide past. Amazing.

"So," he said after a few minutes, "why don't you give me a rundown of where we're going. Not the entire history of New Zealand, mind you. Just the particulars key to the task at hand."

"Sure. We're on the South Island. New Zealand's main export is agricultural goods. Dairy is big, and so is meat. Wool used to be big, but it's fallen out of favor.

"The area on the map you marked is currently a very large sheep station with a lot of rough, hilly country. The feelers I put out say the owner is willing to deal, if he likes you."

Clayton smiled. "You mean, if he likes my money."

She shook her head. "No. I mean if he likes *you*. He doesn't have to sell, and the land has been in his family for a long time. If he thinks you're an ass, he'll tell you to start walking. You need to win him over. Remember, you don't just need a station here. You need *this* one."

"Are we even sure the place we're looking for is on his land?"

"His spread is pretty big, so yeah. It's on it somewhere."

"How big is big?"

"Roughly 25,700 hectares. That's about 63,500 acres. He has about twenty thousand sheep and a thousand head of cattle."

That was a large spread. He'd be paying a pretty penny for this property. If he didn't want to shell out a lot of money, he needed to put his best foot forward. There was a time for being a cantankerous old man and a time for being as smooth as honey.

They drove down the lakeshore for half an hour and then took a boat across. A man in a Range Rover picked them up at the dock.

They drove for a short bit before the house became visible. It was a big one, low slung and spread out. It looked like a working part of the station, based on the number of people doing things. Several large barns seemed integral to their tasks.

The men had a resemblance to hands he'd have expected to see in the old west. That shouldn't have surprised him, he supposed. People dressed in serviceable, long-lasting clothes for work.

Penny put her hand on his arm. "Let me do the initial talking. Mister Durey is a bit of a curmudgeon, and I want to gauge his mood. I'll introduce you, and then you can broach the deal when he seems in the mood to talk about it. Don't rush. This conversation needs to take as long as it takes."

"I'll be good. I promise. If you see me wandering off script or have a suggestion, jump right in."

He climbed out of the vehicle and decided to leave his jacket in the car. It was warm enough without it, though there was a little chill in the air. It reminded him that the seasons were reversed down here. He'd have to get used to snow in July. And warm, sunny Christmases. That was going to be odd.

The main door to the house opened, and a tall rugged man came out. He looked as though the wind had worn all the soft places off him. A large hook of a nose dominated his face, bent a little to one side. No doubt telling the story of one hell of a brawl when he was younger.

Penny took the lead and introduced herself, shaking the man's hand. "Ashton Durey, this is Clayton Rogers."

Clayton stuck his hand out. The two men shook, getting a mild test of strength as they measured one another.

"Mister Rogers," the man said. "Welcome to the neighborhood."

"The longer I live, the fewer people that remember that damned show," he said with a real smile. "My son absolutely loathes it."

The other man grinned. "It was big when I was a kid. I have the whole series on disc. The grandkids love it. The two of you can come on in."

The inside of the house was golden hardwood, and equipment and saddles hung on the walls. A worn and lived-in working home. Clayton approved.

"My wife is in town with the rest of the lady folk and grandkids. I figured we'd best talk without everyone chipping in their opinion. You want a beer?"

"Sure. Whatever is handy."

He gave Clayton a measuring stare. "I'll wager you like that horse piss they sell in the US. Crap, every ounce of it. I'd suggest pouring it out, but then you'd have to fill out all those damned environmental-impact statements. I'll get you something that'll put hair on your chest. Anything for you, Miss Cash?"

"Something without chest hair, please."

He laughed. "I can handle that."

A few moments later, he had some cold bottles out of the fridge. Armageddon Pale Ale made by the Epic Brewing Company. He'd never heard of the brand before. It tasted very much of hops. He wasn't much for beer personally, but something like this might change his mind.

"This is *good*. I'll assume it's made in New Zealand."

The man nodded. "Yup. I'm not surprised you haven't heard of it. All you Americans ever know about this area of the planet drink-wise is Foster's. You can do better."

"I'm starting to get the idea you New Zealanders don't much care for your neighbors."

"You could say that. Just don't call it family issues. You might get into a fight for that."

Clayton held up his hands. "I'm not from around here and have no intention of getting involved in my neighbor's squabbles. The people on Nauru seem to agree with your assessment, though."

"Smart people, sounds like. I've heard a bit about you. That's your spaceship that just landed on Mars?"

He nodded. "My son, Harry. He's a good boy, but not my biggest fan."

The other man leaned back against the counter and took a drink. "Why is that, if I might ask?"

"I made a lot of money running a corporation. You don't get to the top of something like that without stepping on toes. And heads. I hurt people, and he doesn't much care for me because of that."

"You changed much since then? Not sure you sound like the kind of fella I want to sell the family station to."

He saw Penny stiffen a little, probably afraid of how he'd respond.

Clayton gave the other man a considering look. "Not so much, but I'll draw a distinction. I always had the people working for me in mind. I'm not the kind of person to lay off thousands just to boost the stock price. The heads I broke were sharks like me. They had it coming, and I'd do it again in a heartbeat."

Now Penny had the "deer in the headlights" look. This conversation was veering far off the course she'd plotted, but Clayton was going on instinct. This man was a lot sharper than the image he was projecting. He'd have a good bullshit detector.

Durey took another drink and slowly nodded. "I suppose a man who's going to build a secret spaceship in orbit and run off to Mars might walk over a few people on his way to the top of the heap. Why Mars? Why space?"

"Because mankind is choking the Earth. Or maybe it's better to say we're getting too crowded and there are too many assholes in the world making things dangerous for everyone. Mars isn't the goal of my space project. I'm going to start mining in space and building large habitats all around the solar system. It's time to get humanity spread out a bit. One idiot having a bad day could bring society down.

"Or it might come down under its own weight. I don't know. I'd rather see humanity survive whatever nature has in store for it, and that means we need to spread out. If something like a massive coronal ejection takes out high technology down here, I don't want to miss the chance we have."

The other man considered that and nodded. "I can see that, though it confuses me a little. Why are you looking to buy a Kiwi sheep station?"

"I sold off most of my companies and have a lot of cash at the moment. I have some ideas that this property could play into."

"To do with space? Hard to see the connection."

Clayton nodded. "It isn't easy to connect the dots, but they're there in my mind. This looks like a solid business with a lot of family history. I know wool isn't doing so well right now, but why sell? If you weren't already thinking that way, we wouldn't be having this conversation."

The other man grunted. "Coincidentally enough, it's the future that has me in the crack. My kids all ran off to the big city and don't want anything to do with sheep. An occasionally thankless job, I'll grant you.

"And with the downturn, I'm having trouble justifying even trying to get the grandkids interested. They're city born and bred. One year soon, I'll have no choice. I'm not getting any younger."

Clayton could relate to that. "If we can come to an agreement, I give you my word your people will be treated right. And, perhaps, there's something else I could do that might make a difference."

"What's that?"

"I'd imagine your kids have their own lives mapped out, but what if I offered your grandkids the very best education, but one they'd have to work for. One that led to important work in the space program that's going to spring up down here."

Durey seemed to consider that. "Down here? What kind of space work?"

"I'm breaking ground on a major spaceport on Nauru. The space mining industry will be bringing a lot of valuable minerals to this part of the world. That's going to make industry spring up where it never existed before.

"Imagine them as engineers mining an asteroid. Or piloting a spaceship up on a lance of fire. Exploring the limits of the solar system. Surfing the rings of Saturn. Maybe even leaving the system one day. Who the hell knows?"

The room settled into a long quiet spell as Durey considered what he'd said. Clayton knew he'd made an offer that the other man liked, but only time would tell if it swung things in his favor.

"What do you mean when you say an education they'd have to work for?"

He smiled. "Kids don't respond well to having everything handed to them. My son Nathan is the poster boy for pampering gone wrong. They have to work for their dreams. Work hard. That makes an achievement mean something.

"So, I'd pay for their schooling, but only so long as their grades made the cut. B's and above. C's are for people who don't want something badly enough. Then, when they have their degree, a job on the track they're looking for.

"If they want to be an engineer, they'd work with the top men and women in the field. People with high expectations. Ones they'd have to work their butts off to meet. That's how you become the best at what you do."

Durey looked at Clayton, his eyes unreadable. Then he took a drink and set the bottle down. "I think we might be able to come to an agreement after all. Let's go look over the property and see if we can agree to a number we can both live with.

"It won't be cheap. I love this land. But I love my grandkids more."

16

Harry was exhausted. Idiot him, he'd thought they'd land on Mars and go exploring.

Nope. It was dark in the caldera now, and they'd been humping ass to get the camp set up. They'd needed to cart the habitats to a handy lava flow near the crashed ship. That five hundred meters of rough ground meant they'd spent an hour just finding and marking the best path.

Then they'd carried *everything* over on their *backs*. The sun was almost to the wall when they'd inflated the habitat and started moving their gear inside, along with the food and other consumables.

Now that they'd finished, the pilot had cooked dinner. Cooking being boiling water and pouring it into a dehydrated food packet to steam as it reconstituted. Rice and beans. Not bad.

They'd wanted to spend every second moving gear, but he'd put his foot down. So, they'd scouted a path to the wreck too. And to the area beyond it.

The camp was very close to the crashed ship, so it was a safe trip in the dark, as long as they had lights. No big cracks or other obstacles, but they'd still put up ropes to guide them. They'd need them if the lights failed for some reason. It was darker than the cave under the pyramid in Guatemala.

Well, maybe not *that* dark. The stars shone in their unblinking glory. Phobos and Deimos also cast some light when they were in the sky. The closer of the two, Phobos, sped along, making two orbits a day. It was in the sky a bit more than four hours at a time. Deimos took a leisurely thirty hours to circle the planet, so they'd have it all night.

The ship had crashed a long time ago. Perhaps a thousand years. It struck hard and slid right into the wall of the caldera. Part of that intimidating cliff of stone had fallen on it.

If the layout was the same as the other craft, it didn't look as though anyone had made it out. Rocks partly blocked the airlock. If it had opened, they would've fallen in, and no amount of work would have allowed them to close it again.

Someone had almost made it.

Their destination was obvious. A massive hatch about sixty meters to the left meant there was a base built into the volcano. The fact no one had come out to rescue these people said it was probably deserted.

The base would wait for tomorrow, but Harry was convinced they could get into the crashed ship with a little elbow grease. The light gravity made levering the rocks out of the way easy. He wasn't worried about further rock falls. If it hadn't come down in a thousand years, odds were very good it wasn't going to drop tonight.

They moved the stones blocking the airlock in twenty minutes. Harry had to shuck his glove to control the key he'd brought. They'd found others on the comet, so he didn't feel bad about taking it.

The thin air of Mars was cold. Intensely cold. Once night fell, the temperature plummeted. Up here, with the thinner atmosphere, it would get colder than any of them had ever experienced.

The key slid into place, and the airlock opened slowly. It only made it partway before it froze. Harry could see that the frame was warped. He managed to wedge himself inside. He worried the inner door wouldn't open, but it gave him no trouble.

The inside of the ship was a shambles. And a slaughterhouse.

Even before it had crashed, blood had coated the inner compartment. Mummified corpses littered the floor, not in neat body bags but where they'd fallen or been tossed in the crash.

These people hadn't died of blunt force, either. Someone had shot most of them. He'd seen enough wounds like that to know.

Several dozen men, women, and children lay sprawled in whatever angles fate had left them. He could see the pilot's console up front. The stones had come in through the forward roof and crushed the pilots to death. He guessed no one survived the crash.

"We're going to have to take our time in here, Sandra. It's a charnel house. I'll take pictures, and then we'll empty it out in the daylight."

He saw something on the floor and picked it up. A pistol, but not like the ones he was familiar with. It didn't have a slide to toss out the expended brass. He spotted a safety but had no idea which setting was safe versus ready to fire. He'd carry it back by hand. Cautiously.

* * *

"You're what?" Jess asked.

"We're an extended family unit," Crockett said. "It's really not that unusual."

He sat at a table in the area they were using to eat with his wife and—

girlfriend?—at his sides. Neither of them seemed disturbed, so Jess had to believe him, though she really didn't understand.

She nodded. "I've heard about polygamy, of course. I just haven't ever met anyone that practiced it."

"This isn't anything like the terrible things you occasionally hear about in the news," Emily said in an even, matter-of-fact tone. "We're all in this together because we want to be."

"We've been a family for years," Sierra said. "Us and Jacob Danvers back on Earth. He's in the Marine Corps. We're in this for the long haul, and we're not a problem that's about to blow up in your face. The only drama you'll see is Michael when he doesn't get his way."

"Hey," he objected mildly. "I'm not that bad."

Both of the women gave him steady looks.

Jess shook her head and smiled. "I can't imagine how a relationship like that is stable, but if it works for you, I'm certainly not going to judge. More power to you."

"You said something about books and scrolls," Sierra said. "What can you tell us about them?"

"Doctors Powell and Young opened the crates that were in the room we took over for a dorm. They had books and scrolls in sealed containers of their own, and they look intact, so we're assuming they've protected them. There were more in another compartment.

"They also found copies—scans, really—in the computer system. Someone translated the finds to the strange language. So, we're working on identifying where these books and scrolls came from so we can reverse the process."

Michael Crockett nodded. "I should be able to place them in general terms. Sierra is actually more familiar with many of the forms of writing than I am, so she might be able to narrow them down even further."

His wife smiled. "I'll take a look and send some sample images back to *Liberty Station*. They can consult with experts on Earth without implicating us in the outer system. That said, I'll want to examine them as soon as possible."

Jess turned to Emily. "We're also hoping you can help them modify the computer program in one of their phones to do translations on the fly."

The younger woman nodded. "I'll have to take a look, but I'd imagine I can. I think I know the program you're talking about. One that you catch foreign writing in the camera, and it morphs on the screen?"

"That's the one."

Emily smiled. "Then you're in luck. I've already modified a version of it to translate some of the other languages we usually work with. I paid the developer for a copy of the source code, and we work together on improving the program when I push it in new directions. My copy is fully licensed for me to mess with it."

Michael Crockett stood. "So, if we're finished, I've got a lot of work to do. I'll focus on the physical copies. No offense to Doctors Powell and Young, but I want to be certain we don't miss anything that needs to be done to protect these priceless artifacts."

The unspoken implication was that there were plenty of other artifacts on this ship that weren't being protected. Yep, not so subtle.

Emily hung back when the other two made their way out. "You really don't need to worry. We have the same ups and downs as more traditional couples, but nothing that will cause anyone else problems. We've already told him that he needs to keep his roving eye on lockdown while we're in this situation."

Jess rose to her feet and walked out with the other woman. "He has a roving eye? I guess I shouldn't be surprised. I can't imagine how you make it work."

"It does take the right personality for it and the ability to set aside some of the normal jealousy. He doesn't sneak around behind our backs, though. We have a say on who is part of our group, so if we veto, he doesn't pursue someone."

She shook her head. "You have my deepest respect for making that work, and more power to the four of you.

"Back to the crisis at hand, I'm hopeful that you'll be able to get us some translations on the control screens. At this point, so long as we start slowing back down, I'm inclined to let this train pull into the station on its own, but we'll need to know what happened so we can get back home."

"I heard we'll be passing close to Neptune later today. Within visual range?"

"That's what I'm told. We'll be having an escorted trip out to see it after dinner. I'll make sure everyone knows."

"Great! I wouldn't want to miss something like that."

Ray Proudfoot was inside the elevator when they arrived. "There you are, Jess. Miss Adams."

"What do you need, Ray?" Jess asked.

"We found something you need to see. We've explored every section of the base, except for the tunnel with the cave-in. Rex went down to look at it with me and has some observations."

The cave-in had been on the second level in from the surface. It wasn't nearest the surface, so they were relatively confident that it wasn't a threat to their life support. It looked as though one of the corridors had collapsed at some point in the past. She wanted to know what was on the other side of it, which was the only reason they were even considering digging it out.

They made their way up after Emily got off the elevator at the core. The base was huge. Like their own personal Death Star, just smaller.

Rex had dug out some of the area and was standing there with a shovel. "Hey, Jess. I found something important."

She looked over the collapsed tunnel. "I've seen far too many of these in the last few weeks. What's up?"

"See these?" He pointed to a shattered wall beside the area he'd dug out.

"The wall? Sure. It broke."

"No, inside the breaks." He used a finger to pull out a shard of metal. "This isn't part of the wall."

Jess took it from him and looked it over. It was about five centimeters long, bent, and burned. "I'm missing it."

"This is shrapnel. It was involved in an explosion. This was part of an antipersonnel bomb. From the make-do nature, I'd wager this was an improvised explosive. The blast probably brought the roof down."

She shook her head. "What were these people fighting about? Why did so many need to die?"

"I've got another question for you. We found that ship in Guatemala. Harry found one on Mars. Where did they come from?"

Jess frowned. "Is that a trick question? Here, I suppose."

"That docking bay up there had room for one ship. Where did the second one come from?"

"You think it came from behind the collapse? We didn't find any indication of a second hangar when we scanned the surface."

"We didn't land here and look all that closely. What if there was a larger, underground hangar through here?"

She shook her head. "Why conceal one and make the other obvious?"

Rex shrugged. "I'm not sure why these people did anything. Both crashed ships came from here, or there's another place we haven't found. Harry verified they had the same patches, so I'm betting they were crew here.

"This rock looks like a dead comet. Even at very close range. If we hadn't been looking hard, we'd have missed that first hangar. What if there's something larger that they were worried would be found more easily?"

She supposed that was possible. It didn't cost them anything to look. "Have them turn down the gravity here and get some help. Be careful of vacuum. I want this section opened up as soon as possible. I'll take a team up to the surface and see if I can find any sign there's a secret bay."

17

———

J osh Queen had to hustle to make it through the screening process at the White House and only barely made it to the Oval Office on time. As usual, the room never failed to make him quiver with excitement. One day, this would be his. He knew it deep in his bones.

George Blankenship rose from behind the desk and came around to the seating area.

"Josh, so good of you to come over. Tea?"

"I'm good, Mister President. Your call sounded urgent."

The two of them sat on the comfortable couches, and the president leaned forward. "I just had a meeting with the Chinese ambassador and, to be blunt, he was pissed. He said you were threatening to seize Chinese property. I'd like to know what's going on."

"Are you sure you want to know, sir? With the election coming up, you might want plausible deniability."

"I can't deny the man told me you planned on ejecting his countrymen from the Yucatán Spaceport. I might as well know what's happening, because he's going to make a stink about it."

The president smiled. "Son, space travel is dead. We killed it here in this office twenty years ago and good riddance. The money can be better spent earning us brownie points with our base."

"I'm not so sure it's as dead as we'd like it to be, sir. You've heard about the space station that was really a ship?"

"Of course. Some idiot wasted his money building a spaceship and beat the Chinese and Indians to Mars. Big deal."

"There's more than meets the eye. We're pretty sure he has nuclear weapons up there."

Blankenship's expression narrowed. "That's a serious allegation. Do we have any evidence to back it up?"

"He blew up a dead comet on the way to Mars. Destroyed it so completely it went from about a thousand kilometers in diameter to nothing. That seems pretty conclusive to me."

The president considered that and then nodded. "Fair point. So, what justification do we have to seize the spaceport? Clayton Rogers already sold it to the Chinese. They didn't have anything to do with the weapons, did they?"

"Not that we know of. I talked to the AG, and he agreed that the original sale of the ISS2 framework was fraudulent. Rogers's ex-wife bilked the government out of a lot of money for that failed project.

"I think she was in league with Clayton Rogers to make it look as though the project had fallen so far behind schedule and over budget that we'd never see it done. Then she let her ex buy it cheap through the Russians. They helped because they hate us. The US government footed a lot of the bill for that spaceship. It belongs to us."

Blankenship frowned. "That's quite a leap to prove in court. And, it doesn't speak to seizing the spaceport. He also said something about you promising to seize other Chinese companies."

"Well, not precisely. Rogers sold Rainforest to the Chinese without clearing it through the SEC. We're investigating whether the sale was legal and looking into how complicit the company was in defrauding the US taxpayers. With what Rogers has done, there are probably grounds to seize everything he owns, and then the money can go into helping the poor and disadvantaged."

The president smiled. "I like the way you think, but this is a powder keg. Ambassador Chen told me in no uncertain terms that if we carry through on your threats, his government would take everything back. The implications for using force were not subtle. This could all blow up in my face."

Queen leaned forward and gave the president his most earnest expression. "When I spoke to Rogers, he said that he intended to start mining in space. He talked about that being a lot of money. I dismissed it at the time, but now that I've had time to consult with specialists, I think he was underselling things. Intentionally so.

"He stands to make hundreds of trillions of dollars over the next few decades. And, on top of that, he'll crash the precious-metals market. Think of the political position that will put him in. A man with nuclear weapons in space and being by far the wealthiest man in the system. He's got his eye set on world domination."

Blankenship shook his head. "That's jumping too far, Josh. We can't just assume that's going to happen."

"His son claimed Mars in the name of his company. The whole damned planet. Does that sound like someone who's playing small?"

"I saw the landing, but I didn't get that out of it."

"He said Humanity Unlimited. That's the name of the company. First Mars, then the universe. Humanity Unlimited. He's going to claim everything."

"He can't do that. We have treaties."

"With other governments. Guess what? They don't explicitly say a private entity can't do that. And, on top of that, he incorporated Humanity Unlimited in the Republic of Nauru. Perhaps you've heard of it. An island nation that Clayton Rogers owns outright. One that never signed those treaties. And one where he's busy building a new spaceport."

The president stared at him for a moment, rose to his feet, and pressed the intercom button on his desk. "Cancel my afternoon appointments and summon the cabinet and the national security advisor. Oh, and the Joint Chiefs of Staff. This has a military component. I want everyone in my conference room in an hour."

* * *

Nathan stepped off the plane at one of the smaller airports outside of Paris. It was dark, and he could see a fire somewhere in the city. The large number of sirens wailing in the distance seemed to indicate a lot of police. Probably another terror attack.

They were almost a weekly occurrence these days. The French had let the jackals in, and now they were eating France's carcass from the inside out. Now that the militants had carved a Caliphate out of parts of Iraq and Syria, they'd become much more virulent.

Twenty years later and they had conquered half of the Middle East and had their eyes set on bigger prizes in Europe. Then the world.

And the US was milquetoast enough to let them do it too. All that diversity and nonprofiling crap. In the last five years, the Islamic terrorists had managed to strike inside the US three times. That's how it had started here in France.

They slipped across the Mexican border with ease. The federal government did almost nothing to stop the flow of illegal immigrants. The political morons considered them new voters to solidify their hold on power.

Most of the people flooding into the US wanted nothing to do with the terrorist nutjobs, but if you didn't screen them, how could you identify the real threats?

It would only take a few simple actions to set the terrorists back on their heels. Infiltrate the mosques where the radicalization took place, identify the troublemakers, snatch them off the streets, and make them talk. Once they'd given up their friends, give them a bullet and a lonely grave.

Hell, it might not even be too late to save France.

Maybe he could form a team to take care of some of the problems and write it off on his taxes. A kind of community service. Something to think about.

He pulled out his phone and called his mother. "We're in Paris."

"Good. I have two missions for you. First, you need to find some convenient rag heads and plant evidence on them that they were behind the attack on the reactor lab."

He shook his phone. "I'm sorry. Something garbled the transmission. I thought you said you wanted me to frame someone else for Harry's attack."

"I did, jackass. The State Department is snooping around, and the very last thing we want to do is point them at Clayton. The bastard might tell them the truth."

"That's not very likely. He has even more to hide than we do."

"Nevertheless, I don't want to get them looking. Take some equipment or files, pick some people that look like terrorists, and blow them up. Let the police come to the conclusion they were behind the attack."

Nathan wasn't going to argue. His men would literally jump at the chance to screw over some Islamic fundamentalists. "And the second item?"

"I want you to find that place on the map. We're making progress on the ship, but I'd much rather find something bigger. Like a real base. The experts tell me the location is about fifty miles outside of Paris. It's in unfriendly terrain, so it was probably meant to be hidden."

"Then it's done a good job. Have you narrowed the area?"

"To within a mile or so. I'm thinking ground-penetrating radar or something seismic if it's too deep."

"Send me the GPS coordinates, and I'll make something happen tonight. Radar, most likely. Explosives might be a bit much, considering how jumpy the French police are. I'll let you know when I have things arranged."

He ended the call and looked at his Paris team. "I have good news. We need some terrorist patsies, so I've decided we'll kill the real deal."

That earned him smiles all around. It was as though he'd given them a hefty bonus. Perhaps he had.

* * *

KATHLEEN ENDED the call with her son just in time to have a long discussion with her people in India. Unfortunately, the Indians weren't interested in dealing. They really wanted to go to Mars, even if they were in second place.

That was unfortunate.

So, she called the Chinese. They seemed just as uninterested, right up until they learned that Clayton was her ex-husband and a competitor. Then they started bargaining.

The deal still needed work, but she thought she'd be able to pick up their completed spaceship for a reasonable amount. It would just take some finagling. They'd also offered her a very good deal on Rainforest.

Considering that her father had built a lot of that business before Clayton stole it from her, she was tempted. They were having problems with the Securities and Exchange Commission, but as an American, she'd have better luck there.

They talked for several hours, she summoned in a number of people to work the angles, and by the close of the day, she'd made a tentative deal. A very good one, from her point of view.

They, of course, thought they'd gotten one over on her, but they didn't know all the details. In the end, she'd borrowed enough money to make things happen without major sales of her property.

The Chinese got billions for Rainforest, the Yucatán Spaceport, and their Mars ship. She was almost broke, but wealthy in property. She'd get her money back and more. Especially once she was able to turn some of that alien tech into real advances on Earth.

Yes, the US government was currently eyeing her new spaceport, but she could take care of that. She paid enough federal judges to make the correct rulings and issue injunctions. She also had a lot of leverage in Mexico City.

They were the actual government of record over the spaceport. All they had to do was change their minds and tell the US to back off. They'd bitch, but they'd do it.

And China avoided a shooting war with the US. That actually saved her quite a bit of money in the deal. No matter how big a game they talked, she knew the Chinese really didn't want to start World War III. Not yet.

Another positive point would be telling Queen where he could stick it. Oh yes, that was going to make this *very* worthwhile.

Her lawyers burned up the midnight oil getting all the details worked out and all the appropriate papers signed. She wanted everything done before morning. Whatever Queen thought he'd be doing, she wanted to ruin his entire day.

18

Morning came early for Clayton. Too early. They'd stayed up late into the night talking about their dreams, their fears, and whether this sale would happen. And that had been after a long, grueling trip around the spread.

The place was ruggedly beautiful. Not quite mountainous, but more what he'd call hill country. Without good transportation and paths, much of it would be difficult or impossible to get to.

Including the spot he was interested in. It sat in the area farthest back from the lake. His casual questions had gotten Ashton Durey to tell him that they didn't use that part of the farm. Never had.

That was good. It meant that the odds of anyone stumbling across whatever was there were slim.

Clayton showered and came down for breakfast. The sheep farmer looked wide-awake and refreshed. Penny looked a little run down but seemed cheerful.

"Good morning," Durey said. "I hope you slept well."

"Well enough, though I think those late nights are more a young man's game."

"True enough. I've been talking with Penny while Cook prepared breakfast. I think she's talked me over the last hump. I'm willing to sell, but not cheaply."

He mentioned an amount that was indeed on the high side.

Clayton nodded. "Done. Penny will have the papers drawn up, and you can have your solicitors go over them. I'll add in a bonus if we can close the deal quickly. My preference would be to make it all happen during this trip."

"Actually, I passed the information on to your people last night," Penny said. "They had contracts reflecting everything delivered this morning. The young man who flew them out is eating with the hands."

"Excellent. I'll look them over after we eat. Then I'd like to go see some of the less traveled areas of the farm while Mister Durey finds someone to look over his set."

The older man nodded. "I'll have a couple of the boys show you whatever you like. I had a long talk with my wife this morning. She's seeing things my way. One thing. I'd like to stay on and oversee the place. Unless you know someone more familiar with running a sheep station."

"I'd hoped you would. The house and everything else will stay the way it is. I don't need more than a room when I come visiting."

The three of them ate well, and Clayton retired to his room to review the papers. Everything was exactly as he wanted. His people knew their business. The bonus wasn't in writing, but he'd take care of that part himself.

Once he'd locked the papers away, he made his way down to find Penny and two young men waiting for him.

"Clayton, this is Samuel and Mick. They'll be escorting us on the trip."

The young man she'd indicated as Samuel stuck out his hand. "Pleasure. It'll take a bit to get back to that area. It's rough country. No paths to speak of. I suggest we borrow your courier's plane and go that way."

"An excellent idea." Clayton raised an eyebrow toward Penny.

"He's down doing the preflight checklist on the plane," she said.

"Then let's go."

They drove down to the lake where the young man with the seaplane was waiting. "Morning, everyone. Mister Rogers. I'm Liam. I'm afraid I only have room for three of you."

"That's all right," Samuel said. "Mick would be happy to wait here for us."

Mick's expression indicated some disagreement with that assessment, but he nodded. "I can find something to do."

"Excellent," Clayton said.

They all climbed into the plane, and the pilot started the engine. Once the plane warmed up, he taxied onto the lake and took off.

Clayton wasn't sure how to direct the pilot toward their destination without tipping their hand, but Penny had a plan. "Here's a map of the station. We'd like to see this back quadrant over here. We know no one is using it, but we'd like to place a retreat out this way. When Mister Rogers wants to get away from the world, he really, *really* wants to get away."

Samuel grinned. "You won't have anyone disturbing you out there, that's for sure. No mobile coverage and no access by vehicle. Hiking in would be a nightmare. You'd have to drop a team in from helicopters to clear a place to land a whirlybird. Then fly in any building materials. Quite an undertaking."

"Never underestimate the power of getting back to nature," Clayton said. Penny was going to get a nice bonus of her own. She'd been on top of every aspect of this mission. He couldn't have been happier with her performance.

The plane finally arrived over the area he was interested in. It was just as remote as they'd said. While the location wasn't precise, he was certain it centered on a small plateau.

The shrubs would take a bit to clean off, but it would make an adequate landing area. He suspected it might have served such a function a thousand years ago.

One side had a gentle slope down to a forested area that would serve well for a house location. If he was going to do things out here, he needed to make sure no one suspected what the real reason was. He'd actually build a getaway. And he'd probably use it too.

"That spot looks promising," he said after they'd circled it a few times. "I think we could even land a helicopter without any problem. I'll assume there's a place we can rent one at the airport."

Samuel nodded. "I know a guy. Penny said you and Mister Durey have some business to conclude. I can take a trip over and get one back to the house by the time you're ready."

"That sounds capital. I'll send Penny with you to take care of the payment details. I think we can go back now."

He considered the area around the plateau as they flew away. Nothing down there looked like a secret base, but these people didn't want anyone finding them. That much was obvious. They'd arrived on this island before any of the native humans, and still they'd hidden everything devilishly well. That meant something. He just had to figure out what.

* * *

AFTER A GOOD NIGHT'S REST, Harry and his team made their way back to the wreck. The first task in the daylight was to set up the rest of the ropes and lights between the camp, the wreck, and the door to the base.

A second lifter had brought more people and supplies, so he designated the other team to clear the wreck.

He'd had time to examine the weapon overnight. The power pack wasn't like the blue cubes. It seemed to be a variant of the kinds of batteries used on Earth today.

Probably with a lot more juice, but still. They'd cleverly built it into the magazine containing the flechettes. That made sense. If you didn't have ammo, you probably didn't need power.

There was no chamber for a ready round. It fired the top flechette in the magazine. Based on the wounds he'd seen, they probably traveled at high speed. The barrel of the weapon had to produce a strong magnetic field.

All in all, very high tech.

The weak sun was almost directly overhead when he and his people stood in front of the unopened hatch leading into the wall of the caldera. Based on the weathering, it had been here a long, long time. Dust and grit filled the edges and made small dunes in front of it.

The hatch was of a size to accept vessels significantly larger than the one that had crashed. Harry assumed there was a way to open it from an approaching vehicle.

A second, smaller hatch beside that was more like what people would use. There was a metal plate beside it with a standard dimple to allow for manual opening.

The engineer had made a handle for the key. One that would allow him to hold it in his gloved hand. No more cold.

Harry inserted the key, and the personnel hatch slid ponderously to the side. The inner door was open. His suit indicated the area inside was at Martian pressure. Lights came on in the room beyond, revealing a wide space capable of holding a dozen spaceships.

It wasn't empty.

Two ships similar to the crashed vehicles sat off to one side, to all appearances undamaged. A larger vehicle occupied the center of the chamber. It was bigger than the other two combined. It had the sleek lines of a fighter jet and protuberances that looked like weapons.

A fourth vessel sat almost against the wall opposite them. Smaller than the rest, it looked like it could only hold a couple of people. Its shape suggested speed.

The chamber itself was obviously a hangar. Rails above them allowed for moving ships and loading cargo. The back wall had both a cargo-loading area and a wide corridor that led to a large airlock hatch. A smaller one for people sat beside it. An enclosed control area over the loading dock was dark but suggested that it was where people oversaw operations here.

"So, if we have ships, where are the people?" Sandra asked.

"Since they didn't make a rescue attempt, we have to assume that there wasn't anyone left alive," Harry said. "Though I'm not inclined to assume anything. We'll proceed with full precautions and keep an eye out for hostiles. We'll need to search these ships to be sure we're not leaving anyone behind us."

The two ships that looked like the crashed one opened readily enough. No one was inside them, and they looked as though they were ready for flight. The engineering spaces had active blue cubes.

The engineers were going to have a field day. Potentially operational spaceships. This changed everything, depending on how fast they really were. He might be able to go rescue Jess without taking months to do it.

The larger ship was more challenging. It had no key slot. Rather, it had a keypad with what looked like six numbers in the alien language. The orange button under them must be the activator.

Since he didn't know the code, the only thing he could do was see if it was unlocked. He pressed the button.

The hatch slid open on a much different kind of ship. The ceiling was a bit low and the proportions were off. A console near the hatch had a chair that was set low to the ground and was very wide.

Racks on the wall held weapons and armor. The armor told the same tale as the chair. Someone had designed them for beings less than five feet tall and very thick. Squat might be the right word. Not a normal human being. More like a dwarf from the old *Lord of the Rings* movies.

"This matches what Jess said she saw in the gravity controls on *Freedom Express*," Sandra said. "One of the images was of someone from a heavy gravity environment."

"Could be," Harry agreed. "I wonder how they fit into the picture. While I can't read the alien writing, those numbers on the door were the same as what Powell and Young deciphered for us. That implies a connection."

He moved forward and found the cockpit. The pilots' couches were of similar dimensions. No people.

Harry ran his hand over the control console, and it came to life. The layout was different from what he remembered from the crashed ship. That didn't mean much when they knew almost nothing about these people, but it suggested to him that they weren't the same.

After he let his suit camera get a good image of everything, he backed out. The rest of the team met him at the hatch. This ship was clear.

The last vessel was different. It seemed designed for a single person. The cockpit was similar to that of a fighter jet, enclosed in a long, clear canopy. The backswept wings and engines suggested it was fast.

A touch to the control off to one side caused it to rise. The space was long enough for a very tall person, but someone had removed the original acceleration couch and replaced it with one similar to those used in the crashed ships. That left enough room behind it for storage, but that was obviously an afterthought.

He guessed this ship had originally been for the third kind of being Jess had hypothesized. The light-gravity beings, tall and slender.

A touch of the control console revealed a third kind of layout, but once again the same language.

"All clear," he said. "It looks as though they parked their ships and went inside. Odds are good that they never made it back out. We'll need to explore the rest of the base, but I bet the people in here had a little shooting problem of their own. Ready?"

Time to explore the alien structure.

19

J ess was just getting ready to break for dinner when Rex called. "We're almost through, and we've found something."

"I'm on my way."

Ray Proudfoot gestured at the controls on the main console in the core. "Don't forget we're about ninety minutes away from Neptune. You don't want to miss that."

"Trust me, I'll be there. They'll have the first pass at the translation software ready tonight. We'll meet back here once we finish sightseeing. If you'll excuse me, I'd better go see what they've found."

She took the elevator up to Rex's level and made her way to the cave-in. She had to pass through an airtight door, so she put on her suit beforehand. The suit indicated the pressure was the same on the other side, but she kept her helmet on. If there was a blowout, she didn't want to be looking for it.

They'd moved a lot of the debris but not all of it. Rex stood next to a mummified body.

"Who'd you find?" she asked as she stopped beside him.

"You tell me."

The proportions of the body were all wrong. Very short and broad. "You found one of the heavy-worlders."

He nodded. "I think so. And he's a soldier. Look at the armor. It didn't save him from the cave-in, but it did keep the rocks from squishing him like a bug. And we found this."

The object in question turned out to be a short, thick rifle. She'd seen images of the pistols Harry had found on Mars, but this was a completely different kind of weapon. It looked as though it fired something with a lot of recoil, and the bore was large and intimidating. She certainly didn't want anyone to point one at her.

She looked through the scratched faceplate on his helmet. "See the nose and lips? They're shaped the same way as ours. The position of the eyes and ears are consistent too. As odd as this sounds, I'm betting this guy was human."

Rex looked unconvinced. "Built like this? He must be twice my width. That's not normal."

"We'll let the medical team look him over, but I can't see an alien species evolving on another world with such precise features. This guy has some human in him."

She stood and looked at the rocks. "Any idea how much farther?"

"The rocks were shifting pretty easily, so I'm thinking we're almost through. Let's get this fellow out of the way and see if we can break through before dinner."

"Don't forget we're passing Neptune in a bit more than an hour. Plan on eating lunch on the fly or after."

They backed out of the way and let a couple of suited figures load the dead man onto a makeshift stretcher and carry him out. In the reduced gravity, that wasn't much of an effort.

The men got back to work clearing the rubble, and it didn't take more than ten minutes for a gap to develop at the top. Rex peered over the lip with a light. "The tunnel seems to be intact after this. We can get the debris out of the way and brace the ceiling. We'll keep the gravity low too. That should prevent any more collapses."

Clearing everything took about half an hour. The corridor continued on, but the lighting was out. So was the gravity. It would be interesting to watch Ray do damage control on an unfamiliar base without knowing the technology.

"Let's stop now," she said. "We can grab a quick bite and head out for the surface. We don't want to miss this. And since we can't control our course or speed, we're sightseers."

"We need a guard," he insisted. "We have no idea what's beyond this. Until we do, I'll post some people. I'll stay too. Wouldn't be fair if I didn't."

"That's probably a good idea. Maybe we can come back through past Saturn and give you a better show. Thanks. I'll only be an hour or so. Then we can go explore the rest of this base. And find out what was so important they had to fight over it."

* * *

PARIS WAS STILL DARK, but it wouldn't be long before it began coming to life. Nathan's men had found a nest of live terrorists. Not bad for only being in town a few hours and not very complimentary of the French police.

The unprepossessing apartment building was mostly dark. The residents would begin rising for the day in an hour or two. Well, normally they would. In this case, they'd wake up rather more abruptly when his team took out the people in the apartment on the third floor.

They snaked a camera under the door to make sure it wasn't booby-trapped. Then Nathan picked the lock while his people kept watch. They'd avoided the cameras at the street level, and he'd rather the police never knew they were there at all.

Once the door was open, he entered with his suppressed pistol leading the way. Unlike how Hollywood portrayed them in the movies, a shot through a suppressor was hardly silent. It just reduced the noise down to something that didn't sound like a gunshot.

Combined with using lower-powered ammo that didn't break the sound barrier, it was good enough. Anyone that woke up would assume that someone had dropped something. Unless they got into a gunfight, then all bets were off.

Nathan didn't expect anything like that. These idiots hadn't even posted a guard to watch over the bomb-making materials scattered across the kitchen table.

It looked as though they were making some improvised explosives out of chemicals. Nice, but hardly showy enough for his plans. He pulled some C-4 and a timer out of his pack and set it among the jugs and wires. That would get the police a lot more excited.

The charge was small, but he needed to leave most everything in the apartment recoverable. It was hard to frame someone if the police couldn't find the planted evidence.

One of his men was leaving a scattering of papers from his mother's lab in the living room while the rest kept a close eye on the bedrooms. He'd prefer not to kill any of them. That would just raise questions. This was supposed to be a case of incompetent terrorists blowing themselves up.

There'd been a big bomb maker that had killed himself and his entire class of suicide bombers a few years ago. Nathan had laughed for days. Who doesn't love irony?

Nathan pulled some equipment he'd brought along and left it on the other side of the kitchen from the bombs. It had low-grade radioactive material. That would *really* get them excited.

He didn't want to make things any more difficult for the police than he had to. If he could put a signed note confessing to the crime, he would, but that was over the top. They'd just have to deduce his lies for themselves.

A noise from one of the bedrooms captured their attention. A toilet flushed, and the shower came on. Someone was up.

The timer still had fifteen minutes to go, so he'd rather not risk someone wondering where the extra bomb came from. He motioned for two of the men to follow him into the bedroom.

Based on the mess, a man lived in the room. No self-respecting woman would tolerate the filth. He shook his head at the stack of girlie magazines. So much for deep religious fervor. The bastard probably drank and fornicated too.

Not that Nathan objected to any of those things. Hell, he was all about drinking and fornicating. But he didn't lie about who he was, either.

The bathroom door was unlocked, so they got in without a problem. A cheap shower curtain was all that separated them from the terrorist. He could hear the man singing something catchy in French under his breath. Well, Nathan was going to screw up his day for sure.

On a silent count of three, one of his men yanked the cheap plastic barrier aside, and the other shoved the man against the wall of the tub, clamping a hand over his mouth. Nathan planted the end of his suppressor against the suddenly terrified man's forehead.

"Allahu Akbar," Nathan said pleasantly. "If you have a few minutes, my friends and I would like you to settle a dispute for us. Nothing too complicated, but we wondered what really makes shit bags such as yourself blow up schools and gun down random people in the name of God. It really has us confused."

He had no idea if the man understood him, but he obviously comprehended the weapon. That would do for now.

They dragged him out and duct-taped his mouth, hands, and feet. Harry shut off the water as his men carried their struggling prisoner out.

He considered killing him here, but again, that would raise questions in the simple minds of the police. Better to keep things straightforward.

Besides, this had been more fun than he'd expected. Maybe he could get some other names from the bugger and do this again.

Nathan didn't lose any sleep over the things he did, but even he had his limits. Wanton murder of children was a bit much. Scum like this asshole bred like lice here in Europe. He'd never lack for targets. Besides, everyone needed a hobby.

They hustled the idiot into their van and drove slowly away from the apartment building. A wireless camera on the street level gave him a good view of the exterior as the bomb went off. It blew out the windows but left the walls intact. Good.

The interior of the apartment was on fire, but more than enough evidence would remain to nudge the police to the appropriate conclusions.

They might have fun shooting up the remaining terrorists too. The blast hadn't been strong enough to do more than stun them. Well, maybe cause some broken bones and shrapnel wounds. They'd be in shape to resist the police with force when they showed up.

They'd wanted to kill for their god. Now they could die for him instead.

Nathan pressed an icon on the handheld, and the video feed vanished. The microcharge in the camera wouldn't make a mess, and it would hardly draw any attention as it destroyed the camera. Not compared to the burning apartment building.

The sun would be up in a few hours. That left plenty of time to settle their guest in and touch base with the people he'd had scanning the target area with ground-penetrating radar. The plane and equipment hadn't come cheaply. He hoped his mother's money had gotten her some positive results. She tended to blame the messenger in cases like this.

* * *

THE DOOR LEADING into the rest of the base proved more resistant than Harry had hoped. It was either locked or unpowered.

They'd have to do this the hard way. He'd ordered the team to bring up the portable airlock. That meant they didn't have to worry about decompressing the base, if it still held pressure. There was no telling how fragile the artifacts inside were, so it paid to be careful.

Just in case the door wouldn't open because the bay was depressurized, they tried it again once they had the airlock pumped full of air. Still no joy.

Then they started on the wall near the door. People often reinforced the obvious points of entry. The wall might be easier to breach.

Only, in this case, that hadn't proven true. The wall was made of stern stuff.

The precautions proved wise. There was heat and pressure inside the base. The testing unit indicated the atmosphere was breathable. That probably was bad for a lot of potential artifacts, but it meant the base was operational. At least life support was.

They snaked a camera in and looked over the large room on the other side of the door. It was consistent with a cargo-receiving area. He wondered what they brought in from Mars. It wasn't as though the planet had ever supported a population. Still, people didn't build bases without a reason.

The controls to the personnel lock seemed simple enough. They slid a manipulator inside the room and pressed the button beside the door. The inner door closed, and the outer one opened.

"I feel like a B and E man," he said.

Sandra shook her head. "You're a mess."

The chamber was big enough for four people to enter. Harry found a manual lock that he thought had disabled the outer door. He turned it off and cycled them through.

The large room had a number of crates sitting off to one side. A few had fallen and come apart. After a thousand years, it was a miracle any of them were still together.

He walked over to one of the breached containers and examined its contents. Food, maybe? After all this time, it was hard to tell.

So, they'd imported their food all the way from Earth—they certainly hadn't been growing anything outside—or they were shipping it from here to other locations that couldn't grow food.

Outposts in the Martian desert? Again, why? Maybe they'd find out inside the base.

A short set of stairs led up to the room overlooking the loading bay. The lights came on as soon as he stepped inside. The controls were a lot simpler than inside the ships. He could figure out the main exterior hatch and the pressurization controls just based on how they looked.

"I'm going to try to bring up the bay pressure," he said over the suit radio.

He removed his glove and ran the *faux* slider up.

"I'm hearing something," one of the men in the bay said. "I think it's pressurizing."

The control for the exterior hatch went orange. No doubt because it wouldn't open with pressure inside. Good enough. He'd need to station someone here to facilitate entrance and exit until they worked out a procedure to make sure everyone stayed safe.

There were controls for the hoists that lined the roof of the bay. He moved one of them to be sure.

There were displays he didn't understand. Probably communications. A strobing icon there might mean some kind of emergency beacon from the crashed ship.

They hadn't detected one, but that didn't mean it wasn't there. Radio might not be the preferred method of communication for these people. They might use something more esoteric.

"Okay, we need to patch the hole in the wall," he said. "Once we do that, we can go in and out as we choose. With the personnel airlocks, we can leave everything in habitable conditions."

The loading area had two corridors that led deeper into the base. One was large enough for cargo, the other for people. He opted for the smaller one.

They passed two emergency pressure doors. Both were open but would slam closed if there were a loss of atmosphere in the loading area. Smart.

"Are we going to test the air?" Sandra asked. "We could see things a lot better without these suits on."

He was feeling a bit winded. It took a moment to figure out why. The gravity was up. Maybe close to Earth normal. It must've been slowly getting stronger as they walked.

"That might not be a bad idea, but I don't want to do anything until they check for viruses and bacteria. We'd be taking a big risk."

"Sooner or later, someone is going to have to take a chance," she said. "Sit it out in quarantine until we're sure that everything is good. It's the only way."

He stopped her as she reached for her helmet. "You're right, but that's my job."

Harry popped the seal on his helmet and lifted it clear. The air smelled old. He'd traveled by submarine a few times. It seemed like that. Canned and recycled. There was a very faint hint of decay in the air. He couldn't imagine what hadn't already rotted in a thousand years.

A noise caused him to turn and look at Sandra. She was pulling off her helmet and shaking out her hair.

"I thought I said I was doing this," he grumbled.

"Oh. You meant *only* you. My bad."

"You're a terrible liar."

She grinned. "No, I'm a *great* liar. I just don't need to fib this time. It smells as if something was alive in this place in the recent past. Shall we find it?"

They continued down the hall with the rest of the team—still in their sealed suits—following behind. They passed a number of doors with strange writing, but he decided not to stop.

After three intersections, Harry decided the base was huge. At least the size of a stadium, if he believed the curves of the crosscorridors. Though they passed two elevators, he decided to press on and see what was at the center of the base.

There was some kind of noise coming from ahead. He couldn't place it at first, but then it hit him. He just couldn't believe it.

Sandra stared at him. "Am I hearing what I think I am?"

"Let's find out."

They came to an atrium like the one many cruise ships favored, where the interior cabins all faced an open inner area. It was circular and at least a hundred meters across.

Harry grabbed the rail and looked over it. The open area went down dozens of levels. The floor was a jungle similar to the one in Guatemala. Complete with live vegetation, birds, and insects. Now that they were close, he could make out the individual cries of different small creatures. And the occasional roar of something larger.

"How the hell can this exist on Mars?" Sandra asked.

"Damned if I know. I guess we'll need to make our way down to take a better look at some point."

20

J ess made it out of the airlock a few minutes early and got to watch the large, dark planet grow huge above them. She supposed it was pure chance that the base entrance was facing the planet, but it might not have been. Perhaps they'd programmed the computer to do so because people might like watching the spectacle.

And a spectacle it was. They came close enough for the ice giant to fill the sky. What looked like solid color from far away resolved into deep blue swirls that were quite distinct. She didn't see any large storms like the Great Dark Spot, though.

NASA had discovered that original massive storm when Voyager 2 flew by in 1989. Telescopic observation years later showed it was no longer there, but others had come and gone since.

They were recording everything to send back to *Liberty Station*. The NASA probe had visited the cold world, but her people were the first to come in person. They wanted to document everything they could.

At the speed they were traveling, the flyby was over almost as soon as it began. It was still long enough for surprises, though. Someone called out and pointed. One of the moons was just visible. Amazing.

The extinct comet rotated to keep Neptune in sight as they pulled away. That answered the question about the orientation being chance. Neptune shrank to a dot and was lost among the stars. Perhaps they'd be able to come back and spend some quality time later.

Jess waited until everyone else had entered and then made her way to the cave-in. Rex and a couple of men stood nearby, still in their suits, but with weapons in their hands.

"Do you really think those are necessary?" she asked. "I'm pretty sure that nothing is alive in there."

"It never hurts to be careful."

She shook her head. "Let's go see what we can find. Then we can get some real food."

Rex turned on his suit light and led them down the freshly opened tunnel. It quickly turned into the scene of a full-scale battle. Bodies littered the floor, some in pieces.

Jess was glad she had her helmet on. She suspected there was still some kind of odor, even if just the musty scent of mummified corpses.

Most of the dead looked to be heavy-worlders, though she saw a number of normal humans interspersed with them. The regular humans didn't have armor. They wore the same coveralls as the others they'd found thus far.

Why was that? And where had the heavy-worlders come from? None of the quarters they'd looked at had seemed comfortable for someone with that body type.

"Look at how the bodies are laid out," Rex said. "The regular people were overrun. They had no weapons. Most of them had been moving toward the cave-in. Away from the aggressors."

"What about this guy?" she asked.

The dead man in this case looked to be a normal human, but he was in armor and had a rifle. He seemed to have died going the other direction.

Rex shrugged. "If we find more like him, he might have been part of a counterattack. If not, just an unlucky bastard caught in the open when the shit hit the fan. Whatever happened here happened fast."

The corridor opened up into a large chamber. If the area behind them looked as though a battle had taken place, this room had held a war.

A glance around the circular room told her that they had hundreds of bodies. The area looked like a cargo bay. The large crates made that obvious. A number of them had been blown open in the fighting.

It also contained vehicles. Half a dozen ships like the one they'd found in Guatemala. Some were damaged, but others seemed intact. And there were smaller craft that seemed more suited to carrying troops. There had heavy armor and protrusions that looked like weapons.

All of the latter seemed damaged. And there were a lot more regular humans in armor here.

"This is where the main battle took place," Rex said. "The normal guys pushed the heavy-worlders back here, and they killed one another."

The room was big, but Jess could see all the way around it. This was the only corridor leading out. There were a few arched alcoves, but they stopped after a few meters. The ceiling was one large, smooth piece. There was no way for the ships to get in or out.

* * *

Queen arrived at his office early. He'd stayed up late with the military people and representatives from other sections of the government planning what they'd do today.

They'd put those bastards in their places. Clayton Rogers and his ex-wife were going to learn not to screw with the US government.

The look on his assistant's face told him there had been complications. He stopped beside her desk. "What?"

"There have been a few overnight developments. Here or in your office?"

Queen gestured for her to precede him. "In private."

Once he'd settled behind his desk, he gave her his full attention. "Hit me."

"The Chinese made a deal with Kathleen Bennett last night. They sold her the spaceport and Rainforest, as well as their ship. That undercuts the entire premise of the seizures."

That it did. Yes, the original sale to the Chinese was illegal. Or it would be once the Department of Justice got all its ducks in a row. That made this second sale also illegal. Technically.

The problem was that he couldn't just seize control of the spaceport now. The national security aspects of the case had changed. BenCorp did a significant amount of work for the US government. They had all the required clearances.

Without invalidating all of that, and the critical research and production projects they had contracts for, he couldn't just take what he wanted.

That didn't mean he wouldn't get it, though. They'd take possession of the spaceport and Rainforest. And, by extension, the spaceship orbiting Mars.

"Yes, that is troubling, but not insurmountable," he said. "Get Justice on the phone."

The woman shook her head. "There's more. Doctor Scott called. They found the missing comet."

Irritation flashed through him. "You mean it was there the entire time? Dammit, I thought you had NASA confirm it was gone. Damned incompetent bastards. We should've terminated the last of their funding already."

"A different observatory looking at the outer system saw it and word got back to Scott. The comet just passed the orbit of Neptune."

"How could that be? They made a mistake. Comets don't just jump from Mars to Neptune."

His assistant shrugged. "You'd think not, but he claimed it was moving at a rapid pace. And accelerating."

That stopped Queen cold. His anger vanished, quenched like hot steel dumped into a bucket of ice-cold water. "What did you say?" he asked carefully.

"The comet is accelerating. Both NASA and Doctor Scott verified it. Not only is it going far faster than a comet should, it's going fast enough to leave the solar system entirely."

"That isn't possible. Get Scott on the phone. Wake his ass up."

"He said he'd be ready for your call."

Queen leaned back in his chair. This was lunacy.

His mind went around in circles for several minutes before his phone rang. He hit the speaker button. "Queen here."

"Mister Secretary," Doctor Scott said. "I have wonderful news!"

"I fail to see what's so wonderful about it, Doctor. Perhaps you'd care to explain it to me."

"Certainly," the almost bubbly scientist said. "The comet has sped up greatly. That means that they developed a powerful space drive. We're not seeing any exhaust, and frankly, I have no idea how they did it, but this opens up the entire solar system for exploration in our lifetimes."

Perhaps that was enough to excite the scientist, but Queen had more realistic problems to solve.

"What the hell are they doing out there?" he asked. "Their ship went to Mars. Why split up like that?"

"You'd have to ask them that. What I find more interesting is how they moved such a large body without breaking it into pieces. Neptune is thirty astronomical units out. One AU is the distance between the Earth and Sun. That's a vast distance to travel in only a few days, much less on a hunk of rock that size."

Queen suppressed his exasperation. "I'm sure this is all very exciting, but I'm more concerned with the security implications. This interjects a whole new layer of complication into an already chaotic situation."

"I'll say. Such a body would make a most lethal weapon in the wrong hands."

"How so?"

"If it came back to Earth at that speed, it would be a global catastrophe. Greater than the impact that killed the dinosaurs 65 million years ago."

That shocked Queen speechless for a moment. "You're joking."

"Absolutely not. While the Chicxulub meteor was ten times the diameter, this comet is going significantly faster. Speed translates to energy in an impact. I assure you that a one-kilometer comet impact at that speed would cause global devastation.

"Let me put this into perspective. The impact that killed the dinosaurs was off the coast of the Yucatán Peninsula, but the heat flash set most of North America on fire. Think nuclear blast, but on a much larger scale. If that comet were going fast enough, it would be an extinction-level event. The kind that obliterates humanity."

Queen blinked, slow to grasp the full implications of what he was hearing. "You're telling me that they have a weapon more powerful than a nuclear bomb?"

"I'm telling you that they have a *potential* weapon more powerful than all the nuclear bombs on this planet combined. Easily. But I'm sure that they don't intend to extinguish humanity. That's crazy."

"You don't know these people, Doctor Scott. I wouldn't be so sure. I want a complete report on what you've found as soon as possible. Oh. And where are they headed?"

"That comet is going fast enough to leave the solar system, but it would still take a *very* long time to reach the next nearest system. They aren't even going toward any that are particularly close.

"The Kuiper Belt ranges from the orbit of Neptune out to about fifty AU.

It's also possible that they're heading to something in the Oort cloud. They'll probably decelerate when they get there. Once they start slowing down, we can make a more educated guess as to the destination."

Queen vaguely remembered the Oort cloud was where things like comets and Pluto came from. "What kind of time frame are we looking at in general?"

"That's impossible to guess with distances this vast. If the object is close, they'll need to start slowing down soon."

"Stay on top of this, Doctor Scott. I want to know everything we can find out about that comet and where it's going. My assistant will give you my private cell number. Call me anytime, day or night, with any significant events or breakthroughs."

He ended the call and sat back. This game had gotten significantly more dangerous. What was Clayton Rogers doing? And, better yet, what was his end game? There was something big Queen was missing. It was time to disrupt their plans and get inside their heads.

He picked up his phone. Time to start the marbles rolling.

21

K athleen had only begun reviewing the most recent status of the wreck investigation when Nathan called. A quick mental calculation told her it was about 3 PM in Paris.

She picked up her receiver. The phone had military-grade encryption and was untappable. She should know. Her company had developed the technology for the NSA.

"I saw the news," she told her son. "It looks as though the police are coming to the right conclusions. Well done. Maybe that will get Queen off my ass."

"Thank you," he said, "but that's not why I called. The ground-penetrating radar found something. There are hollow areas a hundred feet down."

"Caves?"

"A little too compact and regular for caves, I think. Someone put a small base down there."

She leaned forward. "Are you kidding me? How big?"

"The radar isn't a precise tool at that depth. We won't know until we get into it."

Just the idea of all the potential technology down there made her heart race. They needed to get in there fast. This would really put Clayton in his place.

"What about the property ownership? Can we acquire it?"

"Two steps ahead of you, Mother. I made a generous offer, and the owner sold it with undue haste. The area is rocky and mostly overgrown. I have no idea what he expected to do with the land originally, but it obviously didn't work out. I have the bill of sale and transferred deed in my pocket."

She nodded to herself. "Good. Get busy looking for a way in. And don't destroy everything. We need some of it intact if we're ever going to decipher this technology. How long do you expect it to take you to get in?"

"We'll see. There's no obvious entrance. I'll let you know when I find one."

She'd barely set the phone back down when her disposable cell rang. "Yes?"

"Good morning, Mrs. Bennett. Ethan Wagner here. Might you stop by this morning?"

He wouldn't have called unless he had something interesting to tell her. "I can be there in an hour. Pick me up at the usual place."

Setting up the covert transportation only took a few minutes, but being certain no one was aware of where she was going, or even that she was aboard, took longer. She had to be careful. One slip and the FBI agents watching her campus would know something was up. And that would bring Queen down on her.

Not that she couldn't beat him at his own game, but she had bigger fish to fry.

The transport went off without a hitch, and she was in the satellite facility an hour later. Wagner was waiting for her. She shook his hand perfunctorily. "What have you got, Doctor?"

"It would be best we speak in my office."

This was new. The man usually couldn't wait to spill the beans. He escorted her to his office, a cluttered, disorganized pile of paper and folders with furniture hidden under the ever-changing surface.

He cleaned off a seat by relocating a dangerously unbalanced pile of binders to a side table in even worse shape.

Kathleen eyed the stacks nearest the chair and decided she was moderately safe for a few minutes. She sat and crossed her legs. "Okay, Doctor. What have you found?"

"We've completely deciphered the electrical system. We now know how to read the required power on all the equipment. As the ship is unflyable, we've disassembled it and have the major sections in various labs for analysis. In the process of taking everything apart, we found a hidden compartment with a number of interesting items inside."

She leaned forward with a smile. This was a tremendous stroke of luck. "Tell me more."

"First, we found something the people that abandoned this ship must have forgotten, or perhaps didn't know existed." He opened the drawer and pulled out a glowing blue cube. "This is a spare power supply."

Kathleen gasped and reached for it but stopped. "Is it safe?"

"It seems to be. We're detecting no radiation at all emanating from it. And the area where it normally sat in the ship wasn't shielded."

She took it from him. It sat on her palm, ten centimeters along each edge and lighter than she'd thought. The glow inside it was a deep blue and steady. It was beautiful. "How does it work?"

"That's still up for debate, but I can tell you it's capable of putting out a prodigious amount of power. We isolated the system where it plugs in and pulled as heavy a load as we could. It seemingly had no problems running this entire facility.

"Frankly, that's not surprising. Anything that could lift a vessel off this planet has to be capable of generating much more power than that."

She set the cube down on the desk. "Are you any closer to discovering how they did that?"

He nodded. "The ship's hull had a number of emitters that the team associated with the drives are certain can change the curvature of space. The ship literally creates a slope for it to slide along."

"How fast could it go?"

The scientist smiled. "Ah, now that's an interesting question. And one with an answer that might surprise you. It could probably achieve a top speed of several tenths of the speed of light before a particle of dust destroyed it.

"A better unit of measure might be how quickly it could accelerate. Think of someone in a snow sled on a hill. The angle of the slope determines how quickly they pick up speed. The sharper it is, the faster they go barreling down, and the sooner they reach the bottom.

"This drive most likely operates in the same manner. It creates an artificial gravity slope that the ship 'slides' down. As there is no barrier to higher speeds in a vacuum, that ship can theoretically get very close to light speed, given enough time, but like any sled on the slopes, there are dangers to going too quickly. Like running into trees."

She could see the example in her head and nodded. "That makes perfect sense. Thank you. What about blocking the dust in space? I seem to recall hearing about using magnetic fields to shift it out of the way or screens to block them. Every science-fiction movie has something like that."

"As of yet, we've found nothing that looks to be able to generate such a thing. That would be wonderful, no doubt, but we can't count on having such luck. If such a thing existed, it would allow this small ship to reach speeds approaching that of light. There were no signs they carried enough food or other consumables for such an extended journey."

Kathleen frowned. "That's twice you've said, 'approaching the speed of light.' What does that mean and why couldn't they exceed it?"

The scientist looked smug. "That's an easy trap to fall into. As an object approaches the speed of light, its mass grows. At the speed of light, its mass would be infinite, preventing it from going any faster."

That sounded dubious to her. "It seems to me that a falling object getting more massive helps speed it along."

He seemed unfazed. "I know it doesn't make logical sense, but the laws of nature break down at points like that. In any case, without shielding, a bit of hydrogen is a lethal obstacle at that speed. A tree, if you will. $E = MC^2$ is unforgiving at 99 percent of the speed of light.

"In any case, that brings us to the last few things we found in the wreck." He held up two slivers of metal. They looked like data chips. "These seem to be keys. We couldn't figure out how to open the doors from the outside, but one of the interns found a spot they fit into. They might prove useful in opening other doors."

She took one of the keys. It looked exactly like the picture of the "data stick" Nathan had found. She set it beside the cube.

"What else?"

He brought a deadly looking pistol out of the desk drawer and set it carefully down in front of her. "This is obviously a weapon. It doesn't use gunpowder. The barrel generates a powerful magnetic field that hurls a sliver of metal at high velocity. The magazine doubles as a battery to power the weapon."

"And you know this how?"

He shrugged. "Once we determined what it fired, we read the numbers off the battery and charged it. We fired one round into a crash test dummy. It went through the dummy, causing significantly more damage than we expected, and embedded itself into the concrete wall. It made a very respectable hole, I might add.

"There's a selector that allows for lower speed shots, most likely to prevent damage in a ship like the one you found. One at high speed would go through people and the hull too."

She picked the weapon up. It was light and fit her hand well. After a moment, she set it with the other objects. The only one she kept was a key. He had two, so she'd keep this one.

"I know of some military specialists that could probably help with this. Well done, Doctor Wagner. Well done. There will be large bonuses for everyone."

He smiled. "We also found cockpit and external video on the ship. We saw the man who brought it here. We watched it crash. I had them record both the view and the screens it took to get there. I sent the video to your encrypted email account."

Her cell phone rang. "Excuse me for a moment."

It was her assistant. "We have a problem."

"What?"

"The FBI is back, and that agent you hate is looking for you. They have warrants for every building. And that's not all. They have an order from the Justice Department to expel us from the property. They're seizing it."

Her vision dimmed as she surged to her feet. That caused a catastrophic avalanche of papers that swept around the room. Wagner leapt to his feet with a wail.

"That son of a bitch!" she shouted. "I'll be right there."

"I wouldn't," the man said. "He has a warrant for your arrest. The smug bastard said the charges were legion, but his favorite was treason."

* * *

NATHAN WAS IMPRESSED with how quickly money got the paperwork completed. He held a deed in his hand before 5 PM.

The area over the base wasn't easy to get to, but it helped if one wasn't too concerned about knocking over inconvenient trees. The cover story was that he was clearing the area for a new facility. True enough, as far as that went.

His phone rang. It was his mother. Of course.

"Mother. I just got the—"

"Shut up and listen. Queen pulled the trigger on me. The Department of Justice wrote out an illegal warrant to seize all my holdings. They won't find everything, at least not right away, but you need to keep your head down."

He immediately understood. Like the old Rendition program, they'd have someone snatch him off the street, take him to some off-the-books facility, and question him. Thankfully, no one of import knew he was here. And with his connections, he could vanish like a ghost, if he needed to.

"I'm secure enough," he said. "What about you?"

"I'm on a plane heading for France now. I'm traveling under an assumed name, and my people there will make certain I get into the country unmolested.

"This won't last long, either. My lawyers are burying them in paperwork. I can't begin to imagine how many lawsuits they've initiated. I expect an injunction from a friendly federal judge in Chicago to put a stop to these shenanigans shortly."

He could hear a thread of uncertainty in her voice.

"I'm sure it will," he said. "Eventually. I'm more concerned with how much they find out before someone yanks them up short."

"Nothing relating to the project you're on. I made sure that everyone with need to know was clear and at the facility with the ship. The feds won't find them."

That didn't mean they wouldn't discover plenty of other wrongdoing. Thankfully, he had backup plans in case everything went down the toilet.

"What about dear old Dad?"

"That bastard figured this out before I did, as much as I hate to admit it. He sold everything that the US government could get their hands on. Hell, he sold everything except for the holding company that owns the spaceship. All that money went into the company. It owns the island he's lording it over and the spaceship."

He nodded. "That makes sense. If you're going to stir the hornet's nest, be ready to run. The irony here is that you bought most of his leftovers from the Chinese, just in time for the US to take it from you. He couldn't have worked that better if he'd planned."

"Watch your mouth," she hissed. "I'll get what I own back, along with a strip off Queen's ass. I need that spaceport, and the US isn't just taking it away from me. And Rainforest is mostly international, even if the majority of sales are in the US."

Nathan smiled. He'd hidden his own money very well. He'd do fine, regardless. It was no skin off his back if his mother came out on top or not.

"As you say. I'll have some people pick you up at the airport. You'd never find this place on your own." He got the details from her and hung up.

With the way things were shaking out, he was glad he'd used his own funds to make the purchase and pay the bribes. Interpol was notoriously bad, but they'd eventually unravel all his mother's companies.

And, if things really went downhill, he'd be the owner of record for a very valuable alien find.

He grinned and headed for his car. There was nothing like hedging one's bets. He'd come up smelling like roses on this deal. If his mother went down, he could make a play for her holdings. That would all sort itself out over time.

She'd arrive early the next morning. That gave his people time to isolate where the entrance was and start digging. If it was where he thought, they might get into the place tomorrow.

22

Q ueen stepped off the plane at the Yucatán Spaceport. FBI agents, Mexican police, and more than a few US soldiers filled the airport. They'd already rounded up the remaining employees—both Chinese and American—and were sorting them out. They'd question the Chinese and then expel them from Mexico.

The Americans would get rougher treatment. Some of them were employees of Clayton Rogers. Others worked for his ex-wife. Both sets probably knew things that he wanted to know. He'd make sure they told the agents everything before he charged them with treason.

He spotted Special Agent in Charge Pembroke waiting for him near a cart.

The skeletal man smiled as Queen approached. "Mister Secretary. Welcome to Mexico."

"Not for much longer," he said as he shook the man's hand. "We have an agreement in principle to treat this as a special territory, like Cuba does for Guantánamo. It didn't come cheaply, but it ends up serving both countries' national interests. Have you had any luck finding Kathleen Bennett?"

The tall man grimaced. "No. After she disappeared in Chicago, I thought she might have fled down here, but no one seems to have seen her. We'll have to search the place from top to bottom and question everyone to be sure, but she must have gone another direction."

"I figure Clayton Rogers's people would hand her over pretty quick, if they had any idea where she was."

"Me, too. Come on. I'll give you the grand tour, and then you can sit in while we question the senior flight director."

They climbed onto the back of the cart, and it sped away, taking them to where a car would pick them up.

"Frankly, I'd rather skip the tour and get to the questioning," Queen said.

"These people are up to something. They're playing a game where we don't know the rules, and that has to stop."

In a low voice, he filled the agent in on what he knew.

The man listened quietly until Queen finished and then looked at him sternly. "We have laws against telling tall tales to feds."

Queen smiled. "It does sound like something out of a fairy tale, doesn't it? Let me assure you that I'm not the one making this up. Something odd is happening, and we don't have the full picture. Yet."

They climbed into a black SUV in front of the airport terminal, and it took them to the flight-control building. There were a lot of federal agents and soldiers here too.

Pembroke led him to a small conference room. The feds escorting them settled against the wall as they sat down in front of an overweight man in shirtsleeves. His face was overly red, but Queen couldn't tell if that was because he was angry or had blood-pressure issues. Or both.

"Mister Secretary," Pembroke said, "this is Avery Jackson, the senior flight director for the Yucatán Spaceport. Mister Jackson, Secretary of State Josh Queen of the United States of America."

Queen leaned forward, letting his full title help intimidate the man. "You've got a lot to answer for, Mister Jackson. Your employer—and you—have committed acts of treason against the United States of America."

If that fazed the man, it didn't show in his expression. "With all due respect, Mister Secretary, you're full of shit."

He was holding up better than Queen had expected, but that made sense. He was a flight director, just like in the old NASA days when Apollo 13 had gone terribly wrong. Jackson had to be able to act even when everything was going into the toilet. Especially then.

"You smuggled nuclear material into orbit," Queen said. "You built a spacecraft capable of reaching Mars and turning a dead comet into some kind of weapon. You need to tell me everything, or you won't be going back to the US. They have some very uncomfortable cells in Cuba. Don't make me send you there. Save yourself."

The man shrugged. "So we built a spaceship. Big deal. Other people have too. There's no law against it. Just because the US gave up doesn't mean everyone else will."

"You used an unauthorized nuclear reactor," Pembroke said. "The UN didn't allow for you to have something capable of propelling a spaceship."

Jackson turned his gaze to the federal agent. "So? Since when did the US start giving one rat's ass what the UN does or doesn't do? Isn't the US busy denying them membership dues because they're too corrupt?"

That was *exactly* what Queen was doing, but that was beside the point. "You don't need to be concerned with the relationship between the US and the UN, Mister Jackson. All that matters in this case is that you did a no-no. One that can send you to prison for a very, *very* long time. I want to know what you built up there."

The man leaned back and considered Queen. "At the risk of sounding pedantic, a spaceship. In case the unspoken words 'you idiot' weren't clear, I'll do you the courtesy of adding them this once."

Queen counted slowly to ten before continuing. "Tell me about this spaceship. What propels it? Why go to Mars? And why send a dead comet out of the solar system?"

"I have no idea what you mean about the comet. As for the spaceship, it uses deuterium-tritium pellets as fuel. The reactor fuses them, and the energy propels the ship. Safe as houses. No nuclear bombs.

"Their mission is to put mining outposts on various asteroids and build colonies where jackbooted thugs like you can't go. Oh, and to make an ass ton of money."

"That doesn't explain the trip to claim Mars or sending a comet out into deep space."

Jackson shrugged. "I think you're making that shit up. Not Mars, the comet. I'm not surprised they made a point of going to Mars first. They wanted to show the world they were serious. I don't know anything about claiming it."

Queen smiled thinly. "You didn't see the young man claim Mars for Humanity Unlimited? I thought it was the most watched video ever."

Jackson shook his head. "You just don't get it. He wasn't claiming the planet. He was saying we could do anything we set our minds to. That we didn't have to let ass clowns like you plant your heels on our necks. He was putting you on notice that your time in charge is almost done."

"We'll see who's done when this is all over. Take him away. Lock him up nice and tight. If Mister Jackson keeps up this attitude, we'll be sending him to Guantánamo with the rest of the unrepentant terrorists. I doubt he'd like forty years there, like some of the fellows from Afghanistan have had."

The federal agents dragged Jackson out. Queen listened to him bray about his rights for a moment and then turned to Pembroke.

"I want every computer system in this place searched. Leave no byte unturned. I want the plans for that ship. Anything Rogers can do, we can do better. Let's see how free he feels when we ship a few hundred marines out to take everything away from him.

"And then start on Bennett's people. I want her in a cell beside her ex-husband." Queen smiled. "He's going to be getting an unexpected and unpleasant wake-up call very soon."

* * *

CLAYTON ROSE MORE REFRESHED than he had in years. Perhaps he'd been wrong to dismiss a vacation away from all the stresses of his professional life.

He dressed and threw back the flap of his tent. The sun wasn't quite up yet, but the horizon was brightening. It wouldn't be long now.

They'd switched over to a helicopter and flown back in time to set up camp just up the ridge from the plateau. The helo was nestled below them, all tied down.

The camp they'd chosen would have a stellar view of the rising sun. It had taken several trips to get everyone and all the gear they needed for a few days' exploration out here. Half a dozen tents sat around a campfire. One of the hands was making breakfast, and it smelled wonderful.

He made a trip to the latrine they'd dug the night before, walked back to the fire, and saw it was Mick. The man looked up and smiled.

"Morning, Mister Rogers. It's going to be a nice one. I can already tell."

Clayton sat down on one of the logs they'd dragged up and accepted coffee in a battered metal mug. It was scorching hot and perfect for the chill morning.

"I hope so. Mick, right?"

"You have a good memory. Mick Bird. I'm one of the supervising hands on your station."

He'd signed the papers last night and made the payment. All this was now his. They'd even paid a government clerk to come back into town to register the transfer. He now owned more sheep than he'd ever know what to do with.

"I'll eventually know everyone's name and a good bit about them. Take care of your people, and they'll take care of business. That's a lesson I took to heart and one that will serve you well too."

The man grinned. "Hell, I already knew that. This place is more like family than a business. It shows."

"Then I won't need to do very much at all. You and your coworkers can keep doing what you do. I'll learn as I go."

"Make sure you come down for the shearing. That's a sight you'll never forget."

Clayton could only imagine.

They sat in silence while the sun slowly rose above the horizon. It was glorious. The cold, clear, pure air made for some vivid colors.

"Never will get used to that," Mick said. "I grew up in Wellington. Mind you, it's clean, but it's still a city. You don't get nature like this there."

"What brought you out to work on a sheep station, if you don't mind my asking?"

"My brother. That's Samuel. He always had a hankering for working off the grid. They had a spot open, and he pushed hard for me. I wasn't sure it was the right decision at first, but now I wouldn't trade it for the world."

Clayton smiled. "I hadn't pegged you as brothers, but I see it now. He's a bit bossy, isn't he?"

Mick laughed softly. "You have no idea. Always been like that. It's okay, though. I fight back when it's worth it. He's a good, loyal man to have at your side when things get sticky. What are the plans for the day?"

"We'll eat and then do a survey of the area," Clayton said. "I bet the ridge would be a fine spot for a getaway cabin. In any case, I want to know what's around here first. Plan on being out here a couple of days, at least."

"No worries. Well, if you'll excuse me, I need to wake the sleepy heads."

Mick made the rounds and woke everyone. Penny looked a bit tussled as she made her trip to the latrine, but she had everything in order once she ducked back into her tent, dressed for the day, and made her way to the campfire.

"Morning," she said, yawning. "You're up early."

"I'm a habitually early riser. I hope you slept well. It turns out I should've camped rather than staying in the house the other night. I feel terrific today."

"I think a wolf snuck into my tent and twisted me into a pretzel."

He laughed. "Perhaps a cot would help. It wouldn't hurt to have a few shipped out on the next supply run. Be wary of the coffee. It's hot and strong. Perhaps even corrosive."

She shuddered. "I'll stick to tea, then. What are your plans for the day?"

Clayton checked to make sure no one was close enough to overhear them. He pitched his voice low, in any case. Sound carried in the quiet air.

"A general search of the area. We'll make a map as we go and see if anything jumps out at us. They'd have built this base before humans lived on this island. It's possible we could find some sign of it.

"If we do, we make sure not to draw any undue attention to it. We'll come back another time and examine it more closely."

An unbirdlike chirping disturbed the quiet. His sat phone in his tent. Very few people had the number, so it was probably important.

He rose to his feet and retrieved it. "Yes?"

"The US government seized the Yucatán Spaceport," his assistant said. "They're in the process of locking down every company you sold."

"Then I suppose it's a good thing I sold them," he said with a chuckle. "And an even better thing that my ex-wife bought them from the Chinese. Her bad luck. She deserves it."

"Yes, about that. They've issued warrants for her arrest, and yours, I might add. The charges are numerous, but treason is high on the list. They've seized a number of her wholly owned companies, and she's gone underground."

Clayton considered that. "Treason is a strong charge. Especially for her. She's probably done something to earn it, but they're acting in a much more straightforward manner than I expected. Have they shown up looking for me?"

"Questions have been asked in Australia. They paid a number of people there visits, including the government. They're seeking extradition."

"Awkward when I have diplomatic immunity there."

"I assume that's because they don't recognize it. And we know what the US does when they can't legally take someone into custody."

Clayton looked out the tent toward the campfire. "Yes, they send in a black-bag team and take them. Or kill them. I wasn't obvious about going to New Zealand, but they'll find me. At least they'll learn I'm here somewhere. The land purchase will bring them calling in short order.

"I really shouldn't stay any longer than needed. Send one of Harry's teams to the station. Keep it quiet and muddy the waters with a false itinerary. Only the pilot gets the correct destination along with sealed orders to open them halfway to Brisbane. I'll extract when they arrive."

He disconnected the call and considered the time it would take to fly in.

He had the rest of the day to explore. Even if they tracked him down to the station, they'd never locate him out here in the back end of nowhere.

Mister Durey didn't know precisely where they were and probably wouldn't be very cooperative if nosey people came searching for him.

Meanwhile, he had breakfast to consume, and then he'd start exploring the wonderful wilderness. If Lady Luck showed him favor, he might even find the hidden entrance to the base before he left his American pursuers in the dust.

23

Harry had stayed up later than he should have examining the base. It was significantly larger than he'd expected. It would take them a very long time to explore every nook and cranny. The number of people that had once lived here must have been staggering.

Almost as much as the central jungle.

They'd found stairs to take them down to that level, but he'd resisted the urge. It was late enough by the time they'd worked everything out that the others in the party had been in their suits too long. They'd retreated to the landing bay.

Since Sandra and he had exposed themselves to the atmosphere, he'd had someone bring in cots and supplies for them. He figured that if they hadn't gotten sick in a few days, they probably wouldn't.

Sandra shook him awake far too early the next morning. "I found something funny."

"Oh, good," he said as he stretched. "I needed a laugh."

"Funny strange, not funny ha-ha. Get dressed, have a snack, and come with me."

He took his turn at the portable latrine, dressed, and had a breakfast bar. He considered putting on the suit but decided not to. Sandra wasn't wearing hers. Just ship's coveralls.

"Okay, now tell me what we're looking at."

She gestured toward the larger corridor. The one they believed the original owners had used for cargo. "I took a walk down that way. I found more than I bargained on. I'm not quite sure how to explain it."

"Then let's go solve the mystery."

He followed her down the corridor. It quickly opened up into a larger warren of storage rooms. There were a lot of cargo containers. A number of wide lifts served other levels.

Sandra led him to the closest of them. "I took a ride down in this one."

"That wasn't very bright," he said with a frown. "If it had broken down, we might not have found you for weeks."

"I took my radio, and I left a note on my bunk. Anyway, there aren't any stairs in this segment, so my options were limited. Come on."

He sighed and stepped into the elevator. It looked remarkably similar to the ones used on Earth. Sandra pressed the key for the lowest floor. He was starting to get a drift of the numbering system. This one was fifteen levels beneath them.

That was a lot of cargo for a dead world.

The elevator dropped quickly into the depths of Mars. He wasn't sure what to expect when the doors opened, but the area looked very much like what was above them.

"Okay. Now what?"

"We go on the other side of these crates, and you explain what I'm seeing."

He followed her around the imposing stacks and stopped when he saw the far wall. It looked... odd. Rather than being somewhat curved, like the rest of the walls, it was flat with a series of arches. Three large ones, to be precise.

The arches led into shallow alcoves. He walked over to one and stepped inside. It was a dozen meters deep with metal ribs all along its length. No other exits. Nothing stored there. Each of them looked the same.

Harry turned to Sandra with a shrug. "I'm at a loss. Seems odd, but I'm sure they used them for something."

She nodded. "I know they did. Look down."

The floor was made of grav plates, much like the rest of the base. The scuffs indicated someone had traveled over them a lot.

He felt his eyes narrow. Traveled where? The worn paths led into the alcoves.

"Now you see," Sandra said. "Something was moving crates into and out of the alcoves."

The width was about right for the few cargo lifts scattered about. The thick wheels would fit into the worn areas.

"That doesn't make any sense," he said. "Why move crates into those shallow areas and then take them back out?"

"No clue. Did you notice the floors in there? Stone. Not grav plates."

Harry went back into one of the alcoves and examined the area closely. The wear only came inside a little way. Then it ended abruptly just in front of the far wall.

He went to one of the cargo lifts. It was a one-seat affair much like a forklift back home. He'd had occasion to use one a few times. They weren't that complicated. He was willing to bet this one wasn't, either.

A touch of the screen brought it to life. "These people really built to last. This thing is still operational."

The console was mostly graphical. That made figuring out the controls possible. In short order, he was able to raise and lower the fork, as well as control the angle of the tines. Forward and reverse were simple enough to figure out.

He circled around until he found a crate off by itself and cautiously picked it up. The sides held.

An image of the area in front of the lift came to life on the console. That was useful, since he couldn't see around the crate without lifting it high off the ground.

Harry brought it around to the first alcove, and an alien twelve-digit numeric keypad appeared off to the side of the video. There were twelve spaces above it.

He randomly tapped out twelve numbers. They filled the open area above the keys, but nothing happened other than them flashing orange for a moment and vanishing.

"It's looking for a code. Maybe there's a secret door in there."

"It's solid rock," Sandra said as she climbed up beside him. "What are these?"

The keys she was pointing at sat beside the numeric keypad. They kind of reminded him of up and down arrows with a gray button between them.

She pressed the up arrow, and the code he'd just entered appeared. The numbers flashed orange and disappeared again.

"Invalid code, maybe," she said. "Let's see if there are any others in memory."

She pressed the up arrow twice and a different sequence of numbers appeared. These stayed on the screen and turned orange.

Still, nothing happened.

"Maybe the center key enters them." Harry pressed the gray button, and the numbers flashed and then turned gold.

"What the hell is that?" Sandra demanded. The area inside the alcove was becoming misty.

They climbed off the lift and stared at the alcove as the mist grew thicker until they couldn't see the stone behind it. That made no sense. There had been nothing back there but rock.

Small bits of lightning seemed to shoot through the mist, running from side to side as well as up and down. They backed up a little as the light show got more energetic. Then the mist seemed to puff out and faded somewhat. Enough to see through it, in any case.

The alcove was deeper. Much deeper. Darkness stretched out farther into it than the light could penetrate.

He stepped close and could see misty air swirling inside. The floor in the new area had grav plates. He felt an unexpected chill in the air too. As though the temperature had fallen ten degrees. Or more.

"I'm taking a look."

He stepped into the alcove and almost immediately regretted it. The temperature in this new room felt arctic. He shivered almost uncontrollably as he walked completely into the new area. He felt the gravity drop closer to Mars standard. His breath puffed into a cloud as he gripped his arms around his torso.

The chamber looked more like a lounge in an airport than a cargo area. Complete with a wide viewing port.

He looked over his shoulder through the arch. Sandra stood there looking at him with some concern. The wall on this side was much more artificial looking but substantially the same as the Mars side.

Harry stood shivering in the darkness, staring out the glass at a deep sea of stars. The outside of the port was in space. And he was standing somewhere other than Mars.

* * *

Paulette Young met Jess after breakfast. "I have version one of the translation program ready for testing."

Jess took the phone from her and looked it over. It seemed as though the camera was displaying directly on the screen. "Excellent. Let's go to the core and give it a look."

Once they arrived, Jess sat at the console. A touch brought it to life.

"Now what?" she asked.

"Hold the camera so that the image shows the writing. Keep it as steady as you can."

She held it so that she could see the writing. It morphed as she watched, the letters actually changing to English. It was very finicky, whole words changing back and forth with each movement of her hand.

A two-handed grip proved more stable. Some words didn't change, but most did. The grammar of the translation was terrible, but she could make sense of what she was reading without too much difficulty.

"Let's see. 'Protected terminus track. Assessed period before advent twenty-six qwen.' I suppose that means the course is locked, and we'll get there in twenty-six qwen. Whatever that is."

Paulette nodded. "Based on what you've said, you picked the destination, and the computer locked it in. Like an autopilot. A qwen is a unit of time. My best guess is that it's about an hour and a half."

"So, we get to wherever we're going in almost two days. That's not terrible." She touched the destination icon, and new text appeared. She'd done this before but had no way to determine what it said.

The translation was a little clearer this time. It read, "Abandon automated passage or alter swiftness." She touched the second option, and an up-and-down slider appeared with text beside it. They were close enough that they might as well complete the journey.

Paulette leaned forward and read over Jess's shoulder. "It looks like you can boost speed or slow down. The lower options look open ended, but the faster speed is capped."

"That makes sense. There's a top speed to any vehicle. I do like the sound of four qwen, though. Six hours. And I thought this thing was already hauling butt."

Jess slid the slider up to the fastest speed. A box demanding confirmation appeared. It used the word 'sanction' in the translator window. She gave her permission, and the options disappeared.

"I guess we'll see how accurate the timer is. We'll want to have people here monitoring the console. If need be, we'll cut speed or change course. I wish we had a clue where we're going."

"It seems like it should say," Paulette said. "Let me try something."

The other woman leaned forward and pressed on the destination but kept her finger there. A different screen opened with text in it.

"How did you know to do that?" Jess demanded.

"My phone behaves differently when you press and hold. I figured it couldn't hurt to try. Let's see what we have here."

The text was brief and to the point. 'Investigation transport Padjar. Peril: Ravencraft.'

"What the hell does that mean?" Jess asked. "Investigation transport? What's a Padjar? And it's dangerous because it's Ravencraft?"

"We still have a lot to learn," Paulette admitted. "We're making progress working on the stored documents. As we identify more of them that we can accurately translate for ourselves, we can use them to fine-tune the data this program uses.

"Emily has been a tremendous help. She's working on updating the HUD in a spacesuit helmet to do the same kind of translation."

"That would make exploration a lot easier."

Jess's radio squawked to life. "Jess, this is Ray. I think you need to come up here."

"Is there a problem?"

"No, but we found something I can't explain."

"On my way."

She handed the phone back to Paulette. "Keep working on this. I want as much improvement on the program as possible by the time we get to wherever we're going."

"We'll do our best, but that might not happen in just six hours."

Jess headed up to the battle scene. The bodies and small combat equipment were gone. Doctor Crockett and his wife were cataloging everything. With him grumbling about how much context they were losing.

Liberty Station's chief engineer was standing near one of the arches with Rex. "What's up?" she asked as she stopped beside them.

"This wall," Rex said. "Based on the number of pockmarks all around it, a lot of people were shooting at it."

"Okay." She examined the wall. There were indeed a number of scars all around the arch. Based on the weapons they'd recovered, the impacts came from fast-moving flechettes.

Ray gestured at the alcove inside the arch. "This area, however, is scar free. That seems statistically unlikely."

She shrugged and looked in. It was maybe ten or so meters deep and had metal ribs along the stone. "Maybe one of the vehicles was in front of it."

"Look at the arch itself."

One look told her what he meant. The arch was scarred and chipped. The wall area at the back of the arch was pristine.

Jess put on her engineer's hat and started looking at angles. "The shots came in from several directions. You can tell by how the rock chipped. Yet this alcove is free of damage. It's as though something filled the area. One of the vehicles wouldn't stop a hundred percent of the projectiles."

She stepped into the chamber and examined the arched entrance from the inside. It was stone, as expected, but there were dozens of small projectors on the inside. They looked like little fans, so probably not narrow beams.

"There are some projection devices in here. Maybe they display an image onto the wall. No controls, though."

"We have another oddity," Ray said. "There are definitely no exits for the ships. And no way the heavy-worlders could get in here and surprise everyone.

"And how did they get the cargo inside here? Not through the main entrance. This just doesn't make any sense."

Jess shrugged. "There's no telling. I figured out how to increase our speed, by the way. If the translation program is working correctly, we'll arrive at our destination in six hours. You might want to get some sleep and food. It might get busy in a hurry."

Rex seemed amenable to the idea, but Ray Proudfoot declined. "I don't like things I can't explain. I'm going to borrow that translator and see if I can't turn something up. You might want to take your own advice, though. You're running on fumes."

She smiled at him. "I could use a catnap. Wake me if you find anything important. Otherwise, I'll see you in a few hours for the big reveal."

24

Q ueen stepped off the plane in Chicago, annoyed. He'd barely made it to the Yucatán Spaceport when one of Pembroke's associates called and insisted they come back right away.

He'd demurred and told her that they'd be back as soon as he was done, but she'd insisted—vigorously—that he needed to "get on the damned plane right the hell now." Her exact words.

Pembroke swore she was one of his best agents, so Queen had grumpily acquiesced. This had better be worth the delay in his schedule, or both of the FBI agents would regret it. Deeply.

A short black woman with a no-nonsense air about her waited at the bottom of the plane's steps, a black SUV parked behind her. Queen wasn't attracted to women, but even he could recognize her beauty.

Her professional stance made him suddenly doubt his certainty that this was going to end badly for her. She didn't seem to be the kind of person who panicked and demanded her superiors come running when she hit some minor bump in the road.

Pembroke stopped between the two of them. "Secretary Josh Queen, Agent Brenda Cabot. Lay it on us, Brenda. What's so important that it couldn't wait? And how did you end up here? I thought you were in Michigan."

"I have my sources," she said, her voice a little deeper than Queen expected. "And I *am* the FBI's resident expert in odd cases like this.

"Not that this is like anything I've ever seen before. And I'm hurt you tried to keep me out of it. What we found is probably classified, so we should talk in the SUV. If not, it sure as hell will be the moment you see it."

Queen gestured for her to proceed. "Lead on, Agent Cabot."

She climbed behind the wheel, and Pembroke sat in back with Queen. The SUV took off as soon as they were strapped in.

"We traced a bunch of offshore companies and subsidiaries belonging to or associated with Kathleen Bennett," Cabot said. "We also pulled the call logs from her phones. As part of the monitoring while we were searching the kill site, we got a FISA warrant to capture the phone numbers of every cell phone used in the area.

"We didn't get the contents of the calls, but we got the caller and the length of the connection. Most of them were innocuous, but a few stood out. Burner phones. That was unusual in a stand-up place like this, so we focused our attention on those first."

Pembroke nodded. "I assume that led you to someone interesting."

"Yes, sir, it did. Doctor Ethan Wagner. He purportedly owns a small engineering firm here in Chicago."

Queen smiled a little. "Purportedly. I gather he works rather more directly for Kathleen Bennett."

She nodded. "Yes, Mister Secretary. Once we knew the name of his company, we were able to link them, though it wasn't easy. Someone went to a lot of trouble to bury the connection.

"We got a no-knock warrant and raided the place in force this morning. We didn't find anything connected to the murders, but this might very well be linked to the larger case with the spaceship her ex-husband built."

She handed Queen a tablet that had been sitting on the front passenger seat. "The pictures speak for themselves."

He examined the image on the tablet. It looked like the framework for some kind of aircraft. One he wasn't familiar with. It was either mostly stripped or they hadn't completed it yet.

"What am I looking at?" he asked.

"That's a spaceship."

He felt his eyes widen. "Pardon me?"

"Did you hear about the hubbub in Guatemala? Someone blew up an archaeological dig. Collapsed a Mayan pyramid."

He nodded. "Grave robbers, I assumed."

"Perhaps, in a manner of speaking. Apparently, this was the target of the theft. Doctor Wagner was a little short on details. He only knew bits of the story.

"Mrs. Bennett delivered this craft to him and told him that it had been recovered at the Mayan site. He claims it is far in advance of anything we have, and based on the parts I've seen, I tend to believe him. He also claims that it's a thousand years old."

Queen sighed. This wasn't going to end well. "And you believed that kind of nonsense?"

Agent Cabot gave him a steady look in the rear-view mirror. "Before you jump to the conclusion that I've lost my mind, I recommend you at least see it in person. You're already here, after all."

He couldn't argue with that, so he only nodded.

The SUV made the trip to a nondescript industrial building in twenty minutes. There was no overt sign that the FBI had the place locked down, but he saw a few agents in cars on the street.

"I figured you might want to keep this quiet," she said, "so I have everyone inside."

That was certainly true. There were federal officers packed inside the building, including a heavily armed tactical team. There were no local police. Perhaps she didn't trust them. Wisely so, most likely. This *was* Chicago.

She led them deeper into the facility, using a company badge to get through a number of security doors. They ended up in a wide bay with the skeleton of the supposed spacecraft.

He walked around it and tried to look past his doubts. It was very different in design from the lifters he'd seen in the briefings about the Yucatán Spaceport. For one, he saw no engines. And it didn't seem designed to attach to a rocket.

"How does it move?" he asked.

The petite agent shrugged. "They think it manipulates the curvature of space."

"Seriously? You realize how crazy that sounds, don't you?"

"I do. Climb inside, Mister Secretary. They've stripped everything but the control consoles out. It's on power from the facility, so it's safe enough."

He went up the short ramp someone had built for access and eyed the size of the cabin. Small, but sufficient for some cargo. The two acceleration couches sat in front of dark black panels.

Queen slipped into one, and Cabot the other. She reached out and touched the screen, and the controls came to life. So did the exterior monitors.

The layout was different from anything he'd seen before, and the writing was gibberish. Still, that didn't mean anything.

"How do we know this isn't faked?" he asked. "This all seems within the realm of possibility, outlandish drives aside."

"I asked that very question. It seems they just had a major breakthrough in exploring the ship's computer. It has a bit of flight data from its last trip."

She touched the controls and brought up a new screen. "This is about a twenty-minute recording."

The screens reconfigured when she tapped an icon. The wrap around "windows" looked out onto space. It also showed the Earth rotating serenely in front of them. One small section of the console displayed the inside of the control area. Not as it currently was, but as it supposedly had been.

It showed a man sitting on one of the couches and the controls from over his shoulder. The man was blond and dressed in a set of coveralls. He had a cut above one eye that didn't seem fully staunched. He was... rumpled.

Queen watched him manipulate the controls. He seemed hesitant. As though he was unsure of what he was doing.

He muttered to himself. The sound coming from hidden speakers conveyed that clearly enough. Queen didn't recognize the language, but he could tell cursing when he heard it.

The man guided the ship down toward Earth. Reentry was knuckle biting. At some point, the man made some mistake he couldn't correct, and the smooth descent became a crash. Not a fatal one, but one that left the ship in the jungle after a very hard landing.

The man seemed happy enough to have survived. A very reasonable viewpoint, Queen thought. He unstrapped himself and left the cockpit.

Outside, the jungle slowly came back to life after the intrusion. He was about to turn to Agent Cabot when he spotted a man in the foliage. He looked primitive. Like an indigenous person. While Queen had no idea what a Mayan looked like, he could believe this man was one, based on his clothes.

The man from the ship stepped into view outside and appeared to be speaking to the native. The primitive man seemed quite impressed because he threw himself flat on the ground. The video ceased shortly after that.

"See what I mean?" Cabot asked.

"That is also interesting, but it could be faked. With a lot of difficulty and expense, but it's possible."

She smiled. "I said that too. So, I have one more chance to convince you."

Cabot took him to a room that looked like it held the electrical service for the building. Large switches controlled the power from the city grid. Except they were all disconnected.

Instead, a large, cobbled-together piece of equipment seemed to be providing the power. Its centerpiece was a glowing blue cube ten centimeters on a side.

"We've had our people verify this building really is cut off from the city grid. We shut down power for the area after searching the building for battery backups. There were some but only for critical equipment. They couldn't affect the whole facility. This cube is providing the power this entire complex needs. All of it."

"And it came from the ship?"

"So Wagner claims. If this isn't alien tech, I don't know what is. Look, Mister Secretary, everything I've seen tells me this is real. Crazy, but real. If Area 51 really does deal with little green men, now is the time to call them in."

He had to confess that the preponderance of evidence was on her side. This was insane, but inarguable. What was it the fictional consulting detective Sherlock Holmes said? Eliminate the impossible, and whatever remains, no matter how improbable, must be the truth.

"If you'll excuse me for a moment, I have a call to make. Then I want to speak to Doctor Wagner."

Once she'd left the room, he called the senior Navy commander advising the president, Admiral Paula Hannover. "Paula, Josh. I'm changing the status on Operation Golden Parachute. You are go to execute. Make it quiet if you can, but I want Clayton Rogers in custody as soon as possible.

"Try to avoid killing any civilians or starting a war with New Zealand, but don't let either of those outcomes stop you. Make it happen."

* * *

CLAYTON ROGERS WIPED his brow and rested his machete on his leg. This was more physically taxing than he'd expected. Of course, he'd never forged his way through the untraveled brush like this before, either.

Young Mick had provided a good example of how to do the task. His strokes seemed effortless. He rather reminded Clayton of the character in an old movie set in Australia. Mick was a young Crocodile Dundee.

Not that he would ever say that to him. This innate animosity with their neighbors across the Tasman Sea was almost reflexive. Odd, but he wasn't going to be the one to offend. America was no stranger to regional issues. Who was he to judge?

"This has a right nice view," Mick said when he crested the ridge. "It's wide too. Looks stable. You could build a very substantial getaway home up here."

Clayton stopped beside him and took in the view. It was still early in the morning, so the sun was mostly behind them. The vista was indeed stunning. He'd proceed with building a place, no matter what they found here, he decided. He deserved a place to get away from it all.

Mick sent his men to search the ridge area for weak spots that were obvious enough to disqualify it. They'd clear the brush so that professionals could do a more thorough survey later.

Penny was off with the other team, looking into the area around the plateau. It made sense for the base entrance to be close to the landing area.

And he was convinced the flat slab of rock had once served that purpose. The stone bore some scars that didn't look natural.

Unlike Mars, though, this entrance wasn't in plain sight. Someone had wanted to be certain no one found it. Even on an uninhabited island.

He'd viewed some of the footage from the Mars base. The people who'd built it were more than capable of hiding something like this in plain sight. And with the dead from the battle on *Freedom Express*, he had no doubt their concern for doing so had been correct.

Whatever had happened had been vicious and brutal. There was probably plenty of information on why the conflict had happened in the computers, once they could decipher the language.

It was academic at this point. Those people and their grievances had died a thousand years ago.

The time delay for communication with Jess was about six hours at this point. One way. And she couldn't talk directly to Earth. At that range, there was no such thing as a tight beam. Everyone on the planet would know if she signaled them.

Wouldn't that excite the SETI people?

So, any information from her came through Harry on Mars. He'd only just found out about the remnants of the pitched battle there. The images of the heavy-worlders and their weapons convinced him that they were the enemy these people on Earth feared.

Jess would reach her destination soon, whatever it was. Then he'd hear all about it late tonight. He hoped it was worth the long journey.

His sat phone rang. It was his assistant.

"Good morning," Clayton said. "I hope you aren't calling with more bad news. We haven't seen any sign of trouble. Please, tell me that they haven't come pestering Mister Durey."

"I haven't heard anything from that front," his assistant said. "We just received some information from Mars that you need to see right now."

His gut clenched. Something had gone wrong.

"Then tell me. Is Harry okay?" He was astonished at how level his voice sounded.

"He's fine. All of them are. They found something unexpected and of critical importance. I'm not comfortable with saying what, even over an encrypted line. You need to return to Nauru at once."

His man didn't order him around as a rule, so this must be truly important.

"I'll make arrangements to leave as quickly as I can. I want an encrypted file with the data in my inbox by the time I board the plane."

Unlike encrypted phone communication, he was much more confident of the file encryption. The NSA might be able to crack a phone call. They'd be working decades to bypass his file security.

That would change once his people perfected the quantum entanglement phones they were working on. Using the effect that Albert Einstein dubbed "spooky action at a distance," they'd be able to talk without any concern that others would even be able to detect the communication, much less listen in.

The entangled photons in the source and destination devices would change in exactly the same manner without any apparent information traveling between them. None they could detect, anyway.

It would also eliminate the time delay for long-distance communication, they believed. There was no detectable time lost in the reaction of one photon to changes in the other, no matter how far away. It was instantaneous. No more light-speed limitation to communications.

"The update is already in your inbox," his assistant said. "Also, a US Navy destroyer has arrived in the Tasman Sea. I'd suggest you depart before it lands troops to look for you."

"I'm sure the CIA already has people on the ground that are more than capable of inconveniencing me, if they find me. Stop being such a mother hen. I'll call you once we're in the air."

He disconnected and walked over to Mick. "Something has come up, I'm afraid. I need to return to Nauru right away."

The young man didn't turn his head. "Something is up here too. That's either the slowest plane ever or I'm looking at a drone."

Clayton blinked in surprise. He stared in the direction the other man was looking and saw nothing.

"Are you sure?"

"See the big hill west of here? It's going to be over it in a minute. I saw a slow-moving dot and thought it was a bird, but it's going in a straight line." He handed Clayton his binoculars. "I looked all around so it wouldn't freak out the people manning it, just in case they already found us."

Clayton made a show of looking in a few different directions before he looked at the area Mick was staring at. It still took him a minute to find the drone.

And drone it was. Painted to look like a cloud, the damned thing was almost invisible, but once he was on it, he could follow it fairly easily. It had its camera pointed in their direction too.

"It's the US military," he said. "That means we can expect company very shortly."

Mick nodded as Clayton handed the binoculars back. "I figured that already. You might want to get Miss Penny in hand and scoot."

Clayton nodded. "Let's find her and get the hell out of here."

25

It was late when Nathan found what he was looking for. After nine in the evening. It got dark fast out in the ass end of nowhere. Without the extra lights, he wouldn't have been able to see his hand in front of his face.

The area where the ground-penetrating radar had indicated there might be something was a large hill. One overgrown with trees and vines. Perhaps the idiot that had sold him the land had wanted to grow grapes.

Good luck with that.

They used a portable radar unit to look at the crown of the hill. It told him there was a hollow area to the north side. Once he knew where to look, he found a suspicious slab of rock. It looked native, but it was deep under an overhang.

It took Nathan half an hour of searching to find the hidden dimple where the key went. It turned out to be a good thing he hadn't sent the key to his mother after all.

His phone rang. Mother. She really knew how to ruin a moment. Still, now he could brag.

"Good news, Mother. I found the entrance to the base."

"The FBI raided the lab with the ship. They have everything."

The news hit him like a falling boulder. "Shit! How did they find it? You said it wasn't even connected to you."

"I don't know!" She sounded anguished. "The bastards know everything, or they soon will. Now they'll never stop looking for us."

"Or they'll go after Father with everything they have," he said. "We don't have any more than that ship. Or so they think. Please tell me that the scientists scrubbed the data. And had the courier arrived yet?"

"He hadn't arrived yet. Call him back. As for the computers, my man on the inside dumped the computers when they rushed the facility.

"That won't slow them down too much. They have the scientists themselves to question. Still, they won't know about your base. I hope to God it's worth something, because we won't have a pot to piss in soon enough."

He considered the time. "You'll land later tonight. By then I should have something on this facility. I know you have your personal fortune spread out under any number of fake names, so we'll survive. If we can master this tech, we can use it to force the US to back down. If China finds out about it, they'll give the US a black eye."

"While I have no objection to the US being humiliated, there's no way they'd leave us alone. We need to find a way to keep them back. I'll keep thinking on it. You explore the base."

"Consider it done."

Nathan slipped the key into the dimple he'd found. It clicked into place, and the slab of rock slowly ground its way back into the hill and then whisked to the side.

The stone was obviously only a façade. The back side was metal.

The room beyond the door was small. It led into a short hall with what looked like an elevator door. Then his adrenaline spiked as he saw a weapon above the door, pointed right at him.

* * *

HARRY BACKED out of the strange new area and figured out how to close down the connection. Then they got their suits on and called for backup. If something went south, Harry wanted a full team ready to pull them back to safety.

His idea of a fully prepared incursion team was one in suits, fully armed, and carrying enough supplies to survive if they got cut off. That entailed moving a lot of air, food, and water into the strange compartment before they left it.

Thankfully, they had a forklift to get it all inside in one trip.

Sandra and his Liberty team led the way inside. Some of the scientists followed.

"I wonder how long this contraption can stay open," Sandra said. "If we keep it activated, it might run out of juice and leave us stuck."

"It would be nice to be able to activate it from this side," Harry agreed. He examined the wall beside the transport arch. There were controls, similar to the ones on the forklift. It showed a different sequence of numbers. He carefully wrote them down, not a simple task in his thick gloves.

"Take the forklift back to Mars. If I can't open this in five minutes, use it to come get us."

Sandra gave him a jaunty salute and backed the forklift into the misty room back on Mars. The tremendous difference in temperature between the two locations was causing a fog as the water in the air condensed.

Once the connection broke and the wall went back to being just a wall, he entered the numeric code he'd written down, but nothing happened. It took several attempts to figure out which button was the one to enter the change.

The arch came back to life and opened what his science types were guessing was some kind of quantum tunnel to the destination.

Only it wasn't the cargo chamber on Mars.

The arch led out onto a pristine beach. A wave of fog engulfed them as the wind pushed a lot of moisture into the room. He could still see the suns in the sky, though. Both of them.

"Don't touch anything," he said.

Harry stepped out onto the beach and looked around. Other than the double suns sitting near one another, it could've been a beach on Earth. The portal opened out of a stone ridge and what looked like a patio to the left.

He made his way over to it. The remains of a number of tables were scatted across the open area. Piles of strange-looking leaves and debris covered everything. A stiff breeze blew everything around in little eddies. No one had been here in a long, long time.

It only took a few minutes to record everything with his suit camera. He grabbed some organic debris and put it into a sample bag. Then he returned to the room where his team waited.

"That wasn't what I expected," he said. "Not at all. This transport system can obviously cross incredible distances. There was no telling where that system was."

"Congrats, Boss," Leann Branson, his com specialist, said. "You're the first human being to leave the solar system and explore an alien world. Too bad you didn't have some prepared remarks."

Harry laughed. That hadn't worked out so well for him last time.

"Also," she continued, "I figured out what you did wrong. You transposed two of the numbers. See?"

He looked at the controls more carefully. The alien numbers weren't natural to him, yet. He'd made a rookie mistake. One that led to the greatest discovery in human exploration.

Wasn't that how science worked? Someone tried something, had an unexpected result, or made a simple mistake, and something tremendous happened. He'd take the lucky find.

"Twelve numbers. How many possible combinations is that?" he asked. A lot, he suspected. Millions. Maybe billions.

One of the scientists used a calculator. "8.9 trillion."

"What the hell would they need that many possibilities for?" Leann asked incredulously.

He shrugged. "Aliens. Who can understand them? Maybe they just didn't want to be shortsighted. Like the moron who didn't leave enough digits for the years to roll over on computers at the millennium. When it was only a few decades away. Not smart."

"Wasn't that the same loser that thought 640 kilobytes was all the memory a computer would ever need?" Leann asked. "Wow. Talk about getting it wrong."

"I'm not sure those were the same losers," he said. "Could they really have that kind of need? That looked like a scenic restaurant view, but there was no restaurant. They might need a ton of these tunnels in their civilization, like phone numbers or IP addresses."

Leann looked mulish. "How could they stop two people from calling the same destination? A busy signal? Something doesn't sound right."

"We'll have time to figure it out." He checked his timer. Only a minute to go before Sandra opened up the arch. He'd best try the correct number. Being a bit more careful this time, he entered the correct code.

The arch opened a tunnel, and he was relieved to see Sandra standing there beside the forklift.

"You took your sweet time," she said. "I was starting to get worried."

"I dialed a wrong number. Let's see if we can get the other portals to dial it for us."

They'd experimented with the controls enough to discover how to send a code to each of the three available arches. One of them seemed broken, but the second worked fine.

He left the one to the room with his people open. Hopefully, there wouldn't be any power issues.

Harry started to enter the code combination but stopped. "This goes to a different location. One with an atmosphere of its own. Helmet on, Sandra. It might not be healthy."

The rest of the team was suited, of course. Since he and Sandra had already been exposed to the room they'd found, she hadn't bothered to helmet up.

It only took a minute for her to lock her helmet on. Then he finished entering the code and hit the activation button.

The second arch lit up and opened a quantum tunnel to the beach he'd just explored.

"Holy shit," Sandra muttered. "That's not Earth."

"Not with two suns," he agreed. "I brought some of the plant life back in a sample bag. I accidentally transposed two numbers. God only knows where it is. Or what it was."

She turned to him and shook her head. "How damned big is this thing we've stumbled into? I thought ships were hot stuff, but this is a game changer. It literally opens up the whole universe."

He nodded. "And it's a two-way street. If someone out there has the right codes, they could pop up here. We know there are bases of some kind scattered all around the solar system. These things could connect them all. Hell, *Freedom Express* might have some too."

"Then why even have a ship like that? This doesn't make sense."

"That's what happens when you don't know all the facts. I can see possible reasons why someone with access to quantum tunnels like these might want to get between point A and point B without someone else tracking them. They were fighting a war of some kind."

She shook her head again. "This is too weird. It reminds me of some old science-fiction show I watched once. Star something."

"*Stargate*," he said. "A classic. They had a couple movies and several television shows. I can sort of see some similarity to that. Fiction mimicking reality, I guess. Or vice versa. Let's hope we don't have to fight any ancient Egyptian gods with superweapons."

"Personally, I associate this more with something like 'The City on the Edge of Forever' from *Star Trek*. Without the time travel, of course."

He shut down the tunnel to the beach and handed the samples and codes off to someone who'd be staying behind. "We need to start a database of destinations by code. We know the Mars base code for the first arch. We should get the code for this one. Let's switch the tunnel to the first location over to it."

Once he did that, they had both arches' codes. He made sure every member of the team had a copy. Not the best idea, but they didn't have time to memorize them yet. That would be the next step. If they didn't have a copy with them, an enemy couldn't take it from them so easily. They had to protect humanity.

"There has to be a better way of accessing these things," Sandra said as she walked with him into the compartment with their people. "Some of these arches have controls, but others don't. Surely, the forklift only works on the ones at the Mars base. What if someone got stuck on that beach? How did they open it from that side?"

"Damned if I know. Maybe some kind of controller? We'd have to find one before we would know for sure."

Once everyone was safely inside the compartment, he killed the tunnel. They were alone on whatever this was. Somewhere in space.

They'd look around for two hours and then return. That left plenty of time to get a better idea of where they were but didn't put them at extended risk.

"Hey," Sandra said, looking out the wide window into space. "I can see something."

Harry stepped beside her. "What?"

"There's a shadow over to the right. Something is blocking the stars."

He killed his suit lights. "Everyone, lights off."

The room went spookily dark. It took a few minutes for his eyes to adjust, but he finally saw what she'd seen. There was an oval of dark material there. A slender, curved rod came away from it and led toward whatever this was that they were in.

No. Not a rod. An arm, like they had on *Liberty Station* to hold the mining platforms away from the hull of the ship. Their view of the stars seemed to be rotating slowly, and that thing kept exact pace with the changes.

It was part of whatever they were on. Ship, station, something else. Whatever this thing was, it was big. One more mystery left behind by the people that had watched and mingled with them a thousand years ago.

"Okay, people," he said, turning his suit light back on. "Let's move out. Keep together and don't touch anything without telling me first."

26

Clayton, Mick, and his people made their way back to camp without a problem. Penny was still out with her team, and no one knew precisely where they'd gotten off to.

He told the pilot to go start his preflight inspection while the men broke camp. Mick and he went off to round up Penny and the rest after he grabbed his pack.

He expected to find them close by, but that instinct proved wrong. They finally found them on another wing of the ridge, far above their level in the valley. Some shouting gave them the idea that he wanted to join them, and they directed him to a steep narrow path.

Penny met him at the top of the climb beside a tall-rock outcropping. "We found something promising."

"It will have to wait," he said. "The US military is shadowing us. We spotted a drone. It's time to get out of here."

A shout from below pulled his attention. One glance toward the plateau told him it was already too late. Two men in mottled camouflage had the pilot under the command of their rifles. A look at the camp showed more soldiers herding the men together.

It wouldn't be long before they were on their way to his location. If they weren't already.

The area below them was still clear. He eyed the large rocks overhanging the narrow path. "We might be able to push those over and delay the inevitable, I suppose. Mick?"

"Hang on."

The young man was lying on the ground near the edge of the ridge. He had a rifle with a scope to his shoulder. Clayton hadn't seen him grab it.

"Don't shoot them," Clayton said firmly. "Those men are just following orders."

The man gave him a frown. "I'm not shooting at them. Now, if you'll give me a minute of peace, I might be able to give us some breathing room."

Clayton held up his hands. "Pardon me, then. Carry on." Under other circumstances, this would be amusing.

Mick lined up his shot and squeezed the trigger. The loud blast rolled off the hills around them. Down below, men shouted but didn't fire on them. Clayton backed away from the edge, anyway. Why take chances?

"Got it!" the young man shouted with a grin. "How much does a drone cost, anyway?"

"A lot of money, probably. If we get out of this, I might buy you one. You took it down, I assume?"

"It went right down into the ground," Mick confirmed as he backed away from the edge of the ridge, rose to his feet, and slung his rifle. "Unless they had two, we're not in direct sight of them anymore. And no drone, please. A fast red car would be fine," he quipped with an impish expression.

"I'll see what I can do," Clayton said. "Let's push some of these rocks over and make getting to us more difficult."

The two men got behind the pile of rocks at the top of the path and gave it their all. It didn't budge a centimeter. In the end, it took Penny and the men with her to tip the rocks over.

Just in the nick of time, it turned out. He saw a squad of men round the base of the ridge just as the rocks obliterated the steep path. One of them stood there, looking up at Clayton as the others rushed forward to examine the destruction. A man in subdued civilian clothes came out to join him.

The uniformed man sketched a salute toward them and shouted up. "Clayton Rodgers, on behalf of the United States of America, I'm instructing you to surrender peacefully. No one needs to get hurt."

"And if I choose to do no such thing?" he shouted back.

"Then I'll come up there and take you with whatever force proves necessary. I can't promise no one will get hurt that way. I know one of you has a rifle, and I won't take chances.

"We've already captured your aircraft, and there's a jammer blocking any communication. This only ends one way. I'll leave the other people in peace. Be reasonable."

Clayton pulled out his sat phone. There was no signal. He didn't think they could be blocked. Score one for the US intelligence services.

It was probably the doing of the other man down there. CIA, Clayton wagered. Or maybe NSA.

"We'll see how things play out," Clayton shouted down. "We're not going to shoot at you, so there's no need to do anything hasty."

"Like shooting down a drone?" the civilian yelled. "Do you know how much those things cost?"

"Mick Bird," the officer said. "You're the one with the rifle, right? If you say this is over, then it's over. You and your men will not be harmed. You have my word as an officer and a gentleman. End this before someone makes a mistake that can't be walked back."

"Sorry," Mick yelled. "I don't work for you, mate. The boys and I are loyal to our boss. You want him? Come up and get him."

And Clayton was supremely confident that they would do exactly that as soon as they could.

* * *

QUEEN SAT down at the break-room table. They'd cuffed Doctor Ethan Wagner to the chair across from him. That wasn't strictly necessary, but he thought it would put the man into a cooperative frame of mind.

Wagner looked rumpled and more than a bit frightened. Good. That would smooth matters considerably.

"Doctor Wagner, I'm Josh Queen. You can think of me as your best friend right now because you have the opportunity to help me and help yourself at the same time. Cooperate and we'll forget that you were working for a snake like Kathleen Bennett. It will be as if your treasonous actions never happened. Do you understand?"

The man nodded convulsively.

"And just so we're clear," Queen said genially, "if I find out you've misled me or held something back, I'll lock you beneath the highest-security prison I can find. You'll spend your time in solitary. Maybe you'll never see another human being for the rest of your life. I hope the choices before you are as black and white as I can make them. Choose once and choose wisely."

"I'll tell you whatever you want to know," Wagner said. "This is just a job. I didn't know anything about treason."

"Very good. Agent Cabot, please remove the good doctor's cuffs. I'm sure he won't cause me any problems. Will you, Doctor?"

The man shook his head vigorously.

She stepped forward, removed the cuffs, and resumed her place against the wall.

"Let's start at the beginning, Doctor. When did you first hear about this spaceship?"

"Shortly before Mrs. Bennett delivered it. It came in a cargo freighter. A helicopter lifted it out in the dead of night and brought it here. We landed it out back on a mobile platform and brought it inside."

"She just brought it right in, and customs enforcement didn't find it?" He looked at Cabot. "Find out who signed off on that ship. They're dirty."

She nodded and made a note on her phone.

"I'm told that someone on your staff purged the computers. Now I'm going to have to pull the data out of you one bit at a time. If I find out that you've left any stone unturned in your report to me, the aforementioned bad things will happen. What have you found?"

The scientist licked his lips. "Well, I suppose the big find is the power supply. A little blue cube with the output of a nuclear reactor. More, probably.

We weren't able to stress it enough to determine the maximum throughput. That was going to wait until we had more equipment."

"I've seen it. How can it hold that much energy?"

"We're still discussing the merits of that. Whatever it is, it's been able to hold power for a millennium and still have a lot of kick left."

Queen frowned. "What's your best theory?"

"There's a theory that even empty space has a sea of energy, both positive and negative, that cancels one another out. If someone could tap that sort of thing, a cube of that size would be able to liberate enough energy to boil the oceans off this planet."

"That sounds dangerous."

"It might be. We have no way of knowing. All I can tell you is that every test we've given it shows it's stable. Obviously the designers didn't think it was something to be overly concerned about."

He considered that and slowly nodded. "Perhaps you're right. What can you tell me about the designers?"

"Very little," the scientist admitted. "We recovered three bodies from the wrecked ship. They were in very tough body bags. One female and two males. One of the males was a boy in his teens, and the DNA results indicate the other two were his parents. He even had a cell phone, or the equivalent. Carbon dating and other tests lead us to believe they died about a thousand years ago."

"So they were human? Fully human?"

"The DNA doesn't lie. I can tell you these people came from somewhere in central Europe, probably Italy. They were modern humans that could have walked the streets today and not drawn a second glance."

That was disturbing. "Do you think that's likely? Could we have them among us?"

Wagner shrugged. "Anything is possible, I suppose. If this ship came to Earth, odds are that others did as well. Perhaps their ancestors are out there right now. Some secret society of those who remember the glory days of their people through stories whispered in the dead of night."

"Seriously, why be so paranoid? Surely, if something like that were true, we'd have heard something by now. No one is that good at keeping a secret."

Queen's phone rang. "Perhaps you would like some water, Doctor?"

"That would be very welcome."

He gestured for Agent Cabot to handle that, stepped into the hall, and answered his phone. The caller ID indicated it was his assistant. "Queen."

"A SEAL team has Clayton Rogers pinned down on a ridge in the back hills of New Zealand. They're working on securing him now."

He smiled. "Excellent!"

"Only to a point. We lost the drone watching over the scene. One of them shot it down."

"That doesn't matter, as long as our people get out with Rogers. I'll be back in the office shortly."

He disconnected the call and put his phone away. Things were coming together It wouldn't be long before he had everything well in hand. He'd take the dead boy's cell phone with him to have an independent lab look it over. Just to be certain Wagner wasn't lying to him.

* * *

KATHLEEN FUMED as a private jet registered to an untraceable holding company raced toward Paris. They'd taken everything from her. Everything.

Yes, she still had money. The liquid funds, anyway. But they'd seized her companies. Frozen trillions of dollars of value. They wouldn't get away with it. Of that, she swore.

Her legal team had already filed a blizzard of lawsuits and received an injunction from a friendly judge, but she knew that wouldn't stop the government's extralegal activity. Not now that Queen knew about the ship.

He wouldn't allow the rule of law to stand in his way. Besides, she couldn't even claim the damned thing. It was gone. She had to accept that.

That didn't mean she had to take it, though. She placed a call to a memorized number.

"Joe's Bar, Grill, and Machine Shop. Joe speaking."

Kathleen imagined that was funny to him, though she had no idea why. She'd never met the man and wasn't about to ask.

"I need to order takeout. The account is B-1054."

"Sure. Send me a note and wire the payment. How soon do you want it?"

"As soon as possible. I'll pay the premium for speedy delivery. Also, this has some rare ingredients. Look for the note."

She hung up and brought up an anonymous email account.

Josh Queen, secretary of state. Chicago or Washington. As soon as possible. It doesn't matter how. Twenty percent delivery surcharge if you deliver today. Ten percent for tomorrow.

She deleted the email but didn't purge the folder.

After a minute, her note vanished, and another appeared in the folder.

Hot stuff. I'll try to deliver today. The price is 30 million. Nonnegotiable.

It also had an account number.

The fee was exorbitantly high, but she had no choice. And he'd deliver or wire the money back. His reputation was very solid.

She deleted his note and left her acceptance. Then she logged into an offshore account and wired the money.

Josh Queen wasn't going to be a problem much longer.

27

J ess was just getting up from her nap and grabbing lunch when Ray
Proudfoot called. She grabbed a sandwich and a drink, determined to
be ready when they got to the destination in a few hours.

He wasn't in the cargo room as she expected but was with Doctor
Crockett, his wife, and... his other wife? They were in a room packed with
gear from the battle zone.

"What's up?" she asked.

"This," Ray said, holding up a tablet. "I had Michael look over the
combat armor and found a camera. That told me that they were recording.
Finding the data repository wasn't hard."

He gestured toward the helmet on the table. "We found a port and linked
it up with one of our tablets through a cable we modified."

"You have direct access to their data files?" Jess asked. "That's a huge
breakthrough! How did you even find the video? How did you play it?"

"We cheated," Sierra said. "Emily took one of the helmets apart and tried
possible wiring combinations until she hit one that seemed to give her no
issues. Trial and error got the power levels right. We burned up a few helmets
in the process, but omelets need eggs."

"We'll still probably be able to recover the data from them," Doctor
Crockett said. "We think we only fried the ports."

Emily took the tablet. "The operating systems aren't compatible, of
course. I'm only using this as a dumb terminal, which required some work and
some luck. The helmet is really in control. I installed version three of the
translation software on the tablet, and it's making guesses as to what the text
says.

"As for finding the video, that's where we cheated. We turned on the camera and then went looking for recent files. The basic use of files and folders is intuitive. People want to be able to find things."

"And once we located the file, we convinced the system to tell us what to play it with," Ray said. "Again, this is all running on the helmet, which is not a very complex computer system."

Jess shook her head. "Techogeek gobbledygook. You guys rock!"

"That's not the part we called you down to see," he continued. "Watch this. It's not pretty, but it shows something you need to see."

"Is it the fighting? I've seen people die. I'd rather not do so again, if I don't have to."

"There is some of that," he admitted. "That's not the astounding thing. Watch."

Emily held out the tablet and tapped an icon. The screen changed to a video of a number of heavy-worlders standing in a group. As they were in armor, Jess suspected they were soldiers. They were talking. The language didn't sound at all familiar.

One of the men shouted something, and the guy with the helmet cam turned to face him. His armor was a little different. Maybe he was an officer.

He stood beside one of the small combat craft they'd found wrecked in the bay. He spoke to them for a few minutes and then held up a small tablet. He tapped on it and began walking away from the center of the formation.

The troops readied themselves, but she couldn't tell why. They were facing a blank wall. It had arches similar to the ones in the bay but no hatches she could see.

Then the wall inside the arch turned misty and little bolts of light shot through it. Moments later, it cleared, and she could see a room on the other side. The cargo area on *Freedom Express*. A few men and women were standing there gawking until the heavy-worlders rushed in and began firing.

The fight was as ugly and one-sided as she'd expected from the body count. They quickly slaughtered the unarmed crew.

Emily stopped the video. "We fast forwarded. They ran amok on the ship. This guy went to the core with a team. He recorded one of his friends knifing the woman we found there. Armed defenders finally pushed them back.

"This guy didn't make it, obviously, but we saw some of the troops escape before the friendly forces shut down the arches. On tablets similar to the ones the bad guys used, by the way. They must have locked them down, because they didn't seem worried about a second attack."

"If they won, why didn't they take their dead with them?" Jess asked. "And where did they go?"

Ray shrugged. "Damned if I know. The camera shut off shortly after that. Maybe they went through the arches after they blew the corridor. Whatever happened, the evidence suggests that they went through shortly after the attack."

She struggled to understand what she'd seen. "I guess I'm clueless. Why did they blow the corridor if they locked the transport down? And what *are* those things? How can you just open up a link from one room to another that isn't even on the same heavenly body?"

"It has to be something like a wormhole," Ray said. "You've probably seen a number of TV shows using that trope. They all hit the same theme in slightly different ways. Bottom line, this is a technology that allows people to travel great distances without crossing the space between."

She nodded. "That much is clear. We need to know how to operate these portals. I want the controls found."

"Done," Doctor Crockett said. He produced a small tablet with a flourish. "This particular unit was found in the jacket of one of the people killed in the attack. It matches the appearance of the one we saw in use."

"I pulled the battery and replaced it with one of the ones we've been using for testing," Emily said. "They're rechargeable, by the way. The control came back to life and seems fairly straightforward."

Jess took it. "Let's take a look. Suits and armed guards. You did call Rex, right?"

Proudfoot nodded. "He's already in the cargo area with his people. He said there wouldn't be anyone coming for a visit without getting their faces shot off."

The five of them suited up and made their way to the cargo bay. Rex had all the guards present, armed to the teeth, and suited up.

He made his way over to her. "We'll set up behind the equipment. Do you really think this will work?"

"Damned if I know. If it does, this will be the biggest thing to ever happen to humanity."

Once Rex was ready, she brought the control to life. It had three control icons. She touched the first, and it took her to a screen with a numeric keypad. She'd been working on the alien language and recognized that much.

She backed out and visited the other screens. They were identical, so these were controls for all three arches. Presumably, the first one was on the left, based on their writing.

The keypad had spaces for twelve characters and a number of other icons. One was orange and looked like a knot. She suspected it was the lock for the arch in question.

Jess tapped the icon and an open string replaced the knot. Rather than typing in random numbers, she found the up arrow to check for history. Score one for intuition. A code filled the spaces.

"I'm about to hit Enter on the last code someone used on the left arch, I think. Here we go!"

She hit the key, and mist filled the arch. After a moment of lightning, it cleared to show a chamber on the other side.

One with several armed men in suits who raised their weapons to aim right at her.

* * *

HARRY LED his team down a long curved corridor. The equipment along the bulkheads looked strange to him, but he wasn't a spacer. Not really. The instruments they had along continued to sample the environment.

It was very, very cold but nowhere close to absolute zero. More like North-Pole-in-the-winter cold. The atmosphere was bone dry but would sustain life in a pinch. So long as they didn't freeze to death.

They'd been moving slowly down the corridor for almost two hours. Part of him wanted to go faster, but as soon as he did, they'd find something unexpected and fatal. Better to be slow the first time.

They'd brought chalk to mark the walls. They'd know what was safe next time.

The corridor they'd been exploring and photographing was coming to an end. He could see a large closed hatch ahead of them. It seemed as solid as a bank vault.

He considered turning back without opening it but knew that risked mutiny. After the slow pace, his people wanted to see what was on the other side. So did he.

"There's a touchpad beside the hatch," Sandra said. "Only one button. Shall we ring for service?"

"Get ready, everyone."

He raised his rifle, but the hatch slid ponderously aside without any slavering monsters on the other side. A vast chamber lay before him. One that didn't make much sense from where he was standing. He could see something on the distant ceiling.

Harry walked over to the hatch and looked inside. There was a platform for them to step onto, so he used it.

Once he was out, the world seemed to reorient itself. He was now standing in what looked like a gigantic tube. It dropped away beneath him and rose far above his head. The platform had a gently curved walkway that led to the wall of the tube.

There were buildings all around him. They seemed to rise from the walls of the tube and point inward.

"Hey, I get it," Sandra said. "Watch this."

She stepped onto the walkway and moved forward until she was standing at right angles to the rest of the team. "This thing is rotating, right? Well, I bet that if I toss something I'll see the Coriolis Effect. We're in a giant rotating tube. I could walk around until I was looking down at you from up there."

Harry shook his head and moved out to join her. Once he did so, everything snapped into place in his mind. She was exactly right.

"This is a massive city in space," he said. "A huge colony like my father wanted to build. These people beat him to it and went big. I wonder how far across it is."

One of the men brought up his weapon and triggered the laser rangefinder. "It's more than a kilometer away. Call it 1,300 meters."

They'd never have been able to see the other side of the tube without some kind of lighting. He wasn't sure where it was coming from. There wasn't much. It seemed like twilight.

"I'm not seeing any signs of battle damage. If there was fighting, they didn't blow anything up or set it on fire. There's no telling what or where this thing is located."

"Maybe we should look out the window," Sandra said.

He looked in the direction she was facing. About a quarter turn around the tube and a few hundred meters to the right was a dark rectangle.

"If we go, we'll blow the timetable for our return."

"Only if we walk back like grandpa with his walker," she retorted.

Everyone laughed.

"I suppose we could pick up the pace," he admitted. "At least on the way out. Okay, let's go over there and take a quick look."

They walked between the abandoned buildings cautiously, treating this like a surreal version of moving around in Iraq. Every dark window could have housed a sniper. Every bit of refuse might have concealed a bomb.

Of course, nothing happened. They made it to the window in about twenty minutes.

The transparent plate had a railing to keep people from walking right across, but the presence of gates told him that it was possible. Looking down, he could see nothing but stars. Then he saw the shadow of something dark.

"I wonder why they have these big windows without something interesting to look at," Sandra said.

"There is something," he said after a moment. "You almost can't see it in the dark, but it's there. Look at the line of stars."

The heavens were full of stars, but there was a line where they stopped slowly rotating into view. More like an arc, really.

"I see it," she said. "Is that a planet? It's about the same size Earth was when *Liberty Station* was in orbit."

Harry thought she might be correct. If so, there were no lights on the planet's surface. Not one. And it was darker than even Earth was from orbit at night. It was as though there were no sun at all.

"We need to head back," he said as soon as the planet, or whatever it was, rotated out of sight.

His radio came to life. "Liberty Six, Mars Base."

"Go Mars," he said. Someone had to have come through the quantum tunnel to call him.

"You need to return ASAP. Events have taken a turn for the worse on Earth and for the better up here."

"Way to be obscure," he said. "We're on our way. And you can count our excursion as a turn for the strange."

28

Nathan threw himself to the side and landed hard. The small creatures calling to one another in the dark behind him were the only noises he heard. No gunshots. Nothing.

He cautiously raised himself off the ground and waved a handy stick around the corner. Still nothing.

After a moment's consideration, he called for one of his men to come up and look inside. The man agreeably wandered into the room and gasped when he saw the weapon. It didn't fire as he hurriedly backed out.

"Are you trying to get me killed?" the man snarled.

"Of course not," Nathan said indignantly. "It doesn't work, obviously. I was going to have you assist me in further exploration, but if you're frightened, I'll send you back to Paris to wait for my mother."

The man didn't seem convinced by Nathan's lies. He was smarter than he looked.

"What is this place?"

"An old World War II bunker one of my mother's associates upgraded. She heard about it and some of the things he once kept here after he died."

"I think I *will* go back to Paris. Shall I send more of the men out to help you... search?"

There were three others back at the base in Paris. "Keep one man to watch the prisoner when you go get my mother. Send the other two to help me here. Bring her as soon as you pick her up. I left the data at the hideout. She has the codes for it. And send the rest of our searchers up here to join me before you leave."

The rest of his on-site team came in to join him after a few minutes. He gestured toward the elevator. "We'll go down, if it's working. If not, we'll force it open and rappel down."

They had no real way to search for booby traps, and Nathan wasn't sure there were any. After all, if the weapons didn't work, how dangerous would they make the rest of the place?

Nathan pressed the call button, and the elevator doors slid open. It was large enough for all of them, so they piled in. The buttons had the alien script on them, but there were only six. On the theory that the good shit was at the bottom, he pressed the one he thought corresponded with the lowest floor.

The doors slid shut, and it started down. He'd guessed right. It went down the correct number of floors, and the doors slid back open.

"What kind of writing is this?" one of the men asked.

"Code," Nathan said blithely. "The bugger who built it loved putting things in code."

If he found what he hoped, he'd have to tell them some version of the truth very soon. Or kill them.

The lowest level of the base was a wide, open area. A vehicle park. One filled with what looked like combat aircraft and transports. Ones unlike any he'd ever seen before.

Their wings were short and stubby, swept sharply back. They had racks for missiles and the snouts of guns. They looked exceedingly dangerous. Too bad he wasn't a pilot.

"Nice," one of the men said as they spread out to cover the room with their weapons. "I wonder how they get out."

That was certainly a valid question. They were far too large to go up the elevator, even if the entrance could have allowed them to take off. Yet the room seemed devoid of other exits.

The area around the elevator showed that they had stairs on the interior levels. They just didn't go up to the entrance. That made some sense tactically.

"Look at the floor," he said. "Maybe there's a hidden elevator."

Only there wasn't. The floor was one solid piece of rock, polished smooth and flat. The ceiling was also uncooperative, another slab without lines.

That left the walls. There were three large arches with cavities behind them, but they dead-ended. No exits there.

They looked at one another, confused.

One of the men scratched his head. "Boss, not to tell your friend his business, but he should've left a way out when he built these things."

"Look inside each of them," Nathan said. "Let's be sure no one is hiding behind us."

The craft were all empty. A third of them looked like fighters. The rest were jazzed-up troop transports. The controls came online with a swipe of the consoles, but they made no sense. Perhaps once his mother arrived, she could shed some light on what they said.

"Gather round," Nathan said. "We'll head up a level and see what we find there. I know this seems confusing, but rest assured, you'll hear the real story soon. Just not right now."

The next level up was more interesting. It looked like a mustering point where troops gathered. There were lockers filled with equipment and an armored door with a keypad. No place for his little chip.

He stepped back. "Time for the explosives, boys. Let's open this up without wrecking whatever is inside."

It took three tries to crack the egg. They used wrecking bars to tear the thing open.

The room inside was an armory. One filled with alien weapons and armor.

"Jackpot!" he exulted. "This is something we can use!"

He looked at his watch. The other men should be upstairs by now. He'd bring them down and call his mother before continuing. She'd land before long.

"We'll explore further as soon as we go get the rest of the boys. Come on."

He led them all back up the elevator. Sure as anything, one of them would pocket something valuable if he took his eyes off them. In fact, he'd arrange a strip search when they got back into Paris.

There was no one waiting when he got back to the road. He pulled out his phone and called the man he'd sent back.

"Yes?"

"The boys aren't here. You sent them, right?"

"Oh yes. I sent them. To see their infidel god."

It clicked that he wasn't speaking to his man. Obviously.

"Who is this?"

"What? You break into my apartment, blow it up, kill my friends, and you don't remember me? Allahu Akbar, my friend."

Shit! The bastard had somehow escaped and killed his men. What was he? The Muslim James Bond?

"Well, well," Nathan said. "You're a lot more resourceful than I gave you credit for. That's fine. I did what I needed to do. I'm sure you'll be looking for revenge. Get in line. I don't have time to waste looking over my shoulder for you."

The other man laughed. "You mistake me. I, too, have better things to do. Such as going through all the papers and computers you thoughtfully left behind."

Great. He couldn't remember what was on the computers. Nothing they could crack easily. He'd encrypted the critical data.

"Well, as entertaining as this is, I'll have to let you go," the terrorist said. "I'm picking someone up. We'll meet again soon. Very soon. Until then, sleep well, my friend."

The line went dead.

He frowned. Picking someone up?

His body flashed cold, as though someone had dumped a bucket of ice water over his head. He'd probably questioned the man he'd taken the phone from. He knew Nathan's mother was coming to Paris.

* * *

"WHAT ARE OUR OPTIONS?" Clayton asked Penny. "Is there another way down that we could use to evade them?"

"Not really," she said with a shake of her head. "They've marooned us up here pretty effectively. But that doesn't mean we have no options. There's a cave. It looks to go in quite a ways. It's not very obvious, so they might miss it."

She gave him a meaningful look. There was more to the story than she was saying.

"Give me a moment, Mick. And I won't forget your support."

The man nodded and headed off to talk with his friends.

"What do you really have?" he asked.

"A cave-in. It's under an outcropping and out of sight. I took a quick look inside, and it's an artificial corridor. Based on the amount of water damage, it's been open for quite a while. If there is a base down there, we can probably get nice and lost."

"And they'll eventually find their way in. Then the US government will know what's really going on. Hell. Everyone might know."

She shrugged. "So what? You pretty much have a lock on the good stuff. It's in space. Tell everyone and let the chips fall where they may."

"That might be an option if they weren't jamming us," he grumbled. "Still, my choices do seem rather limited. It won't take them more than an hour to get someone up here. Probably less. Then this game is over, and they cart me off to charge me with treason or whatever. I wonder how the weather is in Cuba this time of year."

He sighed and stared at the clear sky for a moment. "If we take Mick and his men down there, they'll talk."

"Maybe we can kill two birds with one stone," she said. "Come on."

They walked back over to Mick. Penny gestured for the young man to follow her. "Come look at this and see if you think we can climb down this way. I initially dismissed it, but maybe I was wrong."

She led the two of them to a cliff wall on the other side of the ridge. It dropped straight away to a pile of rocks about fifty meters below.

Mick leaned over and looked down. "Sure. Me and the boys do our share of rock climbing. It's not the safest rappel I've ever done, but we can do it. You ever went down a rope, Mister Rogers?"

"No, and I don't intend to start now. Here's what I want to do. Lead your men down the rope and take our pursuers on a merry chase. Penny and I will hide up here in the place she found. Make it obvious how you got down and that should keep everything scrambled."

The young man pulled off his pack and dug out a rope. He tied it off around a handy rock outcropping. Based on how sturdy the last one had been, it was probably safe enough. He used some spare clothes to keep the rope away from the sharp rocks on the edge when he dropped the loose end down.

He brought out a small bag of sturdy metal rings and a second rope that he began cutting into lengths of a few meters each. While he did so, he gave the men instructions on how he wanted them to lead the troops away.

His men got the idea quickly. They all seemed familiar with the process and tied ropes around their waists and legs. The rings both secured everything together and attached them to the main line.

Carefully, one at a time, they dropped down and slid off the end of the rope. In less than fifteen minutes, Clayton was alone with Penny and Mick.

He held out his hand to the young man. "I appreciate everything. I'll make that clear in time, I promise."

Mick shook his hand with a grin. "I'd hold off on that for a bit. You see, I'm staying here with you."

"Why am I not surprised?" Clayton asked. "How loyal are you prepared to be? If you stay, I'm going to have to let you in on a secret that might be more than you care to know. And I'm going to have to insist that you keep it to yourself."

"Now you're going all mysterious. Sign me up. I can keep my trap shut. Just ask anyone. Besides, you have to trust me now or throw me off the cliff."

"That's a good point," Clayton admitted. "Come along, then. We need to get under cover before the young officer and his men get up here. Drop one of those metal rings here, just in case they don't get the idea."

Penny led them off to another part of the ridge and down past a large outcropping. The far side had subsided a little, and a dark opening was just visible. It wasn't large at all.

"You went in there?" Clayton asked Penny. "You're quite brave. I'd have been afraid that an animal was denning inside."

She slid down into the depression. "I think any number of them have over the years. Come on."

Clayton followed her through the hole. He had to shove his pack through first, but he managed to avoid getting stuck.

Mick brought up the rear. He used a leafy branch to rub away the signs of their passage before he turned to look at them.

The only light came from the hole, so it was pretty dim, but the regular lines of the corridor left no doubt they were inside an artificial construction. A scattering of animal bones and other detritus verified Penny's guess that many creatures had denned up in here over the years. The stench was astonishing.

Mick looked around and turned on his light. "This isn't natural."

"Thanks, Captain Obvious," Penny said with a smile to take any sting out of her words. "This is what we were really here looking for."

The young man looked around for a moment and then shook his head. "I know there has to be a story behind this, but we really don't have time for me to hear it. Your secret is safe, though. In for a Penny, or so they say."

Something in his voice made Clayton's eyes narrow. Ah, so that was how things rolled. Mick had a crush on Penny. And, from the looks of things, she wasn't objecting to the concept. He hoped things flourished there.

"Well," he said after a moment. "We need to find our way down into the base without leaving a trail they can follow. Just in case they find the opening."

"I have an idea," Mick said. "Hang on."

He crawled back out through the hole and pulled some loose brush into the opening. "There. Now it looks like a plant instead of an inviting cave. With any luck, they'll go haring off after the boys, and we'll be safe."

"But we can't count on that," Penny said. "We need to get some space."

Clayton dug into his pack and pulled out his flashlight. After hearing about Jess's exploits in the Mayan pyramid, he'd made certain his assistant had stocked it with things that might prove useful in an emergency.

The man had seemed to think it was a waste of time with all the prepared men along for the ride, but he'd done a thorough job of it. Someone else was getting a nice Christmas surprise in their stocking this year.

His light was bright and steady. "Since we know nothing of this place, let's go this way."

He led them deeper into the abandoned facility. He hoped whatever the important information his assistant had found could wait, because he wasn't going to be giving any input for a long while.

29

It was almost one in the morning when Kathleen's plane landed and taxied up to the hangar. Three men stood waiting for her as the steward lowered the ladder.

One of them was putting away his phone as she came down. He stepped forward and spoke in French. "Mrs. Bennett?"

"Yes," she said. "I only have a few bags inside. Be careful of the laptop. If it gets broken, I'll take it out of your hide."

He bowed. "Of course. My men will take care of everything. This way, please."

Her phone rang as she walked with him toward the hangar. Her son. Couldn't the idiot even wait for her to get off the plane before calling?

"Nathan, I'm a little—"

"Don't land. Stay on the plane. Go anywhere else."

She frowned. "What are you babbling about? I'm already on the ground. Your man is taking me to the car now."

"He's not my man. He's a nutjob terrorist."

The man pulled a pistol from behind his back and aimed it at her midsection.

"I'm afraid I'll have to let you go." She disconnected the call and stopped walking. "Whatever you want, I can pay it."

"I'm sure you can," the man said with a smile as he took her phone and removed the battery. "Your son is wrong about one thing, though. I'm not a 'nutjob terrorist' at all. I'm a warrior of God. One he and you have engaged in battle. I am uncertain why, but I look forward to finding out."

Several shots came from the plane behind them. That didn't speak well for the health of the flight crew.

"I didn't send my son after you," she assured the man. "He made that choice on his own."

"So do we all," the man said agreeably. "Perhaps I will release you after you answer a few questions. Walk. Someone will come looking for the customs man soon enough. I'd prefer to be elsewhere by then."

He forced her into the middle seat of the small van. His companions sat on either side of her as soon as they threw her luggage into the back.

The man took them out of the airport and onto the streets nearest it. "My associates and I have a place close by. The trip is short."

Her mind raced as she tried to figure a way out of this. She certainly wasn't going to overpower them. It had to be through skills she actually had.

"I won't give you a thing unless I have a way out. If we can come to an arrangement, I'll see that a large sum of money is put into escrow, only to be released once I'm free."

He smiled at her in the mirror. "Money isn't everything, though it *is* a useful tool. Tell me, Mrs. Bennett, how much is your little toe worth to you?"

"What?"

"How much would you pay to prevent me from cutting it off with garden shears? What would you pay to stop me from pulling one of your teeth out with pliers? The number of parts you would likely wish protected is legion.

"Cast aside the belief that you have any control over what happens from now on. You will do exactly as I tell you, or you will suffer great pain. Allah does not care what we do to the infidel.

"What is the saying in your country? God helps those who help themselves. What happens next is in your hands."

* * *

Jess watched Harry and his people come through the portal on Mars. He shook his head once he had it free from his suit. "You shouldn't have taken your helmet off."

"I didn't know that when we arrived. Too late, now."

He sighed. "Just my luck. Did you turn the ship around?"

She grinned at him. "Nope. We found the same neat quantum tunnel you did. Nice name, by the way. I like it.

"We had an area where there had been some fighting. We found a controller, and this was the first code up. I guess someone from *Freedom Express* came here after the fight."

"And hopefully went on somewhere else," Harry said as he sat down on the tine of a forklift. "This base is huge. It'll take us weeks just to look into every room. And that doesn't even begin to count the place we just visited."

She sat down beside him. "No one here knew exactly what that was. Where have you been?"

"I think it was a big city in space. It's orbiting a dark world, and it dwarfs this base. The central hub is over a kilometer across, and it must be ten times that long. It also has some pods that come off it like branches on a tree. Those alone have to be almost the size of this base. I'm wondering if that's where *Freedom Express* is going."

Jess tried to work her mind around the size of it and failed. "Wow. That's like New York in space. And it was dead? Fighting?" She cringed at the amount of death that entailed.

"More like abandoned. The atmosphere was breathable but cold. Really, *really* cold. Think of the worst the Arctic can throw at you.

"We also visited a world with two suns. Definitely not in this system. So, I was the first man on Mars and the first to leave the solar system. Will they make a statue of me?"

She laughed. "I'll see that we commission one. Emily Adams is an amazing artist. I'll have her draw something suitably heroic."

"We're not close enough to see whatever *Freedom Express* is heading toward, so it might be that city. There are a lot of objects in the trans-Neptunian area. They suspect there might even be one or two the size of Earth. Or bigger. We'll know in a bit more than an hour."

Sandra made her way over to them. "Sorry to interrupt, but we've gotten word there's trouble back on Earth. Harry, your father is up a tree in New Zealand."

Harry frowned. "What?"

"He's on the run. The message just came in. The US military cornered him in the wilds of New Zealand and are working to catch him. Some of the men with him got away and finally called it in to the station on a sat phone."

He shook his head. "Well, isn't *that* just dandy? We haven't found a code that leads us back to Earth, and I'm leery of just trying everything in memory. We've been damned lucky up to this point. All it takes is one wrong number and we're toast. Hell, the entire planet might pay for that mistake."

Jess narrowed her eyes at him. "So. We're just leaving him?"

"Don't think this makes me happy, but yes. Either he'll get himself out of this mess or we'll rescue him when the time comes. Fretting about it now isn't going to do anyone any good. Your ship is about to make a rendezvous. We need to focus on that."

She sighed. "I suppose you're right. I don't have to like it, though. What's the plan for *Freedom Express*?"

He stood. "We'll come back with you and see what happens. If it's bad, everyone can retreat through the quantum tunnel to Mars. If not, we'll make a different call. I want a full report on everything you've found."

She nodded. "Will do. I can tell you that Emily Adams has been a hero. She's working tirelessly with Doctors Powell and Young. They've cracked the language barrier. Mostly."

He grinned. "That's wonderful!"

"Yes, it is. It's still very rough, but it will get better going forward. Come on, let's get everyone together and get back to *Freedom Express*. I want to be out on the surface when we get there."

* * *

QUEEN ENDED the call and stopped Agent Cabot from going back into the room. She'd found some water and was standing there waiting for him.

"I've been called back to Washington. Something urgent. I want you to put everyone here on ice and get every detail you can."

She nodded. "Yes, sir."

"And I'm going to want the boy's cell phone."

She frowned. "The alien one? Alien human? I'm not sure what to call them."

He chuckled. "I feel you. Yes, that one. I'm taking it with me to show some technical people I trust. Get it for me."

Cabot called up another agent and handed him the water. "See to Doctor Wagner."

He followed her to one of the lab areas where she asked for the device. One of the agents found it in an evidence bag. She looked at it curiously for a long moment and then handed it over to him.

It was actually somewhat larger than a modern cell phone, which seemed odd. It had a distinctive logo of a tree surrounded by some strange text. Another line of which was etched across the top of the device.

"Special Agent in Charge Pembroke wanted to talk to you as well. He's looking at the cube, I think."

Pembroke was indeed in the room with the cube. He looked up as they entered. "Mister Secretary. Brenda. Isn't this thing amazing?"

Cabot drew her Taser without a word and shot her boss. He went down before Queen could do more than twitch. He reached for the doorknob, but she pulled her service pistol and jammed it in his side.

"I'd rather not have to shoot you, Mister Secretary. You make the call. Perforated or not?"

"Not," he said, his throat dry.

"An excellent choice," she said as she patted him down. She pocketed the small handgun he kept for protection and the alien phone. "Flip the main power on and then pull the cube. Carefully and slowly."

He pushed the power lever back into the engaged position, and it slammed home with a hum. Unsure of what to do, he tugged at the cube. It popped free surprisingly easily.

She pocketed it too. "Now we go out to the car. Come quietly and no one gets hurt. And rest assured, if you do anything to draw attention, I'll shoot you first."

"Why are you doing this?" he asked, his throat tight. "From all accounts, you have a very promising career ahead of you. Had, I mean. I doubt Agent Pembroke will be in a very forgiving mood now that you've electrified him."

She smiled. "I'm sure that's going to negatively impact my next performance evaluation. Once we get out of here, I'll tell you. I promise it'll be worth the ride."

"I seem to be lacking any reasonable alternatives, so I'm completely at your disposal."

She pushed him in front of her and slid her pistol into her jacket pocket. "I'm aiming right at your liver. Nasty way to die too. I scored top marks at Quantico. Captain of the pistol team. I can hit a fly's pecker at fifty meters. Now, walk."

He exited the electrical room, and she closed the door behind them. They passed several agents, and then she walked him brazenly past the heavy-weapons team guarding the door. She greeted the leader by name as she casually kidnapped him.

Once out of the building, she put him in the passenger side in one of the SUVs. Out of sight of the people watching the building, she handed him a set of handcuffs.

"Not to seem unfriendly but put these on. And don't try to make them loose enough to slip out of, or I'll crank them down. Seat belt first and then put your arms around the chest strap."

He did as she ordered. "What the devil could you hope to gain? Selling this on the black market? I suppose that could net you some money, but we'll come after you like, well, gangbusters."

She climbed behind the wheel and drove slowly away from the building. "Would you believe I'm one of those alien humans? And that we mean you no harm? You can skip the take us to your leader BS. We've seen what douche canoes you are."

He shook his head. "You've lost your mind. I suppose it happens to the best of us. Let me assure you that if you give up now, you'll receive the best of care."

"I can understand your skepticism," she said with a smile. "I don't exactly come across as an alien visitor. That's because we've been here since before America existed."

"You can't be serious."

"Completely. You maniacs have no idea how dangerous what you're doing is. Now we have one chance to keep you from drawing disaster down on humanity's head."

She patted her jacket. "This power supply will be helpful, but the gate controller is really what flushed me out."

"The what?"

"The cell phone. Only it isn't. Our ancestors used it to activate long-range transporters. Not like *Star Trek*. More like *Stargate*."

"Star what?"

She tisked him. "You really should bone up on your science fiction. Especially now that you're dealing with this stuff."

He started to respond, but a vehicle in the next lane drew his attention when the driver rolled down his window and raised a pistol.

Cabot must've seen him, too, because she yanked her wheel over hard and smashed the SUV into his vehicle, spoiling his aim.

The window beside him shattered, and something knocked the breath out of him. The man had shot him!

She stomped on the brakes and used the nose of the SUV to tap the back quarter panel on the car. It immediately spun out of control and went into the ditch, rolling hard. She didn't stop to go after the gunman.

"I'm hit," he gasped. "Take me to the hospital."

"Hang on. I'll get you some help."

She pulled a cell phone and called someone. "We have a problem. I need a pickup and a medic at the alternate location in two minutes. The subject has a gunshot to the torso."

He tried to argue with her, to order her to the hospital, but the world was fading to gray. It went dark before he could tell her that he was dying.

30

H arry looked around the cargo area and hangar on *Freedom Express*. There were a lot of ships. A few even looked undamaged. Sooner or later, they'd have to train someone to fly them. If they ever figured out how.

The crew was ecstatic about the unexpected rescue. He immediately got Doctors Powell, Young, and Crockett moving the most delicate artifacts back to Mars. Just in case. If things went bad, he'd evacuate the crew. Hopefully, that wouldn't prove necessary.

"We went outside to watch the approach with Neptune," Jess said, "but now that I think about it, I'm not sure that's the best idea here."

"Let's go to the command-and-control room," he said. "We can see if the ship itself can look at whatever it is."

She nodded and led him to the elevator. "If we could find a quantum code to Earth, would you save your father?"

He raised an eyebrow. "I don't like the man or trust his motives, but I'd prefer not to have our secrets in the hands of the US government. Hell, any government. But we can't help him.

"Say we found a code for one of the bases on Earth. Unless it's the one in New Zealand, it'll take us hours to get to his location. Perhaps days. Even then, we don't exactly have the forces to fend off the US military. I'm afraid he's on his own."

Jess sighed. "That's harsh, but I understand. It just doesn't seem right."

The elevator let them out into the core. She led them to the control console. Ray was in the chair.

"Harry, it's good to see you."

"And you, Ray. What do you have?"

The engineer gestured at the console. "We're almost to the target. Call it ten minutes until we're at a full stop."

"Can you see what it is?"

The other man shook his head. "I've found the visual system. It has a good level of magnification, but we're only starting to come into range. That little dot there on the right-hand screen is what we can see."

It wasn't much to look at. "Any planets around here?"

Ray shook his head. "I think I'd have noticed one. No, we're approaching something floating in space alone."

"I wonder how this ship knew where it was so exactly after all this time," Jess said. "The orbits of small bodies get distorted by encounters with other bodies over time. That didn't seem to matter. It came right to it."

"Perhaps it's giving off a signal we can't detect," Ray ventured. "God knows there's a lot we don't get about these people."

That was certainly true. The scope of what they'd found made forming a plan to deal with it difficult. It was like staging a raid to rescue a kidnapped child and finding the Doctor's TARDIS. Unexplainable and almost incomprehensible, at least without the Doctor around to tell you what was what.

"We've been reacting since we found the guy in the pyramid," Harry said. "My father's original plan didn't have anything to do with them. We have to make a real set of plans on exploring and exploiting this setup.

"This is dangerous stuff. We can't afford to keep stumbling around in the dark. We need to know who these people were and what they were fighting about before we run into some of them. We had no choice but to come out here after *Freedom Express* got into motion, but it has to stop. We've got to organize and bring others in to help us do this cautiously."

Jess frowned. "Like who? The US? Have you seen the kind of crap they've been up to the last twenty or thirty years? It's a corrupt oligarchy in everything but name. And the UN is even worse. I'm not sure who you'd find that wasn't out to line their own pockets."

"That's my father's problem, once we rescue him."

"We're close enough to see the thing," Ray said.

Harry focused his attention on the object on the screen. It was a ship. That much was obvious. It didn't use a planetary body as *Freedom Express* did, though. It was long and sleek, though obviously not suitable for atmospheric work.

Freedom Express came to a halt relative to the unmoving ship. On the screen, it looked like a derelict. No lights and no reaction to their arrival.

"Do we take a look?" Jess asked.

"We only have the one lifter, and it's all we can pilot, anyway. We'll go over, but this is a cautious reconnaissance. We need to get an idea of what we're dealing with. If it looks dangerous, we leave. Understood?"

They all nodded.

"Good. Have all nonessential personnel move back to the Mars base and take everything that isn't bolted down. If we send word to run, they drop everything and haul ass. Come on. It's time to go check out the spooky ship."

* * *

CLAYTON, Penny, and Mick worked their way deeper into the dead base over the next few hours. There were signs of fighting everywhere. In fact, Clayton suspected the collapsed corridor was battle damage.

On the top level, animals had scattered the bones of the dead, except for the skulls in the helmets. It was horrifying and very creepy.

Mick's skepticism about the whole alien aspect of this changed when they found their first heavy-worlders. That was on the second level.

It was mostly quarters, based on the rooms they peered into. The fighting had been heavy here, and they found a number of regular humans and heavy-worlders in armor. Based on the large divots blown out of the walls, the weapons had been quite powerful.

Mick wanted to test that theory, but the ones he tried didn't work.

"They probably don't have any power," Clayton guessed. "None of the tablets or smaller equipment we've found has worked."

"Do you think they missed finding this base?" Penny asked.

"No way of knowing," Mick said. "Though if we're planning on getting away from them for a long while, we might want to go deep. The more they have to search for us, the less chance they have of finding us."

Clayton led the way to the lowest level. His flashlight revealed a normal-looking corridor as he stepped out of the stairwell. There was a T intersection a few dozen meters away.

"That's a long way down," Penny said. "I counted fifteen levels. What's down here?"

He shrugged. "I have no idea."

"I'll go look." She strode purposefully off to the intersection and looked in both directions. "I'm going a little bit to the right. I'll be back in a minute."

Mick finally arrived. "I heard something upstairs. I think we have unwelcome guests in the building."

"Damn it," Clayton muttered. "I'd hoped to avoid this kind of mess."

Penny stepped back into sight. "The right side leads to a large room filled with machinery. I haven't looked to the left yet."

"Let's take a look," Mick said.

The right corridor led to something more than a machinery room, he decided. The large hatch that would have normally sealed the room was open. As there was no power, that was probably a good thing.

Complex equipment filled the massive compartment, but he recognized what some of it was at a glance.

"This is the power room," he said. "See those machines over there? They are like the devices that held the blue cube on the crashed ship. Only bigger."

They were a lot bigger, actually. The places where the cubes would have fit were empty, so he had no trouble determining how large they should be.

Rather than ten centimeters, they were almost a meter in size. That was a lot of power.

"So," Penny said as she gazed into the empty slots. "I'm assuming this means whoever left took their power supplies with them. Where did they go, then?"

"Maybe they went to the other side of the corridor," Clayton said. "Let's take a short break. I'm an old man and need to sit for a bit. Eat a little food and drink some water. I also should look at my laptop and see what my assistant was all in a twirl about."

They found a handy console to sit at. It was dead, just like everything else. The food and water in the packs were of the travel ration variety, and not so tasty.

He set up his laptop. He'd powered it on when he grabbed it earlier. That meant it had synced his email before the jamming cut them off. Hopefully.

Yes, there was the email. He opened the attached video and watched it as he read the report out of the corner of his eye.

What he saw set him back on his heels. Instantaneous travel. That one thing would make all his work to this point moot. Humanity could go wherever they liked without being bound to one planet like the feudal lords of old had done to keep their serfs on their estates.

If, of course, the universe wasn't populated by bloodthirsty aliens waiting to find humanity and serve them up for lunch. The jury was still out on that one.

The recordings from the strange world with two suns were humbling. His boy had opened the universe up.

"Well," he said after the video ended, "I think I know how these people got out. Though it would seem to require power."

Clayton explained what they'd found on Mars. Neither of his companions believed him, so he played the video again.

"You think the boys from here evacuated through one of those and took the power supplies with them?" Mick asked when the video ended. "Is it safe to go looking for them? Even after all this time?"

"Damned if I know," Clayton said, "but it beats being frog-marched back to the US to stand trial on trumped-up charges. Let's go take a look."

The corridor going the other way led into a vast cargo storage facility. Based on the situation on Mars, that spoke well of their chances of finding one of these quantum tunnels.

In fact, they weren't hard to locate at all. Three arches sat against the most distant wall. A large machine was set up nearby. It was similar to the power systems found on the crashed ship and had a small blue cube.

"Someone rigged up a temporary power supply," Mick said. "Then they went through. I guess they couldn't take that last bit of power and still keep the portal open."

There was a small tablet wired into the machine, and a large cable ran to the arch closest to them. There was a short tunnel inside that had metal ribs all along its length. A touch showed that the device still had power. It must have been drawing energy from the cube.

Using what he'd seen in the report as a guide, Clayton looked over the controls. Only one arch was showing, so only the one with power was online. On the off chance that it had the code for Mars in memory, he scrolled up.

"It only has one code," he said. "The memory is empty of everything except the last portal. Let me see about entering the code for the Mars portal myself. That would make for a handy escape."

Only the control wouldn't let him enter the code. It was as though the others had hardwired it only to allow transit to this one place. He wondered where that was and why they'd restricted it.

The sound of the stairwell door opening told him that he didn't really have a choice but to find out. The US military had almost caught up with them, and there was no other way out.

31

Nathan sealed the facility up and drove with his men to Paris. He honestly wasn't certain what he hoped to do. The bastard had his mother.

He'd already tried tracing the phone. No dice. He must have removed the battery.

A quick stop at the house he'd been using for a holding facility confirmed that the prisoner was gone. He hadn't escaped, though. Someone from outside had breached the building.

The police had everything locked down too. They wouldn't be able to trace it back to him, most likely. He'd been very careful in how he paid for it. They might find his DNA in there, if they got lucky. He didn't recall touching very much, but he must have handled a number of things.

Based on the number of body bags coming out, his people had taken some of their attackers with them. Still, odds were good that none of them had survived.

Pity. Replacing them would be an inconvenience.

A trip to the airport found the scene there undisturbed, though for how long, he didn't know.

The crew on the plane was dead, executed. He found a body in the hangar too. Based on the dead man's uniform, it was someone from French customs. That would be the man on his mother's payroll.

He had his men carry the lone body into the aircraft and clean up the blood. That would give them a little while longer to examine everything. At three in the morning, no one was thinking their best. It might take until the shift change before the people here realized they hadn't seen the dead guy for a while.

Nathan made a call and got someone capable of piloting the plane on the way. If he could keep it from being found, that would lessen the heat on his mother, and thus on him.

The security system hadn't done one thing to protect his mother, but it had recorded the murder of the crew. Now he had faces to go from. Neither of the men was the bastard he'd framed and kidnapped.

The plane had external cameras too. The one on the door caught a good view of the man of the hour waiting for his mother, as calm as could be. She must have been blind. That guy didn't look like a customs man at all.

He was about to shut it off when he stopped and backed the video up. Inside the hangar was a small van. Not the kind normally used around an airport. It hadn't been there when they'd arrived.

He couldn't see the license plate, but the make and model were clear enough to one of the native Frenchmen.

"This vehicle got out of the airport somehow," he told one of his men as the new pilot pulled up. "Someone in security here could get the plate. Find that person. Pay them whatever you need to."

They'd stashed the bodies in the cargo hold. He'd have someone at the new destination get rid of them. As a sop to the pilot's sensibilities, he'd taken the time to wipe the blood and brains off the seat and console.

He'd probably missed some, but it would have to do.

"Take off as soon as you can and go to Moscow," he ordered the pilot. "I'll have someone meet you there. Do what they tell you, keep your mouth shut, and you'll be back here tonight with a lot of money in your pocket."

After the jet started, warmed up, and headed out, his man came back and climbed into the back of the van.

"I found someone willing to work with us. Here's the license number. I made sure he got a good look at the driver's face too. If there are any questions about tonight, he'll point the man out."

"What about us?"

"We'll never come up in his report."

Nathan nodded appreciatively. "Very nice. Now all we need to do is find a dirty police officer with access to the traffic system. Surely every camera in this town is wired to report where a vehicle has gone."

In modern Paris, the nanny state kept track of everything. The same for London and other major cities. That was why he preferred stolen vehicles and hats that obscured faces.

The data on where that vehicle went could tell them a lot. The man had probably dumped it, but that might give them an area to search for clues.

"Already done," his man said with a grin. "They dumped the van, but my guy spotted the driver in another vehicle a few blocks away. He traced the car to an apartment building parking lot."

He handed Nathan an address.

"You've done very well," Nathan said. "As of right now, you're my new team leader. I want extra muscle at that building and for us not to be tracked going in or out."

The man nodded. "We can have everything in place in an hour."

That might just be the longest hour of his mother's life.

* * *

JESS SAT beside the pilot as they winged across to the dark and foreboding ship. In the pale starlight, it was a black shadow. The console on *Freedom Express* must have been amplifying the ambient light. She couldn't see much at all.

She could tell one thing. It was big. Really big. They made passes along its length so the cameras could record everything. It was more than a kilometer from stem to stern.

None of the areas she saw looked to have a docking clamp—and the odds were almost certain that one wouldn't have worked for the lifter—so they landed on the hull near what looked like an airlock. Thrusters held the ship down as they exited. The pilot would wait near the ship for them to come back.

The airlock design was different from what Humanity Unlimited used. The door looked short and wide. That made sense if this was a ship designed for heavy-worlders.

Harry had brought an armed team of his people, Ray Proudfoot, and Emily Adams. They might need their expertise. They didn't need them to unlock the airlock. It cooperatively slid open. The compartment was wide enough for all of them to fit in.

"Everyone, remember where we parked," Ray said.

She had to smile. "Use the chalk to mark any place you turn. Point the arrows back toward the ship."

"Good idea," Harry said. "That will make things easy to understand when we're running for our lives."

"You have a serious case of pessimism," she said. "Be confident."

"I am confident. Confident that we'll be running for our lives. It always seems to go that way."

"Not helpful."

Jess waited for the last of the boarding party to come inside and hit the switch to cycle the airlock. The outer hatch slid ponderously shut, and the inner one opened. The chamber beyond was initially dark, but the lights slowly came up. They were dimmer than she expected and a little redder.

"Maybe the color is indicative of—" she started to say, but the gravity plates came on and slammed them all to the deck. It felt as though the ship were rapidly accelerating, but she knew it had to be the heavy-worlders' gravity.

Even raising her head was a strain. "We should've... thought of this."

"Everyone okay?" Harry asked. "We have to be very, very careful. It feels like I have two people on my back."

Getting to her hands and knees was a strain. "Holy God, there's no way we can explore anything like this. I can barely move."

"I think I can go a little ways," Harry said.

"Maybe I can do something about that," Ray said.

"Anti-gravity belts?" she asked. "Those would be awesome."

He laughed, though it sounded more like coughing. "Nah. I did some looking at the gravity system on *Freedom Express*. Let me try something."

Placing one foot carefully in front of the other, he made his way to the panel beside the door. He tapped it, and it came to life. She couldn't see what screen he navigated to, but the gravity let up until it felt about right.

The relief from the team was palpable.

"That's got it," she said. "Thanks. But won't it do the same thing as soon as we walk out of the room?"

"That depends on what I find in this little locker," he said as he came back over to the airlock. He opened a panel with drawings of the three styles of human. Inside were necklaces. He pulled out a number with regular humans emblazoned on the metal tab that sat about chest high.

"Put these on," he said as he handed them out. "The grav plates are supposed to read them and adjust the field accordingly."

She gave him a narrow-eyed stare. "And why didn't you mention these up front?"

"I forgot," he said sheepishly. "I'm not used to dealing with these things. The findings are in my notes. I submitted them to the scientists to add to whatever summary they put together."

"Any other little surprises we should know about?" Harry asked.

"I'll let you know if I remember any."

He shook his head with a smile. "I'll go test the hall."

A few cautious steps out into the hall proved the engineer's theory. They could walk without gravity crushing them to the ground.

Harry looked both directions down the corridor. "Which way?"

"Damned if I know," she said. "Let's try forward."

She set off toward the front of the ship with everyone else behind her. If they found directions inside, maybe her helmet camera could decipher them via the translator.

* * *

QUEEN SLOWLY BECAME aware that he was alive. His thoughts bounced around inside his head like the ball in an arcade game, but at least he wasn't dead.

He lay in a regular-looking bed with an IV stand beside it. There was some kind of thick mat wrapped around his torso. That didn't seem right, but all he knew about gunshot treatments was what he saw on television.

There was surprisingly little pain. He'd expected something like this to be debilitating. They must have him on good drugs.

Speaking of them, they weren't in the room. Perhaps he could escape while they thought he was out of it.

The only problem was that he couldn't figure out how to get the damned mat to come loose. He'd just have to take it with him.

Pulling the IV needle out was surprisingly painful, and he bled like a stuck pig. The pillowcase was the only thing he could find to bind himself with.

He staggered a little as he headed for the door. There was something taped on the inside. A note.

You shouldn't be up. There's a guard outside the door and no fire escape. Lay back down before you hurt yourself. Cabot.

Dammit. Was the woman psychic?

A look out the window confirmed that they were on an upper floor and he had no way down. He supposed he could shout for help or write a message in blood on the window, but it was dark out, and this didn't look like the kind of neighborhood where people rushed to help one another.

But he wasn't going to sit down like a good boy, either.

He opened the door, somewhat surprised that they hadn't locked it. There was a man sitting in a wooden chair across from the door. He looked like every stereotyped villainous thug Queen had ever seen on TV: short but heavily muscled and bald as an egg.

The only thing that jarred this impression was the magazine the man was reading. It looked like a science journal. High-energy physics or something.

"You shouldn't be up, Mister Secretary." The man's voice was even deeper than Queen had expected. James Earl Jones deep.

"I've had about enough of this," Queen said. "I want to talk to someone in charge, or you can just shoot me again."

The man smiled a little. "From what I hear, Brenda only *threatened* to shoot you. The gunman was with someone else. You're a very popular man, by the way."

He rose to his feet, setting the magazine on the chair. His head was still below Queen's. Short and squat didn't begin to do him justice. The man looked like he could bench press a car. Or tie recalcitrant government officials into pretzels.

"Now, back into the room and I'll call the doctor," the man said. "He can take that off, if it's time, and then I'll take you to see Brenda."

Not happy with the outcome, Queen did as the man said.

A few minutes later, an Asian man in a lab coat came in. "Good evening, Mister Secretary. I'm Doctor Granger. Call me Todd."

His accent was jarring. Queen guessed somewhere in the South. The rural South. Possibly on a mountain where they hadn't seen regular people for a few generations.

"It's the way I talk, isn't it?" the man asked, obviously seeing something in Queen's expression. "Happens all the time. You see one thing and get another, and it makes you feel like you're in the Twilight Zone. Well, maybe in this case, you aren't too far off.

"Before we begin, let's lay out some ground rules. You might decide to get froggy and take me prisoner. Victor won't like that. He's the rather large man sitting outside. Let me assure you, he's even stronger than you think.

"Also, I have a black belt in three different martial arts. See? Stereotypes are good for something. I bet you're inclined to believe me because of my appearance."

Queen was amused in spite of his situation. "You're quite the talker,

Doctor Granger. Allow me to say that the name is jarring too." He sat on the edge of the bed. "How badly am I hurt? I actually feel pretty good."

"I've thought of changing my name to Kawasaki, just to see how many people would buy into my tall tales of being a motorcycle mogul. My friends insist that I have a low sense of humor. I'm not really sure why. Let's see what the autodoc has to say about your condition."

He walked around the bed and looked at the back of the mat wrapped around Queen's torso. "It tells me the damage has been repaired. I'd still be cautious about any sudden movements or heavy lifting, but you're going to live. Of course, I already knew that. Let's get this thing off you."

He did something, and the mat came loose. Queen saw a panel of some kind on the back as Granger wrapped it up and set it on the bed. The text was in the alien script.

"What's an autodoc?"

"You know that story of Brenda's you don't believe? Well, this is an artifact from a long time ago that is still better than any medicine we have on Earth. It can fix so much that we'd be stymied by, and quick too. It's only 10 PM, and you're all better. Except for where you yanked out that IV. Let me tape that up."

A look at his side showed no sign of an injury, other than a healed scar. It looked as though it had happened years ago.

"I'm going to have to believe this wild story, aren't I?" Queen asked with a sigh.

Granger smiled as he stopped the bleeding with a folded piece of gauze. "That's up to you, but I can guarantee you won't be in any doubt by morning. That controller you gave Brenda is going to open a whole universe that we'd thought gone forever. That's going to be for good and ill. Pandora's Box, if you will."

"'Gave' is a little strong of a word," Queen said dryly. "She kidnapped me at gunpoint and stole it. She's going to prison for a very long time when they finally catch up with her. You, too, I'm sorry to say. You seem like a nice enough fellow."

The other man laughed. "I've been in prison all my life. So have you, but you didn't have the perspective to see it. Come on. We'll go open those eyes of yours."

32

Kathleen screamed. She'd never felt such excruciating pain before. No matter how she struggled, it only got worse.

The sorry bastard who'd caused it stood in front of her with a smile. Holding her little toe between his fingers. "You see? I can do whatever I wish to you, and you cannot dream of stopping me."

"I was already going to talk, you asshole! You didn't have to cut my toe off!"

"Perhaps. Perhaps not. At the very least, you'd lie or conceal information. Now you grasp the full penalty for trying to fool me.

"Let us begin in earnest. You had this scanned copy of a document in your luggage. What is it? What language is this?"

They'd torn her luggage apart and found the hidden compartment where she kept emergency identification and cash. She'd stashed a copy of the papers Nathan had sent there for study.

"If you're so smart, you tell me," she snarled.

He nodded, as though she'd shared some deep secret with him. "The arrogance of the infidel is legendary. You think me uneducated because I believe that the word of God came through the Prophet Muhammad, peace be upon him. You think me an ignorant savage.

"Allow me to disabuse you of that notion. I have a master's degree in architecture. I know many languages, at least enough to recognize them, but I've never seen anything remotely like that. Shall I take another toe to prove how little choice you have in answering my questions?"

Her foot was still throbbing in agony from where he'd use garden shears to snip off her little toe. She'd rather not go through that again. Ever.

"It's the language of visitors to our world."

He frowned and shook his head sadly. "You really must think me an idiot. So be it."

"Wait!" she shouted desperately. "I'm telling the truth! All the news about that ship visiting Mars, that's my ex-husband. He found proof of people from space coming to our world a thousand years ago. That's just one piece of it.

"I have a crashed ship in my lab in the United States. The government confiscated it. It's true. Every word."

He set the shears down and looked at the paper more closely. "What is this map? It seems to be of the area around Paris. I've seen medieval documents that had similar drawings of the area. It was founded in the third century after Christ, on him be peace."

"We think there's a base down there. One left undisturbed for over a thousand years." She sure as hell didn't want to tell him that, but she'd like to keep the rest of her toes. God forbid if he started in on her teeth.

"And these markings?"

"Numbers. Twelve of them. These people used base twelve, so like our zero to nine. We're not sure what they mean."

He considered her for a moment and then picked up her computer. "What is on this? More information?"

"Yes. Scans of documents, pictures, reports. It's all there."

"Unlock it."

She typed the password and unlocked the encrypted drive. It booted up.

He set the computer down and handed her a pad and pen. "Write down the password."

His tone really pissed her off. He already believed that he was going to roll over her from now on. No, she didn't think so.

She wrote down the password, but it was a trick. It worked, but after three uses, it wiped the drive clean. And she'd just used it once. She'd had the operating system modified for just such an occurrence as this. Let him think he'd won.

He folded the password and slipped it into his jacket with the map. Then he had her tell him where the images of the ship were.

He stared at them, mind blown. She could see the wheels spinning but getting no purchase.

"Islam does not speak of people from other worlds," he said at last. "I'm unsure if this is blasphemy or not."

"That's your problem, not mine. Sometimes you have to adjust what you believe based on the evidence."

He dug into his pocket and pulled out the alien key. The thin sliver of metal gleamed in his hand. "What is this?"

"It's a key. It allowed us into the ship. The others used it to get into their facilities."

He examined it curiously for a moment and then dropped it into his pocket.

The front door to the apartment blew in with a tremendous crash. The wall of noise stunned her. The only one of her captors that seemed capable of movement was the man with her computer.

He snatched it up and scurried out the back like a rabbit, just missing the men rushing in the front with pistols out. The ensuing gunfight was short and brutal. Nathan came in right after the lead men.

"Where is he?" he shouted at her. He had to. Her ears were ringing so loudly that she thought she might never hear correctly ever again.

"Out the back. He took my computer and a copy of the map. Kill him."

It occurred to her after he'd ran off that the bastard had taken her toe with him too. Like a grotesque souvenir. Maybe Nathan would get it back when he killed the man. She'd like to have it put back on before it rotted.

The thugs with Nathan went from body to body, shooting everyone in the head. She supposed it paid to be thorough.

Nathan was back a minute later. "He got away. We'll have to kill him another day."

He cut her free from the chair and looked at her foot. "One of my guys will sew this up as soon as we get out of here. We need to be long gone when the French police show up. In this neighborhood, they'll come in force."

Two of his men grabbed her and hustled her out of the apartment. Another one came in with a gas can. It looked as though they'd be having a bonfire. Probably to get rid of any DNA evidence. Good.

Five minutes later, they were on the road out of Paris. Fire trucks and police cars raced in the other direction. They'd bound her foot, but it still throbbed in agony.

"Where are we going?" she asked.

Nathan turned in his seat and looked at her. "To the base. We found it and got inside. I'm relatively certain the police won't trace us there. We can make plans on what to do next once we get there."

"We have to find that son of a bitch and kill him. His friends too."

"We'll get payback for what he did to you. I promise."

"Screw payback. He knows about the alien tech. He has the map. He might be able to find the base."

Nathan considered that. "We'll need more people. If he comes calling, we'll give him a big surprise."

After a moment, he smiled. "This is actually kind of refreshing. It's usually Father and Harry we're competing with. All those 'no kill' rules made life boring. Even though you've lifted that, I confess to a certain level of anticipation in struggling against them. These people we can exterminate like rats. That's a nice change of pace."

She shook her head. "You're insane."

Her son laughed. "It's taken you this long to figure that out? I've known I'm barking mad for years. It's really freeing when you don't have to limit yourself to what society finds appropriate."

He turned around and stared out the windshield. "You're going to love what we've found. I'm sure you can come up with a way to use it against the

US. Maybe sink one of their aircraft carriers or something. In any case, the game has changed for us."

It was about time. She was sick of having everyone run over her. It was time to put her enemies in their places. First these Islamic morons, then Queen, and finally her ex-husband.

* * *

CLAYTON HIT the button to activate the quantum tunnel with a mumbled prayer. He caught himself part way through and snorted. A less religious sort than him was hard to imagine. The oldest habits died hardest.

The portal opened in much the same way as those in the video had. At least it opened. He'd really have been screwed if the damned thing hadn't worked.

The other side was dark. Pitch-black. The beams from their flashlights went just far enough to reveal rough stone. The natural kind, like one would find in a cave.

"Through the gate," he said as he walked to the other side. "We'll see if we can't slow them down a bit."

Once they joined him, he tugged the tablet as far over as he could. The short cable meant his arms were still in the old world. He certainly hoped it took as long for a portal to shut down as to open. Otherwise, he'd have difficulty feeding himself.

Clayton unplugged the tablet that controlled the quantum tunnel and jumped back a few steps. Nothing happened. The gate showed no sign of closing.

"Hmm. This isn't what I had in mind."

"We need to get farther into the cave, Mister Rogers," Mick said. "If we're right here when they come along, they'll just drag us back to the US."

They retreated deeper into the cavern. A path showed people had once used this portal fairly regularly, based on the wear. No telling how long ago that had been.

"Off the path here," Penny said. "There's a side cavern without the neon sign saying, 'we went this way,' to lead them in behind us."

Mick scouted and waved them in. It wasn't deep, but there were several columns of stone to keep them out of sight if anyone glanced in. Scuffs of movement told him that the soldiers had come into the transport room.

Too bad. The power room would've kept them busy searching for a long time. Probably long enough for the tunnel to close. He made a mental note to have them test how long a portal stayed open on its own once he got out of this mess.

They shut off their lights and waited. He breathed as shallowly as he could. Sound traveled in silent spaces like this, and he didn't want to attract the notice of the soldiers if they decided to come into the cave.

Of course, they had no way of knowing it was located somewhere else.

Without seeing it open for himself, he'd have guessed it was just an opening in the wall.

The sound of men moving quietly through the unfamiliar caverns grew louder. There were no lights, though. He mentally rooted for them to keep going.

Then reconsidered. How would he rescue them if this was an alien world? These were Americans. He wanted to elude them not leave them trapped. This was quite the quandary.

"You can come out of there, Mister Rogers. We know right where you are."

The voice made him flinch in spite of himself. He made no move and hoped that the others didn't give them away.

"You probably think I'm bluffing. IR/UV goggles. I can see the heat of your bodies around the rocks you're hiding behind. If I have to come in there, I'll shoot first and ask questions later. Toss the rifle onto the ground, and we all walk out alive."

The loud clatter of metal on stone told him that Mick had let the rifle drop. "There you go," the young man said. "I don't have any other weapons that can hurt you from over here. I'm coming out with my hands up."

He also turned his flashlight on and pointed it toward the ceiling. That let Clayton see Penny joining him.

With his options gone, Clayton raised his hands and stepped out to join them. Several men with weapons held up to cover them lifted their goggles and came forward to relieve them of their packs. They then searched them closely for weapons and used zip ties to bind their hands behind their backs.

Their leader—the same man who'd spoken to them from the base of the ridge—came forward. "You sure know how to make things hard on everyone, Mister Rogers. Let's get the formalities out of the way. You're under arrest on the charge of high treason. We'll take you back to our ship and then the US to face trial for your crimes."

Clayton shook his head wryly. "We both know you don't have the authority to arrest me in New Zealand. This is an out-and-out kidnapping."

"Good luck having your attorney use that in court," the young man said. "My name is Lieutenant Commander Karl Krueger. I once had the honor of serving on an op with your son. He was a fine man. This situation pains me because of that."

The soldiers brought them out of the side cavern and started herding them back toward the base. Commander Krueger walked beside Clayton with one hand on his arm to keep him steady.

"What the hell is this place?" the man asked. "We almost missed the opening up on the ridge."

"You're not cleared to hear the answer to that question, Commander," the man in the civilian clothes said. He was standing on the path near where it changed direction and headed off to the portal.

Clayton felt his lips tug up in a smile. "It's a thousand-year-old base left by—"

"Shut up!" The civilian shouted.

"—humans that once traveled the stars," Clayton finished. "I'm not likely to get into more trouble by talking, so don't bother to tell me to shut up, you moron."

"Gag them," the man said coldly. "Not one more word from any of them, or you'll find yourself in a hole with them, Commander."

Krueger stopped and stepped in front of Clayton. "Your authority over me only goes so far, Mister Ulysses. Let me give you a bit of advice. Never give an order you know someone will disobey. It makes you look weak and undermines your authority."

The civilian didn't back down. "I know you military freaks want to feel like you're all that and a bag of chips, but you need to realize what kind of world you live in. You can do it my way, or I'll make a few calls, and you'll be transferred to the ass end of nowhere to await your own court martial."

"You got a big mouth for such a little asshole," one of the soldiers said. "We could have a nice friendly-fire incident, and our problems go away. Or you could slip and fall off a cliff."

"Enough, Gunny," Krueger said. "We don't threaten to kill civilians, even if they are CIA douchebags who deserve a horrible death."

"Laugh it up," Ulysses said. "Your day is coming."

A soldier came up behind the CIA agent. "Commander, we have a problem. We've lost the exit."

"What do you mean? How can we lose an exit?"

"It's gone, sir. Just like it was never there. The center part of the tunnel we came through is just a solid piece of rock now."

Great, Clayton thought to himself. The worst of both worlds. Trapped in an unknown location *and* a prisoner. Could things get any worse?

33

—————

H arry marveled at the size of the ship. It seemed to stretch on forever. The lights came on ahead of them and went off behind them. The atmosphere was cold but had started getting warmer. The ship knew someone was aboard.

The corridor had the feel of a military warship. He'd traveled in enough of them over the years to recognize the frequent placement of airtight doors. On the ships he'd traveled on, those had been watertight. In case battle damage breached the hull.

He hoped this didn't turn out badly. It seemed unlikely that anyone was going to come complain about them trespassing, but if they did, it would get ugly.

"Why is the ship just parked out here in the middle of nowhere?" Emily Adams asked. "Doesn't that seem a bit odd?"

"It does," Harry said. "The most likely answer is that they didn't want anyone stumbling across it. Way out here, there's zero chance anyone on Earth could find it. Not optically, anyway. It's obviously still functional, so it was in standby mode."

"And it's waking up," Jess said. "If the heavy-worlders are the bad guys in this drama—which it sure looks like they were—then this is not the best thing for us. If they come back looking for trouble, then we'll get shot up."

Ray stopped next to a diagram on the wall. "Here's a simple deck plan. Even heavy-worlders get lost, it seems. This says we're a few decks down from the control center. If we're going to find answers, that's one of the places I'd look. Also, if we go down and aft, there are transport chambers. I bet those are quantum tunnels."

Harry liked the sound of that. "If we can open a direct passage to Mars, that might make me feel a little safer. We can send *Freedom Express* a little farther away and not risk so much."

"One thing is bothering me," Ray said. "Where did this ship come from? The drives we've seen all have a light-speed limit."

"Even the grav drives?" Jess asked. "It seems as if altering the gravity gradient should let you 'fall' right up to the speed of light. Infinite mass would help in that case, wouldn't it?"

The engineer shrugged. "If you were falling toward an infinite mass, it might make a difference, but it would most likely prevent a ship from hitting light speed. The natural universe is pretty firm on maintaining the laws on that sort of thing. Above the quantum level, anyway. It sure seems as though the quantum tunnels violate those laws."

"What if altering the gravity gradient takes more and more energy as one goes faster? That would stop a ship somewhere short of the ultimate speed."

Harry tapped her on the shoulder to get her moving again. "So would a bit of hydrogen at those speeds, I bet. I read a humorous article on the internet once about how a can of beans would act at various speeds. A single bit of gas at really high velocity could make a damned big explosion. And before you mention using magnetic fields, I'll remind you that it takes time for something to move."

She nodded and started walking again. "That's true. Atmospheric compression causes the heat a lifter generates on reentry. Most people think it's friction of the ship's passage, but it's not. The air can't get out of the way fast enough and the vehicle smashes it together, causing high temperatures."

"Fine," Ray said. "How did this ship get to the solar system? Sublight? That's one hell of a long trip, even if they came from somewhere close."

A set of stairs led them up several levels and brought them to a large hatch. It didn't open when they approached. There was a twelve-digit numeric panel beside it.

"It wants an entry code," Harry said. "Great. We're not getting in that way, then."

Jess squatted and looked at the pad. "Some of the numbers have odd patterns in the dust. Not from recent use, but from oils on the fingers, I bet. I'm seeing two. It's looking for six digits, so someone was using a really weak code. We just have to guess it."

"Sixty-four possible combinations seem a little weak for security," Ray said.

"That's because no one expected us to be able to dismiss most of the numbers," Jess said with a grin. "Bets on how many tries it takes me?"

It turned out to be seven. "Lucky seven," she exulted as the hatch slid slowly open. "Come to Momma!"

Harry raised his weapon and stepped inside. He had to admit the bridge was a little underwhelming.

The room beyond had no consoles or even chairs. It was completely empty.

* * *

DOCTOR GRANGER LED Queen to the elevator with Mount Victor right behind them. The large man made an impression even when he wasn't in sight. It was as though Queen could feel him standing behind them.

He looked down into Victor's eyes when they got into the dilapidated elevator and started down. "I saw you reading a science magazine. Might I inquire if you're a scientist?"

The large man smiled. "Sort of. I'm a doctoral candidate in theoretical physics."

"Forgive me, but you seem about as far away from my mental image of a theoretical physicist as possible."

"I get that a lot. If it makes you feel any better, I'm also on the university wrestling team."

"That I can believe."

The elevator doors wheezed open onto a large open room taking up much of the basement. Perhaps all of it. There was a large amount of equipment set up, but they'd cleared the right-hand side of the room.

Someone had built a stand that supported a series of metal arches about ten meters deep. It looked very out of place. The metal framework supporting it wouldn't allow anyone to walk through. He couldn't imagine what it was for.

Brenda Cabot stood talking with several men and women clustered around what was obviously one of the alien power supplies. The stolen blue cube sat inside it. Or possibly a different cube. At this point, he wasn't going to doubt her story anymore.

She saw them come out of the elevator and waved them over. "Mister Secretary, welcome. I'm glad to see you on your feet. I have no idea who the shooter was. We're guilty of a number of crimes, but that one is someone else's."

He inclined his head. "I'm willing to grant that possibility. I've made a few enemies over the years. I see you already had a power supply."

Cabot shrugged. "Actually, it's the one I stole from you. We had the unit but not the cube. It's the power source. Forgive my rudeness, but I'm not going to introduce my associates. I'd rather you only come after me once we cut you loose."

At least that supported her claim that she'd be releasing him. It would've been better if she'd not allowed him to see their faces at all. Of course, this could all be a sham, and these people might be of no particular importance.

He inclined his head toward the others. He had the doctor's name, but that was almost certainly fake. As was the wrestler-theoretical physicist's. Meant to lead him astray, no doubt.

That was fine. He'd locate them one way or another. Sooner or later, everyone made mistakes.

"By now, every law enforcement agency in the country is on high alert. They'll be looking for you everywhere."

Cabot smiled. "Good thing I won't be handy, then. You wanted to know if I was telling you the truth. Watch and learn."

She picked up the "cell phone" and brought it to life. Reading from a piece of paper, she painstakingly entered a long series of characters.

"I thought that was dead," he said.

She lifted it to show a cable running to the power supply. "I have it on external power while they refurbish the battery." She tapped the screen one last time.

He wasn't sure what he expected to happen, but the arch filling with mist and lightning wasn't it. He gaped as it grew thicker.

"What is that?" he asked.

"Technology we'd given up hope of ever being able to use," Cabot said. "Without power or a controller, we had no way to activate it. Let's just hope it does what it's supposed to. My people have been waiting a long, long time for this moment."

The mist cleared, and Queen could see the impossible. A large room on the other side of the arch where the scaffolding had been a moment before. Hell, where the scaffolding still was.

He wanted to ask more questions, but Cabot was walking forward, her hands in the air. The room, he belatedly noticed, had a number of armed people in spacesuits. Ones surprised by her appearance.

"I mean you no harm," Cabot said as she passed through the arch. "I'm Agent Brenda Cabot of the FBI. I need to speak to your leader."

Victor nudged Queen forward. As soon as he passed through the arch, he realized the scale of what he thought he'd seen was wrong. The chamber on the other side was huge.

A glance over his shoulder showed an arch on this side too. It was built into a stone wall. There were several others. One of which was open to another place.

He ducked low under Victor's arm and dodged through the second portal.

* * *

NATHAN TOOK his mother inside the base as soon as they arrived. He sent one of his men to move their van somewhere else. He didn't want to lead the bastard right to his front door.

Several dozen of his men were less than twenty minutes behind them. He'd have a devil of a time keeping this place a secret with so many people in the know, but he didn't really have a choice.

"What have you found?" his mother asked as soon as they were inside.

"An armory and a room with combat aircraft. Oddly enough, there doesn't seem to be a way to get them out."

"Then you missed something. These people don't build things for the hell of it. Take me to see."

He tasked one of the guards to watch the approach outside with a radio. If he spotted anyone, he'd call the team leader.

Nathan decided the armory would be a good first stop. He could compare the weapon his mother had brought to the ones there.

She smiled when she saw all the hardware. "Now this is worth something. They tested a pistol back at the lab, and it was quite destructive. I can only imagine how these compare."

"Why imagine?"

He grabbed one of the rifles off the wall and snagged a magazine from the slot it was sitting in. The light below it was orange. He had no idea if that meant it was ready for use. Well, he'd find out soon.

It didn't have a means of chambering a round after he locked the magazine in place, so he looked for a safety. It had a selector switch that seemed to indicate four possible conditions. Odds were very good the first one was with the safety engaged. The next might be single fire and the other full auto. He couldn't guess what the last one was for.

It never ceased to amuse him when the idiots in the liberal media insisted on calling a semiautomatic weapon an automatic. Or an AR an assault rifle. Neither classification was accurate.

On a whim, he'd done a little research on the mass shootings they were always raving about. Based on the number of rounds expended by the shooters and the time they were alone with their victims, a single-shot pistol could do the same amount of killing. Or a muzzleloader. Or a machete.

So, all their arguments calling for smaller magazine sizes and forbidding so-called assault rifles were nothing more than sniveling bullshit. If they really wanted to stop mass killings, they'd outlaw the moronic gun-free zones that attracted the mentally deranged killers in the first place. They usually killed themselves as soon as anyone resisted, the cowards.

He pulled his thoughts back from that particular annoyance. Maybe he could make a public service announcement later.

Nathan aimed the rifle down the hall and squeezed the trigger. The first setting was safe. Or the weapon was broken. He flicked the selector to the second setting. A single shot blasted down the hall.

There was no "bang," but there was a significant kick and a loud "crack" from the wall. The rifle didn't eject a shell casing. The next setting was still a single shot, but the noise of the impact was much louder. He wagered the round was traveling at a much higher velocity.

He flipped to the final setting and braced himself. It was burst fire. Three rounds, most likely. He engaged the safety and walked down the hall to examine his handiwork.

The slugs had torn mighty divots out of the wall, except for one chip he decided came from the weaker shot. "Damn! I've got to get me one of these!"

He walked back to where his mother was sitting and smiled. "These will go through any body armor I can imagine quite handily. The technology will redefine how combat works. And if those rag-headed bastards come calling, they'll be screwed."

"Let's hope it doesn't come to that," she said. "That kind of fight will get the attention of the French authorities. Then they'd take this place away from us too. What's on the other levels?"

"The only other area we've looked at is the bottom level. It has the combat aircraft, but no way to get them out."

He had two of the men carry his mother down while he slung the rifle across his shoulder, found a holstered pistol for himself, and grabbed extra magazines for both. There was body armor, which had to be damned tough, but he didn't have time to try it on.

His mother was examining the arches when he arrived, seated on a piece of equipment someone had dragged over with her injured foot up. "They don't go anywhere," he said as he stepped beside her.

"It certainly appears that way, but what are these? Step inside and look up." He did and spotted some kind of small mechanism.

"Damned if I know. I can tell you it doesn't make solid stone vanish."

"Almost nothing would surprise me about these people. See how all the ships are oriented toward these arches? I think those projectors *do* provide a way out. We just need to figure it out."

His new team leader came up to him. "The extra men from Paris have arrived. Where shall I put them?"

"Get them down here," Nathan said. "Have the cars taken elsewhere. I want as little evidence of this place on the outside as possible. Leave a team upstairs to defend the facility if they arrive in force."

The man nodded and went back upstairs.

His mother insisted the men take her to a ship, even though the movement was obviously painful. Getting her inside it was an ordeal that involved a lot of swearing.

He stood outside one where they'd raised the canopy. It looked like a fighter jet inside. Surely, his mother couldn't make heads or tails of it.

"What are you expecting to find?" he asked.

"I'll know when I see it. I spent a little time going over the console on the crashed ship." She brought the controls to life and moved through a number of screens. She was obviously being careful not to activate anything.

"It would be useful if we could understand what these words mean," he said after a few minutes.

"True. Ah, here we go. This ship has cockpit recording software too. Wagner sent me a video of this from the one we used to have. It showed the man flying it. Perhaps we'll get lucky here too."

She tapped one of the icons, and the console area on the right cleared to show both an interior and exterior view of the ship. A man in a flight suit and helmet was manning the controls while other men worked on various ships on the floor around it. They all looked as human as Nathan did.

The man brought the fighter to a hover. The quiet was astonishing. No roaring engines. It was floating silently above the floor. He edged it over toward one of the arches and brought up a control panel that Nathan hadn't seen before. A numeric keypad.

The pilot referenced a tablet and slowly entered a string of digits and pressed the gray button. The numbers changed to gold, and the arch ahead of the ship filled with mist. Little bolts of lightning shot through it, and then it cleared.

The stone was gone. Now he was looking at a night sky full of stars above a darkened landscape.

Nathan cursed in awe. This wasn't possible. One didn't simply open a gateway to some other place like that. That wasn't science. That was magic.

The man in the fighter edged through the arch and into the night sky. One of the camera views showed the fighter emerging from the side of a mountain. The pilot stepped on the gas and accelerated into the sky.

His mother ended the recording and found a second one. This one was very similar, but the craft didn't come out on the planet but in space. On the moon, to be precise. Nathan recognized the view of Earth when the ship emerged.

His mother turned to him, her eyes almost glowing with little gold dollar signs. "Do you realize what this means?"

"No," he said honestly. "I'm having trouble getting my mind to wrap around it."

"Imagine gates like this that people could use to get anywhere on Earth. Or to the moon. Maybe even farther. Transportation would change everywhere, and we'd get a cut of every transit. We'd be richer than our wildest dreams of avarice."

"Beyond a certain point, it's just keeping score," he said. "Right now, we need to worry about surviving our enemies."

His team leader cleared his throat. Nathan hadn't heard him approach. "We have visitors."

"Don't do anything hasty, Mother. I'll see to our guests."

The two men went back up to the top level. The short tunnel into the hill shielded the exterior door to the facility, so he wasn't worried about intruders spotting light from inside.

He edged out until he could see the nearest cleared area. That was where they'd been parking. The first thing he noticed was the large number of cars. There were hundreds of people out there, all armed.

Nathan watched one man whipping them into a frenzy. It must be the bastard. He knew what the prize was, and he'd called in enough people to take it.

Or so he thought.

With the alien weapons, Nathan was betting he could pull off an upset victory. It was going to be one hell of a fight. That made him smile with anticipation.

34

Clayton laughed. "Well, this certainly changes things, doesn't it?"

Ulysses frowned at the soldier who'd led them back to the arch. "This obviously isn't the same way we came in. Spread out and find the real exit."

The gunnery sergeant shook his head. "This was a straight-line path. No branches. It comes right from here to where we found them. There's no other way to go. This *is* the exit. You can see the support right there."

Commander Krueger stared at the wall for a moment and then turned to Clayton. "Humans that traveled into space, huh? Okay. You've provisionally convinced me. What is this?"

"A means of long-range transport. My son calls it quantum tunneling. A device in the base you chased us into opened a path here—wherever here is—without going through the space in between. Considering that my son went to an alien world, we could be anywhere. Literally."

Ulysses grabbed Clayton by the collar. "Open it back up. Now."

"And if I say no, what will you do, toad? What will these strapping young soldiers *allow* you to do to make me talk?"

The CIA man glared at the navy officer. "Search them. They have something on them to open this thing."

At Krueger's nod, the gunnery sergeant took their packs and patted them down thoroughly but professionally. He paused at Penny. "My apologies in advance for the indignity, ma'am."

"Do what you have to do, Gunnery Sergeant," she said.

He gave her as complete a search as he gave Clayton. He spared no area but didn't linger.

Krueger leaned over to Clayton. "They aren't soldiers, by the way. That's an army term. They're either sailors or marines, depending on their branch."

Clayton nodded. "How should I refer to them, then?"

"Look at the insignia. You can tell one from the other. As a general term, just refer to them as the men."

Once the gunnery sergeant had everything laid out, he started going through it. The haul wasn't much to scream about.

Krueger picked up the tablet. "This doesn't look like something you bought at a box store. Is this alien tech?"

Clayton nodded. There wasn't much point in denying it. As soon as the man turned it on, he'd find the gate controls. "It is."

The commander examined it for a moment and pressed the power button. He frowned. "What am I doing wrong? How do you turn it on?"

"You press the button you just pressed. Didn't it come on?"

The officer shook his head. "Gunny, cut Mister Rogers loose. I want him to show me how this device works."

The large noncom pulled out a wickedly sharp-looking knife and freed Clayton.

After he rubbed his wrists, Clayton took the tablet and pressed the power button. Nothing happened. He held it down, but that didn't make a difference. The device was dead.

"Hmmm. This isn't good. We found it attached to the machine on the other side of the gate. Perhaps it was only getting power from it. That would make sense, I suppose. Every other small device we've found had a dead power supply."

The officer stared at him. "So, you're saying that we're trapped here? Wherever here is."

Clayton stared at the arch. "It certainly appears so. I hope you brought enough food and water for an extended stay. We might be here for a while."

* * *

JESS LED a search around the area near the control room and found a locked hatch that indicated it contained the ship's computer. She suspected that was what was in control of the ship. In some ways that made things simpler, but she really had no idea what its goals and criteria were.

After a half an hour of them searching the various rooms, the computer decided that it should just turn all the lights and heat on. A little experimentation determined that the gravity was now set at what they'd call normal, even without the devices they wore around their necks.

They checked in with the lifter and *Freedom Express* regularly. The ship showed no signs of powering up in a more significant way. If it did, they'd get out as quickly as they could.

One thing was certain after a while. There were no people on this ship. There was no food, either, so that seemed a purposeful decision. Harry thought the ship was sitting here in a mostly powered-down state so that someone could use it at some future point.

She wasn't so sure. If that were the case, they'd have powered the ship down completely. The computer was on, so there was some set of circumstances where the thing would act. And based on the hostility that the heavy-worlders had shown to the regular humans, it wasn't benign.

They eventually found the transport room. It had the standard three arches and was exactly like the images in the dead soldier's helmet cam. This ship—or one much like it—had launched the attack on *Freedom Express*.

They'd recovered a controller from one of the dead fighters. He'd been an officer of some kind, based on the different type of armor he'd worn. The techs had repaired the battery and charged it up, so the lander went to get it.

Once it arrived, she opened a quantum tunnel to *Freedom Express*. They had one open to Mars there, so they now had a quick exit, if they needed one. All they needed now was an address on Earth that was under their control, and they'd be able to move around the system freely.

Of course, that also had its negative consequences.

Such as when someone they didn't know opened a tunnel to Mars and a man ran through the tunnel to *Freedom Express* and then to the alien ship. Like what was happening as she looked on right now.

She knew every member of the crew on *Liberty Station*, so Jess knew right away that this was an unknown person. The way he looked around with a desperate expression helped make that determination too.

Jess pulled her pistol and trained it on the man. She was still in her suit but had her helmet back on the hinged holder. "Freeze!"

The man stopped and raised his hands. "Well, it was worth a try."

Men and women from *Freedom Express* rushed in behind him and looked to her for guidance.

She holstered her pistol. "Who are you, and where the hell did you come from?" she asked as they took him into custody.

"My name is Josh Queen. I'm the secretary of state for the United States of America. Someone kidnapped me, and I just escaped. You work for Clayton Rogers?"

"In a manner of speaking. I'm Jessica Cook. Someone search him for weapons. Who kidnapped you?"

"That's an excellent question. I'm not sure I really know the answer. They're back at the first place these arches led to."

One of the women from *Freedom Express* started searching him. "They're back on Mars. This guy came running through and dodged in here before we knew what was happening. The folks on Mars are trying to find out who the new people are. They're not with Mister Rogers, though."

Jess triggered her radio. "Harry, this is Jess. We have some new folks coming through on Mars. I'm heading back that way to sort this out. I'll leave the search here in your hands."

"Roger that. Call if you need me."

"Will do. Be careful."

They went back to Mars via *Freedom Express*. The new people stood in front of a freshly opened tunnel. The other side of that one went to a large room with curious people staring through.

A confident-looking young black woman seemed to be in charge of the new group. Beside her stood a very large man. One whose body immediately reminded Jess of a heavy-worlder. The third member of their group was a man with Asian features in a lab coat.

The other woman slowly stepped forward and held out her hand. "You must be Jess Cook. Your friends here said you were on your way. I'm Brenda Cabot. I'm with the FBI. Rather, I used to be."

She inclined her head toward Queen. "Once it gets out that I kidnapped him, I suppose I'm just a regular fugitive."

"I'd hardly call you regular," Queen said dryly. "You'll be at the head of the top ten most wanted list. Every man and woman in law enforcement will be looking for you and your accomplices."

Jess could believe that. "Let's go sit down and talk, then. I'm sure you have a very interesting story to tell. Someone will get you settled on *Freedom Express* in the area we use for meals while I change."

Getting out of the pressure suit only took a few minutes, so they'd just gotten tea when Jess joined them. Sandra was leaned up against the wall nearby, so Jess felt relatively confident of her safety.

"Your sudden arrival has my full attention," she said. "How did you get here, and who are you?"

Cabot sipped her tea and launched into her explanation calmly. "My associates and I are descendants of people that fled from the Mars base and this ship about a thousand years ago. We've come to warn you of a great danger."

"That's quite a claim," Jess said, "but your ability to use the quantum tunnels certainly lends credence to it. Why haven't you shown up before now? And why kidnap Secretary of State Queen? If that's who this guy really is."

Queen looked amused rather than offended.

"We didn't have a gate controller or power supply," Cabot said. "Once I became aware of the investigation into Kathleen Bennett and what they'd found, I took steps. Taking him seemed like the easiest way of making contact with the US government while I did it."

"But not exactly in a manner calculated to earn trust," Queen said. "I'm very much afraid that all of you have some explaining to do, and the US government is going to demand some changes to what is happening out here. You can't just claim all of this for yourselves. This is now classified as top secret-SAP and falls under the control of the US government."

Jess gave him a steady look. "Do you know where you are? No? Let me clue you in. Space. Far beyond the outermost planet. This might take jurisdictional overreach to new heights.

"So, let me make our position plain. Your opinion means very little out here. Those things called borders mean something for a reason. Humanity Unlimited is incorporated in a country not called the United States, and even it doesn't control what we do out here. Is that plain enough for you?"

He shook his head with more than a hint of sadness in his expression. "That's naïve at best and foolish at worst. Even as we speak, US military forces are taking Clayton Rogers into custody. This is over."

Jess laughed. "You think that's enough to stop us? Harry doesn't even particularly like his father. Even if he did, the articles of incorporation make clear what happens in that kind of situation. We don't negotiate with terrorists. And that's what the US is acting like. This situation is not yours to dictate."

Queen's expression hardened. "You can act this way now, but circumstances change. At some point in the not so distant future, we'll be out here with you, and we'll take all of this away. By force, if need be. Corporate or personal greed will not dictate national policy for the greatest democracy on Earth."

"Now who's naïve? Corporate and personal greed have been dictating US policies since before any of us was born. You'll do whatever lines your prospective pockets the fastest."

Cabot cleared her throat. "As entertaining as this is, you should save it until later. I need to warn both of you about what you're getting involved with. As powerful as the US is, it's in just as much danger as everyone else. I'm talking about an extinction-level event."

Jess made a point of turning her attention away from Queen. "This has something to do with all the fighting that took place back then, I'm sure. It pains me to ask this, but can you prove any of your story? You have to admit, it does sound a little Dan Brown."

The other woman smiled. "I understand how ludicrous this sounds. One of my distant ancestors was assigned to this very place, I believe. One of the old stories revolves around the huge chamber at the center.

"The gravity is steady all the way around, so you could look up and see people walking over your heads. The elevator let out in the center and stairs headed off in a number of directions like a spider's web. Am I close?"

Jess nodded. "That's all accurate, and not something we've shared, so I suppose you have to be telling me the truth." She shifted her attention to the large, squat man. "Excuse me, but are you somehow related to the heavy-worlders?"

"My name is Victor Holyfield," he said. "And yes. One of my ancestors was a wounded heavy-worlder. They called themselves something different, but that's not relevant right now."

"So, they were human."

He nodded. "Yes, with a little tinkering. I'm not going to step on Brenda's story, but they're humans modified to live and work in heavy gravity. The genes are dominant, so I still have all the traits."

Jess felt her eyes widen. "So, you can move around in the 3G environment on the ship we found out here? It's abandoned but operational. We're not sure what it's doing out here."

"I'd have to try, but almost certainly. I suspect that I'm woefully out of shape for that kind of thing, though."

"That's my cue to jump in," Cabot said. "That ship represents a huge danger to everyone in this solar system. They left it here to monitor us, and if certain criteria are met, it will go tattle. Then the heavy-worlders come back to finish what they started. Only this time, they kill every single human in this system."

35

Nathan watched the enemy form up for a minute before heading back down to the lowest level. Once that bastard figured out where the entrance was, they'd come in faster than he could stop them.

Too bad they didn't have a real clue how the systems in this base worked. That gun mounted near the elevator would be very helpful right about now. At least he could use the other weapons to even the odds a little.

He'd closed the outer door, so maybe they wouldn't find it at all.

It only took a few minutes to gather his men and issue weapons from the armory. They had no trouble grasping how they worked in practice. A few bursts each at the far wall proved that. Their professionalism would make a difference against semitrained illiterates.

The armor was straightforward too. If it was made to protect against these high-powered weapons, it would do well against regular bullets.

As soon as the first group was ready, he sent them up to relieve the men at the entrance. Within fifteen minutes, everyone was armed and armored.

He put most of the men down at the lowest level, but he led the troops at the entrance himself. His hopes of going undiscovered only lasted half an hour. Then someone started pounding on the door. Based on how thick it was, maybe they were shooting it.

It would probably stand up to a few blasts, but nothing was indestructible. He sent most of the men down to the lowest level and set up shop in the elevator. That gave him some distance from explosions and an easy way of getting out of the fight when the time was right.

After a short pause, the door slid open on its own. The bastard had gotten in!

The hallway rapidly became a target-rich environment. One that he and his people used ruthlessly to their advantage, mowing down the screaming idiots as they charged in.

The weapons were significantly more effective than he'd imagined possible. A single burst killed half a dozen men. With the three of them firing, the entrance became a pile of bodies in no time at all.

They weren't unmolested, though. A round bounced off Nathan's shoulder armor. The unlucky man next to him took the ricochet in the side of the head. The other man took a shot to the face a moment later.

Time to head for greener pastures.

He hit the button for the lowest level and stripped his men of their weapons and ammo. They'd moved all of the ammo to the lowest level, figuring the weapons left behind would be useless without them.

It pissed him off that they'd lose the ships on the lowest level. That was a given now. The enemy would pin them down unless his mother had figured out how to open the portals. And hopefully to somewhere more hospitable than the surface of the moon.

How did that work, anyway? Shouldn't space suck the air out of the base?

When the elevator doors opened, he shot up the controls and dragged one of the dead men to block the doors from closing. Let the savages use the stairs.

His men had made barricades with good fields of fire on the stairs. They'd make the bastards pay for every inch.

His mother waved him over. "I have a code to somewhere safe, I think. It was on the papers you found. We should retreat before they get here."

"Where does it go?"

"Who cares? It has to be better than staying here."

The stair doors banged open, and a man stuck his head out. Nathan's troops took it off for him.

He grinned at his mother. "They know where we are, so I guess we should look at making an exit. After you."

Nathan expected them to be hesitant after the slaughter upstairs, but that only seemed to make them rush in faster. Someone led the way with a grenade, which got his people ducking. More men flooded out, found cover, and opened fire on them.

His mother was under cover in the cockpit of the ship. Bullets bounced off its armored hull. She painstakingly entered the code.

"Here goes nothing," she said as she pressed the last button.

The arch nearest them filled with mist and lightning. It cleared to show a room made of metal, like on a ship at sea.

Several of his men rushed through the portal, and he heard gunshots from the other side.

"Great, bad guys over there too," he grumbled, grabbing his mother and ignoring her scream of pain as he yanked her out of the fighter. "Time to go."

His men followed along behind him as he ran through the open portal. His scouts were exchanging shots with someone in a corridor beyond the room. Two people in spacesuits lay sprawled on the floor.

Nathan wished he had time to figure out what was going on, but the enemy pushed through the open portal right behind him. They seemed determined to chase him to ground and kill him.

Thankfully, there was another exit from the room. He ran through it with his mother before more people came rushing out of a second arch. At least these new people were shooting the terrorists.

As far as he was concerned, they could kill one another off.

It was Harry and his people. It had to be, with the familiar spacesuits. Time to close this fight off.

He set his mother down and pulled off his pack while she clutched her foot and moaned. He'd stuffed it full of goodies before they'd left Paris.

Like the disposable antitank rocket he pulled out.

He opened the launcher and leaned out long enough to fire the weapon at the portal the bad guys were coming through. The mighty river had slowed to a trickle. The bad guys were in the room now. He couldn't see anyone past the moron standing in the open portal, looking like he wanted to turn around and run.

The rocket hit the top of the portal and riddled him with shrapnel. The metal wall reappeared instantly, cutting the idiot in half.

Well, that was gory.

That blast sent his brother's people retreating toward wherever they'd come from. Since they were still shooting up the terrorists, Nathan let them take their casualties and go. The less people that stayed, the fewer trying to kill him later. He used a second rocket to blast that portal after they were gone.

By now, he was taking heavy fire from the remaining bad guys. He had to pull back. Just before he yanked his head clear, he saw the bastard that had cut off his mother's toe directing men to go around through the other exit.

He had no idea of the layout, but neither did they. He'd make do.

* * *

THE UNEXPECTED ATTACK caught Harry completely off guard, and he cursed himself for not taking steps to prepare for it. The people from the past had locked their quantum tunnels to keep people from coming at them without warning. If he and his people made it clear, he'd best start doing the same.

He'd spotted his brother carrying his mother and lined up a shot, but as much as he hated her, Kathleen Bennett was still his mother. In the end, he let them escape. Probably a mistake he'd regret later, but he couldn't make himself do the unthinkable.

Then some idiot used a rocket launcher to destroy two of the three portals. Thankfully, after his people had made a clean escape. The men pulled their injured and dead with them on the retreat.

Now all Harry needed to do was get clear with the people left on the ship. He had them rendezvous near the airlock where the lifter sat on the hull. Thankfully, everyone was in suits. That was going to save their lives.

A few at a time, they cycled out onto the hull and into the lifter. A message to *Freedom Express* got him the information that everyone was accounted for.

He went over his helmet video as the lifter was detaching. Who were the people Nathan was fighting? He hadn't heard a word about new players in the game. Were they associated with the people that had the secretary of state?

Probably not, they looked an awful lot like they came from the sandbox. If so, Nathan had opened things up to some very dangerous lunatics.

"Harry, the ship is moving," the pilot said.

He made his way forward in the lifter and saw the ship was getting smaller very quickly. In fact, in less than twenty seconds, he couldn't see it anymore.

"Where's it going? Toward Earth?"

The woman shook her head. "The other direction. The map that Jess showed us had something marked farther out. I think it might be going that way."

"Get us down and safe as quickly as you can." He switched channels. "*Freedom Express*, this is Liberty Six. Over."

"Go, Liberty Six."

"We're coming in hot. As soon as we land, I want you to take off after that ship at max acceleration. We need to keep it in sight and find out what it's doing and where it's going."

"Copy that."

The lifter came in quickly, settling into the landing bay the older humans had used. The outer hatch closed, and the gravity came up to normal.

"Everyone, go get checked out by medical," he said. "I don't care if you feel fine. That's an order."

One he should obey too, but he had more pressing business to attend to. He impatiently took the elevator down to the core and made his way to the main control console. The woman sitting there was one of the pilots assigned to *Liberty Station*.

"Can you drive this thing?" he asked.

"As well as anyone," she said with a shrug. "The handheld translates for me, but I don't know where a lot of the screens are. This is simple, though. I just selected the ship as the destination and ramped up the speed."

"Are we keeping pace?"

"Not even close. We'll get where he's going, but not in time to do anything about it. Not that I have a clue what we'd do if we caught it. We don't have any weapons."

He smiled grimly at her. "This entire comet is a weapon. If we catch them while we have a speed advantage, we can swat them like a fly being run over by a watermelon."

"Nice visual. At this rate, he'll be at the area on Jess's map in less than twenty minutes. It'll take us at least twice that long."

"That a lot faster than I expected."

She smiled and shrugged. "What can I say? This thing moves faster when you know how to give it the gas."

"Harry."

He turned to find Jess and a bunch of people he didn't know standing behind him. Rex and Sandra had a security team watching over them. He suspected Jess hadn't considered that and gave Sandra a nod.

"Harry Rogers," Jess said, "meet Brenda Cabot and Josh Queen. She's a former FBI agent and claims to be part of a secret organization made up of descendants of survivors from this ship and the Mars base. Mister Queen is the secretary of state for the United States."

"Agent Cabot, Mister Secretary," he said politely, "I'm sorry to be rude, but I'm a little busy right now."

Cabot took a step forward. "That's the reason we've come to you. That ship is dangerous. You must stop it, or humanity is in terrible danger."

He shrugged. "That's out of my hands. Once my brother and the people he was fighting came on board, we lost all control over there. We don't have anyone aboard, and it's on its way out of here. Not toward Earth, but something farther out. Can you tell me what it's going toward?"

She shook her head. "Our people passed down as much information as we could through writings and oral tradition, but we only know what the survivors knew. They said there was a ship belonging to the Asharim watching the system. I can't recall anything about bases far out in the system like this."

"Who are the Asharim?" Queen asked. "What's their beef with humanity? What kind of trouble have you people gotten us into?"

Cabot turned toward him. "The Asharim are aliens. Humanoids from a relatively low-gravity environment. They discovered humanity about 900 CE and took samples from various areas of the planet.

"Their intention was to harness humanity as a subservient race to work for them as something of a cross between slaves and indentured servants. I'm not certain that my ancestors really understood the details correctly."

Harry nodded. "We found icons in the gravity controls that must have been for them. Even here, on *Freedom Express*. Obviously, something went wrong. What happened?"

"Rebellion," she said. "The Asharim were in conflict with other races out there, and some of them made contact with humanity. They armed and trained us to take control of our own destiny, or so they said. I'm a bit skeptical. I'll bet they had their own plans for us.

"The Asharim don't have the same moral system that we do. To them, humans are bugs. Or farm animals. Our sentience means very little to them. They only respect someone that competes at their level.

"In any case, there was a lot of fighting, and humanity made its move. This ship was part of an underground inside our system to supply various bases. Just in case something terrible happened."

"And it did," Jess said. "They came in and killed you. But not humanity as a whole."

Cabot smiled wryly. "One doesn't just kill the golden goose. Humanity was valuable, at least potentially so. They modified Victor's ancestors to be heavy-gravity warriors. Indoctrinated them and used them in their fighting as Janissaries."

"I'm not familiar with that term," Queen said. "Is that like mercenaries?"

"Sort of," Jess said. "People raised to be loyal and fight for their masters. Slaves that didn't really know any better."

"The bottom line," Cabot said, "is that the Asharim had too many irons in the fire and thought they might need humanity once everything settled down. They did everything they could to exterminate the rebels. Quite effectively, I might add. Then they left a ship here to watch. If humanity becomes a threat again, it's supposed to go tell them."

"This has to stop," Queen said. "The United States is taking over here. We'll protect Earth. You people have done more than enough."

Harry gave him a flat look. "I've seen firsthand how people like you deal with problems. You line your pockets and then keep things going until you can't control anything. No thanks."

"You seem to think you have a choice in the matter. We'll find our way out here in force and take over your ships. You know how powerful the US military is, I believe. Do you want to fight them?"

Harry shook his head. "No, but you mistake your place in this. Your mandate ends on Earth.

"And I didn't cause this disaster. Something drove my damned brother to bring a bunch of Middle Eastern fighters after him. I don't suppose you know anything about that, do you, Secretary Queen?"

Queen sneered. "You people found this stuff and failed to say one word about it. Now you're responsible for what you've done. We already have your father in custody. You'll join him shortly, and we'll clean up this mess. We'll also put you maniacs in prison for the rest of your lives."

The pilot cleared her throat. "Sorry to interrupt your diatribe, Mister Secretary, but the ship we're chasing just reached the target area and disappeared."

Harry returned his attention to the console. The icon representing the ship they were after was gone.

"What does that mean? Did he go into hiding? Some kind of supralight drive?"

"They don't have faster-than-light drives," Cabot said. "The quantum tunnels are faster than light, but they have to fly a ship across space to get something built at the destination. They use automated ships to handle that kind of exploration. He must've went to the gate on this end."

Harry blinked. "A gate big enough to transport a ship like that? It was huge!"

She nodded. "So the old stories say. The Asharim are very, very advanced."

"Are you going to continue to hold me prisoner?" Queen asked. "This woman kidnapped me."

Harry turned around and fixed the man with a stern glare. "Considering you have my father, I think that might be showing a somewhat hypocritical stance on your part, Mister Secretary. Or is it only kidnapping when someone does it to you?"

"I don't expect someone of your background to understand affairs of state,

Mister Rogers. As the present leader of your company, I hold you responsible for any and all of this, so you'd be best advised to release me."

Jess stepped between them as Harry balled his fist. "Boys. Put them back in your pants. Secretary Queen, you seem to be operating under a mistaken impression. I'm the second-largest stakeholder in Humanity Unlimited. Harry is only a minority partner. With Mister Rogers out of communication, I'm running the company now.

"Let me give you one piece of advice, sir. Your country is attacking us, and if you do not cease, we will feel no compunction against defending ourselves. You and your friends are so corrupt that I cannot and will not trust you to operate in good faith.

"I should just lock you up, but I won't. Against my better judgment, I'll see you returned to Earth."

She took a step into his personal space. To his credit, he didn't back up.

"But let me make one thing crystal clear. I hold you personally responsible for Mister Rogers's safety. If any harm comes to him, the gloves are off. I'll start by making a broadcast to everyone on Earth telling them the whole story. Then let's see you secure any of the sites on the planet. Hell, you'll be lucky China doesn't come after you for real."

Queen smiled. "Now you're in my territory, Miss Cook. If you get the Chinese going, you'd very quickly be wishing you only had me for an enemy. They're ruthless. They wouldn't hesitate for one second before slitting your throats and taking whatever they want."

"So, our little conflict stays covert," she said. "Keep my warning in mind. Miss Cabot, would you and your people be so kind as to return Secretary of State Queen to wherever the hell you found him?"

The former FBI agent inclined her head. "He doesn't know where our base is. After this, we'll relocate it somewhere outside Chicago. The breakdown and move won't take long. Then we can cut him loose."

The short black woman turned her attention to the government official. "One thing you should keep in mind, Mister Secretary. We've been around as an organization for far longer than America has. We've used advanced technology to place ourselves in positions that you wouldn't dream possible.

"Look around, Mister Secretary, and wonder which of your friends is really one of us. Aren't secret societies great? Who do you think invented the story of the Illuminati? People that knew a bit about us. Be warned."

"We're slowing down and coming into visual range of the destination," the pilot said.

Harry turned his back on the others as Rex led Queen away. The small dot on the screen expanded slowly until everything clicked for him.

"I know that place," he said. "We were just exploring that massive tube. The one that could hold all of New York and not feel crowded. It's powered down into standby mode."

They came flying in and got a good look at the massive structure from the outside. It was, as he'd expected, a tube over a kilometer thick and ten times as long. Many smaller branches formed pods away from the hull, making it look like a massive tree trunk awaiting trimming.

It orbited a large, dark globe. He had no way to judge size, but whatever it was looked larger than the comet by a big margin.

"Where did the ship go?" Jess asked.

"The sides of the station look solid," Cabot said. "What about the ends?"

The pilot brought the comet around to look at one of the endcaps. It was solid as well, but they could see projectors similar to those in the arches on the edges, only on a massive scale. That was a quantum tunnel generator capable of taking a huge ship across the galaxy in a moment.

"Well, I suppose we know where it went," he said. "How do we follow it?"

No one had a good answer. Obviously, the ship had sent a signal to activate the quantum tunnel. If it ran like its smaller brethren, it would have a log of the address. They just had to access the system and find a controller to open it for themselves.

And that wasn't happening right now. The ship had escaped. Whomever it was going to warn would soon know that humanity was a threat to them.

"I think that's a planet," the pilot said.

"Excuse me?" Jess asked.

"Look at the distance the station is orbiting around that object. It has a similar mass to Earth. And it's completely circular. A globe. I'm also not seeing any debris. It's cleared its orbital area. That's the definition of a planet."

Harry looked at the screen. "How good is this thing? Can we see the surface?" It was darker than the cave under the Mayan pyramid, so he wasn't sure what he expected, but he was curious.

"Let me try." The pilot manipulated the controls and the view shot down. The sky was clear. Out this far, it might not even have an atmosphere.

Only it must have at one time. The dim light made it hard to see, but he was looking at something that looked very much like a city. One on the surface of this world. It was dark and dead, but once it had supported life.

"Holy cow," Jess said as she took over the controls. "Look at the size of that thing. It's everywhere."

"The planet?" Cabot asked.

"No, that city. I've been moving the view around and it doesn't end. It's as if a massive city is covering the entire surface. Those buildings must be huge."

Now they had another set of questions. Who had these people been, how had their planet gotten here, and what did it mean for humanity?

36

Kathleen hobbled around the small set of rooms Nathan had left her in, both terrified and bored. A length of pipe made a terrible crutch. Yesterday, she'd been a powerful woman with tens of thousands of people jumping to obey her smallest command. Today, her domain was these few rooms that she couldn't even place on a map.

The two men left to guard her were French, hired thugs of Nathan's. Other than him, she had no one to call her own. It sucked.

Nathan was off with most of the men, trying to kill the rest of the bastards that had followed them through the gateway. Only one set of people would control all this. Whatever it was. And she swore it wouldn't be that bastard. She'd cut off his toes and feed them to him first.

Her son seemed to think that outright victory was possible. Perhaps with those alien weapons he was right. That didn't make her feel any better about her situation, though.

Even if they won, she'd watched Nathan destroy some or all of the gateways. They might be trapped on the ass end of nowhere for all eternity.

Harry and his people had been here, but Nathan said they'd gotten away. Was she on Mars? Shouldn't it feel lighter? She wasn't any expert in this, but she thought she weighed about the same as on Earth.

And her foot was throbbing. Gods above, it hurt.

The end of the corridor that she hobbled to was a lab of some kind. She'd seen enough of them over the years to recognize one. Or it might be part of a hospital. Some of the equipment suggested that.

One thing was sure, that thing in the middle of the room was spooky.

It looked like an oversize coffin. Or a sarcophagus. A technological one, with subsidiary machines arrayed around it. The control panel beside it was on and displayed a human form.

She eyed the room again. Lab or hospital? If this was a medical center, she could use some miraculous first aid on her foot.

What she didn't need was any weird experimenting on her body. Or probing. No probing.

Without being able to read the alien language, she had no way of knowing what this was or what it did.

The color of her foot and its size was worrying. If it became infected, she'd have to let Nathan cut it off. That decided her in the end. She'd try the device. Better dead than a cripple.

And without anyone looking over her shoulder, now was the time to try it. Her son would stop her if he were here. Not unreasonably, really.

She sat on the edge of the cavity and put her foot in. Maybe it would work with only that and she could yank herself out if it went crazy.

No dice. She sighed and slid into the cavity. It was obvious by the shape where her head went and where her feet went.

Unsure of what to do, she lay there waiting, more afraid than she had been in a long time. Even counting when the terrorist had tortured her.

The console beeped, and the slab beside her slid over her before she could do more than squeak in terror. She was committed now.

* * *

CLAYTON WATCHED with sympathy as the soldiers struggled to adapt to the idea they were trapped somewhere other than Earth. These men were obviously serious professionals, but the situation was far outside their belief system. It had rocked them hard.

The military men spent some fruitless time trying to get the tablet controller working. Once it became clear that wasn't happening Commander Krueger set two of his men scouting for an opening to the cave system.

Personally, Clayton thought the path was the best clue, but that could also lead them right into some kind of ambush. Based on what he'd seen in the videos, he didn't want even the best of the US forces having to defend him from that.

He stepped over to the officer. "Commander, a word, if I might."

Krueger stepped away from the man he'd been speaking with. "Yes, Mister Rogers?"

"You need to see some of the things we've found. If you'll get my computer, I'll play some of the video for you."

The officer looked at him for a moment and then nodded. "Gunny, bring Mister Rogers's pack."

That also got the attention of the obnoxious CIA agent, but no plan survived contact with the enemy. He walked them through logging on. At this point, every bit of information became a possible key to their survival.

They all watched the videos Jess had taken of the battle scene closely. Once it was over, Gunnery Sergeant Danvers turned to Clayton. "Who were these people?"

The CIA man opened his mouth, but the large soldier held up his hand. "Can it. This is about getting out of here alive now. It's your sorry ass on the line too. Give me any crap and I'll hog-tie you and duct tape your stinking mouth shut."

The other man glared but closed his mouth.

Clayton shrugged. "We're a little at a loss on that ourselves. The large people were from a heavy-gravity world. Very, very strong, I assume. And obviously capable of fighting. They had it in for the normal humans, and the weapons they used were quite advanced and deadly."

"Well, whoever they are, we need to be careful not to meet them," Krueger said. "We're tough, but not *that* tough. Especially when we're understrength like this."

The scouts made their way back, looking a little shell-shocked. "We found an exit at the end of the path, Commander. It's dark out but starting to lighten up. The entrance is on a hill in deep woods. I'm not familiar with the trees. I figure dawn in half an hour."

"Then let's get out of here before full dawn. I'd rather not have an early riser spot us coming from this cave. In the woods, we can hide until we scout a bit."

The military men hustled the three prisoners into the middle of their group and made their way to the exit. The scouts once more led the way out.

It was light enough to see the trees and even the hillside across from them. Definitely a wilderness area. The men didn't speak, communicating with hand gestures that Clayton had seen his son use with his own people.

An overgrown path led to the cave. It ran down the hill like a snake slithering around. Rather than follow it down, Krueger sent his men up the hill. Without a path, that made the going slower, but they had less chance of running into someone who wanted to kill them.

The sun was up by the time they reached the crown of the hill. The trees there were younger than the ones on the slope. It looked as though someone had cleared it at some point in the past.

Clayton could see the remains of a low stone wall. Based on its condition, no one had been up here to maintain it in a very long while. A different path led down on the other side.

"These trees aren't from Earth," Mick said. "I've never seen anything quite like them."

"And there's something wrong with the sun," Penny added. "The shade is off. It's more bluish. Not much, but enough to tell. We aren't on Earth."

"That's not really much of a surprise," Clayton said. "These people obviously had a very large galactic civilization. Based on the condition of the sites we've found, it certainly looks as though something went wrong in the not-so-distant past."

"The war?" Mick asked.

"Perhaps. It hardly seems as though the humans of the time had what it took to fight someone this spread out, though."

Krueger came over to them and spoke softly. "You'd best come see this."

It seemed as though the center of the hilltop had once had some religious significance. At least the large slab of stone certainly looked to Clayton like a massive altar.

What lay on it chilled him, though. Bones. Scavengers seemed to have picked them apart, but it was obvious that more than one person had met their ends here, based on the four skulls he saw.

"I'm somewhat surprised that local scavengers would eat humans," he said softly. "It seems as though something from a different biosphere would be inedible."

Krueger gave him a look. "That's your takeaway from human sacrifice? At least I think those are human."

"We all respond to stress in different ways, Commander. Whoever killed these people did so a long time ago. A very long time ago."

"Sorry to burst your bubble, Mister Rogers," Mick said, "but these haven't been out here for a thousand years. They'd be broken down if they were. They're a few years old, at most. Maybe only a few months. Whoever killed them is very likely alive and well as we speak."

Gunnery Sergeant Danvers came over to them. "We found something to the east. Rather, whatever direction the sun is rising from. The magnetic field doesn't seem to be laid out the same as on Earth, so we're going to have to figure it out at some point . Come on."

They went to the far side of the hill and to the base of a large tree. Someone had built a large platform about ten meters up the bole, but it looked a bit rickety.

"It's more stable than its appearance suggests but come up carefully. The stairs are shaky."

They ascended one at a time until they all stood on the platform. Danvers was right. It was still very stable.

Off in the distance, they could see what the builder had wanted them to look at. A grand city spread out across the hills on the other side of a river. Tall buildings made of metal and glass soared high into the sky. It was magnificent.

But there was something wrong with it. There were no lights. Of course, during the daytime, one wouldn't expect a lot, but the city looked dead. Some of the buildings seemed damaged. One had no facing. He could see the rooms inside it. Another had fallen—though it was still intact—and leaned up against a neighbor.

"I don't think we'll be finding any helping hands over there," Penny said. "No signs of smoke, though. This didn't happen recently."

"Hey!"

They looked down at the hissed whisper. It was the CIA man, Ulysses. "There's something on the other side of the hill."

They made their way down and followed him to where some of the other soldiers were looking out with binoculars. Unlike before, they looked a little spooked. On edge. The sky was hazy over the treetops.

"Is that smoke?" he asked.

One of the troops nodded. "It hasn't gotten heavier, so I'm thinking campfires rather than a forest fire."

Krueger looked over the area for a moment. "That's a lot of people. It might be an army camp. If so, we've stumbled into someone else's war."

Perfect. Clayton shook his head and wondered how the hell they were going to survive this.

* * *

JESS ADJOURNED to the mess hall with Harry and Cabot. Tea and coffee all around.

"As much as I hate to say so, Queen is right in one respect," she said. "We can't fight against a galactic empire with just the few people we have at our disposal. Hell, we can't even read the language."

"I can help with that last problem," Cabot said over her tea. "I can read and speak the language of the Asharim. And I can teach it to you. Some of our overseas folks tell me it's an easier second language than English.

"When it comes to working with the equipment, though, all bets are off. We have some old gear, but nothing like all the things you've found. The gate was the biggest piece of equipment, and it took a lot of trial and error to get it working."

Harry sipped his coffee. "Where did you get it?"

"It was part of a hijacked load of equipment. A lot of human escapees back then were smugglers, pirates, and thieves. They lived on the edges of civilized society. We'd brought it back to the solar system to try to set up colonies that the Asharim didn't know about.

"A lot of worlds were lightly populated in the sphere they control. It's all a hodgepodge of linked places. I've heard of wealthy homes having each room on a different planet, all the gates open continuously. I suspect the lower classes in their civilization are a bit more sedate, but it just goes to show that you never can tell."

"What do we do now?" Harry asked. "I sent a team over to the cylinder. They can see us outside, so we're in the right place. I'm still at a loss as to the planet, though. We need to send a lifter down and find out what it is."

Jess considered their situation. "Clayton is missing. Either the US has him, or he managed to escape but hasn't gotten to where he can call us. At this point, I'm not sure it matters in how we proceed.

"We must find out where that ship went, and then we need to follow them. If we can stop them before the Asharim find out about us, so much the better. The problems on Earth are pressing but not as much as what we're doing out here."

Harry shook his head. "We need to find out where Nathan came from. A base with a gate, obviously. One of the ones on the map we have, most likely. We need to secure all of them we can and destroy the rest. The absolute last thing we need is to have the US government or, God forbid, a bunch of lunatic killers from the Middle East rushing out to all parts of the Asharim Empire, or whatever it is."

"It's a corporate government," Cabot said. "Each business has a vote based on their income. The richest obviously do their best to keep a lock on making money. It's pretty cutthroat."

Jess allowed herself a sigh. "I know letting Queen go is going to cause us trouble, but that was the best of a bad set of options. How do we handle him?"

Harry shrugged. "I say let him blunder around. At some point, we'll need more firepower than we have, and we'll have to go to someone like the US. The key is to stay in control as long as we can. At least until we have some certainty that we can keep Earth safe."

"Why does this feel like an old episode of *Flash Gordon*? With the Asharim playing Ming the Merciless."

He laughed. "I haven't thought of that show in forever. He'd be good, but I'd rather have Buck Rogers on my side."

Cabot grinned slyly. "Isn't your name Rogers? I think you just got a new nickname, Buck."

"It beats the damned song. Maybe folks will stop sending me tennis shoes and sweaters for Christmas."

They all laughed. Jess was glad they could find something humorous in all this. It might get pretty grim before it was all over.

* * *

QUEEN TOOK the bag off his head. They'd slipped it on before they stuffed him into the van and drove him out into the city. It turned the corner just ahead of him, too far away for him to get a look at the license plate.

It didn't matter. The FBI would find them. With all the upgraded cameras that came as a result of the antiterrorism bills, they had eyes all over the place. It made the Patriot Act seem weak. Most ordinary citizens had no idea how much their government knew about them. Or what they could find out, if they really wanted to.

Now he'd turn the full might of the US loose on those crazy bastards. Before they got everyone killed. Or let the Chinese have tech that would let them dominate the world.

Even the conservative loons in Congress would be on board. Wouldn't that be refreshing? The president wouldn't even have to use executive orders to make it all happen.

They'd returned his phone to him, along with the rest of his personal property. He was standing on a street corner somewhere in Chicago, he assumed. People just kept walking, as if a car dropping off a man with a bag on his head was an everyday occurrence.

Perhaps in this part of town it was.

He dialed a number from memory. "This is Queen. I'm safe, but I need a pickup. Trace my location. I also need a plane to take me straight to Washington. I'll need to meet with the president as soon as possible."

These people thought they could get the best of the United States. Well, he was going to prove them painfully wrong. By the time he was done, they'd all be in some unnamed CIA black-ops prison, and the US would have a chokehold on the rest of the world. Then he'd see about extending that hold into the rest of the universe.

* * *

NATHAN CAME BACK to the secured area after he and the men had pushed the Islamic nutjobs back to the rear of the ship. They'd killed a lot of them, but he'd lost some people too. This fight might be more closely matched than he'd expected.

The men guarding the entrance hadn't seen his mother for a while, so he went in search of her.

He didn't find her. There were no other exits, but she was gone.

Or was she? The large sarcophagus could hold a person. The console was lit and showed a general human shape. Was she in there?

"Mother," he said softly, laying a hand on the cold metal. "What have you done?"

He was on a ship going who knew where, fighting enemies that wanted to torture and kill him, and his mother was inside some alien machine. The day just kept getting better.

Well, you ate an elephant one bite at a time. First, he needed to kill the terrorists. Then he could worry about the rest of his problems. Like saving his mother and getting back to Earth.

And just think, a few weeks ago, he'd been bored.

He sighed and sat in the seat. He'd figure it all out. Then he'd get enough people together to kill everyone that needed killing. He'd make sure he and his mother came out on top. They always did. This time it would just be more challenging.

* * *

WANT to get updates from Terry about new books and other general nonsense going on in his life? He promises there will be cats. Go to TerryMixon.com/Mailing-List and sign up.

DID YOU ENJOY THIS BOOK? Please leave a review on Amazon. It only takes a minute to dash off a few words and that kind of thing helps Terry make a living as a writer and gets you new books faster.

. . .

WANT MORE BOOKS BY TERRY? Flip to the next page and grab one.

VISIT TERRY'S Patreon page to find out how to get cool rewards and an early look at what he's working on at Patreon.com/TerryMixon.

ALSO BY TERRY MIXON

You can always find the most up to date listing of Terry's titles on his Amazon Author Page.

Note: the links below (ebook only, obviously) redirect you to my website where you can click a button to go to Amazon. This allows me to participate in Amazon's associates program and earn a little more. Sorry for any inconvenience.

The Last Hunter

The Last Hunter

Bonds of Blood

Alpha Strike

The Enemy Revealed

Command Authority

The Grand Conspiracy

Shield of Humanity

Fog of War

Ships of the Line

Operation Liberty

The Empire of Bones Saga

Empire of Bones

Veil of Shadows

Command Decisions

Ghosts of Empire

Paying the Price

Recon in Force

Behind Enemy Lines

The Terra Gambit

Hidden Enemies

Race to Terra

Ruined Terra

Victory on Terra

When Luck Runs Out

Gunboat Diplomacy

ABOUT TERRY

#1 Bestselling Military Science Fiction author Terry Mixon served as a non-commissioned officer in the United States Army 101st Airborne Division. He later worked alongside the flight controllers in the Mission Control Center at the NASA Johnson Space Center supporting the Space Shuttle, the International Space Station, and other human spaceflight projects.

He now writes full time while living in Texas with his lovely wife and a pounce of cats.

TerryMixon.com

a amazon.com/author/terrymixon

f facebook.com/TerryLMixon

|● patreon.com/TerryMixon

BB bookbub.com/authors/terry-mixon

g goodreads.com/TerryMixon

www.ingramcontent.com/pod-product-compliance
Lightning Source LLC
Chambersburg PA
CBHW060805030726
47503CB00002B/342